LOCK

DEBRA

USA Today Bestselling Author

ANASTASIA

Cover Design: Hang Le
Photog: Mave L Hsiun
Cover Model: Cocoi Castaneda
Content Edits: Aimee Ashcraft of Brower Literary
Line edits: Paige Smith

T, J, and D: It's always for you

1

Ember

TWO MURDERERS WAITED FOR me on the other side of the bathroom door. But I wasn't coming out until the back of my hair laid completely flat. One last look and I was ready to go. I faced the closed door in my brother's mansion. It took another five minutes to get up the spine to open it.

The assassin was completely covered in a skeleton tattoo. From the top of his head to his feet. He was known as Mercy on the street, but I just called him Nix. His best friend stood beside him. A huge, beautiful black man who oozed charm and swagger. He was also a murderer—if he needed to be. And a mob boss, called Havoc by people who were afraid of him. Though I knew him as Animal. The hallway seemed too small for them both, even if the contemporary house was massive. They were a sight that would scare a lot of people. Most people.

They were waiting on me. Havoc aka Animal had one foot resting on the wall and his phone in his hand. And they would wait all day if necessary. I knew they wouldn't approve of what I was about to say. I finally opened the door. Both men looked up in unison.

"Baby Girl." Animal's deep voice was probably half of the reason he was my first love.

"Ember." Nix aka Mercy was my brother. It's hard to see the resemblance between us; I don't have his ink. There's no shading or highlights to make me more menacing. Nix had been waiting stock-still, not leaning. Feet set shoulder width apart. He'd learned an eerie calm at a very young age, when he would keep still for hours to avoid beatings from his father. Under a bed. In a closet. It happened before I was born, and after I existed as well.

Despite this sad history, I was angry with them both. The women in their lives said that I was dragging the drama on too long. And maybe I was. I liked the attention, honestly. But I was still angry that they treated me like a burden, never giving me straight answers. And Nix stayed away from me for my whole childhood. My friends were so jealous that I had these two badasses following me around. They were a pair, for sure. But instead of the instant family I'd always longed for, I was set aside and monitored.

I looked from one face to the other. Blue eyes to brown eyes. "I want to go away to school."

Nix's eyebrows furrowed. "No."

He didn't even give it a second's thought.

"Why?" Animal was always more interested in listening first, passing judgment later. Well, that's how it seemed. But he would agree with Nix. They always had each other's back. And I felt that pang of emptiness. That connection they had—I wasn't a part of it. It came from history. Nix is eight years older than I am. He witnessed his abusive father kill our mother when I was an infant. His father's rage came from my very existence, the possibility that I had a different father. Nix's current girlfriend, Becca, was the one to put a bullet in Nix's father over a year ago when he was trying to kill her; it seemed like the best possible outcome.

But to say our relationship was complicated was an understatement. I knew Nix felt responsible for my safety, but deep in my soul, I was terrified he hated me. If I didn't exist, Nix's father would have never guessed our mother was unfaithful, and she'd still be alive.

Animal was another situation altogether. Nix and Animal spent their teen years in the same home for children. Animal was close with the cop, Merck, who claimed he was my father. At Merck's request, Animal watched over Nix while they were underage. And they became closer than brothers during that time.

While they were becoming blood brothers, I was growing up with Aunt Dorothy, my mother's sister. She loved me in her own way, a way that was laced with a little bit of hate and resentment. She told me often that my mother was the master of her own fate, that going back to the man who killed her was her own fault. Dorothy didn't tell me about Nix. She shooed him away the few times he explored our neighborhood.

I would have given anything to have him in my life. To feel

like I belonged somewhere, even if it was just in his heart. To have an older brother as a kid? It was my dearest wish.

I stared them down, Animal's "why" echoing in my head. I didn't want to get into it with them. It would make me cry, and that made things awkward. I lied instead.

"To get space. From all of this." I didn't say that I wanted to be an equal with them. In on the inside jokes. The easy silence. They were a family, and I was just a job. A girl to keep safe.

I didn't look at Nix's face as he registered the hurt I'm sure my statement had caused.

He'd been my stalker. Still was. I knew about him, but I didn't *know* him. He watched me from behind cameras. He'd covered himself with tattoos and watched Becca and me from a computer or from beneath the shade of his hoodie for years and years.

When we finally connected, when he introduced himself, I was seventeen. Almost done with my childhood and headed to adulthood. The young part of my heart rejoiced when I met Nix. But as I became more entangled in his world, I found that they'd kept the knowledge of who my actual father was from me. I'd spent my life thinking that Nix's murderous father was mine. Instead, Merck the cop was waiting on the sidelines the whole time. Staying away from me. Staying out of my life. To protect himself and his weird, messed-up marriage.

I was lonely. I made as many friends as I could to fill the void. I'd be the life of the party. But at home, Aunt Dor would look at me disapprovingly, telling me I was just like my mom, making horrible choices.

Animal held out his hand, palm up, as if for me to take it. The wedding band clearly marked him as someone else's. But I wanted to cuddle into his warm chest and find comfort there. He would hug me back, because he was that kind of guy.

I hugged myself instead. I needed to block out the impulses

to belong. To find what I needed here. They weren't going to accept me as an equal. I would always be a little kid. Even though I was nineteen. Plenty old enough to do most things. But they clearly wanted to keep me away from their business. And their business was their life.

Nix cleared his throat. "Where do you want to go?"

He was using the big gestures, pointing at random spots in the air like there was an invisible map surrounding us. Animal folded his untaken hand into his pocket.

"I think that's my business." I forced myself to meet his gaze. This was a big moment. I had to be the adult I was demanding that they treat me like.

"Oh, for fuck's sake. I can't have you out there—where in the world? Just–out there without getting to have a say in how far away and what kind of element you'll be in."

He was legit getting angry. Animal stepped between us, his broad back making a wall.

"Sweetness. You got to go for a smoke break." Animal held his hands up.

"I don't smoke," Nix grumbled. I shuddered when I heard the loud thwack. I could tell when Animal shifted that Nix had punched the wall. The drywall now had a ragged hole. There were a few of them in this house, mostly inspired by something I'd done.

"Pretend." Animal whispered a few more things to my brother in that calming way he had.

Finally, Nix stormed off. I felt like my heart was crumpling. Part of me—well, hell—most of me wanted Nix to fight for me to stay. To not understand. Make me part of his crowd. His clique.

Animal would be harder to convince. Nix had a habit of getting angry and going on about things that maybe he shouldn't. But Animal—he'd convince someone on fire that they needed a lit match.

He turned slowly to me, disarming smile in place. This guy was the poster boy for sex. And he knew it. I looked him up and down. Dark skin, thick muscles, and tiger tattoos. He was going to be much harder in general. He was good at seeing through me.

"Baby Girl," he started.

"No. Call me by my name. You're not allowed to sweet-talk me. You're very, very married to a woman I respect. Turn down the porn star dial to like a two." I held up my index finger. I was trying to get a leg up on him, even though I wanted to throw a leg over him.

He tried to appear humble. Less sizzling. He sucked at it.

"Ember." His voice was its own vibration.

"Never mind. Just don't talk at all." My shoulders slumped. He knew about my crush.

"Why do you want to leave? Nix was so excited—when you called today, he thought you were going to announce you wanted to move back in." Animal leaned against the wall.

I shuffled my feet. High heels today. Too high. Tight jeans and a red shirt. My long brown hair was freshly streaked with colors. My going away outfit.

"My friends are all at school. I want to have that experience." That was what I'd practiced saying.

"Now tell me the real reason."

His face was incredibly understanding. I gave up and walked into him. He shoved himself away from the wall to envelop me in the hug. He smelled amazing. Even though his body was rock hard, he was somehow still a soft place to land.

He rocked slightly and patted my back. "Tell me, baby."

I spoke to his pec. "I need to find a life that's mine. I need to find a friend who's like you. My ride or die. I need to start the part of my life that isn't tied up in all the things I've never had."

The tears inspired by my words were welling in my eyes like traitors and threatening my makeup.

"And you can't do that here?" His whole chest spoke, almost.

"I can't do that here." I was sure of that. Here I had to be protected. Here I was reminded so often that I looked like my long dead mother that I was almost numb to it. Here I lived in the shadow of my aunt. My brother.

"If this is what you really want, you know I'll help you with him."

Nix. He meant he was willing to take the brunt of my brother's paranoia and anger so I could leave.

I nodded against him. I knew he would.

"But there's no way you get to walk out of here without protection. Anyone who is paying attention will know that you're in this family. You're a target for any enemies that might want to move on us. Nix won't have it, and frankly, neither will T nor I."

Bringing up T wasn't fair. His wife. My friend.

"T is not going to be my bodyguard." I pushed away from him.

"She's the only one Nix and I trust."

"My choices do not get to take away your wife. No. If that's your only solution, I swear I'll run away and stay away forever. Don't test me. You guys just got married. Happily ever after. Find someone else. I'll allow one person. But not T." I grabbed the front of his shirt and gave him the harshest look I could.

Animal put his hand on top of his head, the tendons in his throat standing out as he swallowed. "You know how he is."

I got on my tiptoes and widened my eyes. "I'm nineteen. What were you doing at nineteen?"

He rolled his head to the side and made a hissing noise. "Girl. You can't ask me that. Different worlds."

"Would you want to have been watched all day, every day?" I let go of his shirt and put my heels on the ground.

"No."

"I'm not taking a newlywed woman with me to watch me walk around a college campus. She deserves to be here with you. She's earned that." Both he and I knew that T would do whatever he and Nix needed. Even if it made her suffer. It wasn't fair to abuse that, and I told him as much.

His love for his wife must have brought the understanding in his face. "Okay. But to go—for him to be able to stay in his right mind, you need security that we choose. He's got impulses like the CIA and KGB had a baby when it comes to you. Have some mercy on Mercy."

Animal was right. And I didn't want Nix miserable. He'd had enough misery in his life already. "Fine. One guy."

Animal's smile appeared slowly and was topped off with lifted eyebrows. "Well, actually, you and I both know T is worth at least three guys. She's ridiculously talented."

His white teeth were blinding and his dark eyes charming. "Fine. Three. You keep T and I get to leave."

He hemmed and hawed and looked like it was killing him, but he agreed to let me leave...as long as I brought three people along with me.

It took me until after he'd hugged me and left me by my old guest bedroom in Nix's house to realize that he'd gotten me to agree to just what Nix probably wanted.

Slick, sexy man candy.

But that was that. I was getting what I needed.

Freedom.

2

Lock

THE PARTY WAS OUT of control, but at this time of
night, that was expected. The house was abandoned,
but in our territory. The backyard had one of the very
few pools in the neighborhood and the only in-ground one.
The cement hole was the scene for skateboarding, graffiti, and
sometimes fires. I ducked under a tree before concentrating on
making sure my gait didn't hitch. No fear. And despite the
jabbing pains and deep bruises, I wanted to prove I was as

close to a superhero as a human could get. Even if that was a huge lie.

A red bandana was wound around my wrist; my arm was heavy with all it symbolized. I'd layered a few leather bracelets around it to make it seem less brand new.

I had a black eye, but most of my injuries were less apparent.

I was sweating with the effort it took to not limp. Not gasping about my ribs as I rolled my shoulders back to enter the crowd with a proud chest was possibly harder than getting kicked in them less than twelve hours ago.

I nodded at the few faces I recognized. The crowd was college-aged, though not all present had academics as a focus.

I took a beer from a guy just after he'd opened it for himself.

"Bitch, what the fuck?" The guy started to protest.

I grabbed the front of his shirt and watched as the anger drained out of his face when he saw the red bandana.

I lifted an eyebrow. "Something wrong?"

The guy shook his head and waved his hands in the universal sign for "I might crap my pants; take whatever you want."

The simple act of showing up for the party was part of my grand plan. No one is expected to be up and walking for at least a week after being jumped into the gang.

The quickest anyone had ever gotten on his feet was three days. So twelve hours afterwards was insane. But I wanted to hit the ground running. This was one shot I wasn't going to miss.

Murmurs followed me as I made my way through the rowdy crowd searching for Dice. My friend smiled when he saw me coming toward him. Dice had a slightly dingier red bandana on his wrist. I threaded my way through groups yelling song lyrics at each other. There was a poker game going on in the old crumbling outdoor kitchen. Three different songs polluted the night, each from a different phone. The air was thick with smoke—cigarette and weed.

"Lock. Look at you. Like fucking Lazarus. Shit, they hit you so hard I thought they killed you. There's no goddamn way you're here." Dice jumped down from the brick half wall he was sitting on and slapped me on the shoulder.

I gave him a hard look. "Don't be a bitch."

We showed each other the gang sign that would now be a big part of our friendship, displaying the right amount of fingers and position to make sure that people watching knew who we were... and who we were with.

"Why, does that fucking hurt, asshole? You want to be a hero, I'm going to bust your balls about it." Dice grabbed two more beers from a cooler by my feet.

We toasted all three drinks we had as I offered, "I'm on so many painkillers I could hammer a nail into wood with just my dick and not feel a thing."

Dice cracked a smile. "You drag your dead ass here because you want to be some sort of legend? You got a long way to go, pup."

"I'll rise to the occasion, cumdonkey." I took a gulp of my beer. I was 4000% sure I shouldn't be drinking on painkillers with a possible concussion, but I did it anyway.

Dice nodded at my drinking, like he knew how much of a defiance it was. "You did good. You knew the rules were simple."

I leaned against the brick. "Yeah. I know. *Don't fight back and don't die.* Pretty sure I did a little of both."

Dice made a few hand gestures at another guy in the gang across the party before returning to our conversation. "That's as true as a goddamn arrow."

"You bastards are vicious." I pressed one of my cold beer cans against my temple. I winced as I used the can as a makeshift ice pack.

"Your father didn't think so." Dice was giving me the business.

"He only thought some of you were worth saving, asshole." I straightened up, my spine making a cracking noise as I did so. I was fucked up.

"Some of *us*, baby. You're all in now. Down to your balls." He pointed between my legs with his pinkie. He was responsible for the soreness there. During the beat-in, he made sure to hit me in the nuts. Asshole.

"Does he know?" Dice was scanning the party while we talked. "Party" was a strong word. A pointed gathering was a better description. We gathered to show our rivals we weren't afraid to meet in public. Daring them to take action. Almost every male here was armed and a few of the girls.

"Nah. Ma doesn't even know yet." Neither of them would be happy about my new life, but what other option was there? "Choice was made, though." I switched to using my beer for its real purpose and took another healthy swallow.

"Your Pops will hear soon. The Cokes on the inside will let him know." Dice met my eyes. A warning. I was making decisions as a man now because I had to. My father was recently indicted on murder charges—*false* murder charges—so I was the man of the family now. My mother and sister were depending on me to save them from slipping into a homeless life.

The only thing I did better than mouth off was stay loyal to my girls. So I'd work in place of my now absent father to keep the peace and the safety in my family.

My father had begged me not to do the very thing I'd just committed to. There was no way out now. Prison, which was just a contained version of the hard fucking streets, or death put an end to what I'd just begun. But I was hard enough. I was mean enough. I'd do good work for my family, until I earned the money to get my mom and sister to a safe place. Maybe get them into a witness protection type of scenario.

At this particular house, the place that had a party from Thursday to Sunday afternoon, there were all the new, fresh young players. Conflicts were started here. Merchandise was exchanged as well. Lives ended here, too. The Cokes wore red bandanas. We were an offshoot of the Dutch family. They controlled all of Valston and beyond. Our greatest local rivals were the Pepsis. Ironically named. They were *not* part of the Dutch family. Loyalty to one or the other was a way of life in my neighborhood.

It was where I had to be until I could run with the big dogs. I started doing what Dice was doing. Watching the scene. I'd have to learn how to notice the slight changes in body language. When a party went sour, it could turn deadly. Fights needed to be squashed immediately, prevented if possible. We'd watch for cops. We'd watch for gangbangers. Girls who didn't belong that might start a war for being in the wrong place at the right time. When I saw her, I knew she was out of the element. There was a way everyone here walked and talked. A guarded type of revelry. But she was scared. And hazy. She kept walking out of her unlaced shoe and dropped her phone three times as she was pushed from behind. Older Cokes were trailing her.

Her long blonde hair was loose and messy. She had on a yellow sundress and black combat boots. Her nail polish was red and so were her lips and she was on something. I just knew how that looked. The neighborhood had addicts. The Cokes sold drugs. I could put it all together.

A group of guys was forming around her, each of them

wearing bandanas in varying degrees of wear and tear. It was off. She didn't seem to be able to focus, twirling in a circle, letting the strap of her sundress fall off her shoulder.

Dice leaned over to me. "Looks like those fuckers found someone to roofie."

Of course. It'd explain her uncoordinated movements.

I took another peek at her. She was good-looking and in a ton of trouble. A girl with a delicate heart necklace wouldn't be used to this kind of trouble. I sighed. The guys were now poking at her, mocking her confusion; it was like watching someone rip the wings off a butterfly.

Dice punched my arm. "Don't. Seriously. They paid money for those drugs. They're going to want to get their money's worth."

I glowered at Dice. "Don't be a shithead."

It looked like I was going to get my ass kicked yet again as I set my beer down and yelled, "Hey!"

3

Ember

HARMONY HILL WAS BEAUTIFUL at night. It was a quaint college town, but close enough to downtown Valston that it was still pretty civilized. There was a makeup store there and a great outdoor mall. And it was a stiff ten hours away from Midville. And Nix. And Animal. And T. And Becca. And Aunt Dor. And my possible father...but that was a train of thought for a different night.

I was almost sure I was the only girl moving into the dorms with an entourage of three guys.

They looked ridiculous, carrying all my pink and leopard-printed suitcases and bags up two stories to my new room. I had no roommate. Nix had done something, or Animal. Well, any of them would know how to hack into a system like Harmony Hill University's dorm assignments. I should've fought it. Stayed in a six-girl suite with one bathroom. Stood in line for my shower in the morning.

But I liked having my own bathroom just off my bedroom. I'd have to go out and get food and stuff, but I didn't have to spend *that* much time with other people. The cover story was that Wardon, Bowen, and Thrice were also enrolled as students. They would hang around with me. They were young enough that they could blend in with the crowd I should be around now. It would look like a rotating group of guys were platonic friends with me.

They were all trained in various ways to kill someone. Hack a computer, canvass a scene. T and Animal approved each of them to be in the entourage, and some of the conversations I'd heard about the rigorous tests they had to complete were crazy-pants. It sounded like boot camp in a dumpster fire.

They were probably making bank. Bowen was lanky and the last guy you'd notice in a crowd, until he locked eyes with you. The crystal blue you found there was disarming. He was currently hanging up my fairy lights and cursing at how tangled they were. I had to explain that they fell like a curtain, not like a string you would put around a Christmas tree.

I hung my pictures and found a good place for my camera. I had the extra lenses wrapped up and waiting in my camera bag if I needed them. Pictures were my art. Well, one of the many different ways I liked to create stuff.

Wardon was cute, tall with curly brown hair. He'd flirted

with me in the past and seemed overeager to help me unpack my clothes. I had to slap his hands when he got to my thongs. I thought Wardon would be in charge, because he'd been assigned to me for T and Animal's wedding in Vegas, but he seemed to defer to Thrice.

And then Thrice, of course. He was the only one who couldn't quite pass for a college student. He was getting to look a little too daddy. But his experience was apparently too amazing to leave at home. He was ignoring my decorations and bed linens to investigate the buildings' floor plans on his laptop, using the box from my small dorm-sized fridge as a desk.

While we unpacked I tried to ask more about the world that Nix and Animal came from. I knew it was sugarcoated and bubble wrapped for me. But I wanted to know what they actually did. Were they really into things that I'd be against? No one took the bait—either brushing me off or ignoring me outright.

After all my bags were in my room, I was starving. Thrice mentioned that he'd seen a pizza place on the ride that looked decent.

I agreed. But grabbing a slice of pizza wouldn't be a simple act of a hungry college student, I found out. It involved an online search from Wardon, who was looking at ratings and reading the one star ones out loud. Bowen was scanning the police reports via an Animal connection to make sure there'd been no criminal activity in the area lately. And Thrice used Google Earth to survey the property.

It was overkill. "Guys. We passed two cow farms on our way here. This place is not going to be a hotbed of criminal activity. Can we just get a slice?" I was shushed.

Wardon went in to scope the place when we actually arrived an hour and half later, though the drive was only about twenty minutes. Finally, I was permitted to walk into the shop with Thrice's arm around my shoulders. Bowen smiled and laughed like I'd told a joke.

Thrice led me to a booth against the back wall and slid in next to me. Wardon was in charge of ordering. We were getting two cheese pizzas. So apparently my opinion was not needed for what I actually got to eat for dinner.

I glanced around the restaurant. There were two booths full of college kids laughing and having a great time. They all had friends; I had bodyguards.

I didn't realize until now how much I wouldn't get to experience. If these three treated me like a president and they were my secret service, I'd never get to make friends. Or go on dates. Or make out with anyone.

Wardon slid into the booth as well, forcing Bowen to put his shoulder against the wall. The waitress brought our pies over. No small talk. The long ride had taken all of that out of us. I stared at my reflection in the pizzeria window. There I was, surrounded by my brother's men, and still lonely.

My image cracked and the glass exploded as a man flew through the window. My comfort was clearly not a concern as Thrice jammed me by my head under the table. My guys moved fast, I had to give them that. People in the restaurant were screaming, some shouting. I thought I heard a gunshot outside.

I knew Thrice, Bowen, and Wardon would be armed. It was the whole reason they were here. I peeked out between Thrice's legs, bumping my head on the support of the booth.

A voice shouted from outside, "The only thing that thick skull of yours is good for is a battering ram." A group of men was staring through the shattered front window into the restaurant.

The guy who had been the projectile pushed himself up a

bit. Before he could respond, he started coughing. He just held up his middle finger instead.

"Oh, that bitch. That's it. He's dead." Clearly, the men were coming in. From my spot under the table, I could make out that they were all wearing red bandanas around their wrists.

Bowen and Wardon moved to stand in front of the man sprawled on the ground.

"How about we move along?" Wardon suggested.

The guys on the outside of the restaurant started throwing things through the window. Rocks, bottles, and a shoe came flying in.

A giant fistfight was about to go down, but my brother's men didn't take out their guns. I studied the guy at the center of the floor, where the glass of the window he'd just been thrown through surrounded him.

Black hair, blue eyes, and a dimple almost made up for the blood coming from his busted lip. From his spot on the restaurant's grimy floor, he gave me the most genuine smile. Like we were friends. Like he was getting up the courage to ask me to dance. Meanwhile, the men wearing red bandanas poured into the restaurant. Bowen threw one man over the counter; the pizzas that were waiting for customers clattered to the ground. Thrice stepped forward and took two other red bandanas to the floor with crackingly well-delivered punches. The other customers were either screaming, fighting, or filming the scene on their phones.

Despite the bedlam surrounding us, the world stopped spinning. I felt my lips part and a smile fight its way to return to him.

Him.

He turned over from his back to his belly and army crawled to me, dragging himself on his elbows, smiling the whole time.

I pushed Thrice to the side with pressure on his calf. Whatever he was dealing with must have been enormous, because he leaned enough out of my way that I could do my best to pull Dimples to cover.

There was blood pooling under his right leg.

"I'd cut my leg off to get here to you."

Sparkling. His eyes were sparkling at me.

I usually had a fresh mouth. A quick reply.

"Hi," was all I could come up with.

He was a lot to process. He was all kinds of handsome, but also all kinds of injured. So, so injured. The black eye made me wince, just thinking of how hard he had to have been hit to get it. There were cuts on his cheekbones and his neck had deep purple marks, almost like he was choked. There was blood from possibly more than his leg, but whatever he had going on under his jeans had to be bad. The blood was changing the deep denim to almost black from the knee down.

Panic welled up in my chest; I was out of my depth. I'd only helped one bleeding person—like really bleeding—when I was a kid. I'd put some mulch on her cut. It wasn't effective.

The color was draining from his face.

He was still hitting on me as he was declining. "So, do you live around here? Do they have a movie theater? If I don't die, do you want to see a movie on Friday? Hell, you're so fucking pretty I'll pick you up even if I'm a ghost."

I yanked my jacket off the bench and tried to tune out the sounds of the battle around us. "Where's this blood coming from?"

He answered my question by grabbing his thigh. The space was tight—our bodies were pressed close together. My jeans would be ruined with his blood. I wadded up my jacket and pressed down on his leg, where the bleeding seemed to be the worst.

Our foreheads were almost touching. The fighting seemed

to be winding down. Customers were coming out from under the tables, and the red bandanas were carrying each other out of the restaurant as best they could. Everything was quieting down, though there were sounds of approaching sirens. It seemed like the tinkling of broken glass would go on forever— the front window had been so large that slivers of glass in the frame kept cutting loose.

"Hey, angel face, if you want to stop the bleeding, you're really going to have to press down on me. Like a lot." His breath brushed my neck.

Thrice popped his head into our alcove. "What the fuck?"

Before I could get a good grip and help, Dimples was dragged away from me.

Bowen had a gun to Dimples' head in a second.

"Stop. No." I crawled out, but Wardon got between the injured man and me.

"Who are you?" Thrice started in with the questioning.

He pointed at me. "Her future husband."

He was cheeky. And still sparkling. Having a gun to his head didn't faze him.

"You don't know who you're talking about. She's so out of your league, you don't even play the same sport."

"I'm Sherlock. They call me Lock." He was giving me his name, not answering their questions.

"I'd call you Shirley," Wardon offered. But Lock didn't respond. His flirty manner fell away as his eyes rolled into his head and his mouth fell slack.

I fought to get around Wardon. "Stop. Help him."

Thrice stood, letting Lock collapse to the ground unassisted. His head thumped on the floor.

"Is anyone dead?" I whispered.

"No. No one is dead. Yet. Maybe this kid." Thrice pointed to another man lying on the ground, who suddenly sputtered to life, and started to crawl away. "Well, that's a lot of blood. We're out. I don't want to deal with the cops. Let's bounce." He pointed to the door with one hand and made to grab my wrist with the other.

I stepped away from Wardon's searching hand. "I'm not going. Fix him or save him. Two choices. That's it."

I felt my spine stiffen. I wasn't going to abuse my power, but I realized how much of it I had as I stood in the pizza parlor. These men worked for me. Sort of. Enough to make me hold my ground.

Wardon attempted to usher me past the situation. Past Lock.

"Don't touch me." I leveled my bitchiest glare at him.

Wardon let go and gestured wildly to Thrice. "What the hell do we do?"

Thrice seemed to time his steps to the pulse of the sirens that were almost on top of us.

I took a look around finally. It was like a tornado had ripped through this quaint mom and pop pizza shop.

"This isn't a game, Ember. We've got to go." He was imploring me to make it easy.

"He comes. Bring him." My demanding voice had a hoarseness to it now. Maybe I didn't know what I was asking from them, but there was going to be a before and an after in this night. I was going to set the precedent now. Chaos and sadness didn't trump my opinion.

Bowen acted, bending low and pulling on Lock's motionless body.

Wardon left my side and helped heft Lock between them. Then he nodded. He escorted me around the counter. The restaurant's workers were cowering behind it. Thrice pointed his gun at them. "You never saw us." When they mutely nodded, he lowered the gun and continued to the exit.

One of the girls was about my age. She had on the apron they seemed to give all the workers. Her shell-shocked face cemented the reality. These people could have died. Maybe even at the hands of the men who protected me.

Shit.

Had my guys escalated it? I mean, Lock had been thrown through the window. The level of violence seemed set when that happened.

Out the back door, Bowen and Wardon put Lock in the back hatch of the SUV. I crawled past them and maneuvered myself behind his head. The rear seats were still set to flat to accommodate the packed bags before.

I focused on the bleeding again. My jacket had been wedged between the men and could still sop up the blood.

Wardon came through the middle doors and sliced up Lock's jeans until he found the wound, a deep, evil-looking gash in his leg.

I rebunched my jacket and handed it to Wardon. The SUV roared and it was put in gear, moving even before Thrice had the driver's door shut.

I focused on Lock's head. Just keeping it still. I pictured his head bouncing off the floor. None of it was encouraging. His body was big. He was lean but strong. What an incredible waste to lose him. I tried to assess what he had going on. The interior of the vehicle was dark, so I used my phone as a flashlight. His face seemed to be swelling as I watched; his hands were battered, like he'd fought for his life. The leg was the worst of it, the laceration so deep. I knew there were arteries that were horrible to sever. I prayed this bleeding wasn't from one of them. I slid my phone back into my pocket.

And what about the other people at the restaurant? I smoothed my hand over his forehead, my eyes traveling across his broken body; that red bandana was still wound around his wrist. The men who'd thrown him through the window, who started the attack, had all been wearing them, too. There was probably a connection. I wondered what it could be. Maybe a gang affiliation?

Nix's voice filled the SUV as the guys recounted the whole incident over speakerphone. He had to be assured twice that I was okay. I even called out, "Hey, Nix," so he could move on.

Lock's eyes opened. "Ember? That's your name?"

"Seriously? You're bleeding out. You're still trying to get with me?"

He attempted a smile. "If I die now, I'll be so pissed."

Nix and Thrice went back and forth about the security cameras. We could all hear the clattering of Nix's keyboard. In between searching for whatever he was doing, he was berating Thrice, Bowen, and Wardon. He was angry. And for the first time ever, I got to feel what it was like to be on the receiving end of his wrath. It was terrifying.

I gazed down at Lock again. He seemed to be forcing his eyes open to stare at me. "Can't believe they make girls this hot."

"Quit spitting your lines and concentrate on not dying."

"Lines are lies. I'm telling the truth."

And like a light switch was flipped, he was off again. His overwhelming presence evacuated, his face went slack, and his eyes rolled into his head. His eyelids didn't even close all the way, showing me a peek of white.

I tuned back into the conversation, gently touching the bruises and cuts Lock had all over. He'd been beaten to hell. A lump formed in my throat at the thought. The violence he'd been a party to was horrifying.

Wardon met my gaze. "It'll be okay."

"Will it?" I knew I didn't live in a fairy tale. This was cold, hard life. People died and almost died all the time.

Nix and Thrice had decided to drop off Lock as a John Doe at the hospital a few towns over. I immediately fought the idea of leaving him by himself. Surely someone should stay, be his voice. Find his family. Nix gave me his rationale: that we were all a party to the violence in the pizza parlor. The police could be looking for me. I had no idea how much damage my guys had done while I was dealing with Lock under the table. I assumed a lot, because we'd walked out.

"It's settled. Drop him off and drive her home." Nix hung up the phone, making my decision before I could add my thoughts.

Wardon touched my hand—the one that was now on Lock's shoulder. "We'll talk to him."

It was nice of him to offer, but this was between my brother and me.

4

Lock

WAKING UP DEAD WAS the worst. I've done it enough times to recognize the metallic taste of blood lining my mouth.

Her.

If I was alive, I wanted to be with her.

I tried to place my surroundings, my brain immediately protesting the horrible game of Twister I'd tried to play with it.

Hospital. ER. Fuck. It was always so expensive here. I knew

not to answer the question about my name out loud. Because that's how they find out who you are. And how to bill you. We had enough bills.

Her.

I met her. The most beautiful girl in the world. Hidden under a table, on the worst night of my life. Well, not the worst. My father getting arrested was the worst night.

Only thing that could've been worse would have been if I'd actually died. Not this time. I closed my eyes. I had to reassess my world. I needed to find out about my mom. My sister.

I replayed everything from the night before. I had started a war with the Cokes—the guys who wore red bandanas and controlled my neighborhood, the local branch of the Dutch family, which basically ran this city. Both legal and illegal ventures. To save a girl that they had drugged.

The fisticuffs I'd started did not end well for me, but she'd gotten away. The girl who had been their prey. I'd caused enough of a distraction that she was able to get out to the road, even as tipsy as she was. A cop had spotted her and helped her into his patrol car.

They'd stopped my beating to tell me they were going to kill me. Which sucked. But when I figured out the reason, I started gloating, telling them that my mother hits harder than they do. That didn't go well either. I have a big mouth and sometimes impulse control issues.

They'd body-slammed me in the back of a pickup truck, and the next thing I knew I was getting tossed through a window. My ribs, which already hated me, actively tried to puncture shit inside me that I needed.

And then there was her. It was well known that the Cokes weren't the brightest crayons stuck in the toolbox. But tossing me into a pizza parlor made no sense at all. That was asking for more trouble in a night already filled with it. First, the cops dealing with the drugged girl—and now making a spectacle out of teaching me my lesson by trashing a pizza parlor. Anyway, I had a feeling I had accidentally been the beginning of the end of the Cokes. I'd been a member for less than twelve hours.

Fuck.

But her.

Under the table. The long brown hair streaked with a rainbow of colors. Her huge blue eyes wide with confusion at our surroundings. The bloodshed and the violence. But that was my baseline. It was my home. I could help her. When I got to her, she was full of concern for me, pulling me to her. Embracing me to try to keep me safe of all damn things. Her hands were a bit cold, but so, so soft. Her lips had been very close, plump and ready to be kissed. I've heard my whole life that beauty is only skin deep, but it turns out my balls were deaf. They only responded to the visual. And she was extraordinary. Just the shape of her face and the way the dice was rolled in her favor genetically was captivating. The slope of her nose, the shape of her brow. Her very, very comfortable tits that I got to put my dead head on. Long legs. Her voice with a hint of wiseass.

Seeing her was like falling off a cliff. Stepping in lava. After it happened, everything else was different. My DNA was changed. My actual human existence was altered. And she was feisty, too. I'd heard her bossing around the guys with her. She had no fear of them. It was hot.

Love, or more likely *lust*, at first sight. I opened up my eyes. Slowly. I was delirious with the need to see her again. I was ready to make even more stupid decisions to get closer to her. I remembered her hair falling over my face as she checked over my bleeding limbs. And my balls only imagined one other scenario where that could happen again. When she was sitting on them.

Thinking about sex right now was stupid. Blood was not meant to rush anywhere after you'd been through what I'd been through.

It made me lightheaded. I was going to die getting a boner. And if it was embedded in her, it would be worth it.

The nurse was in my hospital room now. I heard her humming the latest Kendrick Lamar song to herself. She had good taste. I was still going to pretend that I was unconscious. She checked my vitals, I was guessing, before leaving.

I had to sneak out as soon as I could. But first, I had to nap for a few hours, or days. When I could walk, I would find her. No matter what.

5

Ember

NIX AND ANIMAL WERE standing in my dorm room. Just another way to solidify my image as the really, really weird girl who had swarms of deadly looking guys around her on campus. I'd been here three days and I already had a reputation. The other students would cross to the other side of the road when they saw me with my three (yes, always the three—no one was allowed to take turns anymore after the pizza parlor) bodyguards. An assassin and a mob boss sent out "get away from me" signals even if they weren't trying to.

Nix had his arms crossed, dark jeans and a hoodie, but the hood was down. I could see his whole tatted skull. "Listen, you being this far away is a liability. That's all I'm saying. I can't get here. I mean, see how long it took me this time. I need to be close enough to get to you."

He'd started most of his sentences with the word "I" in our conversation—the control freak.

"Can you update me on Lock?" I wanted to get that out of him before I tore into him—and I would. It was coming.

Nix scowled at my change of subject, but Animal cut in, "He bolted from the hospital in the middle of the night. We perused the camera footage. He played dead when he arrived on the gurney. Then snuck out safely. No one was waiting on him or anything. So we have to assume he's safe."

I'd find out more from Animal in good time. At least *he* was able to treat me like a person.

Nix was winding himself up again. "If I can't get to you, anything can happen. I don't even know who's in charge of the criminal element out here. Just come home. Let me do research and I'll pick you a school that ticks all the boxes I need ticked."

I thought of Lock being here. Ten hours away. I sat down heavily on my bed as Nix exhausted his speech. Animal made a face; both he and I knew I wasn't about to accept the new gospel according to Nix.

"How many times did you start a sentence with the word 'I' in this diatribe?" I met my brother's gaze.

Nix blinked a couple of times.

"I'll save you the counting. A lot. You put yourself and your needs first in this scenario." I crossed my arms across my chest. "I know I'm one of your stalkees. I'm one of the women you feel like you need to control. But I'm also a person."

"You're my sister. My job."

"But not your friend." I lifted my eyebrow.

He put his hand on his chest. I knew my name was inked under the fabric there. Embedded in his skin. It was a measure of his devotion, but he wasn't allowed to turn it into a leash for me.

"You've stayed out of my life. You've left me out of some of the most important decisions of my upbringing. Not anymore. This is not a democracy. I'm nineteen. I'm in charge of *me*. And I know you're paying for this place..." I gestured to my room. "But I don't need you to. I can get a job, take out student loans. And I will. Having three men with me is not realistic. And frankly, it's making me more of a target because everyone is wondering about me. I just want to blend in. And it's what I *will* do."

It seemed like the veins in his neck were feeding piping hot water straight to his brain.

Animal stood and put a hand on my shoulder. "Baby Girl, this isn't the best town if you're in a gang fight a few hours in. I mean, sure, you should have your autonomy, but you have to see things from Nix's point of view. There are only so many options he and I have when it comes to you."

I turned to Animal. His deep brown eyes were inviting. I gave him the once-over I always did. He was a visual gift to girls everywhere. I'd be wasting my vagina if I didn't indulge in a tiny bit of eye screwing. His smile slid to the side—he knew what I was doing. His devotion to Nix made me jealous. Their bond was unflinching. And I knew Animal would be here for me forever, if only because I was related to Nix. I wondered what it would be like to inspire such devotion on my own, just because I was who I was. And what did they do that made them so bound to each other? Were they killing people? I mean, I assumed as much. Maybe selling drugs? Though that didn't seem likely. It was out of character for my brother. Nix seemed to want to do the wrong things for the right reasons. And drugs hurt a lot of people.

"I'm not yours. And I'm not his." I pointed to Nix. "And don't punch the wall. I'm not interested in paying for that. Or for having your anger as a permanent decoration in my place. I'm staying." I held up my hands, warding off Nix's immediate negative response. "Nineteen-year-old girls all over the world are in school. Doing their thing. Getting their education. And I'm going to be one of them. No men lurking. I want parties and study groups and walking home from the bars at ungodly times in the morning."

Nix was just repeatedly shaking his head, a small, furious movement. I had compassion then. T had told me how it had been for him—that he could love anyone after what he'd been through was stunning. He barely survived. And kindness was not a thing he got to experience on the regular. Animal and Merck were his family, or at least the closest he had to one. Which was ironic, given that Merck was possibly *my* dad.

I stood up from my bed and walked up to him. "Thank you. Thank you for caring this much about me. I never had a dad. Or a brother around. But this?" I touched his chest where I knew my name was inked. He covered my hand with his. I watched his anger ratchet down notches. "Makes me so whole. In places I didn't know were broken. Because this control shit? It's how you love. And you love me. And you've pissed me off, but you won't lose me."

Nix cracked then and pulled me into a hug. I wrapped my arms around him, knowing that under the hoodie his spine was intricately etched with ink. There was ink covering every inch of him— the barrier separating him from everyone else.

"I can't. I'm sorry that's not normal. And I can't promise normal. But I can't lose you." Nix kissed the top of my head.

"This isn't losing me. It's me finding who I am. Putting me in a cage doesn't help me become an adult. I need to make decisions that have real consequences. I picked this school because it has a great art program. I want to expand my mind. My experiences." I tilted my face toward his. "You're going to have to let me fly a little."

Animal excused himself from the room. He was good at knowing what state Nix was in, and apparently my hug had de-escalated the tension enough for him to leave.

"Ah, shit." Nix patted my back as he released me. I sat down next to him on my mattress.

"Your knowing where I am all the time eases your mind, but it isn't making my life full. I'm not a bird in a cage or a gerbil on a wheel." I touched the back of his hand to make him look at me.

"I'm not good at this, the part where I hear what people say. I'm still learning about that."

I put my head on Nix's shoulder and sighed. Nix knew more about my mom than I did. Well, *our* mom. He was young when she was murdered but had spoken to her. Laughed with her. Sang with her. Maybe. I didn't know. I was desperate for information about her, but the climate of Nix's house didn't leave space for questions about her.

But now felt right. "Tell me about her."

Nix cleared his throat. It took him a few moments to either think of something or gain his composure. Maybe both.

"Uh. She looked like you—you know that. She was soft." He threaded his bone-tatted fingers together. I stayed silent. Because I was asking him to remember the before. Before the murder.

"We spent so much time together, wondering if he would be home. If he'd be angry. I remember hugging her and knowing that when her heart started to race, when the thumping in her chest was frantic, it was time to hide. I wish I hadn't hidden. What I expected to do, I don't know, but still. She was protecting me. When I should've been protecting her."

"You were a child." I had to defend him—even to himself. I was seeing his weakness now, this protection he took so seriously. It was obsessive because he was always picturing the worst. The things he saw on the daily—memories painted on the back of his eyelids.

"You know, looking back, I feel like I'm timeless. Ageless. When I think about her, I picture this version of me. This size. This knowledge. It wasn't that way. Of course." He shrugged. He made eye contact. "She had a beautiful singing voice. Sang for me. Not in front of anyone else. Said I was part of her so she'd never be embarrassed to sing in front of me."

I liked that. Picturing her singing. There were so few actual photos of her, like her murderous husband had stolen her identity along with her future. "Wish I could have heard her."

"She sang to you when you were in her belly. Had a song. Let me think."

He warbled an off-key song.

"Baby, you are the reason
Time to change the season
I'll hold you all day long
Until you're nice and strong."

I smiled. It was nice to think about her thinking about me. "You have a horrible singing voice."

Nix started laughing. "That I do." He stood, pulling his hood up and zipping his jacket.

I folded my legs and stayed on my bed. "So, we're in agreement? I stay here and you take your goons back with you?"

He looked at the floor for a few minutes. I let him have the time.

He cleared his throat. "I don't want to lie to you, Ember. It's impossible for me to stop. You'd have to shoot me right in the heart. My brain requires me to watch over you."

I sighed dramatically. Before I could start arguing, he added, "Our mom only asked me to do two things in my whole life. The first was hide. When she told me to hide, I had to do that for her." He fisted his zipper and ruffled his hoodie like he was hot. "And the second, with her last breath, she looked at me and said, 'Ember.' And I knew what she was asking. As long as I'm doing what she asked, she's still with me. With us. I'm sorry, though. You deserve a normal life. A normal brother."

When the tears crested my jaw, I wiped them away. Picturing him getting her last word. And then being alone in the room with her murderer. For years afterwards.

He held up his hands as if he was surrendering.

I stood and took his hands in mine. "It's okay. It's okay." His face was strained. I let go of his hands and laced my fingers behind his neck. "It's okay. We'll figure it out. Maybe make them less obvious? They should be good at tucking themselves away."

Nix hugged me. "I wanted anyone who saw you to know that you were untouchable."

I stepped back a bit so I could see his eyes. "Makes it kind of hard to go on a date."

"I'm all right with that."

When he grinned, I knew we'd make a compromise that worked. I was getting less angry with him. With Animal. They'd kept shit from me, but I was only seeing it from my point of view. Not his.

Animal rapped on the door and let himself back inside. His eyes sparkled at our reconciliation. "Should I book you two on *Family Feud*? I mean, T and I can be there, too."

Nix rolled his eyes as Animal stepped into the affection and wrapped us both in his huge arms.

After laughing and disengaging himself from the awkward huddle, Nix patted my shoulders. "Want to visit home Saturday morning? I'll come get you."

"Yeah. I'll come to your house." I leaned toward Animal, who put his arm around my shoulders.

"Does that mean we can love on each other again?" His deep voice was a rumble.

"Stop. I love your wife and you're too sexy to talk in my ear."

Nix shivered and held up his hands. "Enough of that."

Animal and Nix had a quick powwow about the new logistics and how to get my bodyguards near me without interfering in my life. It was nice but strange, seeing them trying so hard, making new plans, just to make me happy.

I hugged them both goodbye. They left happy. My heart felt lighter, too. Ever since I learned about Nix, I wanted to have him as a confidant. When we met, I was seventeen and had just sold my phone to two hookers. I'd wanted to get some quick money to go to a music festival. Instead of meeting my first scalpers, I met Nix and Animal. I still had the selfie I took of the two of us saved as the wallpaper on my phone. My Aunt Dor had told me Nix had left town with his father, and I lived most of my life believing that lie. It turned out that he had grown up an orphan instead. I was an infant, but Aunt Dor hadn't wanted to have Nix in her house. I'd spent my childhood imagining what it would have been like to have a friend in my brother. And for the first time, even though it was so many years later, I could almost believe that could happen.

6

Lock

AS FAR AS I knew, I was out of the hospital clean. Dice picked me up when I texted with the last two percent of my phone battery.

He was still wearing his bandana. He flashed the sign.

"How bad is it?" Had to be the first words out of my mouth.

"Bad, brother. They're pissed but..."

"But what?" I adjusted myself in the seat of his old Mustang. The gang was life. I was worried for my mom and my sister. I had no way of getting them out of the neighborhood yet.

"Well, it turns out the girl that you saved? That was Booker's niece. So..."

"Shit." Booker was the upper echelon. He was one of the top dogs, if not *the* top one. Positions changed a lot.

"They disciplined the guys that attacked you. Hard. I'm supposed to take you to Booker now. But you need to know the guys that got jacked up? They ain't fans of you." Dice tapped on his steering wheel. "I got something for you in the glove box."

I was fully expecting a gun. Instead, it was a new red bandana.

I wrapped it around my wrist but didn't knot it. Dice's gaze went from the fabric to my face and back again. "They are so fucking grateful, you could prolly get out. If you wanted. They might even pay you."

It was a lot to think about. "Can you take me home first? Like tell them I'll come in, but I needed to get clothes or something?"

Dice made a face.

"You look like a minivan-driving dad being asked to stop the family vacation so everybody can take a piss." I patted the dashboard.

"Fuck you very much. I'm trying to stay on the right side of wrong around here." He gave me the middle finger anytime he didn't need his right hand to drive all the way to my place.

"Thanks. I owe you." He rolled up to my apartment building and I hopped out --tucking my bandana in my pocket as.

"You fucking do. You should be my geisha girl for a few years or some shit. Text me when you're ready. I'll bring you in. Maybe work as hard at keeping me alive as I have you."

Dice peeled off, burning rubber. I was pressing my luck a

bit, but I wanted the pain meds to completely be out of my system before I faced Booker.

I made my way to the apartment carefully. I was something special fucked up. I dragged my leg behind me like a sack of potatoes. My face felt swollen to the brink. I wondered if I could burst out of my own skin. I knocked on the door.

I had my keys in my pocket, but I'd been gone. I knew what was next. And if I used my keys, my mom would be spooked when I just appeared in the living room.

I waited. This wasn't the first time I'd been missing for a few days. I knew she hated it. And she would show me how much.

The door swung open. My mother's eyes were wide, anxious; she smacked me right across the face. "Sherlock Sonnet! I buried you a million times in my head."

I took the slap I deserved. I knew she worried.

"Look at you." She fussed over my injuries and slapped my arm at the same time. People would think she was being violent, but she wasn't putting hate in the swings. I shuffled in, absorbing the love for what it was. "Sorry, Mama. You know it's crazy and all."

I had to look at Rhyana. After all my violence and hospital time, I wanted to reassure myself she was fine. She was curled up, asleep on the couch with her favorite stuffed bear. I pulled out my phone and took two pictures. The way the sun was hitting my sister made her look like an angel. My mom, even though she was worried, knew to wait. When I showed her the pictures, she softened, hugging me around my middle. I winced but put my arm around her.

"You smell awful." She patted my face. I grabbed her hand.

"Mama, I met the prettiest girl. She's so beautiful. And feisty. Like you."

"No! No? Really?" My mother dragged me into the kitchen and pushed me into a chair.

"Does she have anything to do with all these things that happened to you?" Mom wet a dishrag from the tap. She wiped my face, cleaning me like a mother cat would her kitten.

I looked around the apartment. The worn couch had a busted leg that was propped up with random old books from an ancient encyclopedia set. The curtains were sun-faded. The table had deep scratches. I needed to slap another coat of paint on the walls of the living room. If I could get to the home improvement store... Maybe I could make Dice take me.

We were doing the best we could. My father hadn't made much as a pastor, and my mother supplemented as much as possible with her sewing.

Dad had been in prison for six months now. It showed. There was a layer of inattention. The tap was dripping. The fridge wasn't really doing the best job of keeping things cool.

I got jumped into the Cokes to try to make some money. I had no other good ideas. In my neighborhood, you either got out or you were embedded in. My sister was beloved, the people in our neighborhood didn't have much, but they were loyal to their own. And for them, Rhy was an emotional touchstone of unconditional love.

My father had been an outlier. A man of God. Of the people. I still wasn't 100% sure what the hell had gone down to land him in prison. He was accused of killing three men. My father would move worms caught in the morning sun into a shaded area so they wouldn't dry out. My father would never kill people. Even if they were trying to kill him.

My mother smacked me on the back of the head again. I rubbed the spot. I took after her for the most part, with her fast temper and big mouth. Somehow she did it all with love. We were in purgatory without my father. I'd been out of high school for almost a year now. The plan had been to go to a community college. Dad had taken a part-time job there, working in the cafeteria on top of his regular job to get me a discount on tuition.

But with him in prison, my mother and sister needed me to work. I glanced at my student ID, which Mom had turned into a magnet on the fridge. I'd never actually used it at the college cafeteria. Because my sister—my sweet, amazing sister—had special needs. Right now, she was in the local elementary school finishing out the summer program, but she was due to transition to the much bigger middle school in September. The medical bills from the last three procedures she'd needed weighed heavily on us all. We didn't even open the bills that came anymore, because the amount owed to the insurance company and, in turn, the hospital made us all want to puke. Tylenol cost fifteen dollars a pill. The cup they brought it in cost ten dollars. Rhy had needed tubes in her ears and had to be put under to get them. I needed to win the lotto, not put groceries into a bag to help my girls. The moment I decided to quit school and turn to the Cokes was as clear as day. I was home and I overheard my mom on the phone, trying to get more time from a creditor. I was holding a list of the expensive books I needed for my first semester at school. I couldn't bring myself to lay problems on top of her problems. I'd crumpled up my list and realized that every-thing was truly different. The hopes and plans I had before Dad went to prison were tossed into the trash, along with the reading list.

I'd talked with Mom about the situation. Right now, Mom was researching homeschooling Rhy. Which would be a shame, because the social aspect of school made a light shine inside my girl.

Mom set a peanut butter sandwich in front of me and

grabbed the red bandana from my pocket. "No. Sherlock. How? Why?"

The simple fabric took the steam out of her. Like a balloon that came unfastened. She flopped in the chair across from me.

I was planning on telling her. I mean, she had to know... Depending how my meeting with Booker went, maybe I could get a hustle on, really start providing. If I stared down at my feet, I wouldn't see the hurt in her eyes. "We need money, Mama."

"Not like this. Never like this. It's...wrong. Your father would be so..."

I covered her hand with my scarred one. "Rhyana needs to go to the good school. You know? The one with the bus with the flowers on the side? Blooming Flower School! That's the one. I've been looking at it online. They have the headquarters in Midville."

My mother jerked her hand out from under mine and covered her mouth.

I continued, "That's it. I just want to support you guys until we get Dad out. We know he's innocent. And until then, I'm the man of the house. I can't get her to that school bagging groceries."

My mom uncovered her mouth. "I'm going to take care of it. You're my child."

"I'm a man, Mama. Any guy worth his salt does everything he can to keep his girls safe. You need to be here with Rhy. We both know it." I tugged the red bandana out of her left hand and wound it around my wrist. "The medical bills..." I stopped talking about them and instead pointed toward the basket we collected mail in by the door. I watched the worry climb up her expression. The bills were so scary, they felt like a noose. "This is my path for now. When we get Dad out, he can get me free. You know he can."

It was my father's specialty, counseling the young people who felt like their only choice was the gang. And understanding, like I did, that the gang had a purpose in the neighborhood.

My mom was so full of personality and vigor people mistook her for my older sister most of the time. But not right now. She looked older now. Worried. Worn. I stood and wrapped my arms around her, pulling her head against my chest.

"Nothing's going to happen to me. Or you. We're going to make it. We're a great team. And Sonnets never give up." I rubbed her back.

We stayed like that for a long while before I heard her whisper, "Thank you."

I took to one knee, gasping a bit at the movement, and grabbed her hand. "No, thank you. Together, Mama. We'll do it together."

I ate my sandwich after that, somehow always the perfect amount of peanut butter. Mom grilled me on the girl I'd seen, asking how we met. I told her the full story, from beginning to end because we were close like that. I made her laugh a bunch, even though I couldn't get rid of the sadness that creased the corners of her eyes.

I looked at my sleeping sister. Long black hair was twirled around her shoulders. She had to wear a bib, because she smiled so much she leaked a little. My heart swelled. She had been my tiny buddy my whole life. I could tell her all my stories, and she'd listen with big eyes. Sing her songs, even if they were off-key. I never felt alone after she was born. Making her smile and laugh was the best feeling in the world. There was a new feeling now: the fact her happiness now rested on me—though as a big brother I always felt responsible for her well-being. It was a heavy feeling. I imagined my father sitting in prison knowing his family was on the other side, fighting to survive.

My mother put her palm against my cheek. "You look like him now. A bit."

I covered her hand with mine. "We'll get it all back—all of it. So help me God."

She nodded.

I had a huge job ahead of me. And a girl on my mind.

7

Ember

I went to my first class on Monday. My three bodyguards were doing a much better job at keeping their distance. I could always find them if I scanned the area, but they were far less obvious. I was to give them a hand signal if I needed them. Wardon was staying closer than the other two, but it had been a good day. Two classes in the morning and one in the afternoon almost took my mind off Lock. I had syllabi and outlines and books to buy.

Three different freshmen and I talked in a nervous, trying-to-make-friends kind of way. It was exciting. After my afternoon class, I navigated the dining hall. I found a chicken dish that was somewhat tasty. I was also really, really hungry.

After I took my last bite, two other girls sat across from me. The brunette smiled brightly. "Love your hair!"

I touched it. "Thank you! And I love your tattoo." She had a hummingbird on her wrist.

Being available and open was making me much more accessible. The blonde introduced herself as Cady and her friend as Heather.

Heather started eating her sandwich, but asked, "So, are you a freshman, too?"

"Yes. It's all pretty intimidating. Getting to classes and stuff." I piled my trash in the center of my tray.

Cady splayed all her possessions on the table: her food meal card, her phone, her lipstick, and a flosser. "Seriously. I have no idea how to keep all my shit together. I locked myself out of our room three times this morning."

Heather nodded. "It's like fast-tracking adulthood. Snorting up responsibility. At least we don't have to cook."

"I'd burn the whole dorm down trying to make that chicken I just had." I pointed to the wrapper. Commiserating with girls my age about stupid stuff felt right. And made me feel less alone. I sat with them while they ate.

We all swapped contact information and promised to meet up later when I found out we were all in the same dorm.

I ignored the bodyguards and went back to my room in the evening. I spent time organizing my desk and my folders. Even though I was a year behind everyone else, I felt like I was going to be okay.

I lay in my bed that night, staring at my ceiling. I had my phone in my hand. It buzzed. Nix.

> How was your day?

> You're gonna pretend like you don't know?

> Well, I know you're okay, but how were your interactions and stuff? Did it all work out?

> Yeah. Thanks for pulling them back. I talked to a few people and had a very chill day. How's the crew? What did you guys do today?

> Everyone here is great. Night. Love you.

I smiled at the phone, not expecting the softer side of Nix. I bet Becca had put him up to it. She was good at bringing the best out of him. It wasn't lost on me that he didn't tell me what they did today. Didn't clear the cobwebs I had as far as their actual daily routine.

> Love you, too. :)

I added a smiley face.

The phone buzzed again. I chuckled when I saw who it was. Animal.

> Hey, Baby Girl. How was your day?

> Aren't you guys in the same house?

> At night we're usually in our own spaces, wiseass.

> Yeah. Okay. That makes sense. I did great. Thanks for asking.

You see anything weird, you know what to do.

Goodnight. Kiss T for me.

;)

I turned and looked out my window. It was just getting full dark outside. Maybe it would have been nice to have a roommate, after all. It'd be nice to chitchat now. Have a girl to confide in. My phone buzzed with another text. I held it up to my face. Unknown number. But the message had me curious.

Hey. I'm alive. You're beautiful.

So glad you made it. Who is this?

Your knight in shining armor? Someday, I hope anyway. As it stands, you kinda saved my life.

You could still be anyone. I have very busy days.

chuckling smiley and a winky emoji

Middle finger emoji

It's Lock. I had to beg quite a few people to get this number. Ember? Right?

Middle finger emoji

I'm sorry. Is this the wrong number? You have to forgive me. I met the most beautiful girl the other night. But then I died. Probably because she's so hot. I'll text every combination of every number until I find her.

You're dramatic. But I'm really glad you lived.

A line of dots popped up and down while he typed. My heart rate quickened.

He was determined. How the hell had he gotten my number? Nix would be pissed. I said a silent prayer that Lock wasn't sending me a dick pic. That would really, really mess with the vibe he was laying down.

A picture sprang to life. I looked through my lashes. Upon closer inspection, I was very relieved it wasn't a penis. It was what seemed like a handful of daisies.

I'm going to put these in water and I'd love to give them to you before they die.

I felt my nose wrinkling. That kind of sweetness hit me right in my girly parts.

That sounds more like a threat than a promise.

The reply took even longer. Then I had a video. Again, the dick pic fear made my finger hesitate, but I pressed play anyway.

It was his face, illuminated in blue from his screen. His face was beat up, mostly on the right side. I remembered how his hair felt under my fingers. He grinned into the camera and sang a really off-key version of "Unforgettable."

Then another video popped through almost immediately.

"I'm sorry. I shouldn't have sent the song. Maybe it's the

remnants of the concussion? Don't judge me yet. Not on that. You wanna Facetime? Too soon? Can I get a date? I mean, is that allowed? Just tell me where to find you and I'm there."

He was wearing a baseball cap backwards and took it off during his monologue. I saw a hint of his dimples while he talked. Only this guy would be flirting while looking like an extra in a zombie movie.

I hopped out of bed and flicked on the light. I messed up my hair a bit and put blush on my cheeks. After sliding back under my covers, I hit record on the video.

"I don't date strangers and I don't Facetime strangers. How are you feeling, anyway?" I hit send before I could come to my senses and squealed after it was done.

I waited for his response with butterflies in my stomach. There was something about him. Dangerous, but safe somehow.

I hit play on the video the moment it appeared. "Ember. I see you, girl. Prettier than I remember, which seems impossible. Lord, you are gorgeous. You in a dorm at Harmony Hill? I'll be by as soon as I can this week. We can get to know each other so I'm not a stranger. And then I can get that date. Sleep tight, sexy." He gave me a wink and a kissy face.

"Cheese Ball." I knew not to respond to that last one. It would be giving him too much. I looked around behind me before I noticed that my tank top had given me away. I'd bought it before lunch after getting my books and digital codes. "Harmony Hill College" was printed in bright yellow letters across the maroon fabric. I'd given him a clue. Though, if he had my phone number, he had enough leads on me to find me I bet. How determined was this guy? I'd been in town less than a week and he'd tracked me somehow. Nix would blow his stack.

8

Lock

I GOT DRESSED IN the morning, trying to look as sharp as I could. I even dipped into my dad's closet and snagged a tie. Rhy clapped when she saw me, and even though I was all business in my head, I had to stop to hug her. Mom was helping her eat. She was doing well. I checked the plate. There were usually apple slices on there with breakfast. I looked from the plastic plate to my mom; she shrugged. Fresh fruit was expensive. It hardened my resolve. I kissed Rhy and my mom on the top of their heads. As I locked the door behind me, I had to step over a basket of muffins someone in the building had made for Mom and Rhy. The neighbors pitched in where they could. Their kindness just made me more determined.

I was fixing this. Not entirely sure how. But today. Dice was ready to meet me, but pissed it was so early in the morning. I wound my bandana around my wrist while Dice and I rolled up to Booker's place. It was an apartment building that was in good condition. He rented out some of the apartments. Mostly it was a place to do business for the Cokes.

The men at the front door gave us a ration of shit. I didn't even know how many people were pissed at me for getting them a beatdown. I was guessing the ones with facial lacerations were the first to suspect. I got a few hisses and "Here, kitty, kitty."

I pretended not to hear them. I was made of metal. For my girls.

I went in the elevator and gave Dice a look. Dice was a good friend, but certainly not a best friend. This could be a trap. A setup. I knew my pulse was banging away at my throat. The elevator door opened and we were frisked by the goons there as well.

It was a horrible fucking life. I was betting anyway. Surrounded by all these shitbags. Well, not all of them were shitbags, but we all started out in the neighborhood and evolved into the soldiers that we were now. Two more pat-downs and one very violent frisk and the door was opened.

Booker was dressed in a suit. It was clear he was projecting a certain image, but there was something...off about him. Like a kid picking from his grandfather's closet. I smoothed my father's tie and realized I was the last person who should be judging.

"You're an asshole. For starters." He stood and put his hands on his hips.

"That's fair," I responded and tried to look tougher. I wasn't sure if I should shake his hand or just stand there like a dung pile. I held out my hand and Booker barked out a sharp laugh, ignoring my offer. I dropped my hand.

The scene was odd. The setting was clearly aspiring to be an office. But it seemed more like a yard sale. There was an odd assortment of bulk food. Soda, chips, and crackers. Clothes were hanging off of furniture. There was a black bedspread covering the two windows. But he had a desk and chairs set up for meetings.

Booker had to be thirty. He had tattoos on his fingers and neck, but he wore them well. They were old enough on his body that they seemed to be seeping into his skin instead of decorating it. His shock of blond hair was dyed that way. There were pictures on the walls of various men and teens. The frames were all a little crooked. It was unnerving.

"My niece was in the process of being attacked by our very own. And you stopped it. I have one very important question for you. And you need to tell the truth because it will tell me everything I need to know. And I will eventually know everything, so spare us both the time."

I swallowed and nodded. I had a feeling I was about to lie.

"Did you know Keely was family?" He waited with the patience that likely got him to the top and kept him alive.

No, I didn't know jack about his niece. I was stopping them as best I could because I couldn't live with myself if I saw a girl hurt like that. Should I lie or not?

"I suspected something like that. Family resemblance." I shrugged.

"She's adopted." Booker's face was a mask, unreadable.

"Oh." I put my hands into my pockets. "Well, no then. I didn't know."

I could see Dice flinch out of the corner of my eye.

"Shit, I told you I'd figure it out. She's not adopted. But you're a fucking liar. Tell me why you threw down after getting jumped not even twenty-four hours earlier?" I thought I saw Booker's left lid twitch.

"'Cause it wasn't a fair fight. And I don't treat females like shit." I tossed up my hands. I fucked it all up. Now Dice and I were going to die and who the hell knew what would happen to my mom and sister.

"You goddamn dumbass. Why you lying to me then? I told you to speak the truth. I don't give a shit how much trouble you're in. To get here, to stay near me, you gotta tell me everything. You got a pimple on your dick? I need to know. You got family in Detroit? I need to know." Booker got close. Real close. In the personal bubble close. From his breath I was guessing he had some sort of spicy sausage meat for breakfast. "You feel me?"

I nodded. Because I got it. Tell him everything. Which I wouldn't, but I'd nod all day long if I had to.

"You got to promise. You're a tough fucker. Hard to kill, have something to prove. Weirdly righteous about shit. I have a sense about people. And I think you're either a diamond in the rough or a huge mistake. But I like to gamble. Do you?" He got even closer. I could count his cavities if I cared to.

I didn't.

"See all these freaking pictures?" Booker waved his hands, gesturing at the walls around us. "These are the people I've had to kill."

He pointed to a tiny part of the wall; it was blank except for a group of naked nails. "And that's where I'll put the pictures of the people I kill next."

He stomped over to the desk in the room and shuffled through some stacks of frames. "Here you fucking are." Booker tossed the frame at me. I caught a picture of my own face. It was lifted from my Twitter profile. Dice caught a picture as well. I glanced to see that he had a picture of himself. He gave me a very dirty look.

"You come here, I make you hang your picture, then I kill you. The last thing you do is this. Decorate my fucking office."

It made sense why the pictures were all crooked now. My blood ran cold; I was holding a prepared makeshift gravestone with my own face on it.

"You could hire a decorator. I mean, save some lives." I smiled and held out my photo so he could have it back.

Booker set his lips in a long, flat line, not taking the picture. We stood, contemplating each other for a few heartbeats before he burst out laughing, his guffaws heaving hot breath over me. "Son of a bitch. We're gonna have to take bets about how long I can put up with you."

Dice was giving me cold death in a stare. Clearly, he thought I was taking risks that shouldn't be taken. That was fine. I had to be me.

"You're going to die sooner than you expect. As soon as my mood changes. I recommend getting out of my sight." Booker pointed at us both using his two index fingers. We put our pictures back on his desk.

I nodded and followed Dice out of the office door.

"You fucking dumbass," Dice growled in my direction. Before we could get to the front door, we were stopped by two huge dudes in suits. I put my hands into my pockets. This place was crazy. I had no idea which way was up.

The shorter one held out two crumpled manila envelopes. "Boss wants you to have these."

I took the package held out to me. I ripped it open; inside was a stack of hundred dollar bills.

"He also showed us the pictures we have to hang before he kills us."

The taller man snorted. "Don't bother buying a coffin with your new money. We toss everybody into the river."

I pocketed the money and gave them both a curt nod. When we were back in Dice's car, we drove about three blocks before pulling over and counting the money.

I had ten grand. Dice had $4,567.

"Let's make it even." Dice reached for my money.

"Hell no." I slapped his hand away.

"I'll fight you for it." Dice put his money into his jacket pocket and held up his fists.

"Bitch. No."

Dice fumed from behind the wheel, "I have it worse because being your friend has put a target on my back."

I gave him the middle finger. We drove in silence on the way home.

I hopped out at my apartment building and called back to Dice before I slammed the passenger door, "That place was confusing as fuck."

But I had money now. Accepting it seemed to bind me to Booker. But there weren't many options. Rhy was happily watching a video on her iPad, an older model that didn't hold any charge and needed to stay plugged into the wall. I opened the money in front of my mother and passed out less than half. I wanted to get Rhy a new iPad right freaking now and told my mom as much. "The rest gets her into the Blooming Flower School."

Steel reserve filled the formerly hollow space in my spine. I would provide for these women. My ladies. Starting today.

9

Ember

OKAY, NOW I WAS making a few friends. There was a guy in my biology class, three girls in my English class, and the girls in my dorm whom I'd met in the dining hall, Cady and Heather. Numbers had been shared. This was how I'd find my tribe. My bodyguards kept their distance. I'd even lost Wardon on one occasion. I'd gotten four text messages from four different people to not let that happen again.

I didn't make any promises because I wanted to try out this new life I'd given myself. I did a few reading assignments and decorated my walls with some dollar store finds. I needed a better, Instagramable wall.

There was a party tomorrow on the quad. Well, all the sororities, fraternities, and clubs were recruiting for new members. I'd seen the flyers, but it wasn't until the three girls I met in English pressured me that I decided it was a great place to pop by and see what I could get involved in.

I wanted the whole experience. Late library study groups, keggers in a basement, and cold nights in the bleachers watching football games. I texted with my girls from home. Also sent an email to Jet. We'd spent our senior year of high school exploring our wild sides, going to concerts, and trying to vape. I was horrible at smoking anything. I wished I could shake the lonely feeling, despite having a phone full of people who cared about me.

Patrick Merck had sent a *thinking of you* card to my dorm address. It had a twenty-dollar bill inside. We had a past, he and I. Actually, unfinished business. Animal and Nix had kept the information that Merck might be my father from me. When they finally told me the truth, and that they'd set up an evening for us to get to know each other, I blew out of the house and started couch surfing. I hadn't really handled the information. I didn't want a paternity test. I didn't think I wanted one anyway. It was complicated. Animal had insisted that Merck was a good guy, but I had animosity left over that I didn't know how to place. The lack of my brother. The lack of my mother. The fact that Merck was out there and knew he *could* be my father—and didn't try to step forward in my life when I was younger. Well, I took the twenty. And tossed out the card. So that was how maturely I was handling things.

The pebble that hit my window made me pause for a

second. Then I went back to my phone. Then another pinged the glass. Then another. It was clearly happening on purpose. Which was weird. Another hit. I turned off my bedside lamp. Now I could see outside better, instead of my own reflection as I pushed the curtain out of the way. A guy was standing outside my window holding balloons.

Oh God. Not a clown. But no, just a man. I opened the window, and when I leaned out, the man below me let go of the balloons. I was able to snag them when they reached me. A bouquet of very wilted daisies was tied to the balloons, surely the same ones from the picture Lock had sent. I knew by the time I had them secure that the guy below me was for sure Lock because he was singing my name. And I was delighted.

"This is wicked creepy. I thought you were a clown and these flowers are dead." I let the balloons go into my room. They bounced off the ceiling. "This seems like a death threat."

He laughed out loud. I felt myself smiling in response.

"Man, you can really bust some balls." He shook his head.

It was a gorgeous night out. The stars were clear and the air had a hint of crispness.

I made sure to point out the obvious. "You brought your balls here willingly. Like, went through some serious effort."

"You got me there." His white smile was obvious even two floors up. "You're beautiful. Worth it."

Why weren't any of the guys tackling him to the ground? This was an interesting development.

"You sneak on campus? Because usually loiterers aren't treated too kindly." I was actually concerned that he could be a target.

"I've got moves. Don't you worry about me, pumpkin." He stood taller. "I know, protective friends."

"Who will want to know how the hell you got my phone

number when I tell them you are enemy number one." I went to close my window.

"Wait, what? No, Ember, wait." He held up both his hands like he could stop me from leaving with just the power of his mind. "I know a guy who knows a guy."

"Who has my number? That's even sketchier." I was glad it was a still night so he couldn't see me blushing. I could hear him clear as a bell, his voice echoing off the cement and brick.

"Okay, no. I know a guy whose uncle works in admissions. Ember isn't a common name. He gave it to me because he owes me a favor." Big smile again. Those dimples again.

"He's compromising student safety so you can get laid?" I tossed my hair over my shoulder, but I was still listening. I loved the pull I felt from my center at the sight of him. Like my nervous system was replaced with tingles.

"I'm getting laid?" His hopeful face was lit up.

"No." I gave him the middle finger.

"Dammit." He kicked his foot behind him. "No, I wouldn't want it like that anyway. You deserve champagne and fancy shit."

"So you brought me dead flowers after you robbed a clown for his balloons. Seems like you're on the right track." I stepped back.

"Aw. Don't be like that, beautiful girl. I'm going to be rich someday. I'll fill a swimming pool with champagne. Tell me, you got a boyfriend?" He stepped closer to the building.

I leaned out the window again and folded my arms on the sill, considering him. He pressed his palms together so it looked like he was praying. Still with the giant smile.

He stepped forward into the streetlight. I could still tell he'd definitely taken a beating. I narrowed my eyes at him. He was trouble. Not dangerous, as far as I could tell, but he wanted in my panties and was used to getting what he desired —or at least I guessed he did.

"Not yet." I smiled back at him when he jumped in the air after the words registered like he'd just won the World Series.

I closed the window on his joyful cursing. He was for sure trouble.

10

Ember

I FINISHED OUT THE week with no other contact with Lock. Which was what I expected. A player knows how to play the game. His lovesick act was just that. When I got a message from Nix reminding me to come home for the weekend, I knew it was a good idea. None of the friends I'd made were party friends yet. I was hoping that they'd turn out that way. Who knows though?

Apparently, Thrice wanted to meet with Nix and Animal. It

was probably about me. Which made the ride home awkward. I stuck to playing games on my phone. Thrice dropped me off. He didn't even help me with my duffle bag. Nix was waiting outside, but I didn't see him at first as I walked to the door. From slightly behind the hedge near the front door, he coughed and I shouted.

"Sorry. I'm so used to staying quiet I forget."

I gave him a hug. "Where's everybody?"

"I asked them to leave us be this weekend. I was hoping we could just do you and me."

My shock must have shown on my face.

"Unless that's too weird. I wanted to just do a brother-sister weekend." He jammed his hands into his pockets. "But it's totally cool if you want to do something else. No pressure."

Delight zoomed from my toes to my mouth, which shouted yes before he could change his mind. A whole weekend with Nix to myself was something I never imagined could happen. I wouldn't take him away from Becca like that. And he and Animal and T were running a whole business. Entertaining the needy nineteen-year-old sister was a low priority.

"That's great. Yeah. I'm down." He motioned for me to go past him, but I caught a glance of his relieved grin.

He reached past and locked the front door behind me. The interior was decorated with streamers and balloons. Balloons seemed to be a theme for this week.

"Whose birthday?" I twirled to take in all the decorations. He had giant silver balloons that spelled out EMBER.

When I saw my name, he shrugged sheepishly. My birthday is in March. He was way off.

"It's, uh, sort of my way of celebrating all the birthdays you had when we couldn't be together. Is that stupid? It feels stupid now."

I stepped farther into the house. The dining room was

laden with a ton of cakes, all with number candles in them. Pictures of me were blown up big and taped around the room. Newspaper clippings. Screen grabs from websites. I wandered closer and saw he had every time I hit the honor roll saved. The last time I'd done it was freshman year in high school. It struck me that the edges were neat. Carefully nipped out with scissors.

The TV had video clips, silent, merged together. Snapshots of my life. A set of pictures showing my rollerblading routine in the elementary school talent show. A small clip of me making a snowman. The newspaper article about the time I found a wallet in the street and turned it in to the police. Probably to the same precinct as Merck, come to think of it. Picture after picture of me playing alone in the backyard. A snapshot of me through the window, the only child at a table of my aunt's adult friends. He had a recording of me standing in front of my photographs that were displayed at the county fair, boasting I had gotten four ribbons.

Nix took my duffle bag out of my hands. "Come with me."

I followed my brother, bewildered and touched at the incredible documentation of me in his house. We went to the basement together and he opened a door. He swung it wide and stepped back. The room was a gorgeous setting of grays and pale yellow. My name was painted on the wall in a beautiful font.

"What is this?" I mean, it was obviously for me, but I was thunderstruck.

"You said you were lonely. You said you didn't feel like you belonged. And I was always watching you. Never knew we would meet. I was saving all this stuff for you. Like a time capsule. Part of my will was to have Animal bring all my surveillance to you. Every year I bought you a birthday gift. Just because that's what brothers should do. You live here. This is your home. It's always been your home, and I know it's probably too late, but this room is yours until the end of time."

He brought a paper out of his back pocket. He unfolded it and tapped it in the middle. My name and his name were on a deed to a property.

"It's in our names now. You will always have a home. And that's all I've got."

His jaw twitched.

A million thoughts ran through my head. Happiness was the current frontrunner now. This was incredibly unexpected.

"What about Becca?" The thought of his girlfriend and soul mate gave me pause. I didn't want her to resent me. This seemed like a lot. Too much.

"Half of it was her suggestion. I realized I've been treating you more like a visitor and not a sister. I never told you that this was where you should've been as soon as I had the money to support you. For a long time I thought I wasn't something to be inflicted on others. So..."

"You're not a something; you're a someone. And thank you for this. All of it's so thoughtful. It's like my wildest dream just came true." I dropped my duffle bag at my feet and approached him with my arms extended. We hugged for a few minutes. He was right. This was what he should've done first, because right in that instance, we became family. I didn't need all his opulence. That didn't matter. But a place in his house meant everything.

"I love you, Ember. I've loved you your whole life. Even when you were alone, you weren't."

"I love you, too."

We explored my room. He showed me how they'd added windows to the room. A bathroom had been constructed and was attached to my bedroom. Just beyond that was a little efficiency kitchen and reading area. My own wing in his house.

My name or initials were in three different spots. He really wanted me to know this place was mine.

Becca and T had stocked my closet and my bathroom. It was like winning the best prize. Nix and I went upstairs and he had my favorite pizza warming in the oven. While munching on slices, we toured my life. The presents were wrapped, sitting on the chairs or the table. Nineteen cakes. Nineteen presents. The wrapping got more elaborate as the time passed. I went to the first one and touched it. It was wrapped in stained brown paper.

"You don't have to open that. I mean, I was just a kid. I didn't even know what..."

I put my hand on his shoulder. "It's okay." I picked it up.

I carefully removed the stiff paper; beneath it was an empty toilet paper roll with the ends bent to create a canister. There was something small rattling in it.

I carefully opened the end. Into my palm tumbled one gold earring. Well, gold-plated. There was a small section that was rubbed off near the front, revealing the silver underneath.

"It was Mom's. I could only find the one. I was just a kid, but I made sure to save it. I didn't know then it was fake. You don't have to wear it or anything."

I stared down at the earring, and it went out of focus as my eyes began to tear up. I didn't have anything of hers. But this was hers. "When did you get it?"

"I found it under the bed when I was hiding one time from him. I kept it in a sock in my room. When it was your birthday, I made it a present that year. You were turning one. So that's what I got you."

I touched the toilet paper tube. It had my name written in pencil. The letters were big and jagged—a little kid's handwriting.

I asked Nix to open up his hand and I placed the earring

carefully in the center. I took out the hoop I had in the piercing in the shell of my left ear. It was real gold, ironically. I couldn't care less. Nothing was more valuable than the stud I affixed there how.

"Baby Ember would've been very grateful." I nodded at him.

"I didn't know then how little of Mom we'd have left. Pictures. Anything."

"You were a genius then, saving this." I touched my ear. I'd never remove it. My heart swelled with pride. I was wearing something that had been my mother's. Given to me by my big brother. My whole life I'd waited to feel like I belonged. And tonight I was getting everything I wanted with royal flourish. I was giddy with the rush of it. We ate a slice of every cake. I opened every gift. The last one was a diamond bracelet. So different than the first gift. They escalated in price as the age on the front increased. The younger ones were my favorite. The thought of a sweet, kid-shaped Nix thinking about his sister every year and keeping track of the small pile of presents made my heart ache.

The pictures and surveillance that he had pinned up as part of the declaration would work just fine as props in a serial killer movie. It all looked obsessive. But watching Nix detail when and where he got the footage and images revealed such a different side. He boasted about the ones that captured moments that would be in a memory book. The sweetness factor was off the charts.

I spent my first night tucked into my new bed. The room was so peaceful, even though it was in the basement. It felt more like a beach retreat than anything else. The rest of the weekend was an unabated brother and sister fest.

I showed Nix two of my favorite movies; he introduced me to a few of his favorite bands. He told me stories from his childhood, and as many things about Mom as he could remember. He even told me how terrible her murderer was. And that I was lucky I never knew him. He told me about dropping out of school and how much the skull tats meant to him.

After hours of bonding, Nix finally brought up Lock. He scooted up to the edge of his chair and tented his fingertips. "So, the kid you met at the pizza parlor? He was under your window."

"Yeah. I was surprised he was allowed to get that far."

Nix bit his smile and shrugged. "He was allowed to talk to you. Anything else, and well..."

"Thanks for that, though. It was nice to get that time to talk to him." I edged up on my seat as well. "It felt super...normal."

"It'd be great if all your relationships could be conducted like that, though. Him on the outside. Passing gifts up on balloons." Nix made two finger guns in my direction.

"Yeah—not likely. By the way, I've been meaning to ask. You don't have any cameras in my room or anything invasive like that, right?" I'd assumed as much, but before I got deep into my college social life, I wanted to make sure.

"Oh no. Never. You have complete privacy. I'd never..." He stood and seemed upset, shifting in his seat.

I stood as well. "I didn't think so. Don't be worried."

He nodded a few extra times and I changed the subject— reminding him that Thrice wanted to talk.

He had to make time to talk to Thrice, but other than that, it was our own private vacation.

The weekend was everything. We had inside jokes now. A special sibling handshake that he didn't even make me feel silly for wanting. My cheeks hurt from smiling. Before it was time to go back to school, he and I played my favorite video game, Spaltoon 2. He told me he would make a profile and we could play it when I was at school.

Everything was amazing. So, so perfect. This was what was missing in the hole in my chest. I told him so as I said goodbye.

"Good. That was the hope. Thank you for letting me in there."

I was smiling the whole ride home, as Thrice drove and Wardon sat next to me. I forgot I had homework, so as soon as I got back to the dorm, I had to settle in and read a few chapters and answer questions. True to his word, there was a friend request from Nix waiting for me on my Spaltoon profile. I accepted and messaged him there. He was totally down for playing a few rounds. He was getting better with each round and we were turning out to be a great team. This time, he was the one making me regret moving so far away. But maybe me doing that helped him come to the conclusion that I need a home with him.

And now I even had my name all over it. I touched my mom's earring. I wondered if she would be happy. And something inside of me said she would.

11

Lock

I QUICKLY FOUND OUT that the Cokes treat guys who save their potential victims like a snitch. Booker made it clear Dice and I weren't to be touched. But like doing a magic spell, it was all about the exact wording used. And the Cokes were allowed to *say* anything they wanted to us.

In my neighborhood you become a man when you get a street name, and boys spend their short childhoods wondering what their names will be. From about third grade to the fifth, I wanted to be Deathblood with everything in my soul.

Dice was always happy with his own last name, and over time, I realized Lock was badass enough. So when the guys started in on us, calling me 'Pussy' and Dice 'Ball Sack,' a part of our souls died.

It was "Hey, Pussy" and "Looking good, Pussy." "Oh, Pussy and Ball Sack, a match made in heaven." They threw rubber balls at Dice and wet tuna at me the last time he and I went out to meet up at the party house with the empty pool. It was humiliating. Dice was furious with me still. He loved Booker's money, though. Spent it all in two nights.

Not me. Mom and I went down to Rhy's new school. I called a service to drive us, and it was handicap accessible. Now, the school she was leaving was public, but small. The administrators were super creative with getting funds. But the Blooming Flower School? They had money to burn. It was incredible. The amount of programs and equipment would be downright life-changing for my sister. I knew I had to keep money flowing. I saw the envy in my mother's eyes when she took in the zero entry pool. Rhy loved water so much. Having it as part of her physical therapy would be a game changer.

Dice could spend his money on detail work for his car. I wanted to give my sister the world.

Booker sent us jobs. They were the peach ones, though. Easy. Checking on old people and making simple transactions. This made the other Coke guys even angrier. I texted Ember late one Wednesday. Keeping my distance from her was killing me. But she needed to miss me. And, in a giant stroke of vanity, I wanted to get my handsome back. I knew I was pretty good-looking. Girls always perked up when I was around. Dice and I had been lifting for a few months. I was already fairly lean, but now I had a bulk of muscle that I'd accidentally on purpose flash from time to time when I lifted up my T-shirt. The ab flash. So the girls knew I was worth all the preening.

She was a different set of beautiful, though. One time there was a movie filming a few blocks over from my neighborhood. I happened to see the actress as I walked by one day. And it was like she glowed. Every set of eyes had to follow her. There wasn't even a choice.

Ember was even prettier than that. Her beauty was a spectacle. The only reason she wasn't wifed up on some old billionaire was her age. Maybe. Now don't get me wrong. I'm deeper than all that shit. I need more than just pretty. But her lovely profile made my balls ache, so when she was feisty, too? I knew I'd go for her. As hard as I could until I got her.

We'd flirted over text. And went a little deeper, too. She'd volunteered some information about herself and what was important to her. Her counselor-in-training job in the summer was her favorite. She shared pictures of her with her campers. Hung up on her wall in place of pride. And the campers—they got me right where it counted. They were in wheelchairs—like Rhy. The crew she was with in the summer? And that she loved it? That sent my heart soaring. Because Rhy was everything. And if Ember understood the very basic principle that I was lucky to have a sister like Rhy, then it was going to be all aces. We could have a future, maybe.

I knew I was going to the library that Friday afternoon, because she'd mentioned that she had a study group. But first, I had to get through the week. I sent her an artsy picture of my sneaker near a puddle with my face blurry in the water's reflection.

She responded quickly with a shot of a tree that had a yellow balloon trapped in it. The way it was framed told me she knew what she was doing. The composition for the quick snap was in the rule of threes. The main subject of the pictures had to line up in a certain way. She didn't seem to have any filters on it either. Raw talent. I told her so. It seemed like we had pictures in common.

I popped into Target and grabbed a Polaroid camera. They were all the rage with the teen girls now. Which was helpfully pointed out to me the next time I got hit on the back of the head with a blob of tuna. But I liked the idea of it. For her. Everyday I would old-fashioned take a picture and then old-fashioned mail it to her at her dorm. Everybody loves mail, right? So by the time Friday rolled around, she'd know I had some fucking depth. I wasn't just looking to screw her. I was going to woo her.

12

Ember

I WAS LIVING FOR these pictures that Lock was sending me every day. It was charming as hell. He probably knew it. Instead of dick pics, I was getting actual art. The back of a little girl's head as she gazed out a window on a rainy day. A half-mast flag with a morning moon behind it. A close-up of a brick patio with a sunflower bursting through. And he jotted something on the back of each. And signed his name.

When I saw him over the top of my book in the library on

Friday, he fanned a bunch of Polaroids in front of him. He was healing even more. I could see more of his cheekbones now. Lock was hot. And now, he was headed straight for me.

He made his way toward me, and it was like he was tasered with happiness. His hands kept moving over the pictures he set down in front of me like an offering.

"You're beautiful." He shrugged.

"You're trouble. I think." I reached out to touch the Polaroids.

"I'm into you, not trouble." After spinning a chair around, he straddled it. He looked a lot better actually. So much better that it made me wonder how badly he'd been hurt.

"Where do you go to school?" I started some small talk while looking at his latest portfolio. He was talented.

He cleared his throat and drummed his fingers. "Um. Hey, you know this library has a great selection of art books. You wanna come with?"

He held his hand out to me. I stacked the pictures and tucked them into my backpack. His lifted eyebrows and hopeful face broke me. I liked to play much harder to get than this. But he was an open book. His smile grew wider the longer I stared at him. "Come on, Ember."

I stood, and before I could grab my backpack, he snagged it. I took his hand. He lifted it to his lips and kissed my knuckles. "You don't have to go to this school to look at the books. Just to check them out." He bopped on his toes, excited. "I used to sneak in here as a kid sometimes, if we were around here, and go to the art books for the boobs."

"The boobs? Where are you taking me again?" I hesitated and stopped walking.

"Art? Boobs are all over art. Stone boobs, painted boobs, even pictures of nudes. Come on. You didn't know that? Artists are pervs. But eventually I started noticing details. And falling in love with some of it. Not just the titties." He tugged on my hand again.

"If you could stop talking about breasts at top volume here, it'd be awesome."

He ducked low and whispered into my ear, "Sorry, sunshine. I'm just ready to be around you so hard right now."

"What do you mean, hard?" I laughed at him when his cheeks flushed.

"Like a lot. Not hard. Not erection hard. Not that I can't get hard. I totally can. Drop of the hat. Want me to show you now?" I watched as he squinted, seeming to finally hear what he was saying. He covered his mouth. He mumbled behind his fingers, "Am I blowing this? Oh God. Blowing. I'm such an asshole."

He was nervous. Like visibly nervous to be around me. It was low-key adorable. I pulled on his hand and led him to the library's escalator. He followed and stuck out his chest like a proud turkey. He started stage whispering to the people coming down the escalator.

"She's into me. Letting me hold her hand and everything." He held up our clasped hands and then kissed mine again. "See?" He waved to the first group of students going down and then brought the group of guys positioned behind them into it, too. "I thought I'd shot myself in the foot because I was talking about boners, but nope. She's still here." He waved his other hand at me like I was a prize he won on *The Price is Right*.

"Stop." I was laughing, but he needed to tone down the chatter. The guys passed, each of them holding up a hand to be slapped.

"My man."

"Boners forever."

"Do you know these guys?" I tilted my head so I could see his face.

"No. People like me. It's just my animal magnetism." He looked me up and down. Again. He kept doing it, his eyes lighting up like I was his own personal Christmas morning. Mentioning "animal" made me think of the man with the same name. I glanced over my shoulder and tried to find my bodyguard.

"He's down there. One of the three guys that have been following you? I recognize the same guys from the pizza parlor. I'm thinking that they're meant to protect you. I wouldn't be surprised to find one of the others upstairs by the time we get there." He was unworried by my security detail, which was oddly relieving. "Will they warm up the condom for us and everything, when the time to come comes?"

I slapped his bicep. "Don't be crude." I was surprised he had figured out that I had my brother's men with me. I thought they were a little better at blending in than that.

"I'm sorry. I think about sex with you a lot. It's pretty much all I think about." He rubbed his thumb on the palm of my hand.

"Since when?" I stepped off the escalator. Lock stepped off as well.

"Since I laid eyes on you, back when I thought I was dead." He towed me toward the fourth stack. "Literally hard as a rock when I met you. Like a fire alarm went off in my body." He bit his tongue.

"Keep talking about sex and I'm out. I get that enough walking across campus. Be different. Don't disappoint me by being a douche. I have hopes for you." I gave him a hostile stare. I wasn't kidding. He was cute. He was funny, but if he was slimy, I was gone.

He dropped to one knee in front of me. "I'm so sorry, beautiful Ember. I'll shave my head like a monk. I'll never mention that your rack looks even more spectacular from this angle. We can chop off my nuts together. I'll sing to you in a gorgeous, clear soprano forever."

I grasped his hand, out and out laughing now. "You're insane." I touched the red bandana he wore almost as a bracelet. "What's this for?"

"Brings out your eyes." He stood and put his arm around my shoulders. "This way. I'll now show you pictures of the greatest riches and art in the world."

True to his word, he took me to the art book section. He did seem very comfortable in it. After he'd plucked four huge hardback books from the stacks, he sat on the floor and patted the spot next to him.

And then we really enjoyed the books. He described his favorites. Using his index finger, he "censored" any nudity. We both puzzled over *David's* tiny penis, though. Lock was truly excited by the art. Depth. That's what it was. I thought I had him pegged and he was showing me more than that. I was into it.

He stopped when describing a landscape. I could tell he loved to stare at my lips. His eyes were bright with all the jokes he was maybe thinking of sharing in the future. He leaned nearer to me, moving the book reverently to the floor, treating it like it actually contained all the treasures pictured.

A man clearing his throat startled me. I jumped and Lock put his hand on my arm. Campus security was there. Two security guards, one tall and one short, dressed as knock-off state policemen.

"What's going on here?" The tall guard pointed at us with his baton.

"Um. Learning?" I offered. My adrenaline was spiked from the scare.

"I was about to try to steal my first kiss, sir." Lock stood and offered me his hand. I took it and pulled myself up.

"Bet that's not the only thing you steal." The guard bristled.

I was confused. First, I wondered if the guard knew Lock and was messing with him. When I flashed to Lock's face, I saw that his whole demeanor was different. Instead of playful, he was hard. Closed. It happened like the flip of a switch.

Lock stopped talking. Didn't offer that this library was his safe spot as a kid. His getaway. His treasure trove.

"How'd you get that bandana?" The short guard nodded at Lock's wrist, where the red bandana was wound.

Lock was true to his nickname now. They weren't getting him to talk.

"It's my headband. I use it to hold back my hair when I take off my makeup." I actually did have a white bandana in my dorm for this exact purpose.

The tall guard snorted. "When it's knotted like that? It's nobody's headband. He's in a gang. You should find a guy from around here to sneak into the stacks with." He tilted his head and gave me a once-over from my toes to my tits.

They were judging him. They were checking him out because of the color he wore on his arm. It clicked. I was so used to security people being on my side I didn't recognize their hostility.

"He's my fiancé." I was getting angry for Lock. All we were doing was looking at books in a library, which is literally what a library is designed for. I told them so. They were unmoved.

I turned to Lock, went to my tiptoes, and kissed him right on the lips. The zap was emotional. His lips. So soft. So interested. He angled his body toward me, grabbed my hips, and caged me in. When I went to pull back, he stepped even closer, making our bodies touch.

Lock was one hell of a kisser.

"All right, enough of that. We don't need a show." The tall

security guard rapped his baton on the metal bookshelf, making me jump and breaking our contact. Lock didn't react to the loud noise. His eyes were fire and focused only on me. A chill went down my spine.

The guards began approaching, crowding us. Lock acted like they didn't exist at all.

"You kissed me."

I nodded. Our engagement ruse was not going to fly if he continued to be amazed by our kiss. I couldn't even blame him. It was the beginning. I don't even know what of, but nothing else in my life had been so definitive. Ever.

Finally, when the security guard almost put his hand on me, Lock snapped out of it. He put his body in the way so the man couldn't touch me.

"No, man. I don't think so."

Lock was ridged. Ready to fight. I said his name a few times. "Come on. Let's go home. We don't need this crappy place."

His focus went from the guards back to me. His hands had to touch me. One on my shoulder, one on my hip. The fire was coming back to his eyes. He was letting our current trouble roll off his back. I distracted him.

I stepped backwards on the escalator, and he steadied me. I knew he wouldn't let me fall. While he held me, I gave the security guards two middle fingers.

He laughed. "Feisty. And you kissed me."

I turned and leaned back against him until the escalator dumped us off. The guards were watching from the floor above. When we went outside, Lock caught my arm and pulled me under his own.

He touched my cheek. "You kissed me."

It was like I'd given him the dearest gift.

"I was protecting you," I offered.

His smile was blinding. "My entire body feels very unsafe now. Do what you must to protect me."

I glanced over his shoulder, trying to see if the guards were following us outside.

"Don't. Don't stop looking at me like that," he murmured as he ran his palms down my arms.

I made him the center of my attention. It was like he was seeing me for the first time. "You kissed me. Do it again. Come on. I already miss it so much."

He had no game in that request. It came from a genuine place in him.

I felt tingles all over my skin. Anticipation was creating goose bumps. "Maybe I took a chance already. Maybe you should take one now."

Surprise etched on his face, still bruised but healing, put an emphasis on the sparkle in his eyes. His hair had a slight curl to it. His forearm was strong as he twisted to put his hand on my lower back. I felt his palm cradle my neck. He traced my lower lip with his index finger. "It isn't fair. How pretty you are. You don't know how incredible it is that you're so..."

He came in for the kiss, and I expected it. And he treated my lips like the most expensive wine. Gentle, at first, then deeper. A nip, his hands steady—his kiss was the only thing that mattered to him. Getting it right.

Before it got more intimate, he stopped. I was searching for more and opened my eyes. He was gazing at my lips and then touched his head to my forehead. "You're ruining me, Ember. There will be no topping this. Topping you."

He smiled, almost sadly.

"What's wrong?" I didn't understand the switch in him.

"Those guys are right. You should date someone else. One of these rich bastards in this school." He stepped backwards and offered me his arm. Like a polite escort.

I swatted his arm away. "Don't tell me what to do. I suck at following rules."

Lock stayed close, the appearance of his dimples revealing the smile he was planning.

I planted my feet and pointed to the place in front of me. "Kiss me more. I wasn't done."

He rolled his head back, running his hand down his face. "Aw, fuck."

And then he was on me. He lifted me up, making me straddle him as he walked me to the closest brick wall. And then I knew what getting ravished was all about. My lips, my neck, his hands running the length of my sides. He was on me like I was oxygen on Mars. It was a sensory overload. He protected my head so I didn't bang it against the brick.

"You two. Get out of here. I swear..." The guards had followed us outside and were looking grim. Lock had no snappy comeback; he just took my hand and pulled me behind him. He was a man on a mission.

13

Lock

IF I WAS OLDER or more powerful, I would revel in being able to get the guards fired—having that loud of a voice. But, now I had much more important things on my mind. Ember's lips. Ember letting me touch her. It was different than the way it was with others. She was like touching a mythical being. She was so gorgeous. The way her face slid from one emotion to another was mesmerizing. Definition of beauty. Her eyes letting me in, her soft curves at my fingertips.

I needed distance. I wanted her, of course. But somehow, I needed her. An injection of soul. Tumbling destinies. I didn't feel like we were meant to be together forever. She was someone else's. I wanted to steal her from whatever fate had planned. I'd be her thief as long as she let me. I hoped to fuck it was more than just tonight.

I led her through the woods near the campus library, toward her dorm. Twigs snapped behind us when I remembered her bodyguard detail. I stopped moving forward and wrapped my arm around her shoulders. "They're following us."

Ember shot me a confused look and rubbed my hand. My brain wanted to snap. Her touch was like gasoline, setting fire to the place in my center that her kiss had shred open.

She stole my attention. The slope of her nose. Her jaw. Another snap of a twig brought me back to reality. "Your bodyguards. I don't want to scare them. So we'll just wait. I don't want to get shot on the best night of my life."

"Oh. Yeah. The guys. Wow." She blinked a few times, like she was under the same spell I was. My heart hoped like an asshole.

Sure enough, two of the guys burst from behind us. "Oh. Hey!" The bigger one staggered to a stop.

Ember held my hand still. "This is Bowen and Wardon. They watch me..." She trailed off. No real explanation there.

I shook their hands. "You guys usually don't lose her, do you? What happened?"

Bowen rolled his eyes. "We set those guards straight. Even though our direct orders are to be invisible."

"They were being jerks," Wardon added, shrugging.

Ember let go of my hand and stepped up to hug each of them. "Thanks. It's nice to know if I was going to wind up in college jail, you guys would help."

Bowen and Wardon were very much in love with Ember. I could see it in how they watched her. I got it. It didn't even make me jealous. No single man in her vicinity would have a choice.

"Yeah. So, where you headed?" Wardon's jaw twitched. I was a problem for him. But she was a job.

"To be alone." I held out my hand again and waited. She would maybe come to me. Maybe.

"Mercy wants to talk to her. For tonight." He turned to her. "It's a thing, Ember. Your brother was adamant." Wardon stared at me.

The conflict was written across her face, but she nodded. She kissed my cheek. I held her body so she had to stay near. "Your brother?"

I knew of a Mercy. A fairly famous murderer. He stood out in street lore thanks to his skeleton tattoo. That he was Ember's family made sense from a security perspective. Of course she'd have guards if he was her brother. But from a potential boyfriend's perspective, it was ball thunderingly terrifying.

"Yeah. He's known as Mercy. And his best friend is Havoc. We're reconnecting. It's important. But I want to go with you. If it counts." She smiled.

I nodded and let her go. I was so possessive over her immediately. She was mine, for this fleeting moment in time. And I didn't want it to pass. But I had a sense that she'd bolt if I was clingy. I caught her jaw in my hand and kissed her lips one more time for our audience. After seeing her swoon a little, I took in the bodyguards. Pain. Residual pain from what they had just seen. I was too proud. To be hers.

They escorted her out of the woods. I had no good way home. I'd taken three buses to get here. I was pretty sure that two of them weren't running anymore.

It was worth it.

14

Ember

THE GUYS WERE GRUMBLING about Lock being a punk, but I ignored them. Lock was catching me. And I hadn't even realized how hard I was falling until we kissed.

So hard. When I was back at the dorm, Wardon insisted on walking me up and checking out my room, even though there was no way the library security guards would still be a threat. When it was all secure, Wardon sniffed and nodded. "Your brother is waiting. Just Facetime him. He's alone. No Becca. He thought it'd be good to have brother-sister time." I lifted my eyebrows in surprise. He really was serious about making time for me.

Once I had my pajamas on, I propped up my phone and hit the button to call him. His video popped up almost instantly. "You good?"

"Hey, bro, it's great to see you, too." I wiggled my fingertips at him.

He was in the basement, judging from his background of claw games. The shadows made his skull tattoo more pronounced. "That kid you're with? He's a Coke."

"What does that mean?" I liked drinking Coke. Maybe he meant the drug.

"No, it's a gang in downtown Valston. A pretty vicious one. Deep Dutch, and indirectly even Feybi family ties." He watched me, his eyes on the screen concerned.

"Do you know everything there is to know about him?" I was getting frustrated again.

"Yes. His father's in prison and he's got a sister..."

He stopped when I put up my palm. "No. He gets to tell me his shit. Not you. In his time. If I want to hear it. You can't stalk him like you do me. I mean, I can't stop you. But I won't listen to reports. Seriously, Nix." I studied my comforter. I knew my face was getting red. After the weekend we'd had, I thought he'd know me better than this. I felt the years between us then.

I found him staring back at me. "I'm sorry."

His voice had a rough texture, like his apology went against his very makeup. The word "gang" was foreign to me, really. In Midville, it wasn't something we dealt with. I'd always looked at gangs as private backyard groups. But the tone in Nix's voice had me thinking about how little I actually knew about what a gang did. What they were for, what they were expected to do.

I put my fist to my mouth. There was a knock on my dorm room door. I was confused. Nix offered, "Animal was in the area."

I looked out my window, shaking my head. "You can't do it like this. I have to be able to go on a date. Kiss a boy without you sending in the troops."

There was another light knock. I put my hand to my hip before hopping out of bed and swinging open the door, shuffling my phone to my left hand so I could still see my brother. "You were in the area?"

Animal's huge body blocked out the light from the hallway. "I was."

"That's a hairy pack of bullshit." I turned as Animal walked into the room, swinging the door closed behind him.

"I did have a business dealing in Valston. I was on the highway just off the exit when Nix told me guards were giving you an issue. I was here to make sure everything went your way." He sat in my desk chair and kicked out his feet.

"I met a boy. I get to meet a boy. And get in trouble with him. Like the most innocent trouble in the world. The two of you... I swear." I flopped back on my bed. My phone bounced flat so I couldn't see Nix anymore.

I could almost hear my brother giving me a reprimanding stare until I righted him. He had his hands in his hair when I did. Frustrated. He addressed Animal as if I wasn't in the room.

"She doesn't want to know about the kid's past. Or, like, all his shit."

Animal nodded. "Yeah. I can see why she'd say that."

Nix sighed so loudly the phone's mic picked him up. "I'm not good at this. Worrying. Not being able to be there."

I felt for him. Slightly. Even though I was pissed again. "I know. But you might try listening to me. Campus police weren't going to hurt me. I was okay. I was getting kissed. And liking it."

Nix leaned forward and banged his head on his desk.

Animal arched a brow and lifted his mouth in a hint of smile. "Let me talk to her, Sweetness. I'm here. Go find Becca in that giant house and let her love on you."

Nix picked up his head and nodded. Before signing off, he added, "Love you, Ember."

I returned it, because no matter what, that was important to me—the fact that we could say those words to each other and mean them.

Animal tilted his head. "That was sweet. I'm happy for him that you aren't a shithead."

"Thanks. I think." I plugged my phone into its charger. "Were you killing people tonight?"

It felt weird that murderers were my parental figures. Sort of.

"I want to talk about you. And this boy you're kissing." He leaned forward, resting his elbows on his knees. He had on a business suit, which somehow made him seem even bigger. Broader. I couldn't spot any bloodstains. Only deep brown skin and a stunningly handsome face.

"He's cute. I like him." I tucked my legs under my covers.

"That sounds low-key. Doesn't explain all the glowing you're doing." Animal squinted at me.

"I'm not glowing." I tugged my hair over my shoulder and started to braid it.

"You're glowing like a brand new neon sign." Animal stood and took off his jacket. I had an extra bed in my room and he was eyeing it.

"You think you're going to fit in there?" I was skeptical. Dorm rooms had extra long beds, but they were still twins.

"I'll do what I have to. Things have been picking up on our

end, and I think T, Nix, and I will all sleep better knowing I'm here." He took his tie off.

I flopped down in my bed. I would sleep like a rock with Animal here. "Do I want to know what it's about?"

"Can't tell you, Baby Girl. It's been a long day, that's a fact." Animal unbuttoned his shirt and I was treated to the sight of him in his sleeveless undershirt.

I lifted an eyebrow. "How much of a show am I getting tonight?" I don't know if I could ever stop flirting with him. It was so easy to do.

"That's it." His smile picked up on one side. "Don't be a dirty old lady." He made sure to lock my door and switch off my overhead light. I watched as he tried to get comfortable on the old mattress as the frame groaned.

"How hard is it to have me here?" I touched my lamp and it turned off. I was afraid to hear the answer; I didn't want to leave college, but I also understood that I was putting them out.

"We're managing. I'll tell you if it gets too messy. I promise."

I was quiet for a few minutes and then I heard Animal's light snores. I rolled on my side and thought about Lock's kiss.

15

Lock

DICE WAS PISSED AND in pajama pants, but he picked me up anyway.

"You need to find a girl closer to home. Snickers with the great knockers has been asking about you." He rubbed his eyes with his left hand.

"This girl's got me so fucked in the head. She's all I can think about." Before he could start listing the eligible girls in the neighborhood, I changed the subject. "What'd you get with your cash?"

"Hookers. Two beautiful hookers that could suck like vacuums." Dice rolled his hips and groaned.

"What's the latest with the Cokes?" I rolled my window down a touch. I loved the night air as it whipped past me.

"Weird shit's going down. Booker's been having meetings. We're supposed to go in next week." He pulled a cigarette out from the pack in his cup holder. I grabbed his lighter and held the flame steady.

"Any news from the other guys?" I put the lighter back near his pack. The smoking was new for Dice. He illustrated this fact by coughing like a grandpa. I was kinda sure he was allergic, but apparently he wanted to find out the hard way.

"Are you kidding? They ain't sharing shit with Ball Sack and Pussy. We'll find out when Booker hands us our pictures in his office." Dice seemed like he wanted to say more, but the coughing took over again.

My mind was clouded with Ember. I had to force myself to think about the very real, pressing things in my life. Rhy and Mom were ready to start in the school. The schedule was an all year round number. Which was great for my sister. Rhy flourished when she had activities every day. This new school even had weekend activities where the parents and the kids attended. Ma was wondering out loud last night if she'd get any pointers from the other moms.

The weekend cost extra as well. I grandly stated that she should sign up for everything. Like the lump sum I'd been handed from Booker would be a regular feature in our life. The stress of not knowing how much of that was true—mostly knowing that it wasn't—was making a mess of my stomach.

Dice stopped at the all night gas station to buy more cigs,

which was dumb because he still had over half of his first ever pack left. I sat in the passenger side and waited.

I borrowed Dice's charger and plugged in my phone. I was busy staring at one of the few pictures Ember had sent, replaying the way she stood up for me in the library over and over when a loud rap on my window made me jump.

I was expecting Dice and immediately tensed at the blue bandana wrapped around the guy's wrist. A Pepsi. Shit.

I'd seen some in my neighborhood growing up. And my father counseled a few, even bringing Cokes and Pepsis together in our living room once to mediate a misunderstanding. But still, the red was what I was used to.

He gestured for me to roll down the widow, which I did. It was then that I looked past him. There were at least ten guys. My nervous glance turned up four more blue bandanas.

I looked back to the store where Dice was. He was about to pay and caught a glimpse of the ambush I was dealing with. He dropped his purchases and headed deeper into the store.

The other Cokes were right. He *was* a Ball Sack.

"Can I help you, gentlemen?" I wasn't getting out of this, so I might as well face them.

"You lost? This isn't your territory." I knew the rules. Stay in your lane. Don't rock the boat. I needed time to come up with a plan. The keys were still in the ignition. If I could get the vehicle in motion...

The driver's side door opened and a wrist wearing a blue bandana pulled the keys out. And effectively pissed all over my hastily organized exit plan.

"You guys own gas stations now? And we're like another ten minutes from home. You expanded lately?" I tapped my fingers on the armrest. Like a conversation with a mob of guys who wanted to wear my balls as a hat was totally normal.

Puzzlement crossed his face. "For like the last seven years. Are you two newborns or something?"

He used his index finger to hook my bright red color. "Did you get bled in like forty-five minutes ago?"

I shrugged. He had my number.

"'Bout that. Listen, I'm not trying to get involved. You give me the keys, and imma roll out. No harm, no foul."

The Pepsi laughed at me. Loud. He bent over, making sure it was so loud the other guys had to join in. "This prick right here?" More laughter. "He's letting us know that he won't hurt us if we give him back his keys."

I darted my glance at the store. Dice wasn't bursting out of there with a fire extinguisher and a bazooka. I was on my own.

"Looks like he loses fights for a living," another piped up from the back.

All the Pepsis laughed then. The one closest poked me on the bruise on my cheek. Ember was never going to get to see how handsome I was if I kept getting my ass kicked.

My door swung open and I was grabbed up out of my seat, my arms restrained behind my back. Just before they could land the first punch, which was going to be a beaut by the way, the guys on the outer part of the pack around me started to fall. With my arms pinned behind me, I could make out that the men were starting to fall. I prepared for the first wallop, but the Jurassic-Park-in-the-dark lighting only allowed me to make out outlines and hints, and my attacker stopped, puzzled.

The noises the Pepsis were making were not the normal ones I'd heard in a fight. The cracks and gulps sounded like dying, not a fisticuffs.

My attacker hit me in the stomach and I bent. The noises only intensified, louder than my own groans. Like extras in a movie, the men began collapsing. When the guys holding me up let go, I rotated with a punch ready. I'd at least try to take someone down. But my punch met only thin air. I turned again, and my attacker was in a pile at my feet. Only then did I see the hooded figure trotting off in the distance. I was too puzzled to even call after them. I couldn't tell if it was a man or a woman. Or a robot. Holy fricks. They had decimated an entire mob of fighters. And left me standing.

Dice came out of the doors of the gas station, his mouth hanging open. "Lock? You do this shit? Holy crap." He pulled his phone out of his back pocket and started filming. I crossed my arms in front of me and mugged for the camera. Dice then helped me move the people away from the Mustang so we could get the hell outta Dodge. They were all pretty much still alive. Which was probably even harder to do than killing them.

"You took us to Pepsi territory for the fucking cigarettes you can't even smoke?"

Dice's eyes were still huge. "What the hell, dude? When did you learn to fight like that?"

I considered him for a minute, then told him the truth. That a mystery person had saved our asses. I didn't want him choosing to stop in Pepsi territory thinking I was some sort of superhero and wanting to see my work.

"Who the hell was it? That Ember chick's security?" He slapped his steering wheel.

"I don't know. All I do know is that I was in trouble and they fixed the hell out of it." I gave him a disappointed glare.

"Sorry, dude. I saw what was going down and thought I could get vengeance for your death or something like that." He patted my shoulder.

I couldn't expect him to get involved in a beatdown willingly. But I hoped I would've at least tried something if the situation had been reversed.

By the time he dropped me off, I was exhausted off my ass. I barely thanked him before I closed the door. I needed some reliable transportation that wasn't Dice. I needed to see Ember more.

I made it only to the couch before I collapsed, clothes and shoes on. I probably should have called Booker right away and told him what had gone down.

I didn't.

16

Animal

I WOKE AS THE sun came up. My lower back wanted to die. The mattresses in that place were shit. God knows how many college kids had screwed on it, never mind slept on it. Ember was almost smiling in her sleep. I checked my phone.

I'm outside.

The text had been sent an hour ago. My bride, my babe, T, was waiting for me. She wasn't even in Valston as far as I knew. There was nothing from Nix, which was either bad or good. We had two families that reported to us: the Feybis and the Kaleotos. We had the Kaleotos in line. They were smart enough to recognize all the beautiful things we did for Midville.

But the Feybis. They were acting up. Hence my meeting in Valston. The family was branching out. Looking to expand to the surrounding cities. It didn't help that their relationship with Nix was strained at best, but that's where I came in. I interrupted a power grab last night. Reminded a room full of men with guns that they were my bitches. In my special way. They were all smiling by the time I was done. I reminded them all that I could charm about half of their men to come to my side, work for me. We had benefits that were appealing. Like a way to get out. Clean money if needed. I was known for rewarding respect and common sense. No one would have ever imagined I could have two crime families agreeing that I was in charge. Hell, I didn't even have a blood family. Just the people I deemed important enough to die for, the people held close in my heart.

I texted T back:

Yeah, on my way.

I pulled Ember's blanket up around her shoulders, tucking her hair behind her ear. She was vulnerable here, and it was killing Nix. I couldn't blame him. Her independence was colliding with Nix's former worst enemies, the Feybis, acting shifty. He'd killed the patriarch in a very violent and disrespectful way. Don't get me wrong. It was more than old Bat Feybi deserved. It seemed like a million years ago, but to the families involved, change usually moved like glaciers. Slow. It took generations to move things differently. As they slowly rebuilt their organization in the aftermath of Bat Feybi's death, they agreed to our terms. They worked for us now. But something was simmering with the Feybis. T had discovered that the Feybis might be connected to the Dutch family—the ones who were running the gangs in the Valston area. Including the Cokes. Ember's new little boyfriend's gang. It was all bubbling too close to Ember now.

Nix wanted to kidnap Ember and keep her in her new bedroom in his basement. It took Becca, T, and me to force him to understand that wasn't a great option.

I made sure Ember's door was locked. I knew that Nix would set his own alarms when he saw me walk out. He had the place wired. I strode out of the dorm building, where I found my beautiful bride sitting on the hood of her SUV.

Her brown hair was pulled over one shoulder and she had shades on. Jeans and a sweatshirt never looked so sinful as they did on her. I leaned in and kissed her cheek. I didn't come at her unless I had a nice, clean mouth. I hadn't been planning on crashing overnight, so I wasn't ready with my toiletries.

T grabbed my belt buckle and smirked. "Miss me?"

I groaned. Being near her started things that would need to be handled. "So much."

She allowed me to cuddle her into my chest.

"How is she?" T lifted her chin in the direction of Ember's dorm.

"Ah, shit. She's got a crush. She was glowing and everything." I ran the back of my hand down T's beautiful face.

"Would he happen to be a Coke?" She tossed her hair and I saw a fresh scratch on her neck.

If she was harmed, she'd been in some shit. Because she never missed a punch. "How many?"

She shook her head. "I followed that kid last night. He

damn near got himself killed. Parked in the Pepsi territory. Was about to get jumped. Dumbass."

"How many did you kill?" I wasn't accusing her; I just needed to do the accounting on how to fix it. She was the closest thing we had to a hit man.

"I didn't kill anyone. I just stopped the situation so the kid and his friend could get away." She put her hand on my shoulder.

"You're perfection." I kissed her forehead. "Do we leave now? I'll text Ember." I stepped back and pulled T with me. I had another car, but I wanted to ride with her. One of our guys could pick it up later.

"I guess. I kind of hate it, despite what we tell Nix." She hugged my middle. I agreed. It felt super wrong, letting one of our own dangle out in the middle of nowhere.

Wardon walked up and touched my fist and then T's. Ember wasn't alone. And these security guys were earning their money. We were tense, though. Two recent murders of Kaleotos men were weighing on our minds. We suspected the Feybis were involved. Despite the fact that they both worked for me, the Kaleotos and the Feybis had a long, bloody history. When one moved on the other, the delicate balance I maintained threatened to wobble. And wobbling was scary. I didn't want more people dying.

17

Ember

WHEN I WOKE UP, it took a text from Animal to remind me he'd spent the night. He'd even made the bed he'd slept in. I missed him, but was also glad to be alone. Because it was time to put on the falling in love songs. Not that I was in love. I wasn't. But Lock's lips were on my mind. I loved this part. When everything was new. When we hadn't annoyed each other yet. Before we knew each other's favorite color. All the newness. I set up a playlist on my computer and danced around for a bit, singing into my hairbrush.

Lock hadn't called or texted, but I knew he would. I felt the electricity between us last night. I painted my nails, did a mask, and used my favorite moisturizer. My hunger became an issue, and I finally got dressed for the day.

My new friend Heather agreed to meet me at the dining hall. The food was subpar, but it got the job done. She wanted to work out in the afternoon, but I passed. After we parted, I strode outside and looked around the courtyard. I spotted Wardon in the center of the patio surrounded by shrubs. I headed his way.

"Hey." I tapped my fingers on his picnic table.

It was one of his favorite places to "study." He could watch the entrance to my dorm and monitor me at the dining hall from there.

His eyebrows came up past his sunglasses. I wasn't supposed to talk to him, not really.

"I was wondering when Animal left?" I shaded my eyes like I might catch sight of him.

"Real early. T was here. They went home." He put his hands over his iPad. "Thought he'd text you?"

I sat down on the other side of the table. "He did. I was wondering how things went. Like I know Nix is probably mad at me."

I didn't know what I expected to get out of Wardon. He was here with me. "Ember, his life is crazy. Probably far crazier than you know."

I tilted my head, thinking about it. "How'd you get involved?"

I was picturing Lock and his red bandana. What made a guy decide to deal on the other side of the law?

"I came out of foster care at eighteen. You leave with nothing. Not one fucking thing. So I wanted work. Do you know how much fast-food restaurants pay?" He flipped his iPad over.

"Not a lot, I'm assuming." Wardon always had on a nice, stylish outfit. An expensive watch. He noticed my assessment and spread his arms wide for the inspection. "He pays you enough? For like, stuff?" I knew Nix had money. But as I thought about the amount of people I'd met who worked for him or with him, I realized he was maintaining quite a payroll.

He grinned at me. "Yeah, kid. I get what I need."

I reached over and punched him on the arm. "Don't call me kid. You're barely older than I am."

He flexed just when I went in for the punch, so I got to feel the wall of muscle.

"I'm twenty-five. You're a toddler to me." He snatched off his glasses and hit me with his baby blues. He was good-looking and knew it.

Before I could respond, Thrice came up on the scene and cleared his throat. "Shift's up."

Wardon nodded and slid his glasses back on; I could have sworn he blushed a bit.

After he'd left the table, Thrice sat down. I decided to rib him a little, too. "You know no one's buying this grandpa goes to college routine you have."

"Listen, I know you want to play and be a student and all of that, but our job is to keep you alive. And you had Wardon distracted. I'll deal with him later. But he didn't even notice I was approaching you both. He wasn't paying attention. And that can get you both killed. Can you do me a favor and just do the school thing? And less of the flirting?" He folded his arms in front of his chest. My skin burned. I felt like a kid getting scolded.

I stood. Chastised was not my favorite feeling. I watched as Thrice sighed deeply, ruffling his hair.

Without another word, I returned to my dorm. I didn't like feeling like I was putting everyone out. That Nix, T, and Animal were making big life changes to accommodate me. That these bodyguards weren't really here to be friends with me. After I closed the door, I sent a message to Nix.

> Hey, maybe you need to pull these guys out of here. I don't like getting lectured by them.

I expected some back and forth, maybe even a Facetime video. Instead, the reply was quick.

> Sorry. I'll tell them to keep their mouths shut.

That wasn't what I'd intended, and now I felt like a huge tool. Like the flouncy, spoiled sister who used her position next to the boss to intimidate the guys underneath him.

> Don't. It's fine. They are just trying to do their job.

I texted a few pictures to Lock, but I had no response. Loneliness was a wave for me. I hated it. Could barely keep my head above water when it came. It took me back to my childhood. I knew I was being unreasonable, that the high doses of attention I required were hard to maintain. But I felt it all the same.

I curled on my bed and tried to remind myself that I would outlast the feeling. I would be okay.

18

Lock

I FIGURED OUT THE worst possible way to wake up. At seven o'clock in morning with a shirtless Dice over my head. "Dude. Booker wants to see us. Fuck. Wake up, for Christ's sake."

I rubbed my palm over my face. It was early. Had I slept four hours? Maybe less.

My sister and mother were probably still asleep. I reconsidered letting Dice have my extra key. I could sleep through banging on the door. And text messages.

"If we don't get there in fifteen minutes, there *will* be consequences." Dice farted. "I'm nervous. Come on." He slapped the couch near my head.

I sat up and scratched my nails over my scalp.

I whispered, "They're asleep. Shut your face."

Dice seemed like he just realized he was in my apartment. "You got a shirt? I forgot to get a shirt."

At least he was whispering too now. I stood and stretched. He pretended to punch me in the stomach and I flinched.

"No stretching. We have to go. Now." Dice had wild eyes. Being in the Cokes was exhausting. I trotted past him and padded into my room. Mom and Rhy shared the other. We were crammed in here, but it worked. It was shelter. I grabbed the first shirt I found, a yellow T-shirt, and threw it at Dice, gesturing for him to follow me.

After we were back in the car, he pulled the T-shirt on and started driving before he even had his door all the way closed.

I cringed at the shirt I had found for him. "I love llama lips" was emblazoned on the front. It was one of the shirts I regularly wore as pajamas. There was a cartoon llama making a kissy face. Mom had grabbed it for me at the local thrift store a few years back. It made Rhy laugh sometimes, so it stayed in the rotation.

Dice followed my gaze to his chest and made the angriest face. "You fucker."

He farted again. I rolled down my window in response.

"Listen, you told Booker about the confrontation last night, right?" He was sweating. And driving pretty shitty.

"I fell asleep when I got home. And the next thing I did was look at your ugly mug. Why?" I rolled the window back up.

"Shit. Well, that's like a huge thing. We ran into a group of

Pepsis and you came out the victor. This could start a war, you know?" He drove even faster.

I hadn't thought about it that way. "Shit."

Moves like that between gangs were usually highly orchestrated. In retaliation to a slight. Or a death.

My heart started pounding, too. There was no other choice. When you're in, you're in. We arrived at Booker's and his goons were waiting. We were frisked and patted, but in a gentler way than usual. Maybe it was my imagination. But they didn't call us Pussy and Ball Sack as much. Maybe they were more respectful just before you die.

When we were in Booker's office, he wasn't there, but we were instructed to sit. It was fuck early and all these people were up, dressed and speaking. Then it occurred to me that they'd never been to bed. This was the end of a night, not the beginning of a day.

Dice sniffled and farted again. I shook my head.

"I think there are more pictures on the wall."

There seemed to be a million pictures on these walls. All crooked. It was so incredibly disarming. Then I noticed our pictures were on the desk. I didn't mention it to Dice; I wasn't ready for more of his bodily reactions.

Booker burst in with two women. Both smelled like weed and had on basically dental floss and tissues with sequins.

"Ladies, this is Pussy and Ball Sack." They gave us both a hazy once-over. One put her hand to her mouth. "Ugh. It smells in here."

He kissed them both then sent them back out of the office with punishing ass slaps. Both tittered like they liked it, but his handprint was immediately visible on their skin. It had to have hurt.

Booker slammed the door. It was then that I realized Booker was drunk off his ass. His motions almost seemed blurry, his gait a bit offbeat. Which was wonderful. I'm sure the delicate conversation about whether Dice and I lived or died was best held wasted.

"You fuckers. Again. I feel like I just had you here." He grabbed our pictures off the desk and handed them to us. I had Dice's and Dice had mine. I had a flash of terror that Booker was going to make us kill each other, before he shook his head and switched them back to the correct way. That was when I knew we were holding our death sentences in picture form. The thought of us decorating his office as the last thing we did beat in my head like a drum.

Booker leaned against his desk and crossed his legs at his ankles. He squinted at Dice's shirt, slowly reading the saying out loud. His silence only made the tension in the room mount. All the men we encountered were in some version of their going out clothes. Dice looked like a slob. I looked wrinkled.

Before we died, I was going to ask if I could switch shirts with Dice. I would take Rhy's llama with me to the grave.

Then Booker burst out laughing. "I fucking donated that shirt to Goodwill like ten years ago. What the hell? I love llamas. So much."

He started laughing and slapping his thighs. "You bitches are hilarious. Now." He rearranged his face into a sober expression. It was chilling how quickly he could switch. "Tell me what the fuck happened last night."

Dice launched into a long, rambling description of how he was trying to take up smoking and we wound up in Pepsi territory, but in our defense, there were no signs stating what belongs to whom, before Booker held up his hand.

"You're fucking exhausting. None of this explains how I have video of this one," he pointed at me, "standing over a pile of Pepsi bodies a few hours ago."

Dice studied his lap when I turned my head. There was

only one person I could think of who would have been able to take a video. And that was Dice. So he took two. Instead of helping me.

"So first, don't fucking take video of business going down. That's a rule. We never know what will wind up on a huge screen TV for the prosecution, if you get my vibe." I was still keeping watch on Dice. His picture frame was shaking in his hands. I almost forgot I was getting ready to die, because I had questions. Instead of helping me, he was hunkered down in the convenience store, trying to get some Internet fame PR brownie points or some shit. I needed better friends in my next life.

"Second." Booker snapped his fingers. "I feel like you might be a problem, Pussy. How you taking down over ten Pepsi guys by yourself? You got something I need to know?"

And this was the gamble. Tell the truth, or let the falsehood that I was some sort of superhero stay floating in the room. I shook my head. "No, sir. Just being myself." Which wasn't an exact lie.

"Well, that's neither tits nor taints. Decision made. Go hang your pictures on the wall. Pick an open nail. Make sure you like where it is because I never move them."

I froze in place. I couldn't even look at Dice. I was shocked. I thought for sure we'd get out of this. I mean, it's not like we'd hurt Cokes. Booker casually pulled out a handgun.

I stood first. I was going to hang my picture in the dead center of the open nails. And it would be straight. As I lifted my picture, it was like I was experiencing my own personal earthquake. And when it was hung, it was the most slanted one on the entire wall. Dice's hands were shaking, too. He managed to hang the frame fairly straight, which pissed me off. I heard the cock of the hammer of the gun. Dice started farting and farting.

They weren't even going to take us somewhere else. Put down a tarp, nothing. I looked at my picture. I could see my reflection in the frame's glass. I was scared. And the room was getting more and more rank as Dice dealt with his fear digestively.

Time stretched on. I was actively trying not to shake like a leaf. I pictured Ember's beautiful face. Tried to force my mind to relive her kisses.

Dice and I jumped when Booker slapped his hands on both of our shoulders. "You little shits. I'm not killing you today." The gun was still in his hand, the safety off, so I wasn't 100% sure we weren't still getting shot. On purpose or thanks to a stupid accident. "Get those pictures down and put them on the desk."

I did so warily. Dice was more exuberant about it. We were both directed to sit again. Dice farted some more. Relief gas, I was figuring.

Booker actually sat on his desk, still holding the gun. I wasn't ready to let down my guard. Though what I could possibly do to a man with a gun from a seated position was beyond me.

"Listen, I was in talks with the Pepsis last night. And it went well. We were working on a truce, their leader Doc and I. And then I get the news of this whole fucking debacle. That two assholes in red bananas were crossing territories and flashing colors. Effectively screwing up everything Doc and I had just settled."

I watched as Booker scratched his head with the loaded gun. I had serious doubts about the intricacies of the meeting he'd had with Doc.

"And then, as everything is going to shit, and the whole gang is getting ready to war up? I hear that you, Pussy, somehow got out of a gang beating without killing a single

soul." Booker gave me a gummy smile. "That's fucking amazing. So then I say, because I know what I'm fucking doing,
'Yeah. I instructed my men—no death. I'm putting my balls
into this truce, Doc.'

And then Doc? He gave me those two ladies you just saw.
And he's downstairs right now. Pepsi and Coke drinking
together. Because somehow you're talented enough to save
lives instead of just dying like you were supposed to, Pussy."

Booker gave me a look of wonderment. I gave a terse nod.
Because he pointed his gun at me. "You're the real shit. I'm
impressed. And this is the second time. Either you are the luck-
iest shit in the world or I stumbled on a real soldier."

He swung the gun at Dice. "But I still can't find a reason he
should be breathing."

Dice's eyes went wide.

I tried to quickly smooth it over. I didn't want Dice to rat
me out and say that I wasn't the one that took down the gang.
"I asked him to video. So you'd have proof that we were serious
about not killing. Just wanted you to have the receipts. I had to
beg him to stay out of it. Ball Sack is a ride or die Coke."

I took a deep breath and leveled a stare at Booker. Dice
started agreeing to my version. If Booker hadn't been wasted, I
had no doubt he'd see through my lie. But this morning, I'd
passed muster.

"Well, I got to say. Booker shares," Booker said, talking
about himself in the third person. "Pepsis gave me a nice
consolation prize slash thank you offering. And I'm gonna
share with you. Because I'm not a fucker." Booker pushed
himself off the desk and set his goddamn gun down. Finally.

He flashed two manila envelopes; both thick with what
looked a hell of a lot like a stack of money. He shuffled the
money around after opening them. "Adjusted the payout a bit.
Because turns out, Dice isn't a fuckhead, according to you."

Booker tossed the envelopes to us. Horrible tosses, but we managed to catch them. Neither of us attempted to count their contents.

Booker dismissed us by opening his door and calling for his new women. We couldn't get out of the office soon enough, and had to ease ourselves past his now exposed boner. The women pushed passed us like their lives depended on getting their mouths around his dick. And as Dice and I damn near ran outside, it occurred to me that they probably did.

———

After Dice dropped me off, I walked in on Rhy's morning routine. I was wearing her shirt, even though it smelled like Dice's sweat. He'd gone home as bare-chested as he'd arrived. Rhy's laughter peeled out when I pointed to the llama and made the same face at her. I didn't count the money yet, but it was a larger amount than last time. I kissed my mother on the head, and then Rhy, tickling her a little just to get more laughter. The money was literally burning a hole in my pocket.

I took a quick shower before tucking the cash pile into my underwear drawer. I dressed in a fresh outfit. I wanted to get down to the registrar's office as soon as possible. When I skipped out without breakfast, Ma questioned me. I didn't want to tell her my stomach was still churning from almost being killed, so I told her Dice and I had gotten a bite out.

I took three buses to the Blooming Flower School. After waiting in the foyer for about ten minutes, an older lady in a plaid skirt ushered me into her office. She was older than my mom, maybe. I asked her how much it was for the rest of the year, plus the weekend program for my mom and sister. After I carefully counted out the cash on her desk, covering the whole amount, she touched my red bandana. I slipped the still half-full envelope into my pocket with my other hand.

She was ignoring my money. I met her eyes. "My son was in the Cokes."

I wasn't sure what the protocol was in this situation. I knew I wasn't supposed to talk to anyone about the Cokes or the members. Just always wear the bandana. No matter where I was. Who I was with. So I nodded. Maybe I'd met her son. Who knew?

"Rest his soul."

I exhaled at her reveal. I expected the speech that came.

"If he had known how it would turn out, how much pain it'd cause, he wouldn't have done it. You have this money. Take it and go. Go far away. Be a different person." She was almost in tears.

I shouldn't say anything. But then all at once I wanted to defend myself. Maybe it was the exhaustion, or the roller coaster of the last twenty-four hours, but I gave her the explanation that was on the tip of my heart.

"My sister? She needs this school. And my mom? She deserves to come here in the fancy bus with her beautiful girl. I'll hustle any way I have to so they have what they need. So maybe, just maybe, your son had his reasons. I know I have mine. No disrespect, ma'am." I pushed the piles of money toward her.

She nodded over and over until she finally stood up and held out her arms for a hug. "Do you mind? You remind me so much of him. And I'd do anything to hold him again."

And I saw my own mother in her then. Maybe in the future. So I stood and hugged her with all of my heart and kissed the top of her head. Mamas were mamas. I knew her son missed her, wherever he was.

19

Ember

LOCK HAD SENT ME more pictures. A few video clips. Enough back and forth that when he asked to visit on Friday I knew I'd accept. Nix and I were messaging back and forth as well. He warned me twice to stay away from Lock. I quickly changed the subject both times.

Otherwise, I was doing well, hanging with new friends. I ignored the security, but didn't actively try to lose them. For the most part, the loneliness was held at bay. It was going to be hot this weekend, so I was going with my favorite sundress for the Lock date. I took way too long doing my best to look effortless. I straightened my hair, which took forever. It was almost down to my ass. The little rainbow streaks showed up better that way. I even added two sparkly tinsel pieces. I knew the sun would catch them when we walked around town. He wanted to take me to dinner. And then we'd walk it off, and maybe go to a bar or two that was lax about the age limit.

I used a light spritz of my favorite perfume and a hint of makeup. Just enough to show I cared, but not enough that he would taste it if we made out. I was really hoping we'd make out again. He had some seriously talented lips.

I messaged T to tell her I had a date. I confirmed it was with Lock. I didn't want to have to hear it from Animal or Nix, but was trying not to be a jerk about my safety.

I locked the door behind me and brought my cute small purse. I met him outside the dorm's entrance. He was holding a handful of pansies. As I got closer, I could see he'd healed even more. The smile on his face when he saw me was breathtaking. Like I was the only thing that mattered to him. I had to return it.

When he handed me the pansies, I noticed they had the roots attached to the bottom. "Did you pick these from the landscaping?"

He cringed and then leaned down for a kiss on the cheek. "If they didn't want to be picked, they should have a fence around them. Like you."

"Are you saying I need a fence?" I felt all the common sense escape me as his lips made contact with my skin.

His low chuckle revealed his white teeth. "Of course not. I suck at quick player lines. I'm not smooth, just crazy about you."

I smiled at the flowers and set them down by the front

window. "If these are still alive when we come back, I'll take them upstairs."

"Great plan." He gently patted the pansies. "Sit. Stay. Good flowers."

"Where are we headed?" I was curious how much forethought he'd put into this date. He at least looked nice, wearing dark jeans, a black T-shirt, and the red bandana.

"Well, this is your hood. Show me your favorite places. Then when you go there, you can think of me." Lock held out his hand, his blue eyes sparkling.

I took a breath and then put my hand in his. "All right. Let's see what you got."

We strolled down to Main Street. Lock was a chatterbox. He also called out to anyone who would stand still, telling him or her we were on a date.

Some ignored him; others wished him luck. He was over-the-top. I felt my face flush a few times. In between, he cracked jokes and told me how beautiful I was. The sun was filtering through the trees and sending patterns on the sidewalk. I felt like my whole body was connected to my hand.

We sat on a bench and people-watched. He slipped his arm around my shoulders and I snuggled in closer. I inhaled the scent of his neck, a warm musk that would be hardwired to my definition of the word "happy" from now on.

A woman who reminded me of Aunt Dor passed, and I pointed her out to Lock. "She looks like the woman who raised me."

He put his hand on my knee. "Was it good? The way she raised you?"

I frowned, coming up with a way to explain what my heart always knew. "I think she tried her best. She didn't want to be a mom. Never wanted kids. But she took me in. I think she loved my mother more than anything. So losing my mom... I think she relived that loss whenever she looked at me. Maybe even blamed me for Mom's murder."

"Wait, what? Your mom was murdered?" He touched my shoulder.

"Yeah. I never knew her. The man she was with—when I was six months old, he killed her in front of my brother. I was at my aunt's. Being with her probably saved my life."

I turned my face to his and watched the empathy furrow his brow. "I am so very sorry. That's rough."

I wasn't sure how to respond. I didn't have to tell many people when I was growing up in Midville. Everyone already somehow knew my mom was gone.

I patted the center of my chest. "One of my best qualities was finding the worth in a day that didn't have a ton of good parts. Insisting that I'd be grateful for what I had. I mean, I had toys, clothes, and stuff. But I'd have given that up in a hot minute to have a mom that lit up when I walked into the room."

Lock brushed my cheek with his fingertips. "We didn't have much, but I had that. My mom loves me like crazy. She'd fight a bull for my sister or me."

"Then you had everything you needed." I let my thumb rest on his chin. "I'm glad that you did, too."

We told each other some more anecdotes, letting the history of our upbringings come to light.

Soon enough, it was time to make our own good memory. I decided to take him to Scoops, a neighborhood ice cream shop I wanted to try. I had no idea if it was good or not, but it's hard to screw up ice cream. But before we walked a dozen steps, he stopped in his tracks, pulling on my arm gently.

"Can we just do this? I keep thinking about kissing you." I turned to face him, looking at his lips.

I nodded once, biting my lip quickly. His sigh of relief made me wrinkle my nose. He let go of my hand and bounced on his toes.

"Okay. Okay? Okay. This is going to happen. Again." He rubbed his hands on his jeans and then came in closer. He looked into my eyes and slid his hand to my shoulder. With a gentle pressure he drew me in. He touched my jaw with his other hand and his brows furrowed.

"How are you even prettier than last time?"

Before I could thank him for his compliment, he tipped my chin up and leaned down. And then he kissed me.

Butterflies in my chest, electricity on my skin—he kissed me. I loved how his lips tasted, which was crazy. Like the composition of him and the composition of me were flavors that matched. Mint chocolate chip. Honey and lemon. And he didn't get handsy. He was just into the kiss.

He stopped and took a few breaths, looking at the sky. "Sweet Lord. I could do that all day."

Lust in his eyes then. Fire all over my body.

This was chemistry. I'd had dates. A few boyfriends. But this was tipping me off my axis. A roller coaster drop into a pile of cotton candy.

If I was drinking, I'd blame it on that. But we were stone-cold sober. The breeze picked up my hair and he pushed a lock of it out of my face, letting his palm rest against my cheek.

Comets falling to the grass. I touched his face, too.

"This is real, right?"

Wonder in his face. "From here it is, Ember."

My name on his lips was the start of something. I took his hand again. We started this walk on a date, and somehow, halfway to Scoops, he became mine.

20

Lock

MY HEART HAD TAKEN off like a rocket. Her name was appropriate. Because she started it. Why it flipped, right then, I didn't know. I was good with the girls. They liked my smile, my swag, usually. But this was a whole new level. I wanted to see us in matching Christmas sweaters. I wanted to find a dragon and fight it for her. Intense. To have her feel the same way would be the most incredible gift from fate. Well, that and the money I kept falling into for Rhy and Mom.

She was leading me somewhere. She could take me right off a cliff. I'd follow. I kept looking at her, like my eyes couldn't get enough. We hadn't even had sex, but that wasn't my only focus. Which was probably alarming and confusing. I mean, of course, I wanted to smash, but I wanted to cuddle, too. Have her head on my chest. The need for that very thing made me put my arm around her shoulder. She reached up and linked her fingers with mine like it was the most natural thing in the world. Like we'd done it a million times.

Her hair was the prettiest, soft against my skin. Across the street there was another couple just holding hands. In this college town, they'd probably get married after graduation and have a few kids and a dog.

The way the other half lived. Not worrying about the electric bill getting paid. Not wondering how good-humored the landlord was this month. Could we get a few more days? Maybe they'd never even tasted generic cereal.

Ember was destined for that life. Somehow, she was at this expensive school. Her sandals weren't cheap. The fabric on her sundress was so heavy. The good stuff that Ma loved to find in the thrift store. I bet Ember was the first person to wear her clothes.

"So, Mercy? He's your brother?" I saw suspicion creep into her expression, her narrowed eyes, and flat lips. "Honest—just making small talk. Not trying to farm info out of you about him. It's just—even here, he's fairly famous. The dude with the skeleton face. He even burned a mob boss in his favorite chair."

Her expression fell a little. Maybe she didn't know that detail. I instantly racked my memory to see if I could remember where I'd heard it. When I couldn't put a name or place to it, I waved it off. "Probably an urban legend. I mean, people think I'm some sort of genius in the Cokes now."

Ember looked at my bandana. "I honestly don't know what he does—detail wise. But I know that I'm safe with him. What about you? Why the Cokes? Did you have to join?"

I blew my breath into my hair. "It's hard to explain gang life if you're not in it. In my neighborhood it's almost like a rite of passage. A way to belong. Being born male where I am from comes with expectations. My dad—he was different. He wanted to break up the gangs. Help our men go to school. Elevate and still maintain the connections in the neighborhood. Just without violence."

"What kind of violence?" She looked to me for an explanation and I hesitated. Gang life was confidential. And she didn't even seem to know much about her brother's business. I didn't want to scare her away with the details of what I was expected to do. Hell, I didn't even know how I was going to manage doing the shit that I wasn't morally comfortable with yet.

"Let's not get into it." I leaned down and pressed my mouth to hers. I used a tongue sweep to force away the train of thought we were both having and guide it in a different direction. When her hand curled in my hair, we were carefree again.

She laughed out loud, no good reason. But I knew. It was that helium balloon feeling in the chest. I was having it, too. I joined her. The rush of it all felt too good. I wouldn't acknowledge the difficulties. We were just a guy and his girl walking into an ice cream shop.

She got vanilla, and I got chocolate, both in cones. I paid for it, of course. We sat on the same side of the booth. I snuck a lick of hers, and she scooped a bit with her finger and then dabbed my nose. She kissed it off, so I was willing to do that all day, too.

Her security was following us. I'd spotted them a few

times. And the fact that she had them at all should have been more concerning than I let it be. But in a way it made sense; she was so special. I wanted to know what she was thinking. Her opinion on everything. It was dizzying. Being with her was all I really wanted to do.

She was into kissing me. Kept finding a reason to lean in, looking from my lips to my eyes and back again. The cold ice cream made the kiss even better. Warming her up that way.

After our ice creams, she wanted to show me the river. We took the long walk. I peeked over my shoulder from time to time. We still had the tail. But it was cool. They were cool. They weren't trying to stop us.

I wanted more privacy, but the two glimpses I got of one of the guards showed their burning jealousy. And I can't even lie. I liked that a lot. If I wasn't me, I'd be jealous, too. The way her sundress swished at her calves was mesmerizing. The way she'd dip one shoulder when she turned to look at me. I could feel my soul carving all of this, every freaking thing right into itself. Her beauty was the blade.

I could just hear Dice making fun of me in my head. Calling me a pussy. The brief thought of hers blinded me for a minute. She had one. And I was going to see it or die trying. I reached for a lock of her hair—streaked bright red—and rubbed it between my fingers.

"Do you do this yourself?" I dropped the red and picked up the purple.

"No. Can't see the back of my head very well. I have a lady who does it for me."

It reminded me of unicorns and rainbows. I wondered if Rhy would like it. I had no idea what the process was like. I asked her how to get it.

"You want rainbow streaks?" She ruffled my hair and I kissed her a few times.

"No. For my sister. She might like it." I shrugged and led her to a nearby picnic table where we sat side by side staring out at the river.

And that's when we had the conversation. I wasn't about to hide Rhy and who she was. She was exactly who she was supposed to be.

I watched Ember's face as I told her how different Rhy's life was than maybe she was used to. I had a spike of fear. Because Ember had to be chill about Rhy. My sister would be a deal breaker. Even for this incredible feeling I was having. But the picture she'd showed me in her dorm of her favorite campers brought me a glimmer of hope.

"Can I see her?" Ember gestured to my pocket.

I pulled out my phone and unlocked it. Our most recent spate of family pictures had been taken just before Dad was arrested. From the time we went swimming in the zero entry pool. Rhy loved it. I called her my little mermaid.

"She's an angel." Ember stopped my hand and used her fingers to zoom in on Rhy's face.

"Oh yeah. My little buddy. I'd do anything for her. Will do everything I can for her." I felt my chest fill with pride.

Ember took the phone right out of my hand and slowly slid through the pictures there. Mom. Dad. Rhy and me.

"You look like your dad. And Rhy looks a lot like your mom." She handed me back my phone.

After careful consideration, Ember suggested hair chalk instead of permanent dye, mentioning that the process was long, and the chalk could get immediate results.

I kissed her again after that. Because she was treating my sister like anyone's. The fear spike was gone. We made out for what felt like hours, sitting on the picnic table, stopping every so often to look out over the river. We watched the sun set. She told me her favorite song and I made her listen to mine on my phone.

Once our stomachs were rumbling, we walked back to town. Now her security had moved to cars. The headlights were bouncing behind us a block or so.

I held open the door for an Italian restaurant; Ember said she heard good things about it. Again, we stayed on the same side of the booth. The reviews online were a mixed bag. So we passed judgment on the meatballs and spaghetti. It was good enough that we asked for a box to take home what we couldn't finish.

It was the perfect day. I had no way to get home, which seemed like I was hoping to get laid, but honestly, I was so excited I forgot to set it up. We laughed at the dead flowers on the windowsill, and she made fun of me for being a plant serial killer. Then she took the stairs in front of me up to the second floor. She opened her door and towed me in.

I locked the door behind us. Being alone like this was nerve-wracking. And exciting. She sat on her bed and held out a hand to me.

After taking her hand and sitting next to her, I wanted to say something awesome. Something worthy of this moment. I had nothing good. I told her she was beautiful about five times in a row until she put her index finger over my lips.

"Show me." And then she lay back. The world could have blown up then. It certainly felt like my mind was doing that very thing.

She lowered her lashes. The opportunity was presenting itself and I was going to take it. I ran my hand from her ankle to her knee. My foot slipped on the sandal she'd kicked off. I fell on top of her. Her peals of laughter broke the tension that was building. I collapsed next to her on the bed. It was narrow, so we were wrapped up in each other. I put my arm behind her head. The fit was meant to be. Her ceiling had glow in the dark stars stuck to it. I nuzzled her temple. Her hair smelled faintly like the restaurant we'd been in.

"You like the stars?" Stupid question. Clearly she did.

"I pretended the stars were my friends when I was a kid." She pointed at a pattern.

"You had to have a ton of friends. You're so freaking likeable." I touched the end of her nose. Her lips curved into a smile.

"I did. I missed a family, though. I was alone a lot." She shrugged.

It hurt my heart that she had pain. Ever. Irrational. I recognized that. Too much. But it was her.

"I'm sorry," I offered. I meant it.

"Do you think we would have been friends back then?" She turned to me. And I kissed her. How would I ever stop kissing her?

Eventually, I answered, "Probably not. I was getting in trouble a lot."

I traced her shoulder with my finger. The neckline of her dress. I didn't want to rush her. Have her think I had a goal for her body. Even though my dick certainly did.

"You think I didn't get in trouble?" She rolled over onto her stomach, resting her head on her hands, feet kicked up behind her.

I took my knuckle from her temple to her chin. So fucking lovely.

I shook my head. "No. I can't imagine what a kid version of you looked like, but damn, if anyone had the heart to do anything but make you smile."

I meant it. She was enchanting. The way she moved was delicate.

"I talked too much. A lot. I had trouble sitting still for a few years there. Had in-school suspension a few times." Ember put her palm on my chest.

I wanted to say more. Say that it was kind of awesome that she broke some rules. That maybe she didn't have the world hand her anything she wanted. But her hand was on my chest.

I flexed. Couldn't help it. I wanted her to be pleased with what she found under my shirt. And then she slayed my balls with a naughty smile. She fisted the fabric of my shirt, pulling it up over my abs.

"Careful, I don't want you to start something I can't stop." It was a real warning. Because she *was* so special. But there were parts of me that would not hold back. The repetitive lust my mind had for her since I first laid eyes on her. On the floor of a pizza joint. Thinking I was dead.

"You underestimate what I can handle, Sherlock." She licked her lips.

I felt my eyes roll back into my head as a tsunami of sex hit my imagination. I ran my palm over my mouth. My body tensed. She pulled my T-shirt up farther. My nostrils flared when her soft hand was skin to skin against me.

"Ember." I was trying to warn her. Promise her. Not rush it.

And then I felt her tongue on my stomach. Licking a pattern. The rainbow streaks, the huge, cat-shaped eyes. The lips that were like a pillow my dick wanted to lay its head on.

I slid out from under her touch, feet on the floor.

I was tremendously satisfied to see the disappointment flit across her face. "Oh no, baby. I got so much more." I tossed my shirt aside. Ember's naughty smile was back.

21

Ember

MY MOUTH WENT DRY at the sight of Lock in only his jeans. His bare chest was his best outfit. It shouldn't ever be covered. Lean muscle. He was the kind of strong that running and climbing got a man. He flipped open the button on his jeans and started the zipper.

I stilled his hand. "Don't open my presents for me."

His smile tugged up on one side and I got to see a dimple. It was incredible to watch that whatever I said was reflected on his face. I stood up and ran my hands over the edges and ridges that made up his chest. His biceps, his forearms, a few veins there. I put my hands in both of his and kissed his chin.

He leaned down and put his cheek against mine, whispering into my ear, "If today's a dream, don't wake me up."

My sensitive ear and the sentiment made me laugh. I realized this was too fast. If it wasn't so different than everything else, I'm sure I'd have been rational about it. About him. I looked into his eyes. Limitless. The way they pierced into me. Like they would never look away.

It wasn't love at first sight, or maybe it was. The tingles. The way I wanted to protect him even though I didn't know him well.

And he snapped. All the discipline he was showing wasn't evident until he stopped restraining himself.

The kisses we'd been sharing all day went from sweet to carnal. The way he swept me back up on the bed confirmed the strength in his muscles. He was taller than me, just enough to feel a bit overwhelmed when he put his weight on top of me. I opened my legs and he put his knees on the mattress. His palms ran up my inner thighs as his tongue dipped between my lips. I wanted him between my legs because that's where he belonged. He took those palms and ran them up my hips, under my dress, and spread his fingers across my stomach.

His mouth moved to my jaw and down to my neck.

There was no more flirting. Lock was determined to take all I had.

It became about feeling. His touch was burning through my body. By the time he had his hand on my breast, I was panting for more. He was working on the buttons of my sundress, and the way we were situated, I could feel what he was offering against my thigh. I heard the groan before I realized it was me.

The banging on my dorm room door startled us both. Lock hopped off of me and walked to the door. "No peephole on this fucking thing?"

He grabbed my lamp off of my desk and stood to his full height. "Who is it?"

His voice was three octaves deeper than it normally was. And I halfway hated myself for getting even more turned on at his protectiveness.

I slipped out of bed. He was overreacting, of course. The knock sounded again. "It's Wardon. Let me in. Nix wants a welfare check."

My jaw dropped. I pushed past Lock to open the door. Lock didn't put down the lamp.

He stood behind me as I opened the door. "Someone better be on fire."

Wardon looked miserable. He held up his phone. The contact on the top read "Boss." I assumed it was my brother.

I took the phone and slammed the door in Wardon's face. "What?"

I heard a sigh on the other side. "You okay?"

"Seriously, Nix?" I flipped the light switch by the door.

Lock put the lamp down and then ran his hands through his hair.

"You weren't responding to my texts. I wanted to be sure."

"I was making out with my boyfriend."

Lock high-fived himself.

"Yeah. This is probably not what I should be doing. My head just went places and I know he has a reputation and everything." I could hear the clack of a keyboard through the phone; Nix was typing while talking to me.

I sat on my bed and fiddled with the buttons on my sundress. The top four were undone. I wasn't wearing a bra.

Lock and I should have been knee-deep in seriously good sensations.

"You don't have a good reputation, and I hang around with you."

Lock was trying to find a comfortable position to sit in. His obvious, huge boner had to be uncomfortable in jeans.

"I shouldn't have sent Wardon. I'm sorry." Nix's voice was suddenly muffled like he'd put his hand over the phone to talk to someone else.

"Is everything okay over there?" It was dawning on me that there was a hint of panic in his voice. Which was rare.

"Yeah. Fine. I just lost track of someone and then I needed to know you were okay. I was thinking there might have been a few hits at once, you know?" More muffled speaking.

"Okay. Well, now that it's settled, I want to get back to my date." I winked at Lock.

"Listen, you can hate me all you want, but T will be there in like four minutes. I need her to stay with you tonight. It's not up for discussion. I'll let you know when it's all clear." Nix hung up and I stared at Wardon's phone.

After the disconnect, I was looking at my own face, captured on my guard's lock screen. I must have seemed confused enough for Lock to get curious, because he peeked over my shoulder.

"Wardon's fucking obsessed with my girlfriend." He took the phone from my hand.

Before I could protest, Lock opened the window and tossed the phone out onto the pavement. The crunch echoed in the night.

"Your girlfriend?" I bit my bottom lip and wiggled my eyebrows.

"Yeah. We've already been engaged, right?" He ran his hand across my collarbone.

There was another lighter knock on the door. I knew it was T. I recognized it from when we were living in the same house. Instead of waiting, she let herself in.

T glanced at the opened window and then to Lock. He seemed to want to explain.

"I had to get rid of that creeper's phone. Ember was his lock screen."

T shrugged and raised her eyebrows. She didn't offer her opinion, just walked past me and shut the window. She cast her gaze around the room like she expected to find people hanging out in the corners.

"I gotta stay." She walked over to the bed Animal had so recently slept in and sat on it. She did not look comfortable. It was twelve thirty in the morning. Lock took the hint that the sexy times were over because he put his shirt back on. I buttoned up my sundress.

Lock's face said it all. He was curious about T. I didn't blame him. She was gorgeous and quietly demanding. I liked her a lot. She didn't feed me bullshit and kept Animal and Nix safe. Animal told me once T was the most dangerous of the three of them. She kicked back on the bed and crossed her ankles.

"Lock, this is T. And T, meet Lock." I pointed from one to the other. T nodded and looked at her feet just as Lock stuck out his hand. He slid it back into his pocket, unshaken.

I shrugged and pointed to my bed. Lock nodded at it sadly like it was a dead squirrel. Once a happy place, now, it would not have the same joy.

I grabbed my pajamas from my dresser and asked T if she needed some. She turned me down and assured me she wasn't sleeping.

So Lock and I weren't even going to get to fool around on

the down-low. When I came out of the bathroom, he was already lying on the bed, ready to be my big spoon.

I took the bait. I curled under the covers. He was on top of them. But his arm went around me and his voice filtered through my hair in a whisper, "This is just as good. I really love being with you."

All the butterflies he kept fluttering around in my belly settled down just like me. His arm was my pillow. It took a while, but eventually, I fell asleep in his embrace.

22

Lock

I GLANCED ACROSS THE room to T. She was impassive. Like she could offer to grab me a coffee when she went to get hers or shoot me dead right here. Neither would cause her any hassle. I could be wrong, of course. I had a knack for reading people, but sometimes they puzzled me still. This girl in my arms had a complicated life. I thought I had a surprising background, but when she reminded me that her mother had been killed, I knew we were on equal footing. Hell, at least my dad was still alive.

She had people, though. And that was good, but I needed more information about how they fit into her life. T caught me looking at her and tipped her head like we were two cowboys in a hallway. I gave her a tight smile.

Our day had been bliss. She was so captivating and funny and perfect. I tried to turn my brain off so my boner didn't wake Ember up by jabbing her in the lower back. It didn't work so I slid my hips back. I looked at T and she was looking at me again. Clearly, I wasn't getting any funny business done with her around. And that's when it hit me. Had she been sent as a specific cock blocker? I glanced around the room as nonchalantly as I could. I didn't see any obvious cameras.

Then I put my head deeper into the pillow. Obviously, I was allowed to lie here with Ember, so I was going to keep doing that as long as I could. The thin strips of color threaded through her brown hair were tangling together. Even that was amazing. So artsy and craftsy. Different, yet alluring. Oh, I had it bad. This girl was hitting me in the heart like no other girl ever had. Legend style. I was pretty fucked. Because whatever hoops she wanted me to jump through, right now? I would do them all and beg for more.

———

I must have drifted off a bit because I woke to T rustling around. When her eyes met mine, I realized she'd made a noise just for that purpose.

She mouthed to me, "We're good. I'm leaving." She flashed her phone's screen at me as well. It looked like it was on the text-messaging screen, with "Boss" listed as the contact.

I nodded and gave her a wave. She locked the door with her own key on the way out.

I put my head back down on the pillow. I was still spooning Ember. Even the back of her head was attractive. I leaned down and sniffed her hair. Amazing.

I was lying in a girl's bed sniffing the back of her incredible head. I was so, so done. I would've made fun of Dice so hard if he came to me saying the same thing. Maybe my nickname of Pussy was actually appropriate.

I didn't want to wake her because she seemed so peaceful. I did want to, though, as well. My boner wasn't backing down.

I lay still. After flipping through my phone for about ten minutes, I fell asleep on my back. I woke up with the sun in my eyes and Ember pointing her phone in my face, laughing.

"What? Hey, beautiful. What, are you videoing me?" I propped myself up on my elbows.

She turned the phone. I was snoring in the video like a ninety-year-old dog. At the end of every snore, there was a tiny little scream like I had a dying elf living in my nose.

I snatched her phone away from her.

"I have a deviated septum."

She was laughing so hard she was holding her stomach and tearing up.

I bit back my smile, trying to stay offended, but I couldn't. I laughed, too. I used her phone to video her laughing, criss-crossed legs on her bed. Her hair was all ruffled up. It must have been a full sixty seconds of her cracking up. I air dropped it to my phone right away.

After I was sure I had the video on my phone, I drew her in again, shifting my weight so I could pull her under me. That sobered her up. Her gorgeous face this close to mine was making my heart pound.

She covered her mouth and shook her head. I heard her muffled, "Toothbrush."

I let her roll out from underneath me, but my hard-on was really hoping I'd use it as a peg to hold her in place.

She started brushing her teeth and rolling her hips at me. Teasing. Smiling around her foam from the toothpaste. I hopped up and inched past her slowly, letting my dick drag across her lower back, my own form of teasing.

I put some toothpaste on my finger and joined her. We looked at each other in her mirror. Man, I could be crazy, but she seemed just as excited to be around me as I was her.

Too fast. Too soon. But damn, if this wasn't love, then I wasn't sure I wanted to know what it was.

She shimmied around me and rinsed her mouth and brush. I did the same, and then snatched her before she could leave. I held her against me.

"That was the best sleep of my life. With you in my arms."

She beamed back at me. I wasn't going to force her to kiss me, but she put her hand on my face. "Same."

She went on her tiptoes and kissed me. The minty breath we both had was a turn-on. Well, pretty much anything right now would be. My stomach whined like an angry whale.

She put her other hand on my belly and laughed against my mouth. "I guess I should be a better host. Want some breakfast?"

I could do without food, that was for sure, but her stomach grumbled as well. She twisted out of my arms to grab her lanyard with her keys on it. As she led me out of her dorm room, I told her how T had left early after getting a text message.

We held hands all the way to the dining hall. I spotted two of her bodyguards on the way over. They could've pointed their guns at me; I wasn't letting go of her.

Her brown hair tickled my face as the breeze picked up. The colors streaked, though it would help me spot her in any crowd. I held the dining hall door for her and made sure she made it up the stairs without tripping. She helped me grab a tray and made sure I had utensils and a napkin. I grabbed a plate of eggs, bacon, and pancakes along with a cup of tea. She had French toast and a cup of cocoa.

I teased her for not liking coffee and she swatted my arm and teased me for my tea. While we waited to pay, she leaned back against my chest like she was mine. I kissed the back of her head. This is what it would be like. This wholesome. To go to this school with her. Study together. Make love all day long. Hell, she had room for me in her place.

It was wishful thinking. I had to be a member of the Cokes and do the things they were going to require of me. But maybe, maybe I could nip up here during the week. Sneak into some classes. Learn. I gave her the kiss she pouted for. She had swiped her meal card and paid for both our trays before I even knew what she was doing.

"I got it. I don't eat enough here anyway. Got to use up this card." She winked at me. I thanked her but really wished I'd been able to pay. I had the money. I told her as much.

She shrugged like having money wasn't a big deal. And maybe to her it wasn't. But I felt like I was standing one hundred feet tall with money and this girl letting me hold her hand in between bites of breakfast.

After we ate, we strolled her campus. I took a few selfies of us in nice spots. And more than a few photos of her. There was a group of guys playing acoustic guitars. One with a fairly decent voice was singing along. A group of girls was kicking a soccer ball around. This place seemed like heaven. Even the bodyguards blended into the tapestry of the day.

Her hand was like satin. I rubbed it with my thumb. She

kept smiling. And it clicked. This was it. The best day. Her. I wanted the rest of my days to equal this with her.

She drew me down for another kiss right in the center of the quad. I could feel the eyes of all the jealous motherfuckers on the back of my neck. I actually wasn't surprised when I felt a tap on my shoulder. I finished up my kiss and then turned.

Thrice was there. I was expecting a lecture. Some sort of warning.

Instead, he delivered a frantic, "We need to get inside."

I joined the bodyguards as we flanked Ember. I'd take a bullet for her. Hell, I'd take a few.

23

Ember

WE WERE GETTING WHISKED back to my dorm, which was fine. But then Bowen sent Lock on his way—not even letting us say goodbye. I really thought it was another false alarm or power play from Nix. Until I saw Thrice put a hand on his gun. This motion, which clearly gave away his cover, set off alarm bells. By the time I was in my room with Wardon and not Lock, everyone seemed calmer. I called Lock and sat on my bed. He answered before the first ring finished.

"Hey, beautiful. They said I had to get out for a while. So I'm going to go home and check on my mom and sister. You okay?"

I heard talking in the background. It sounded like Thrice. I agreed that he could call me later and hung up. I met Wardon's gaze.

"What the hell was that all about?"

Wardon shrugged. "Stuff's going down. Boss wanted you here."

"Seems like *boss* always finds a reason to get involved when I'm about to be alone with Lock."

I launched my suspicion at him to see if I could gauge the truth from his response. Nothing gave him away. Wardon held his hands, palms up, face innocent.

I sighed. There would be other times. But I wanted the now with Lock.

Thrice and Bowen came to my room, presumably after Lock was off campus. They requested to search my room for bugs and cameras.

It wasn't until I saw Bowen entirely ignore an ant that I realized they meant a *bug*, like a tiny microphone hidden in something. They combed the place, and finding nothing, left. Wardon stayed, sitting in my desk chair with his elbows on his knees and his hands folded.

"So he's your new boyfriend. You're all in?" Wardon was interested.

I gave him a shrug that matched the one he gave me earlier. "Maybe? I like friends. He's a friend."

"That you kiss. Are we friends?" His eyebrows lifted around his hopeful gaze.

"You're a friend. For sure. But I'm all kissed out, sorry." I sat on my bed and gave him what I hoped was a moment to leave. I wanted to be alone. Instead of taking the hint, Wardon seemed to settle in. "You got any snacks around here? I'm feeling munchy."

I pointed to my stash of pretzels and water bottles. Instead of asking Wardon about why he was still in my room, I texted T.

Is everything okay?

T returned my text right away:

Sit tight. We are dealing with something. Need to have all the assets safe.

I said my text out loud, "Okay."

I narrowed my eyes while watching Wardon eat my pretzels. "You're my only hope. Tell me what's going down."

"Are you kidding? I like my balls right where they are. I'm not trying to piss off your brother or Animal or worst of all T. My job is to sit here and shoot anyone who messes with you. Including me." He stuffed four more pretzels into his mouth. His crunching was driving me crazy, so I cued up a few songs on my phone to drown him out.

I contemplated texting Nix or Animal, but if T wasn't telling me anything, the chances of them explaining the situation were slim.

I picked my history textbook up off the floor and settled into my required reading. I'd never been as closely watched at home before. It made me wonder what the hell was going on.

24

Animal

WE WERE NOT THRILLED to say the least. The Feybi organization had been on the fringe as of late. Striking out on their own. Doing a few gigs without approval. It was almost like they had someone else giving orders. Not us.

I was the ultimate boss, in the eyes of our enemies and allies. Of course, anyone that knew us knew Nix and I functioned as one entity. Our close bond was unfailing. But the

Feybis had been a simmering pot ever since Nix killed their patriarch. I knew this. I knew they had weak links in their personnel. Family was family. When you burned a man alive in his favorite chair with his favorite alcohol, even the second cousins seemed to hang onto a grudge.

After the third murder of a Kaleotos man, it was time to buckle the fuckle down. Nix, T, and I were in the basement war room, where we had the most sensitive of documents. I could also see Ember's new room from where I sat. Maybe it was time to relocate our base of operations.

Nix stood, hood yanked over his head. "I think it's time I paid a visit to the Feybi compound."

T crossed her legs. "Do they have a new one yet? Because they're still rebuilding most of the one you burned down. Contractors keep coming up missing."

"What have you found out in there?" I pointed to the computer. Nix knew how to get to the shadiest parts of the Internet with ease.

"That's the problem. Nothing. I'm not seeing any coordinated movement on their part. If this is a parting of ways, they're being uncharacteristically quiet about it." He picked up a pen and started clicking it repeatedly.

We were all silent for a while. I looked at the various surveillance monitors around the room. I recognized Ember's college dorm. I watched as Becca tatted a female client down at the shop. And then there was a camera on a house I wasn't too familiar with. Christina. A while back, Nix rescued her from kidnappers. She was little, and very fond of her skeleton savior. Her name was inked on his heart, along with Becca and Ember. Nix viewed the monitor that had my attention.

My unasked question was, *how's the girl?* Nix answered it, guessing it correctly. "They just moved into that place. Christina went with her mom after the divorce. They've moved to Maine. I kind of like that she has some distance from her father's family now."

I nodded as I processed this. We had a lot to juggle. But right now, the most important knowledge was that downtown Valston just had a few buildings snapped up by Feybis. New money. No approval from us.

It was a guess, but an educated one, that they were looking to expand their territory far enough away from us that we couldn't be involved.

Nix didn't like how close they were getting to Ember. And he didn't believe in coincidences— we'd both come to trust his gut. He was leaning toward pulling her out of school and bringing her home.

I knew she was seeing that kid. And that she was head over heels.

Nix was going to get kickback from her. I looked at my gorgeous wife. She was more of a roll with the punches kind of person. Nix, if he could, would rather know the future.

It didn't bode well for our little independent coed.

25

Lock

I SPENT THE REST of the day lurking around Ember's campus with my hat pulled low. I wanted to see if we could get more time together. Dice kept texting me that I had to get back, that there was a meeting in the morning. I ignored him.

I liked it better here. The grass was like a carpet and everyone was walking around like they had all the time in the world. It just felt...privileged. Calm. It reminded me of the art section in the library. I was drawn to it. And, of course, she was there, too. I could barely think of anything else. I kept chuckling out loud, thinking of something she'd said when we were together.

I didn't know that love would make me a big pile of cheese, but it did. I caught myself walking with my chest puffed out, so proud that she'd kissed me and liked it. Seemed like she wanted more of it.

I wandered around until sundown. I inched under her window. Surely, the guys were watching, but were letting this happen. I hoped desperately that she would tell me to come up. I wanted more of her. More of her skin. Her laughter. Her sex. I scooped up a handful of pebbles and began the process of annoying her enough to open her window. It took seven tries. The large glass was heaved to one side and her head popped out. There was a light two floors up and to the side of the building, beaming down on her, like she was on stage. Just for me.

"Romeo, Romeo, wherefore art thou, Romeo?"

"Here. Down below your gorgeous fucking face."

"Don't curse at me." Even from this far down I could see her fluttering her eyelashes.

I immediately apologized until she laughed. "I'm teasing you, lover boy."

The old-fashioned nickname had the word "love" in it. I wanted more.

"Can I come up?" I took my hat off and held it in my hand. I tried to do it with flourish, because if she wanted Shakespeare, I could try to be as fancy as possible.

"You can't. But I wish you could." She rested her chin on her hands, looking legitimately disappointed.

"The guards say no? 'Cause I'm pretty sure I can climb

this." I walked up to the brick wall and slapped it. I tried my luck on the grooves and edges. I got about three feet up before I was forced to hop down. The side of her dorm would not be something I could free-climb.

"Why do you want up here so bad?" She shifted her arms so her boobs were propped up on them.

"Aw. That's not fair. Shit. Those tits. I want to just live in between them." Then I remembered the fancy Shakespeare and added, "For your bosom is like two setting moons on heaven."

It took a second but Ember disappeared and reappeared with an apple core. She threw it at me. "Boo! You're a horrible poet."

I caught it; it looked fairly fresh, so I took as much of a bite as I could. "Thanks, baby! I love snacks."

"I want to see you again. Soon. When can we do that?" She flipped her hair so it was tumbling over one shoulder.

"Let me up there. It can be now."

She didn't elaborate but shook her head.

"I have a meeting I have to get back to, but if I don't have anything lined up, I can be back two days from now."

Her smile started out as a peek of her tongue between her lips until she was full-out grinning. "Sounds good. You've got my number." She went to close the widow and I threw a panicked question at her.

"What's your favorite color?" She stopped and shot me a funny look before answering, "Purple. What's yours?"

"Whatever color your beautiful pussy is." I gave her my biggest smile.

"Oh stop. The flattery is so overwhelming." She tossed her hair behind her shoulders and went back to closing the window.

"Favorite animal? Favorite band? Favorite guy?" I came up to the bricks again, gazing up at her.

She leaned out. "Panda, 30 Seconds to Mars, and..." She reached over and grabbed the window; just before she closed it all the way, she tossed out her final answer, "And you."

I flung my hat in the air and then caught it. Me. I was her favorite. I waited a few more minutes to see if she would come back to the window. She didn't. I walked away backwards just to be sure.

It felt like the start of everything good. And she would be in it. I had money for my mom and sister, a beautiful girl who was looking like my future, and forever in front of me.

———

I made the last bus to the train station, so Dice didn't have to pick me up this time. It wasn't too bad of a ride. I was getting in my mind, making sure I could allot the time for commutes. Back to Ember.

I just couldn't wait to kiss her again. I kept imagining her naked body and making myself uncomfortable in my pants.

When I let myself in my apartment, I was ready for a nice long, alone time shower. My mom was asleep with Rhy. I checked on them and felt a pang of guilt. Mom's only real break on weekends came when I was around to take over. The light knock on the door behind me had my guard up. I grabbed the baseball bat by the front door. It was our alarm system and defense all in one.

The peephole revealed two guys from the Cokes, Snake and Fat Tony. It made me nervous. They knew where I lived. Of course. We all knew where everybody lived. It was how the neighborhood was. I cracked open the door and found a few more guys standing in the hallway. I didn't slide the chain.

"What's up?"

"Let us in." Snake curled his lip up.

"No can do. My sister's asleep." I wasn't letting these guys in my home if I could help it.

"Man, his sister's got problems and stuff." Worm, a guy that I hadn't seen in the peephole, spoke up. I recognized him from downstairs. He was a year younger than me. Normally, I'd take issue with a statement like that, but not this time. Because Worm was trying to protect Rhy, and I appreciated that. I gave him a man nod.

"Booker wants to see you. Now," Snake demanded.

They all seemed to accept Worm's assessment that no one was getting me to open my door.

"I just got in. What time?" I set the bat down and let them see me do it through the crack. I wanted them to know I was willing to participate. Just not right now.

"What the fuck with this prick? I swear to shit. If he doesn't listen one more fucking time." Okay. So Fat Tony wasn't so thrilled with me.

"I need to make some things happen in here. And it has to be me. My ma has to do the food shopping and everything. I'll see him after that. What the hell does he need me for when he has all of you guys? Seriously. I'm the lowest person on the totem pole. Every single person outranks me there." I was busy putting myself down, but hopefully letting them feel bigger in the meantime. I wanted some sleep. And I wasn't lying about Ma needing to go to the store.

Fat Tony grabbed the back of his neck. "Well, after your mother is home, you do it. Get there. And bring Ball Sack with you." He pointed at me through the crack. I nodded and thanked them for the message.

My response clearly baffled them. They had come to deliver one message and left with another. This was not a game I could play for long. Soon, I'd have to step up and earn the money I was getting. I closed the door and locked it back up. I hoped that I could stay the same person with what they were going to make me do. Schoolyard brawls and late night fights were child's play for the Cokes. I'd have to make it to the big leagues for Rhy to get what she needed. I was going to have to move merchandise. Threaten storeowners in our territory to buy our "protection." People I'd known my whole life would see me in a different—probably much worse—light. I would now be an enforcer and a protector. No longer a kid from the neighborhood. It was a tricky transition for everyone.

———————

In the morning it was my turn with my sister. She was patient with me. More so than with Ma. It took me longer to swap out her shirt. Usually she would start fussing as soon as her head was in the body of the clothing, but for me she would hold.

I appreciated it; I always went slowly. I didn't want to hurt her. Her limbs were rigid and didn't bend easily. So the process took a bit. Of course, I cracked jokes and made her laugh the whole time. Then the bib. Then the readjustment from her wheelchair to the table to eat. It was part of her routine and very important. Some people would think that once she was in the wheelchair, she'd stay in it for everything. That wasn't true. She used different muscles to hold herself up at the kitchen table.

It took her about thirty minutes to get her special cereal down. That part was my favorite. For some reason, when it was mealtime, we had more eye contact. And there was a special zing when she looked at me and I knew that she saw me. She'd hum and bounce her fist around. I'd always say hello to her, every time—like we were seeing each other for the first time all day. And she would laugh. Because she knew it was a joke. I'd had friends in the past that had come over to my house and wondered why we worked so hard with Rhy. But they didn't know how smart she was. How in tune she was to Ma and me and Dad, when he'd been around. We knew when she was happy or sad and vice versa. She was part of our family unit. And she did even more for us than we did for her. She was sunshine and hope. And endless joy. I touched her fist to mine, encouraging her to eat more. Keeping weight on her was vital. Life in a chair was best when she had a little bit of cushioning.

When Rhy was finished, I cleaned her up again and set her on the couch with her iPad. It took a few minutes positioning it before I could put on her favorite show. Ma and I knew all the words and songs by heart. After she was settled, there was a thump against the door. I answered it, ready for the groceries. It had been a good haul. Ma used coupons and everything, but she still had bags on top of the pull cart she used.

She smiled at Rhy and gave her a huge hug as soon as her arms were free. "Missed you, pretty girl."

Rhy giggled in return. We listened intently over her program. Sometimes when Ma came home from the store, it seemed like Rhy said "Mama." Today was one of those times, so we danced around to make her laugh before putting away the groceries.

Lots of fresh food. There was a fruit or vegetable in almost every color of the rainbow.

"So many vitamins, Sherlock. Look at all of this stuff. Thank you." Ma grabbed me by my face and shook it with love.

I was both proud and scared at the same time. I wondered if this was how my dad felt before going to prison. I let myself out of the apartment after saying goodbye to my girls. Mom wanted to know if I'd be back for dinner, but I didn't answer. I had a meeting and I wasn't sure how it was going to turn out.

After I was sure she was set, I texted Dice. He seemed to be waiting for it, because he hit me back quickly. Not with the normal ball busting though. The hair on the back of my neck stood up when I got into his car. He was stiff. Formal. Like he was on a job.

"We going to Booker?" I needed to connect with him. Get an idea about what the hell was going on.

"Yeah." He didn't look at me. His knuckles were white. I fixed my gaze out the windshield. I knew it then—Dice had flipped on me somehow. Probably to save his own life. I forced myself to stay calm. Rhy and Ma. They wouldn't have me anymore. Dice was driving me to my execution. I could tell.

At least I'd paid in advance for Rhy's school. But if they couldn't buy groceries... I had to stop myself from going down that path. Weakness would be feasted on where Dice was taking me. Then there was Ember. Couldn't do that either. I was tempted to run, but they knew where I lived. They would make my loved ones pay if I ran. So I sat through the red lights with Dice instead of popping open the door to escape.

When we got to the building, the guys out front weren't wearing red bandanas. Dice's brow furrowed. The tallest opened Dice's driver's side door and gestured for him to get out. I got out of my side, because I knew my lot. We'd go up together.

These guys were different from Booker's usual goons. Their suits were superb. Crisp. Expensive. I took a deep breath. Instead of getting shit thrown at us, we were stared at. This was a whole different crew. My heart was in my throat as a group of them led us into the building; the only red bandanas in the whole place were on Dice and me.

I wanted to ask what the fuck was going on, but clearly

Dice was thrown as well. Another perfect suit admitted us into Booker's office, but instead of the man we feared, a stranger had his feet up on Booker's desk—a stranger wearing a white suit and an orange tan.

I nodded. There was a sense of control and power coming off of him. His steady hand was holding a crystal tumbler of what must have been whiskey. Dice clearly didn't get the same vibe; he started in immediately.

"Where the fuck is Booker? Are you his goddamn grandfather? Shit. This is what happens. Booker said he'd pay me to bring him in." Dice gestured at me. "Now Booker's gone."

I swiveled my head in his direction. "You were going to get *paid?* Where's the goddamn loyalty, Dice?"

Rage boiled that he'd accept money for a bounty on my head. I looked back at the old man. A new picture caught my attention. Actually, a ton of new pictures. But the biggest was just behind the stranger's head. It was Booker's picture in a huge frame. And it was hella crooked.

Dice pushed forward, yelling at the man. A quick glance and I took in all the pictures of the men who'd called us Pussy and Ball Sack in the recent past. I tried to signal to Dice to shut the fuck up, but he was going all in.

"...you old, dried-up hag. What the hell do you think you're doing, sitting in Booker's chair? I'm his best guy. "

The man tilted his head, listening. Amused. A slow smile spread across his face. "So, you're loyal to Booker? Through and through? All Coke?" He swirled the amber liquid in his glass.

"Fuck yeah. Coke till death." Dice threw up the Coke sign.

I didn't join in.

The old man swung his feet off the desk. When he stood, I realized he was wearing his suit jacket as a cape. Between that oddity and the pictures of the other men, the strangeness was overwhelming.

He gave me a slight bow. "I'm Olin Feybi. Formally Olin Dutch. Are you loyal to Booker, too?" He looked me over like I was a hooker he'd just paid for.

"No." A gamble.

The old man's mouth opened a smidge. I heard his teeth clack together when he closed his jaw.

"You from the Feybi family up north then?" I'd seen that last name mentioned in the newspapers my father would read in the morning. Back before he was in prison.

"That's a great question. You pay attention to current events?" He rubbed his palms together and his dry skin made an audible swish.

"I like to read." I could feel my heart beating in my ears. "Don't know too much about Dutch family, though." This was a lie, of course. The Cokes were an offshoot of the Dutch family, after all. But the longer I could keep the old man talking, the longer I could keep Dice and me alive.

Olin bared his teeth in what was an obvious attempt at a smile. "Oh, let's get into my family history. I *love* dragging ghosts up out of their graves. My older brother, Bat Feybi, was the family prince. Our father revered him. But I, I was revered by my mother. Thank heavens. Where Bat was dipping into the illegal pursuits, I learned at my mother's feet. The Dutch family was better at making legal money, though we used *gangs* every now and again. After Father died, he of course put Bat in charge. But I accumulated wealth. Power. As head of the Dutch family, I have connections he couldn't possibly have."

Olin slowly paced the room, his cape/jacket swishing menacingly. "I even brought our youngest brother, Felon, into the fold. He was my father's bastard child with the housekeeper. But I know how to *not* burn bridges. I had everything Bat thought he wanted. Now that he's dead, I'm taking the one thing he had over me: his name. I'm taking the business that's owed to me. And these gangs?" He snorted derisively. "These Cokes and other neighborhood gangs that were beholden to my mother's family, that protect our interests neighborhood? They need guidance. And that's why I'm here. Now, you say that you are not loyal to Booker? Tell me more." He stopped pacing and stood before me, offering his hand, palm up, like he was hoping I would hold it.

My father often said I'd been a details guy when I was young. I'd see things other people skated over. I was good at puzzles. I never missed it when he and Ma fought, even when they did their best to hide it.

How Dice had missed the giant picture of Booker over Olin's head was beyond me. I wondered how much money he'd been promised to bring me in. I hoped he'd been paid at least some of it up front and given it to his family. 'Cause this shit was about to get bloody. Pledging allegiance to the Cokes seemed like the wrong lean. So I jumped the other way.

"Booker was brash. He couldn't decide what the hell he wanted to do. Threw money around. Didn't know how to make a good deal to save his life." I folded my hands in front of me.

The silence was as thick as a noose.

"You say *was*. Booker *was*. Do you know something I don't?" Olin dropped his hand and twirled, cape/jacket flaring out.

"Booker's dead. You killed him. He hung that picture first, though." I lifted my chin in the direction of the big, gaudy photograph.

The old man started clapping loudly. His age-spotted hands almost curved like bowls. "Clever. You've got balls, kid. I like it. I might take in a few of Booker's guys here today to help me with the new Feybi buildings around Valston. You want in?" Olin swayed in front of Booker's chair before sitting.

I nodded. "Yes, sir."

I glanced at Dice. He lost all the color in his face and the rage in his fists at the same time. He'd flipped on me, but I still didn't want to watch him die. And I had no doubt that the old guy was worse than Booker had ever hoped to be.

"Dice is good, though. Like, he's solid. Follows directions. Even if it means turning in a friend." I held out my fist and saw the gratefulness in Dice's face. Apology, too. I knew he'd done me dirty and I was still trying to help him out. Maybe, if my choice was the correct one. He tapped my fist in an apology.

Olin crossed his arms in front of him and nodded.

I knew we weren't in the room alone, but I was still startled by the quick movement to my left. I flinched and crouched, but Dice never saw it coming; one of the men who'd led us into the room put a gun to the back of his head.

I wished I'd closed my eyes and not watched how it ended for Dice. He was there, lights on, and then he was gone.

He was gone before he hit the floor. Olin had blood splatters on his pants; he flicked his hand at them like they were breadcrumbs. I'd seen dead bodies before. My neighborhood was like that. But always covered with a blanket. Always with the story of what happened filling my ears from the surrounding crowd. Never like this.

The numbness that followed, the instant anesthesia from reality was a function of my nervous system. A protection.

I was escorted out of the room. My fight for my friend became dust on my tongue. I was hustled out of the building bodily and pushed into a black SUV. Olin walked easily, despite his age. He was already on the phone, talking and laughing. He ordered directions that I couldn't hear. I wasn't sure where I was headed when my SUV pulled out to follow the procession, but when I turned my head, I watched the building that had been Booker's headquarters going up in flames.

Survival mode. I had to switch it on, and soon. But I couldn't get my hands to stop shaking. And every time I blinked I saw Dice's end.

I tried to picture Ember, just to make it stop, to think of someone beautiful, but I couldn't bring her to mind.

26

Ember

WARDON HAD SLEPT ON my extra bed for a while. That bed was getting a lot of use, but not the way I'd intended. It was *supposed* to be the kissing bed. For kissing the hot guys at college. But instead, it was a free hotel room for my gatekeepers.

The increased proximity of Wardon's actual body was a concern. Nix was going to have to explain himself to me. I wanted space and this was far from it. He refused to tell me anything, the same as the night before.

Just when I was about to say something, Wardon's phone buzzed and he excused himself.

Finally alone, I checked my phone. No texts or pictures from Lock. None. I curled on my side and snuggled into my pillow. It took me a bit to fall asleep.

I wasn't sure what made me wake. A noise? The feeling of not being alone?

The man standing over me was a stranger. Another person was right behind him. My scream was almost out of my mouth. Instead of noise, I had a mouthful of a disgusting cloth. My lips went numb and my nostrils burned.

My last thought was of Nix. This would unhinge him. And then I slipped into unconsciousness.

———

When I woke, I was in the back of an SUV. My head was pounding. I was still in the clothes I fell asleep in—low-slung sweats and a tank top. It hadn't been too long, because it was still dark out. Or it had been really long and it was dark again. There was a guy sitting next to me. He noted that I was awake and offered me two white pills and a bottle of water. Like he'd been waiting for that exact moment. I looked at his face and hands a few times before shaking my head. And then regretted it instantly.

"Fine. Have it your way. Boss wanted you to be comfortable." He put the bottle in one cup holder and the pills in the other. They clearly said Tylenol on them. The water bottle still had the safety seal. After a few more splitting, sharp pains, I caved and took the pills. There were two more men in the SUV.

The driver and the front passenger hadn't said anything to me, acting like I wasn't there at all.

Dark suits. No music. It was very businesslike.

My mouth was dry. I drank the rest of the water.

"What did you do to me?" I coughed.

The man next to me gave me a blank stare. Not answering.

I set down my bottle and held my head. Soon, I was going to have to pee. Anxiety clawed its way into my chest as I came out of whatever drug they had given to me. This was a clear kidnapping.

Nix would be unglued; the bodyguards would be sounding the alarm.

I said as much to the man next to me, but he ignored me as the SUV slowed down. We stopped at what looked to be a warehouse.

The men hopped out and held open the door. I folded my arms. I wasn't going anywhere.

Never get taken to another location.

One of the men took a gun out of his holster. And I got the hell out of the SUV. The location thing was great advice unless someone was armed. My heart was hammering in my chest, the drugs lifting completely. Actually, I think this was considered the third location. It didn't matter. This was it. I was done. They were going to kill me. Maybe do worse. Maybe they were Nix's enemies.

The man who'd sat beside me in the back seat grabbed my upper arm. I kept my arms folded. I didn't have on a bra. A rock bit into my foot. I didn't have on shoes either.

I started fighting then, the pain in my foot spurring me to action. I swung at the man holding my arm. I tried to kick his leg. He backhanded me across my face. I stumbled, but his viselike grip on my arm kept me standing.

The man next to him stepped between us. "Asshole. She's not to have a mark."

Then the driver simply scooped me up into his arms and continued the march toward the door. There was a light on in the building; it almost seemed welcoming.

I tried struggling out of the driver's arms. He leaned close. "Hey. Pretty. No one's going to hurt you again. But this place is covered with our guys. Snipers. Don't waste your energy. If you impress him, you live. If you don't... well... I wouldn't concentrate on that part."

Before I could formulate a response, I was through the door and placed on my feet.

The warehouse was huge and hot. The guy who'd been holding me hadn't been wrong. There had to be fifteen men in the room. There was a single chair in the center, and an old man sat in it. He was wearing a white suit, the jacket draped over his shoulders like a cape. He was a sickly color of orange. Or, at least he looked orange under the burning lights.

My blood started to pound in my head. Sheer panic was starting to win. I put my hands on my knees like Aunt Dor had taught me when I was a kid. Deep breaths. Focus on the in and the out.

"She's scared. God, I bet if I still had a dick, that would be arousing, you know?"

I peered up at the old man. He got out of the chair like a showgirl. Elaborate steps. Deep knee bends. He came close to me and I could smell his cologne. Something was familiar about the scent, but I couldn't place it.

As he approached, I straightened up. I willed myself not to cry. The tear that streaked my cheek was not a great listener.

He circled me. "You say she was sleeping? That's wonderful. Can you imagine? Cosmo getting to wake up next to this sight?"

He ran a hand across the tops of my bare shoulders. None of the men around us said anything. He stepped in front of me and pulled at my arms, clearly wanting me to drop them. I struggled, but the men around me shifted their coats, showing off their guns.

I let my arms dangle on either side.

"I'm Olin Feybi, by the way. Let's take a look at what we're getting. 'Cause sometimes, you get this kind of face..." The man touched my cheek and I flinched. "The body is shit, you know? But if we're going through all this trouble..." He started to lift up my tank top from the hem.

I grabbed his forearm and snarled at him. It wasn't the first time a guy had done something stupid to me. I reacted on instinct.

"That's fine, you're shy. But still." He used his other hand to pull out the neck of my tank top and peer down it. I felt the fire of embarrassment fill my cheeks.

"Oh. Those are spectacular. Cosmo will love me for those." He let go of my shirt and grabbed at the waistband of my sweatpants.

I clamped my hand on his, holding it there. "No. You creepy old fuck." I heard the shuffle around me. The men were pointing their weapons at me again. I didn't budge. "Find a new hobby."

The old man burst out laughing. The men around him joined in, their laughter sounding almost canned, mechanical.

"This is good, no? I mean, Cosmo needs a challenge. Make him fight for it a little, you know?" He was using big gestures to the men in the circle. "While I'm here, I'm noticing she has a mark on her face. Where'd you get that mark, sunshine?"

He rubbed his palms together.

The men were a blur now. I shook my head. I couldn't remember.

"Who was it, Volt?" He pointed at one of the men.

"Files." The answer came quickly. The guy presumably called Files stepped forward.

The old man flicked his hand toward him. Volt pointed his gun and shot Files in the leg. I jumped. The bang and the instant blood were a slap to my entire being.

Files fell to one knee but did not fight back or even scream. He stammered, "Sorry, sir."

"Sorry sucks a lot of dick, you know? The plan will only work if we put her back in her bed in just a few hours. How will she explain the mark you put on her?" He came closer to me and touched my cheek lightly. "Someone get her some ice. Maybe we can bring the swelling down."

I watched him like he was a venomous snake. Getting to go back to my dorm alive was not something I thought would happen. Hope was growing. If I could get back to the dorm, I could tell Wardon and the others about what had happened. I could be safe again. Warn Nix and Animal and T.

The old man handed me my ice. It was really just a water bottle frozen solid, but I did as I was asked and put it to where my face throbbed.

Files had his head down like a kid getting scolded, blood seeping onto the floor.

When Volt walked up to him, I thought he was going to hit him. Instead, he lifted his hand close to Files' chest.

A pop from the gun and it was over. Files' knees bent and he fell to the ground like a robot that had been unplugged.

There wasn't a ton of blood, so I wondered if it was just a warning. But his eyes stayed open. And didn't blink. When the frozen water bottle exploded at my feet, I jumped back, scared. I had to look at it before I could tell what had happened.

I wrapped my arms around my middle and started to cry. I

had dropped my bottle. Then I flat out sobbed. I wanted it all to stop, this nightmare where I had no control, no friends.

The old man patted my back. "I guess we forget how it was at first? Right? God, seeing our first man killed? Hits us all right in the balls." He put pressure on my shoulders, making me stand.

I couldn't take my eyes off Files' lifeless body. The old man sidestepped, blocking everything but his face.

"You're an innocent. That's unbelievable. I knew you and your brother were separated for a long time. Wonderful."

My brain snapped back into focus.

"Oh, yes. Your brother? I know just who he is. And who you are to him. You don't get to be related to murderers and have a normal life. He has sins he needs to pay for. And you're the price." He touched my chin.

I was out of my depth. I thought of T and how she'd handle the situation. I came up with nothing. I'd been protected. Always protected. I wasn't prepared for this. I didn't want this.

"Still tears. My son, Cosmo, is a lucky man. I've picked the perfect girl for him. We'll have you meet, of course. Set a date, will you, Volt? Fill her in on the way back."

The old man twirled and smiled over his shoulder like an evil cover girl. "Can't wait until we're family, little one."

He strutted out the side door and four of the men went with him.

I hugged myself again. It was cold here. Or hot. I couldn't tell. I started shaking.

Volt wiped his gun on his shirt as he approached me. Another guy had a rag he wiped on the center of Files' chest before also heading to me.

I knew I was next. Volt was going to kill me. I closed my eyes. Despite the old man's assurances, I knew this was a deadly situation. I didn't want to watch. When he took my hand and I felt the hard metal in it, I looked.

He was pressing my hand all over the gun. It made no sense. Then the other guy brought the towel to me. He wiped it down the front of my shirt and across my hips. Then with a devious smile he dragged the cloth to my right breast. Before he could start fondling me, Volt slapped his hand away.

"You asshole. Girls don't kill people with their tits. Why you putting his blood there? And Olin said no one touches her. What part of that don't you understand?" Volt let out an exasperated sigh. "I'll fucking take her back. You fuck twits can follow. Butch and Echo, clean up Files."

Volt grabbed my arm and handed the gun to one of the more alert looking men. I staggered as he pulled.

"Listen, I can't carry you now. You've got his blood on you. Don't make me use the sedative again." Volt was tall, with thick hair and a low forehead. I concentrated on walking. My tank top was covered. My hand was covered. In blood.

I couldn't get one straight thought to hold any weight in my head. I was still shaking. Volt stopped outside of the SUV and told me to stay like a dog.

I should maybe run. This was technically taking me to a fourth location, but the old man had said I was going home. Maybe that would actually happen. Before I could figure out any kind of plan, Volt had the front seat covered in trash bags. He made me sit on top of them.

He didn't buckle the seatbelt and I couldn't find it. The trash bags were a bad sign. Maybe that was how they planned to dump my body. I was crying again. I almost put my face in my hands but stopped when my fingers stuck together. The blood. Volt started to drive. The first part of our drive was dominated by the seatbelt alarm. He ignored it. He tossed a bag to me.

When the alarm stopped dinging, he started talking. "Put these clothes on and put what you are wearing into that bag and zip it up."

I did as he asked. I kept on my underwear and covered my breasts as best I could. I now had on leggings and a T-shirt.

"Okay. To anyone that investigates it, you just killed Files."

"What?" That was the exact opposite of what had happened. "No one would ever believe that."

"Really?" He glanced back at me. "Your old clothes are covered in his blood. Your prints are all over the gun that killed him. And by the time I get you back to your dorm, your obsessive text messages to him can be all over your phone and in your email with the snap of a finger."

"But I never. I don't. I didn't even know him!" I couldn't put things together. Nothing made sense.

"Listen, you don't need to talk right now. You're probably in shock. All you need to know is that you're guilty. And we have proof. We're good at this. You're not the first and you won't be the last. If you tell your brother about any of this, or anyone at all, we will start the process of killing people you love. It's horrible watching someone die, isn't it?" Volt turned on the heat.

I was still shaking.

"I don't understand. Why?" I put my hands on my pants.

"You will tell no one about any of this. Go on a few dates with Cosmo and then drop out of school. You need to distance yourself from your brother and his associates. Make them believe it. You tell anyone else, someone dies. Someone you love. And you *will* be framed for Files' death." Volt seemed to be delivering a script.

I put my hand to my chest, my heart pounding. I thought I might pass out.

"You'll know how serious we are in the morning. Get into

that dorm. Figure out how to get rid of the evidence you have on you. Protect yourself. You're ours now. Remember that." He pulled over to the side of the road and hopped out of the car. We were back in Harmony Hills, near campus, by the pizza place. He opened my door and hauled me out.

"Get home. We'll be watching."

As he rounded the car, only one clear question came to mind.

"I've got bodyguards. How do I get past them?" I shouted.

Volt ignored me and drove away. I had no choice. I had to walk. I let my hair fall over my face. It was all a nightmare. I would wake up and this would all be a giant brain spasm. I told myself that with every step I took.

27

Animal

N IX AND I WERE already on our way. Early this morning, Bowen was found dead in his car. Thrice and Wardon had checked in and Ember was fine. Still in her dorm room; she'd been there all night. She'd even answered their frantic knocks. Her hair was wet like she'd just taken a shower. Wardon said she looked exhausted and spooked. Even more so when they told her Bowen had been killed and she needed to stay in her dorm room.

T was headed to the new Feybi buildings to see what she could scope out. Because Nix and I both knew to start where there was smoke whenever we wanted to find the fire.

Nix had a laptop and two phones with him and he was disappointed. The security cameras he had in place showed nothing. More importantly, when after viewing the footage, we could see that Bowen got into the car and died with no interference at all.

Thrice was on speakerphone. He moved the car with Bowen's body so we could determine what the fuck had happened. Wardon was sitting with Ember in her dorm room.

She was barely talking; both Nix and I wondered how close she had actually been to Bowen. Maybe they'd been friendlier than it seemed. Of course, she wasn't as used to the death that came from being in this business. And that was purposeful.

From Thrice's guesses, it seemed like Bowen had been poisoned. Foam around his mouth was the biggest indicator.

Nix wasn't even talking. His fingers were flying over his computers. Becca was on lockdown in the house. He had a visual on her from his smart watch.

A ten-hour drive took us eight hours. I wondered how Ember would take to getting packed and brought home.

28

Lock

A T EIGHT IN THE morning, I let myself into my apartment. My mother was waiting.

She sobbed in my arms, "I thought it would be you. This time. So many boys are missing. So many. What happened, son? What happened?"

That was a great question. One I'd never answer for her. I pulled a wad of cash from inside my jacket and put it on the kitchen table. It landed with a loud thwack.

"Where did this money come from, Sherlock? Where are all the boys?" She rubbed my arms and hugged me again.

As far as I could tell, they were all dead. All the ones that reported to Booker yesterday had been wiped off the face of the earth. Certainly not *all* the Cokes, but enough of them that the neighborhood would feel the loss deeply.

"I got a new job, Ma. I'll be making money. You and Rhy will be okay." I hugged her back.

"Why are you crying, sweet one?" She wiped at my cheeks.

She used to call me "sweet one" when I was little. I had to give her something. She needed to know that I might be marked now, working for the new guy.

"My smart mouth got me a new job. I grew up last night." That was as far as I was willing to go. Knowing crossed her face. She'd lived in this neighborhood her whole life. She'd seen a lot of people learn a shit-ton of life lessons in the span of twelve hours.

I saw regret. "I wish I'd have gotten you out of here. A long time ago."

"Nah. Dad had work here. He was helping. And this is where family is. You did the best you could, Ma. No regrets." After she sat down by the money, giving it a dirty look, I went to my dresser. I filled a duffle bag with my favorite things. It was hilarious how much of it wasn't the least bit useful now. I would be in suits. I would have an earpiece and a gun. I untied my Coke bandana off and left it in the top drawer.

Olin Feybi wanted me. Felt I'd be an asset. Could tell I wasn't loyal to the Cokes. Or so he said. I would work for him. Well, not directly, but he was the boss at the end of it all.

After getting to the former Feybi compound last night (well, now it was the hybrid Olin had created for himself—Dutch/Feybi), I knew I was in. There was either death or this job. No other choices.

Ironically, you could get out of the Cokes. It wasn't easy, but it could be done. The minute I got the tour, I knew this wasn't any kind of neighborhood setup. These were contract killers, earning the kind of money that only could be minted in evil. Details. The cost of the vase by the front door was probably more than I'd ever seen in my entire life. It was an afterthought decoration. It wasn't even given a prominent spot.

The floors were marble. This was a level I'd never seen. I'd only get paid for as long as I lived. I didn't think it would be too fucking long either. But at least with my mom's long history here and the fact that the community loved Rhy, I knew they'd be relatively safe when I was gone.

I slung the bag over my shoulder and walked back to Ma. I wasn't coming back anytime soon and told her as much.

She stood and put her hands on my face. "Sweet one. This happens to most of the young men I've known. And everything changes. Stay true to your heart. Your community. Live for your sister. When I'm gone, she'll need you. Even if it seems hopeless. *Live*. Promise me?"

I drew my mother close with one arm. She was so tiny. Such a huge personality but really, she was delicate. I knew I had to stay away. And I also knew, as my nose itched, that I would cry. I didn't want to. But heading to this future, leaving what remained of the Cokes, it brought me to my knees when I was begging my mind to be strong.

And then she wasn't delicate at all. My mother pulled my head to her stomach. "Son. I'm so sorry. Let's go. Let's pack up, take this money, and go. We can live in a nice coastal town. Just you, me, and Rhy."

I wanted to leave with her. Stay with her. Help with Rhy. Oh God, Rhy would be devastated. So few people in her life understood her. I'd never been so confused. I started to sob, my tears coming from a young, vulnerable place. With matchbox cars and cartoons.

My mother cried with me. She was quieter about it. Maybe she'd had more practice. I had to stand up. I forced myself to do it. After hugging my mother one last time, I picked up my bag, which had slipped to the floor. I was going to leave. I couldn't face her. Not Rhyana.

But my mother grabbed me by the ear. I'd even miss this. She pointed to her room where my sister was. I glanced at the time. Rhy would just be waking.

I hesitated.

Ma offered, "She won't believe it unless it comes from you."

At least Ma still had fight in her, even though I felt like mine was dying. I tossed my bag at the front door. She was right.

I knocked on the door and pushed it open. Her wholesome brown eyes lit up when she saw me. My buddy. My throat started to close. It was killing me, the prospect of telling her. Even worse than Ma. Rhy was still in bed, on her side because it was the safest.

I got on my knees and shuffled over to her. I took her hand. She was brave. Braver than I'd ever be. I had perfectly working limbs. I could walk. Her challenges were seemingly insurmountable. And yet she was here, smiling at me first thing. Maybe I could have a bit of her courage. I was related to Rhy, after all. I had to have something of her.

"Hey. I have to go to a new job. And I won't be here anymore. At least for a while." I didn't have the heart to tell her forever. Because I was pretty damn sure my tenure at the Feybis' was going to be short and brutal.

Her smile ticked down a bit. People didn't think she understood, but she did. "Don't be sad. I'll send mail and stuff as often as I can. I love you so much."

She swatted at me with her hand. I grabbed it up and kissed the back of it. I leaned over and gave her a hug. She did her best to hug me back in the way she had. I had to leave. I was going to break and I couldn't leave her with that.

As I walked out, my mother held out her hand. I squeezed it, but I had to get out the door. My heart was crawling in my chest, scrambling to stay in my old life. In this safe place. I felt it die a little bit as I let go of my mom's hand and grabbed the ball cap from its place on the hook by the door.

Tears were coming now as I stepped outside, but I wasn't sobbing. The older people from the neighborhood were out and about in the morning. Harsh stares in my direction. Some gasps. This would be a broken place in the coming days. And I was headed to work for the enemy.

A few blocks away from the place I grew up, I grabbed a cab.

The driver didn't mention my tears and neither did I.

29

Animal

NIX DIDN'T DO WELL when he couldn't be in control. He knew all the girls he watched were okay, but something was off about Ember. He was stuck on the fact that when Wardon went to check on her, her hair was wet. Ember always slept in. She was a wonderful sleeper. Nix told me three times that he could always count on Ember to sleep through the night during surveillance.

I was going to check on Ember before heading into Valston.

T had some leads on the new buildings. The Feybis were definitely showing more activity than they should.

But first, I had to make sure my boy didn't destroy this tender new relationship he had with his sister.

When we pulled into the campus parking lot, he hopped out before I could even stop the car. His hood was down, too, rocking the full skeleton face. He growled at two college kids on their way across campus.

I double-timed it so I could be at Ember's door with him.

After entering with his own key, Nix pointed at Wardon and then motioned for him to leave with his thumb.

Ember looked different. Her hair that was usually styled carefully was in waves and flyaways. No makeup, just sweats and a tank.

She didn't stand or acknowledge us, offering a blank stare.

Nix sat down next to her gently. I stepped all the way in and closed the door. While Nix comforted Ember, I was checking the interior of her room. Typical mess. Nothing out of the ordinary. The window was locked. Computer looked fine. But the girl—she was as white as a sheet. Her left hand was shaking.

I didn't like it. Finally, she focused her gaze. "Why are you here?" she snapped. "I'm fine. I need to get to class."

She pushed away from the bed and grabbed a sweatshirt off the back of her computer chair and yanked her phone off the charger on the desk. After cramming the sweatshirt over her head, she snatched her notebook as well. I stood and put my hand on the door, keeping it closed.

Nix was watching her calmly. "You don't have class for another hour."

"I want to study." She pulled on the door she had no hope of wrestling away from me.

I expected hugs. Tears even. But this anger was out of place.

Ember seemed to get more agitated. "What do you think this means? One of your guys gets killed and I have to end my whole student career?"

Something wasn't adding up for Nix either. T had warned me recently that Ember was going to have growing pains. That being nineteen wasn't easy. She was going to test limits. Maybe this was like that.

"We had a guy die. That's it. You're coming home. I have a room for you. This has gone too far." Nix put his hand on Ember's shoulder.

"No!" She twirled quickly, bouncing off my chest. Nix steadied her and still she tried to get away. "I'm not going anywhere."

The whole scene was feeling very, very wrong. If we pushed her now, I had a feeling things would go even more haywire than they already were. I pulled open the door. "Okay. Have at it, Baby Girl. You go to that class."

Nix didn't even argue. He just drew his hood over his head and made to follow her out the door. Clearly, he would be her tail for the day.

"I don't want you following me around. This changes nothing. This is my place. Where I need to be. I'm not in danger." She stomped a flip-flopped foot.

Two kids walked down the hallway, peeking into Ember's room as they went by.

Nix laid it out for her. "Either I'm here with you or you're home with me. Those are your only choices."

I saw her anger fall for a second before she rallied it back up. "I'm not going home with you. And you can't make me. That's actual kidnapping. It's illegal. And it would make me hate you."

That verbal blow was too much. Nix could take anything normally. But he was sensitive when it came to his girls. They had more power over him than they knew. Becca was always careful with him, but Ember was too young to understand how his life really worked.

I growled as a warning to her. She flashed her eyes in my direction. "Don't you try to intimidate me. That's not fair."

Feisty. And angry. And pretty fucking bitchy as well. I glanced at Nix; I knew he was going through all the different emotions and action plans. They were as plain as his face wasn't. Ember had mentioned kidnapping, and I knew that was something he was considering. Because he knew Midville back and forth, we had people everywhere. We called the shots. We knew who was buying what building and then some. Here, so close to Valston, we were at a huge disadvantage.

"Nix, we let her go. She goes to class. And fuck if Wardon's grieving for his friend. He can report to work." I texted the guard while watching her over the top of my phone. Regret passed over her lovely features and then resolve again. I hadn't actually known Ember for most of her life, but I'd known *about* her all these years while Nix watched her. And Nix would tell me proudly all the different things she'd done. This wasn't like her. This girl would have empathy for the devil. It was like her superpower. That she wasn't sad about Bowen, nor apparently giving a rat's ass about Wardon's mental well-being was an issue.

Nix nodded once before adding, "Make Thrice go as well. And get me Slice down here. All hands on the fucking deck." He was simmering mad. Just holding off on his boiling point.

As soon as we cleared her, Ember left without even saying goodbye. I closed her dorm room door firmly; I knew we'd be tossing this room hard.

Nix ignored her possessions and used her desk to prop up his laptop. He plugged into her computer as well. "Every time she uses her computer to charge her phone, I get a report. I'm going to pull her text messages."

I wasn't about to stop him. Nix couldn't stop the stalk. It was deep inside him.

"So she's been messaging a kid—this Lock," Nix muttered, typing away furiously. "And that seems like some harmless flirting, but she's also been in contact with a kid named Coz? And things look way more serious than I..." He trailed off, staring at his screen before reading her texts out loud.

> You are so sexy. I need you all night.

> I miss you, too.

"And then the next night," Nix continued.

> Girl, I want you so bad tonight.

> You'll get me, too. I love you. Here are a few pictures to hold you over.

Before Nix could snap his computer closed, I saw some female skin. I assumed Ember had been sending pictures to this Coz guy. I knew kids were attached to their phones, but I was hoping that Ember wasn't the type to make that mistake. She was still young, though.

Nix did some more research, avoiding any pictures. "This might be more the reason for the attitude. Holy crap."

It was clear she'd been getting in deep with the Coz guy before she even started college. Hell, she'd only been here two weeks. Was *he* the reason she'd picked this school in the first place?

When Ember came back to the dorm, the guys were right behind her. She slammed the door in their faces.

She sighed when she saw us. "Why are you still here? Going through my stuff?" She tossed her book onto her bed.

"When were you going to tell us about Coz?" Nix flipped his screen around to show her the messages he'd been able to retrieve.

For a few beats I saw the girl I knew as confusion danced across her face. She took the computer and read through what was there, for what seemed like the first time. Then she settled her face in the bitch look she'd been rocking since we got here. "No one you need to know about." She exited out of the messages. "Could you not do this? Go through my personal things?"

Nix stood. "These guys stay with you. If one more thing happens, I'm pulling you out of here. Or moving in. Your choice."

It was a shocking decision, though one I agreed with. Clearly, they both needed a few hours apart to cool down. I knew Nix would want to investigate this "Coz". Dating that Lock kid was one thing, but she seemed to be straight up in love with Coz and was hiding it so hard she was dating someone else just to throw us off.

I tried to give her a hug before I left, but she stiff-armed me, and not in the funny way she did sometimes when she said I was too sexy to touch. I shrugged and followed Nix out the door.

We both got into the car and he started to steam. "I'm losing her and I don't even know why."

Our complicated lives had just become more so. I sighed. We needed to meet up with T as well. She texted me that she had some more information. Maybe she could shed some light on the situation.

30

Ember

I KNEW BETTER THAN to cry after Nix and Animal left. They'd be watching me more than ever now. The texts I never sent were yet another message from the men who'd taken me last night. I'd never met a Coz, but we had traceable conversations where the few racy pics on my phone had been inserted. That particular breach of privacy stung badly.

The situation was terrifying. I didn't think I'd be able to fool Nix and Animal. I'd always been a shitty liar. But maybe keeping them safe was the best motivation. I'd touched my mother's earring more than once for strength.

It occurred to me that when Nix was young she probably told him a lot of lies to keep him safe. The men from last night were murderers. And they wanted to hurt my people. I was going to have to roll with their punches until I had an out. Being in the same room as my brother, a freaking hit man, and his mob boss best friend wasn't the time or place to mention it.

I overheard Thrice and Wardon and how puzzled they were about Bowen's death as they trailed me on my way to class. My biggest fear right now was that knowing me equaled death.

I couldn't stop picturing Files getting killed. My left hand wouldn't stop shaking, so I kept stuffing it places. My pocket, under my butt, just anywhere. I didn't hear a thing my professor said during her lecture. I went through the motions of being attentive.

When I got back to my room, I had a text on my phone. It was from a new contact. Whatever messages they had pushed onto my history weren't really on my phone.

> This is Coz. Please respond.

I wanted to send a picture of my middle finger, but my left one might be shaking too much. And I didn't know what set these people off. They were capable of taking me, unbeknownst to Nix, overnight.

They could be capable of anything.

I responded:

> Ember here

> Good girl. I'll be picking you up for a date tonight at 7p.m. Dress hot.

Sure

I was going to meet the mysterious Coz. There had been no
pictures of him. I missed Lock, but my phone was quiet from
him. And that was probably for the best. The less people
attached to me right now, the better.

31

Lock

MY FIRST OFFICIAL JOB for the Feybis was standing outside a refurbished, expanded garden shed on their compound grounds. No one was in it, but it seemed like it was set up to be a guesthouse.

My head was dizzy with the swift change in my entire existence. I tugged at the suit I was wearing. It was expensive. The earpiece that connected me to my current supervisor was high-tech. I didn't have a gun yet; I had to earn that.

My job was to keep watch and report anything out of the ordinary. It was hot and I wished I had sunglasses like the rest of the guys. The mosquitoes were aggravating as shit. This was the way it was. My new life. I was in the lowest position in the organization. And it was huge. It was so big and well-funded, I could almost believe it was a real business. There were files and secretaries and mini fridges with water.

And they'd slaughtered almost all of the Cokes in one evening. Then they had coffee in hand the next morning, like they'd played a great round of golf the day before.

I ached with the need to see my mother and Rhy. I felt young. I knew I looked young. But I had to stay on the grind if I was going to send money to Ma. I thought about Ember. We were supposed to meet up tomorrow, but I was pretty sure this place didn't allow time off. I lived behind the Feybis' compound walls, which until recently, had been the Dutch family's compound walls, now renamed and rebranded. There, I had a bed and a hook on the wall to hang my stuff in an outbuilding. The golf carts and ATVs were there, too. The bathroom had a pony wall that only covered you from your knees to your neck. Privacy was nonexistent. I was a soldier here, but instead of having a greater good to hold on to, these people were evil. Loaded, clearly. And their money was very real. They weren't generous with it, but I was supposed to get paid on Fridays, like a real job.

Every fifteen minutes a guy called Volt drove by in a golf cart and gave me and my surroundings a dirty look. I was starving by eleven a.m. No one gave a shit. When Volt drove by at three p.m., I told him I had to take a leak. He swapped places with me and told me I had ten minutes. I took the golf cart back to the warehouse and had myself a non-private piss.

On my way back, I snagged a warm water bottle and a box of takeout food that the guys before me had left on a card table.

It was a sandwich—cooked ham—and it looked decent. I wasn't sure if it was supposed to be refrigerated or if I was even allowed to take it, but I ate it like an animal on the way back to the shed.

Volt tapped his watch. "Nine and a half minutes, asshole. You almost got your dick blown off. If I tell you to take ten, be back in five."

He grimaced at me as I apologized.

This place was as far from warm and cozy as a person could get. I saw gardeners in the afternoon. The grounds' land-scaping was like a resort. I could hear water somewhere, so I assumed there was a pool or fountain or something nearby.

I was daydreaming about swimming naked with Ember when two men headed my way in a golf cart. I tried to stand up straighter.

The driver was a guy a bit older than me and dressed fly as fuck. Every hair was in place and his outfit was casual but obviously all name brand and new. A diamond-encrusted letter C hung from a gold chain around his neck.

The passenger was Olin Feybi, the old fart who'd had Dice killed. My revenge senses started tingling. Sure, Dice had betrayed me, but shit, it had been a horrible situation either way. I didn't have ill will toward him.

As the golf cart came to a halt before me, Feybi was finishing up what could only be a lecture.

"...legacy has to be maintained, Cosmo. You know this. And I've given you time. Too much time. I could die at any minute." Feybi hopped out of the cart with the energy of a much younger man.

The guy called Cosmo was pouting a bit. "Whatever."

"I've found you a great one. And she'll stay here. You'll learn to love one another. She's gorgeous, by the way. Never seen a prettier girl in person. Good grandbaby recipe, you know?" Olin dug into the pocket of his white jeans. He had a Hawaiian shirt on, too. Party Feybi, apparently.

I let my gaze focus past them like I was watching for danger, which I guess I was.

"He's new." Cosmo was staring at me. I could feel his attention. I kept my face blank.

Olin stepped into my personal bubble. I knew better than to level a stare at him. I was taller; he'd take it as aggression. I set my eyes on his white tennis shoes instead.

"Yes. Good attention to detail, son. I acquired him recently. Remember that gang that was interfering with the development in West Valston? Well, they won't be in the way anymore. But I kept this one. Might have been a mistake. We'll see." Olin gently slapped my face three times in a row almost like Ma would.

"I could give three shits about your development in Valston." Cosmo waved his hand dismissively.

Spoiled and unafraid of his father, if I was reading their relationship correctly.

"And this is why your only job is going to be a breeding stud for me. You could've had a head for business, if you didn't party all the time." Olin walked past me to open the door to the shed.

Cosmo followed his father through the open door and shut it behind them. I couldn't hear anymore, though I gathered things from the pieces of their conversation. Olin had found a girl for Cosmo. And Cosmo really didn't care. This was next level matchmaking bullshit going on here. I accepted the shady practices for the money, but kidnapping? That would be hard to swallow. God, I hoped the girl was of age and had decided to come here of her volition. This horrible job would be even worse if I was hurting innocent people, even if all I was doing was guarding them.

The men came out and Feybi locked up, shooting me a look while he did so. I averted my gaze to the distance again. Cosmo still seemed pissed and mostly unimpressed.

"When you meet her, you'll understand. She's perfect." Olin and Cosmo slid back into the golf cart.

"I want that guy at my party this weekend." Feybi pointed at me. "He can be a guard. The girls will like him. He's eye candy." I tried to hide my shock.

"Maybe. He's got to prove himself first. I'll get reports on him and..."

Cosmo rolled his head on his neck and gave his father a disrespectful glare. Instead of the slap I expected, Olin relented. "Fine. You can have him. But you have to have at least a few of the older guys, too."

Cosmo seemed happy enough with that to let his father off the hook. It sure seemed like the much younger Feybi was in charge in that relationship. Not that I cared. They were both shitbags as far as I was concerned.

This job blew. I knew it was my first day, but I wished it could be my last. As long as I could keep from leaving in a body bag as well.

I couldn't even dick around on my phone; they'd made me throw it into the river so no one could trace me. I guess money grew on trees around here because it had taken me almost a year of saving to afford the freaking thing.

For the rest of the day, I tried and failed to avoid thinking about my mom as she called that number. I was feeling sorry for myself again. Volt drove up after dark and told me to get in the cart. I was puzzled while he drove me back to the warehouse. "Aren't you staying here?"

It was a clear change of the guard. He laughed at me. "Listen, pup, you think we'd give you something real to guard? Shit. You'll be watching garbage pails and empty rooms for at least a year before you get anything important."

It sounded boring but safe. As I pictured Rhy and Ma, I knew that was preferable.

32

Ember

I WAS GOING TO HAVE to make Nix and Animal believe I hated them. It was the only way. With something as simple as a fake conversation with "Coz," I knew that Olin had me. He'd framed me for murder and killed Bowen to make a point. I was ready to cower in a corner. Of course, that would be a tip-off. If at any point I let Nix know I was scared, it would be over. He would keep me in his basement...well, our basement. And who knew what Olin Feybi would do to get to me even then. I was going to have to be a brat. And unreasonable. And mean. I had to put my hand on my heart as it started to hurt. It was the exact opposite of what I wanted. I mean, I wanted independence at school, but I wanted this relationship with my brother, too.

But I had to push them away. Olin had my loved ones and me by the throat. Their safety depended on me.

I dressed for my "date" with Coz. Or whoever was on the other end of my phone. I went with a black dress. It felt like a way to mourn Bowen. I hadn't slept, and I wasn't tired yet. Maybe it was the adrenaline.

I texted the number again.

> How am I supposed to get out?

The response took so long I almost put down my phone.

> Walk out the front door. Tell your bodyguards to stay put. Make sure to put effort into your appearance. Also, send me a picture of the finished product. And leave your phone in your dorm.

I didn't respond but walked woodenly to my makeup. I did a basic smoky eye and added a light gloss. I loved makeup, but tonight it felt garish. I took a lifeless selfie and sent it out.

I wanted to crawl into bed and cry, convince myself this was all just a terrible dream.

I brushed my hair until it was soft. By seven p.m., I was standing outside, arguing with Thrice. I bet Nix was calling my phone at the same moment Wardon forbade me from getting into the limo that pulled up. I warned them both to leave me alone and give a girl space as the driver closed the limo door behind me.

When I slid inside, a girl dressed just like me was sitting there. She didn't look like me in the face, but her wig had my colored streaks applied.

When the limo turned into a parking lot, the fake me was shuffled into a waiting SUV, which then peeled out.

The limo driver told me to stay put. After some time, he backed out. I heard nothing that indicated Thrice and Wardon had fallen for the ruse, but when the driver swiveled his head to the right, I noticed he was wearing an earpiece.

It was miles before I was actually switched to an SUV. I wondered what kind of chase Wardon and Thrice had endured. I hoped that they were safe.

When I got in the back, I recognized Olin in the passenger seat. This whole thing was so well-thought-out. So seamlessly maneuvered that I had no choice but to truly believe his threats to my loved ones were just as real. Fear and foreboding lodged in my chest. God, I was in deep, and my heart slammed with the realization. My palms moistened and I wiped them on my dress.

Olin was talking to the driver and one of the men in the third row behind me. I was like an afterthought, even after all the effort that had gone into getting me there.

Finally, Olin twisted in his seat. Maybe I was too tired, or too overloaded, but my fear was slipping away. I was getting angry.

"Well, we'll stop and get a new outfit for her. I want Cosmo to see what she's got." He stared directly at my chest.

"Who's Cosmo?" I figured it was worth an ask. I was getting primped to meet him.

"He's your future boyfriend. If he likes you, that is. You better hope he does. If he likes you jumping, you better figure out how high. And don't stop until he tells you." Olin laughed at his own crass words like they were a joke.

Before the death I saw and the one I caused, I would've been fighting my ass off to get out of this vehicle. Out the back window, I saw that no one was behind us. We weren't being followed. This man could do exactly what he wanted, apparently. And that meant until I could come up with a solution, my loved ones were in danger.

This man had a plan for me, and it sounded like I had to be alive to fulfill it. So I'd do as much. Stay alive.

The vehicle came to a stop behind a building that was clearly very busy. People were coming in and out of various doors and car doors were slamming. Olin got out of the front seat and held open the door for me, his hand extended.

I ignored it and got out of the car without his help. The slap across my face was a shock; no one treated me like this. Ever. And it hurt. I touched my face, covering the pain. The streetlight created a shadow puppet of my form, hunching over.

"If a man offers you his hand, take it. Don't act like a hussy. Think of yourself as royalty, if that helps. If I offer you something, you take it. Understand?" His hand was still extended. My pride didn't let me cry. I thought of my mother. How many hits she had to endure in her life. I stared at him as defiantly as I could while I took his hand.

He nodded and smiled as if he hadn't assaulted me. "Now, we visit Ann. We make the best of what we have here."

Olin held my hand up the back stairs of what seemed to be a club, his entourage of suited guards trailing us. At the top of the stairs, a uniformed doorman let us into a very chic apartment. It had a sophisticated beach vibe, like a magazine spread. The bass of the music playing below seemed to be vibrating the furniture.

Olin found an armchair and gestured to it with flourish. I sat and didn't let go of his hand until he released mine.

He leaned next to my ear. "You're learning. That's fabulous."

I closed my eyes. Maybe that's how Mom did it, too. Maybe she closed her eyes. I steadied my breathing. In and out. In and out. When I opened my eyes, I was calmer. Just a touch. My heart was still hammering away, but I wanted to pay attention to details. Names, if I could. Places.

When I was little, I would play elaborate games by myself. Dolls, forts, drawings. I'd create a whole universe. When eventually Aunt Dor would make me clean it all up, I'd feel like Godzilla wrecking it all. The point being, I could play pretend hardcore. And I had a feeling that I'd have to tap into that tonight. And maybe tomorrow, too. Mom's last word was my name. Nix had been keeping true to what he felt was her request. But I had to reciprocate, and that meant surviving. For him. Somehow, I had to whisper his name back to my mom's intentions.

A woman I assumed was Ann breezed into the room and gave Olin air kisses on both cheeks like they were meeting up in a French bistro.

"Darling. Such an unexpected surprise. A gift?" She gestured to me. I tried not to react. I didn't want to be a gift. None of that had a good connotation.

Ann had a short bob and was wearing a linen shift with nude heels. She could easily be running a company. She seemed out of place in the same building as a nightclub.

"Not for you, this time." Olin half-bowed before snatching her hand up and kissing it. "I need a favor. Can you give her a transformation? I'll be back in an hour. I want Cosmo to really like her."

Ann nodded with all the gravity and understanding of a brain surgeon. She came over and asked me to stand. She ran her hands over me like I was a statue. "I can make some miracles happen here. She's got a lot of resources to play with. Can you give me an hour and a half?" She lifted my hair from my shoulder and rubbed it between her fingers.

"I can make that happen, but that's it. I need her outside ready to go in ninety minutes." Olin patted my ass as he went by. "Play nice with Ann. I'll leave a few men in this room to keep an eye on you." I flinched at his touch, which Olin followed with a slightly harder warning slap. "You better get used to a Feybi touch."

And with that, he was gone, though his guards remained. In his absence, Ann's demeanor didn't change. She was haughty and professional, but I soon gathered that she treated women like a product. I gleaned the information from the comparisons of me to other ladies. She had three laptops and two assistants and they all got on their computers. One was researching Cosmo's Instagram and another clicked through pictures of a girl who had similar bone structure to me. I recognized her when I glimpsed the screen. I think it was the girl who'd acted as my double earlier. The last was pulling up inventory they had on hand. They spent far more time than I expected on the computers. I stood waiting. They hadn't told me to sit and would occasionally ask me to turn or face a certain light.

Ann gave her interpretation of what she felt they could do to me to make me appeal to Cosmo. "We don't have time to dye this hair, but I want it in an upsweep. Tuck as many colors as you can underneath. Maybe get a brown mascara wand to touch up. Cosmo seems to like a more classic profile. Think Hepburn."

And then they started. Ann made the men turn around, at least. She said that their testosterone would affect my femininity. And when the three ladies set to work, I became a product manipulated to the way they wanted me. It was a flurry of tugging and pulling and brushes and poking. At one point, I was lying on a couch with just Spanx on and Ann was doing my makeup as one of the assistants tackled my hair. The other was making sure my feet looked great. Apparently, Cosmo had liked a few open toe heel pictures, so they figured he might have a toe fetish. After they stood me up, there were three dresses to choose from. All of them were put on me and photographed. Ann grumbled about not getting enough time, but having Olin on the hook for a favor was worth the hassle, or so she quietly told her helpers.

We were almost done, with me finally in a tight short black dress with complicated straps and heels. Ann couldn't bring herself to put me in out-of-season open toe shoes, but she knew my feet were ready to fuck if need be. At those words, everything sank in; I was being made into a sex object. During the test to see if I could stand and pose the way they thought best, the door to the apartment burst open.

Two girls were helping a badly beaten woman into the room. Ann went immediately to them. "Set her on the tile. I don't want blood everywhere."

I felt my jaw drop. Instead of being brought to the couch I had been laid on, the woman was brought to the kitchen. She was softly moaning. I choked on a sympathetic sob. There was so much blood; the poor girl must have been in misery.

Ann pointed at me from her crouch. "Don't you dare cry. I don't have time to fix it. Laura, take her to the curb for her ride. Feybi men, go with."

Before I knew it, I was being led down the staircase. "What's happening to her?" I was too shocked to keep my mouth shut.

Laura answered softly as she guided me outside and began checking my hair and makeup beneath the light from the streetlamps. "We have a customer who's known to do that if a girl doesn't follow the script he lays out. She was new."

"This is a theater?" I couldn't connect the dots. A script to me meant a play.

Laura acted like I was speaking a different language. "This is a brothel. Ann is a madam."

And then it all slammed into place. Why they were good at makeup, the pounding music below, even the late hours everyone here seemed to be keeping.

"You didn't know?" Laura patted my hair again.

"No. I don't even actually know what a script has to do with any of this. Does this mean I'm a hooker now?" I was getting ready for Cosmo. Maybe he had bought me, or at least thought he had.

"Not you. Not yet anyway. From what I overheard, you're getting ready for Cosmo Feybi. We would kill for that chance. He's made of money. His father, Olin, is particular, too." Laura pressed her lips shut when one of the men guarding me shook his head.

Olin, of course, would have a connection here. He'd murdered people. Sex had to be part of it. Sex sells and all that. And I was being painted up for Olin's own son. My stomach lurched. I was already overstimulated by this evening. New situations, giant heaps of uncertainty and fear. I had to make this okay in my head and keep moving forward. I pictured Nix and centered my fear. At least I could stand here and not scream at the top my lungs. That was something.

The headlights pierced through the night, and I knew it was the limo. Olin got out of the car after it stopped. "Nice work. I would've thought a little less coverage in the bosom area."

Laura put her head down like she was a prisoner talking to a warden, "Sir, Ann was sure that Cosmo would like this classy ensemble judging from his social media. We can change it, of course—"

Olin let her stir in her fear for a few seconds before forcing a laugh. "I'm sure she's right. Maybe I'm just a breast man, you know?" He reached out and grabbed two handfuls of Laura's.

I could tell her body was stiff with fear. I reached out and slapped his hands away.

"She's not meat."

And then he whirled on me, letting go of Laura. He grabbed the back of my neck and stuffed his hand under my dress between my legs. "I take what I want. Got it?"

I couldn't move. He was horrible. I hated him viscerally. I glared at him. A tiny voice in my head told me not to, but my temper got ahead of me.

"Don't you rear up to me. Say it. *I can take what I want.*" He increased the pressure on the back of my neck.

"Sir. Please, her hair. We can't mess up her hair. Or make her cry." When Olin let go, relief swelled in my chest. It was short-lived.

"Beat her until she's unrecognizable." I thought he meant me, but the bodyguards grabbed up Laura and started in on her. I felt my knees go out from under me. The violence was so swift and cruel.

Olin grabbed my upper arm and steered me to the back of the limo. The last glimpse I got of Laura, she was getting kicked in the stomach.

I felt sick to mine.

"Tell me, darling."

He was sitting next to me. I faced him. I think I knew in that second life wasn't fair. That the rules in books and movies didn't apply to this man. No one was promising me a happily ever after.

"You can take what you want." My mind hated the

sentence, but my survival instincts made me appease him.

I was numb now. I had to be. Because I wanted to cry. I wondered if Laura was dead. If she would die. And what about the other girl at Ann's?

This was the brutal underbelly. I wondered if this was what Nix and Animal did. And maybe T. Were they nice to me and then kicking innocent people in the stomach to make a horrible point? I couldn't imagine it. But all at once I could. All the money Nix had came from somewhere. Was it coated in blood? Did he inherit more from his father than I cared to see? I was growing up in minutes. And I hated it.

The limo rubbed up to a curb in downtown Valston. Olin couldn't stop bouncing his left foot. It was shaking the car subtly. He seemed agitated, like he was waiting for a prom date that might not come through. When we were parked, he nodded at the guard in the passenger seat. No words were needed for this; it was something everyone was in on—everyone but me.

Olin reached up and touched my chin, tilting my head this way and that. I didn't flinch and he noticed. A slight smile parted his lips. "See. I knew you were perfect. Good stock and all that."

I didn't ask him to elaborate, but his anxiety seemed to make him a talker. "Your brother, right? He's like a myth. That's the thing that people forget. Siblings are from the same makeup. You have similarities. Extreme circumstances made your brother what he is. But you've been spared. Until now, anyway. I have to watch for any violent tendencies, you know?"

Olin got a signal from the driver and he hurried to open his door and help me out of mine. This time I took his hand, though his touch was like sticking my fingers into a box full of spiders.

He smoothed my dress and patted my hair, but without understanding the work that went into my appearance. Like he was playing with someone else's toy without an instruction book.

I followed where his focus was pinned. The side door of the club burst open and a group of men came toward Olin. I read the anticipation in his eyes. He hissed a few last-minute details at me.

"Be pretty. Be nice. But have fire. Your life depends on it." As soon as he was done threatening me, he smiled in the direction of the group headed our way. "Son. Can I get a word *without* your friends?"

At the center of the group was a man who had to be Cosmo. Everyone else seemed afraid of Olin, but this guy, who was taller than Olin and smoking a cigarette, only seemed aggravated.

He took an inhale and held the smoke in his mouth, looking his father up and down like he might want to fight him. Then he exhaled a ring in Olin's direction.

For a tense moment it looked like Cosmo might turn around and ignore his father.

I held my breath. My safety depended on this prick.

Cosmo nodded and the seven guys around him fell back. I wondered what it was like to live like this, with other humans treating you like you were some kind of god.

Olin reached for my wrist and twirled me into an uncomfortable dance spin that I wasn't expecting. The heels made me falter a little, but the old man was able to right me. "Her name is Ember. And she has connections that would benefit our family."

Cosmo didn't rake his gaze over my body like his father had. Instead, his eyes searched my face. He was handsome. Dark hair, brown eyes, and great cheekbones. His outfit seemed like he spent a lot of time trying to look like he hadn't done just that.

I couldn't find a ton of interest in his face. My stomach dropped. I pictured the two bloody women I'd seen tonight. Things came in threes. Maybe I would be next.

For a moment, Cosmo's gaze connected with mine. I caught a glimpse of compassion in him. And then it was gone.

"She'll do." Cosmo tossed his cigarette to the side and turned his back on his father and me.

He reunited with his group like he hadn't made a monumental decision about my life.

"She's good? It's okay?" Olin called after his son, but didn't receive a response.

I wondered if Cosmo would get the beating for disrespect that I had witnessed with Laura. But instead, Olin just waved and spun.

"Finally! You're the third girl. And honestly, you might be a little bony for him, but that freaking face of yours. Show-stopping." He took my hand and led me to the vehicle. "Get her back to her dorm. Help her pack. She moves in tomorrow."

I knew my face registered how surprised I was when he started giving me instructions. "You make sure that no one thinks this is anything but a girl falling crazy in love with Cosmo. If they take you? Everyone you love dies and you go to prison very quickly. Head spinningly quickly. Do you want me to prove it? I can."

I shook my head no. Bowen had been proof enough. I didn't want to lose anyone else. I had to stay with this man. There was no other choice.

33

Animal

AT THIS POINT ALL we could do was wait. Nix, T, and I were holed up in a hotel down the street from Ember's school. We couldn't keep this up much longer. There were so many parts and pieces to our daily business that all good intentions at respecting her wishes aside, Ember had to come home. Nix had a hair trigger and it was far from sprung. He and T spent time on their laptops, sometimes switching to their phones in their research.

I was working the phones to keep in touch with all my contacts in the area. We weren't turning up anything but a few rumors. Nix was scanning security footage he was pulling from God knew where. Finally, T cleared her throat.

"Okay. I've got some intel, not on Ember, but on who we might be dealing with." T took a deep breath then unloaded. "A guy was interviewed years ago by the cops after he was willing to accept a plea deal. He was dead the next day. But he left a bit of knowledge. Bat Feybi, you know, the original head of the Feybi family who Nix turned into a human flare, has two other half-brothers. Same father, different mothers. One is named Olin Dutch, but recently has been going around town calling himself Olin Feybi. He's used his mother's Dutch family money to cultivate his own business that bought other businesses that were failing. Olin would then money launder and use those businesses as fronts for his illicit, more lucrative pursuits, like selling arms and classified information. Seems like he used local gangs to protect his businesses in their part of town. Olin pits the gangs he's used against one another, or in extreme cases, goes in and wipes them out when he shutters a front. No witnesses to testify against him."

Both Nix and I nodded, struggling to see how the pieces of this fucked-up puzzle fit together.

T glanced at her computer screen, then continued, "Felon Dutch-Feybi is Feybi, Sr.'s third son that he had with his housekeeper. It looks like Felon stuck close to Olin after his mother died when he was a kid. According to rumors, Felon fell in love with Olin's wife, who had Olin's only son. But despite that, Felon is always with him. Word has it that Felon doesn't speak. And has no designs on being any kind of boss. Just wants to make Olin happy. Maybe Felon stayed to watch over Cosmo after Olin's wife died. They all live together on a big piece of property that's been in the Dutch family for generations."

Nix said, "Coz," out loud.

The mysterious new boyfriend in Ember's contacts.

Nix's fingers flew over his computer by way of response. It was a straight five minutes of typing before he offered more. "He's been in and out of a few countries. Mother passed away a decade ago." He nodded at T, confirming her intel. "If I were to guess, she was probably trying to keep him out of the family business."

T added, "A failed attempt. Although he's been referring to himself as a Feybi now, there's tons of property in the area under Olin Dutch. He's really making himself a dynasty here."

"So, Ember's now involved with his kid? What does this mean?" I folded my arms and watched my phone. Wardon, Thrice, and Slice were canvassing the area for Ember. She'd assured them she was leaving of her own accord and now it was all about waiting for her whim to return.

A text flashed on the top of my screen. We've got her. She just pulled up to the dorm.

And then we were out of the room like a SWAT team. Nix was a bundle of nerves. And Ember didn't know how very deadly that was. He was a quiet guy. A thoughtful one. But this had gone too far.

When we knocked on her dorm room door, we had to do it a few times. Nix tugged out his keys, about to force his way in when she swung it open.

"Me being on my own is really fucking hard to do with you guys always here." She held up a hand, blocking our entry.

Nix touched the doorknob, the tendons flexing beneath the bone inked there. "Let us in."

She shook her head. "I'm packing. Tonight. I've had enough."

"What do you mean?" Nix tilted his head and tipped his chin down.

"I'm going. Now." She twirled and I noticed her hair was twisted and tucked into an elaborate knot. I couldn't see any of the colors she normally had.

Nix followed her in. T met my eyes. *Should we join in or wait it out?* I held my hand out to my wife and we watched the door swing closed. We'd wait in the hall and let Nix have his time with Ember.

And then the fighting started. Ember was hissing and whispering at Nix. I couldn't make out the words. I loved Ember, but my blood was starting to boil. And then Nix went back at her, his deep voice murmuring with a definite edge to it.

T pulled on my hand. She was torn. This might be the wrong way to go about it, especially if Ember was in love. But it was too dangerous. We didn't know enough about the new situation with Olin Feybi.

The fighting wound down a bit. I thought maybe we were in the clear, until Nix threw open the door. Slung over his shoulder was Ember, kicking and punching.

"Come on," was all he said. We were straight up kidnapping Ember, physically taking her.

I knew I must have winced because Nix narrowed his eyes at me. This wasn't a great way to foster a healthy brothersister relationship, as far as I knew.

Ember was straight screaming now. Not even words. T made sure Ember's door was closed and I followed, helping Nix open doors on the way out of the building. The kids who lived there were peeking out of their rooms in curiosity. Some of the boys stepped forward questioningly, and one girl came out with a field hockey stick.

It could almost seem like we were playing around until Ember started screaming fire. Nix dragged her off his shoulder in the stairwell and put his hand over her mouth to quiet her down. He used his other hand to hold her swinging hands behind her back.

Finally, she stopped attempting to scream. All she did was look at him with complete hate, tears falling from her eyes to his hand. He removed his hand and she sobbed. "You're hurting me. Stop."

Nix let go of her hands and she rubbed them. Sure enough, they were all red.

"I hate you," Ember choked out, looking at the floor.

Ember staggered away from him and toward me. She hugged my middle, begging me to not let him hurt her anymore. I hugged her back, rolling my eyes. The whole fucking situation made me want to knock them both out. He was overreacting and she was overacting. Something didn't feel right about Ember's response. I didn't like it.

Nix looked at his own hands and then curled them into fists. He spoke softly now, "Ember, please. Come home."

A crowd was gathering around the stairwell. I reached past Nix's shoulder and pulled his hood over his head. I guided Ember to T and she wrapped her arm around Ember's shoulders.

"Let's let T talk to her for a while, go for a walk." I walked past Nix and headed down the rest of the stairs.

A girl who didn't look much older than Ember came forward with her shoulders back. "Can I help you gentlemen? I'm a resident assistant and I couldn't help but notice that Ember seems to want to stay here."

"We're on our way out," I supplied. Nix covered his mouth for a few seconds; there was murder in his eyes. I wasn't going to let him do anything, but my man was jumpy. I grabbed his elbow and squeezed.

He shook his head and let me lead the way. T huddled Ember up the stairs and back to her dorm room.

When we were outside, we could hear sirens in the distance. We walked our way to the car, and then I drove us back to the hotel. We knew Ember would be safe with T. Nix said nothing for a good half hour as we sat together in the hotel room. Every once in a while he would type on his computer. Then he would punch something. Then type. Then curse. Then stare out the window. Finally, he sat, and that's when I knew he was ready to talk.

"It should be easier than this. I mean, I know how to kidnap someone. Shit." He ran his hands through his hair, knocking his hood off with the motion.

I cracked my knuckles and sat in the chair opposite the bed. "I don't know if you can, Bones. I mean, this someone is really, really important to you."

He hung his head. "I hurt her. She's going to hate me forever now."

"She was fine. Overacting. I don't think she'll hate you. But she's nineteen. An adult. Instead of forcing her to do shit, maybe we should explain *why* we need her to come home. Something felt a little off in there." I twisted my silver ring on my finger.

"She knows why we need her to come home. Christ, Bowen's dead. I mean, how much more serious do we need to be?" Nix punched the mattress, getting revved up again.

T's number came through on my phone. I answered on speaker. "Baby."

"The cops are making me leave. Ember told them I..." There was a brief rustling as T talked to someone else, "No. I'm going. I heard you."

A man was talking about trespassing. This was bad. Finally,

T was back. "Ember told them I was a stalker and needed to be removed."

Nix tossed his hands in the air and then set to work. While I got the details of the latest development from my bride, Nix began packing a duffle bag with weapons.

He commanded, "Tell T to stay on her from a distance. We're making a plan to take Ember that'll actually work. No half-assed nonsense."

Nix slung the full bag over his shoulder while palming ammunition. I knew T heard what he'd said, so I ended our call. I didn't agree with kidnapping Ember, but Nix was beyond reason anymore. It was going down.

34

Ember

I WAS IN DEEP now. I had told my brother I hated him. But I understood him and his world better than ever before. If Olin wasn't holding his life and T's and Animal's hostage, I'd go home willingly. We'd talk about it, figure things out. But Bowen was dead and that was on me as sure as if I had poisoned him myself. And they would be next. I wasn't taking a chance with their lives. They all had a conscience. Something in their hearts that guided them. Not Olin. He was broken. I could tell by the way he made me feel inside. That gut intuition they say women have. He was beyond repair, or had maybe never been right from the start.

I opened my suitcase and started tossing things inside. The officer in the room with me believed that I had family coming to pick me up. Instead, I'd texted the number I had for Cosmo, telling him that if I didn't have a ride out of here as soon as possible things would be out of my control. I got a text back that a car would be downstairs, waiting for me.

I left my cell phone, because I knew Nix would track it, would follow me to his death. The phone was full of lies anyway. I had some makeup. A few bras. Stupid stuff. I couldn't concentrate. I stuffed the handful of Polaroids from Lock into the suitcase as well. I rushed past the cop, telling my RA that I was going to a place that could keep me safe and that my ex-boyfriend was dangerous. Outside, I told the cop about my boyfriend's friends and gave him the location where Wardon and Thrice normally waited. It could possibly buy me some time.

They bought it as far as I could tell, but I was so focused on getting away that I really didn't care. The cop watched over me as I jumped into the back seat of the waiting SUV.

Once in the vehicle, I knew they would get me to Olin. And hopefully, it would be enough to keep Nix, Animal, and T safe. For at least tonight.

I wasn't crying. None of it seemed real. I tightened my grip on my suitcase handle. Olin was nowhere to be found as we passed through the compound's gated driveway. There seemed to be a lot of buildings on the property, but we cruised right past the obvious centerpiece. The mansion was a cross between a Disney resort and the Lincoln Memorial. It was excessive to say the least.

We took a back driveway that turned into dirt, bumping along until we came to a stop at the end of what looked to be a garden path. There were pretty solar lights running down either side of the path, illuminating it. The scent of flowers was cloying as the man in the passenger seat opened my door. Another man in a suit was already there, reaching for my suitcase. I recognized Volt as his hand closed around the handle. I held it a moment too long and he had to tug to get me to release it.

"Where's the new kid?" the man who'd been in the passenger seat asked as he offered me his hand. I took it. Olin had taught me that lesson already.

Volt laughed. "Sent him off to guard the septic. Thinking thirty-eight hours of guard duty will toughen him up. Reminds me of when you started here, Bezy."

"This is Ember." The passenger, Bezy, passed my hand to Volt.

Volt lifted his eyebrows. "We've met."

Bezy acted like he was going to pinch my bottom. Volt pulled me closer to him

"Shit. Go back to the warehouse. You know if you try anything, Feybi will wear your balls as a mustache." Volt cut off Bezy's disagreement with a harsh hand signal, then set down my suitcase and dropped my hand as Bezy got back into the SUV. Another man in a suit appeared behind Volt. We all walked together down the path, arriving at a little cottage.

"You remember me? I'm Echo. I'll be outside your door all evening." He grasped my elbow while Volt trailed behind.

Echo went to the door and unlocked it for me. Opening the door to the cottage, he switched on the lights, then Volt set my suitcase inside.

"Let me know if you need anything. The place is wired, alarmed, and has surveillance. As of right now, you have become Feybi property. Don't do anything stupid," Echo offered.

I nodded once and stepped inside. Echo closed the door behind me, locking it from the outside. I didn't need to pull on the door to know that it was sealed tight. I wasn't getting out. I hugged my middle and turned slowly. The place reminded me of Ann's apartment. I even saw a few of the very same decorations. I thought of Laura and the girl who had to bleed on the tile.

Maybe I had mental whiplash. Everything had changed so quickly. I should've gone to college in Midville. I should've lived in the bedroom Nix had made for me.

I wanted space, and instead, I found myself a cage.

Crying was all I had now. I sat down so I could do it properly.

35

Lock

I HUNCHED IN MY cot, cursing my lot. I didn't want this shit position, watching things that didn't need watching. I hoped I made it to the first payout. But I wasn't too sure. Volt seemed like he had an itchy trigger finger.

I rolled over, trying to get comfortable. The phone they issued me was basic, but I could still connect to the Wi-Fi. After enabling the private browser, I took a risk and accessed my cloud storage; sure enough, I was able to view my video of Ember laughing without downloading it.

It was a mistake. My balls and heart ached in equal measure. We were supposed to meet up. I couldn't even text her to tell her I wouldn't be there. Her bodyguards would be there to watch her, though. Maybe even hit on her.

But I wouldn't see her again. I turned up the volume a touch and put it to my ear, like she was in bed with me and we were cuddling. Damn. I wanted that. I wanted her. The life I had not even forty-eight hours ago. It had changed so quickly. Like those summer thunderstorms.

My father used to tell me all the time that there was a price you pay for the easy money. And he was right. I guess I never expected that the people I loved would pay as well. My sister. My mom. Now alone in the neighborhood, trying to get Rhy everything she needed.

I was pretty much sucking. Or paying. Or sucking karma's dick. I took another look at the most gorgeous woman in the world before listening to her laugh like it was a shell from the ocean, whispering my dreams instead of the sound of waves. I exited my cloud account. I needed to not draw her into any of this, of course. My father's advice would be to never talk to her again. I'd never felt more alone. I pictured Dice falling to the floor again. Maybe I was in shock. Emotional shock. I knew gang life was hard, but it seemed far away sometimes when I was growing up. The deaths were of guys much older than me. But now I was of age. And I was certainly in a place where escape was impossible. Hell, living was almost impossible.

Volt slammed open the warehouse door and flipped on the switch. I realized as I sat up to see what the hell was going on that I had fallen asleep. Volt was my alarm clock.

"Come on, new kid. We got to run a few jobs."

"In the middle of the night?" I shook my head. I was disoriented.

"It's six in the morn, fool. Get up. Slap yourself in the nuts and meet me out by the van. You've got two minutes to get there." Volt went to the tiny kitchen and started working on a cup of coffee.

After splashing water onto my face, I tossed on my suit jacket. Whatever material it was, it never wrinkled. I met Volt as he poured each of us a travel cup.

I didn't drink coffee, but I knew the caffeine would give me a boost. I thanked him and took my first sip as we walked to the van. It tasted like crap. Volt sucked at making it even more than I sucked at drinking it.

I climbed into the back of the van. There were five other guys, including Volt. We pulled out of the compound and onto the main road. They were speaking quickly and clearly primed for something to go down. I was trying to catch up mentally. I slugged some more hellish brown liquid.

"So we have to get in and get out. Make sure we get a few guys intimidated. The same ol' drill." The guy in the passenger seat was giving a commentary. The guys called him Skinny. Super creative street name.

I didn't see any visible weapons. When we got to a parking lot, the van pulled beside a white pickup truck. There was an older man inside.

"Aw, fuck, Dumbo is here." Then Skinny covered his eyes. "Why wouldn't he be in his creepy art cabin?"

"Hell if I know." Volt brought the van to a complete stop. The excitement in the van was turned down as if it had a volume switch. Volt caught my eyes in the mirror. "This old bastard doesn't talk. Just so you know."

I nodded, not entirely sure why it mattered. Volt hit the button for the van door to slide open and everyone squeezed together on the bench seat. The older guy transferring to us took his sweet time getting on sunglasses and locking things up before heaving himself into the van.

Volt closed the sliding door with the button and then started to fill the old man in. "You know how the Vapors have been stalking the docks? Well, we got to get in there and scare them off. We have a huge shipment later this week, and if they..." He trailed off when the old man lifted his hand.

"You don't want me to tell you? Fine. Have it your way." Volt switched the music on and abandoned his catch-up report.

Which I had been appreciating. I didn't think going into a situation like this as the new kid made sense without at least a little knowledge telling me what it was all about. I was going to have to think on my feet. I was okay at it, at least in the neighborhood. This was the big league.

Volt drove us behind a liquor store and told us all to hold still. I tried my coffee again. The colder it got, the more it tasted like licking the back end of a turtle. The older man opened the side door and got out. He left the door ajar and took a few steps to light up a cigarette.

The guys in the van started talking to each other about him.

"Imagine being Olin's brother and being that fucking stupid. I mean, he runs with us lackies when he could be on a yacht getting his dick team sucked by an entire herd of women." Skinny had aspirations.

"I think they say he was dropped on his head."

"As a baby?"

"Naw, at like thirteen."

They all tried to muffle their laughs. I watched Olin's brother through the window; his jaw twitched. They didn't think he could hear them, but he could. The shitheads in the van with me made the obviously stupid assumption that just because someone didn't speak, they couldn't hear you. It was like that for Rhy. I couldn't even count how many people I put in their place because they spoke as if she wasn't right there, listening.

The old man flicked the ash off of his cigarette.

"I wonder what his real name is." Skinny rapped his knuckle on the window and waved when the old man looked around. "*Felon* can't be his given name."

"Sure as shit could. Legend has it that he was born in prison and he wants to die in prison."

The guy next to me spoke up, "He's like giving an octopus a gun."

Their blatant shit talk was pissing me off. The words escaped from my mouth, "Octopi are smart, asshat. And I'm betting Felon can hear you just fine."

All eyes in the van focused on me, even if it required the owners of said eyes to swivel all the way in their seats.

Skinny sneered. "Shut up, new kid. Fucking asshole whiney baby shithead. You'll wear my taint as a fucking ski mask if you utter one more word today."

"Ugh, that sounds more painful for you than it does for me. But have it your way." I sipped my coffee again. Out of the corner of my eye I saw Felon's lips turn up a bit. Almost a smile.

I resigned myself to listening to Skinny and the guys debate how long I would live. The consensus seemed to land right on two weeks.

Which was longer than I was expecting, honestly.

36

Ember

I WOKE UP TO blinding sunlight. I'd fallen asleep on the couch in the cottage last night, still wearing my clothes. I sat up slowly, not totally sure if I was alone. As I looked at my surroundings, I noticed a few obvious security cameras pointed at me. And I knew from my brother that not all security equipment was obvious. I walked into the small kitchen and opened the cabinets. Healthy snacks. All plastic kitchenware. They didn't want me getting any good ideas about escaping. I went to my suitcase, unzipping it to see what I'd been able to grab in my rush. Clearly, my whole pajama drawer made it. My makeup. Lock's Polaroids. I tucked them into the edge of the mirror above the dresser in my room. A picture of Nix and me. I slipped that into the lining of the suitcase, not sure why, but I felt the need to protect the image. I touched my face. It was all puffy. That was from the crying. Even my throat was raw.

I couldn't even imagine what was going on back at Nix's place. Surely they knew I was with Olin now. I doubted I was convincing enough to stop my brother's need to track me. He'd watched me my whole life. I was a routine, if not a responsibility.

I was out of my depth. Had I made a mistake by not filling them in on what was happening? I shook my head. Trying to turn back time was pointless. My silence had protected them. I had to use the bathroom, and I was dreading whatever surveillance was in there. The mostly white motif there didn't reveal anything out of place. I did my business and considered a shower. Just as I had come to the decision that I would try it later, there was a knock at the door.

I padded back to the front of the cottage. The knocking was a surprise; I had no way of letting anyone in, but once the guard, Echo's replacement, saw me through the glass, he threw the lock. I waited as the door swung open.

Laura, the girl who'd done my makeup for Cosmo, was standing in the doorway with a garment bag and a small black duffle bag. "Hey. I'm here to get you ready for Cosmo's party this evening."

She was still swollen, but she was alive. And I was grateful for that. She didn't seem angry with me, and that was good as well. Or maybe she was a better actress than I was. I nodded at the guard like I had a choice of who came into my cage. He locked the door behind Laura.

"What's tonight?" I was still reeling from the change of my entire world.

"Uh, I have here that you're going to dinner with Mr. Feybi and Cosmo. Isn't that correct?" She pulled out her phone and seemed to check something on it.

"I'm sure it's right. They're not really telling me anything." I shrugged when she made eye contact. She was noncommittal and gestured to the table, holding up her bags.

I moved the flower centerpiece to the counter and she took that as permission. Her simple duffle bag was a marvel, unzipped to reveal a portable makeup workstation.

"While I set up, do you want to shower? We're required to make sure you're smooth...everywhere. Do you need help with that?"

I shook my head so that my hair fell in front of my eyes. Prepping me like a meal for Cosmo. I felt my stomach turn. Laura handed me two bottles, one for shampoo, the other for conditioner. She'd thought of everything.

As I disrobed for my shower, I tried to mentally prepare myself for whatever was coming my way. I had to cry some more. Because there were no tracks for this roller coaster ride. No safety harnesses either. As I stood beneath the hot water, I longed for my childhood. The person I was before I saw a man die. Nix's anger at me moving away made so much sense now. And I didn't even know my true fate yet. I could only guess. I was really afraid that I wasn't nearly as creatively evil as the people who held me now.

When I turned the knob off, halting the water, I made sure I'd done everything that was expected. I never wanted to be the reason Laura was beaten again. I wrapped myself in the robe that was helping the bathroom imitate a five-star hotel and stepped into the kitchen. Laura had been busy in my absence. The colors and implements she had laid out seemed to match my skin tone.

She patted the back of the chair near the table and I sat. She asked a few small talk-type questions, but I stayed quiet. I didn't want to say anything that people who might be listening would misconstrue.

She worked on me without a mirror, so I had no sense of what she was actually doing.

I never would've thought I needed three hours in a makeup chair, but when I had to request a bathroom break, I knew a chunk of time had elapsed. When I spied the clock on the wall that had been behind me, it was inching near lunchtime.

While I washed my hands, I inspected my face. Flawless. So flawless that it was unnerving. Ann had complained that they hadn't had enough time before, and now I saw why. The eyebrows that I was particular about appeared like they were painted on by an artist, or maybe even computer generated. The whites of my eyes looked brighter. The pout of my lips just a hair fuller. There was gentle contouring that was making everything right about my face pop.

The blush was blended in such a way... I knew enough about makeup to know what I was seeing now was the result of years of training.

When I returned to the table, I thanked Laura. She murmured, but it wasn't an acceptance. We locked eyes and I saw that she regretted what she was doing for me. This wasn't a spa. I was prey being offered to a hunter. I was a thing, and not a person. A pawn in a chess game I had no idea how to play.

The door was unlocked again and the guard walked in with a tray. We had some turkey, cheese, and grapes. No carbs, which I was figuring was on purpose. I was being kept to look a certain way. A different guard presented Laura with more garment bags. She hung them from a curtain rod before we snacked for a few minutes.

We were quiet as she did my hair. The only time she spoke was to tell me this current dye job wasn't permanent. It wouldn't last more than a wash or two. And they would take out the rainbow in my hair on a different day. The dress was next; she was torn between the brown and the black one.

They were plain and seemed identical. She went with the brown, not asking for my opinion. After I slipped it on with a tight pair of Spanx that I'd never needed to wear before these people were in my life, Laura actually sewed me into the dress. When she was all done, we went in search of a full-length mirror. She had me spin. The entire effect was gorgeous. I realized then the difference money made when getting made up. The fabric of the dress was exquisite. The makeup on my face was so smooth it was like a photoshopped and filtered version of my face. My hair was a shade darker and straight as a pin. I wet my lips and nodded.

She'd done what she'd set out to do. She risked a comment then, near to my ear, "The better you look, the longer you'll live."

I knew she was trying to reassure me, but a chill rolled down my spine. Death was clearly an option. It was on the table.

Laura patted my shoulder and turned to clean up the area that had been the center of the attention.

"I'll put the black one in your closet. Tonight, wear the brown heels and the jewelry I've set out on your vanity. There is perfume as well. Just a touch." She stopped and fussed with my hair one more time. "There'll be a guard by in about an hour. Please try not to move too much."

I didn't want her to leave, but eventually, she gave me a wave and knocked on my door to be let out.

37

Lock

THE MORE TIME I spent with these assholes, the more apparent it became that I was going to die a very, very stupid death. Skinny had trouble staying in his lane and kept looking at his phone while driving. I glanced at Felon a few times. He seemed chill. Like nothing could bother him.

I also began to realize they had a lot in common with the

Cokes, despite the fancy suits. Lots of bullshit and appearances. But everyone only actually knew so much.

I watched the route we took, trying to memorize it. I had no doubt that these guys would lead me to the slaughter or leave me behind. I was somewhere between being their enemy and their prisoner. We rolled up to a squat brick building. Behind it was a large, flat yard, and behind that abutted the docks. If the Vapors wanted to watch for shipments, this was prime real estate.

Volt cleared his throat, then gave us directions. "Right now, we need to just intimidate this gang. Pull the circle, no eye contact. I do the talking. New kid? Don't fuck up."

With that, the van door slid open and we all tumbled out. I knew dick potato about this shit, but seeing a fuck-ton of jack-offs falling out of a minivan seemed like the least intimidating thing I could dream up.

I waited until Felon got out. As we walked forward, I mumbled to him, "Damn. I woulda come up in here in a fleet of cars. We're as scary as a poodle in a tutu."

Felon lifted his sunglasses and gave me a look that clearly told me he could hear just fine and that he thought I was right.

I shrugged and followed the group as two men emerged from the brick building. I had no weapon, and I looked like a nineteen-year-old kid in a suit. I looked like an inexperienced, dumbass nineteen year old in a borrowed suit.

But I stood shoulder to shoulder with these guys as they formed a circle around the men.

Olin's men grew tense. But the guys we were surrounding? They were as cool as cucumbers. I felt a gentle tug on my suit jacket. When I turned my head, I saw that Felon was right behind me. He tugged on me again. He motioned with his head that he was leaving. That gut instinct. It kicked in. Whatever he wanted from me, I needed to follow him. Volt was starting up the "talks."

I stepped backwards and toward Felon. As simple as that, he started walking away. I trailed behind. Everyone was far too involved in Volt's conversation to pay attention to us. The house next door to the brick one had clearly been abandoned.

Felon headed straight for it. I glanced over my shoulder. The docks had a beautiful breeze coming off of them, smelling of salt and sand. Armed men were slowly surrounding the Feybi guys, though they didn't notice. The Vapors came prepared.

I followed Felon into the house. It looked ramshackle, but he pulled a key out of his pocket and unlocked the door. He said nothing as he stepped inside. I followed anyway. He acted as if I wasn't there. But he was showing me a secret he had cultivated. On the top floor, he had a bedroom with another lock. After he let me come in behind him, he locked the door from the inside.

We could see the confrontation between the Vapors and the Feybis easily from the window. Felon had prepped this room before today; a suitcase was already waiting there for him. Felon meticulously unpacked and set up his sniper rifle. I did my best to pretend like I felt calm. I didn't. I didn't know which side he was on. I was following my gut and my love for my sister and mom.

Felon took out a handful of Tootsie Rolls and unwrapped them. He set them, naked on the sill. He stretched his neck and cracked his knuckles, then he ate one roll.

After he swallowed, Felon lined up the site and squeezed the trigger. I ducked low and peeked out a window. One of the Vapors went down. I couldn't tell if he was dead, but he wasn't moving.

The crowd of men, all of whom were already on edge,

reacted. Some dropped to the ground; others whipped out their pistols. Felon finished chewing another Tootsie Roll, and then he went back to the rifle. Another Vapor went down.

Chaos reigned below us. It became a close range fight. Our small group of guys was far outnumbered, especially with Felon and me hiding up here. Felon took three more Tootsie Rolls and then somehow was able to focus in on the men below, only tagging Vapors with a bullet.

He was making his one gun seem like an army, and he was making time to eat candy. Volt grabbed Skinny, who was limping, and they dragged themselves toward the van.

"All our guys gone?"

I was so shocked to hear Felon speak that I didn't answer him for a minute. When he pointed in the direction of the scene, I snapped myself out of my stupor to look for him.

"Yeah. They all just got in the van." I could see the vehicle from my angle.

Felon nodded. He started zipping up the tools of his trade as the van peeled out of the neighborhood.

I didn't bring up that we were now stranded in the enemy's territory with no wheels. Felon didn't seem like he was in a rush. I went from window to window as discreetly as I could, keeping watch.

This was it. Vapors were going to firebomb this old place and roast Felon and me like marshmallows.

Felon didn't seem concerned. Once he was packed up, he offered me the last Tootsie Roll. I hesitated. It seemed like each candy corresponded with a death, and I didn't want it to be mine.

His smile lifted up on one side. "It's okay. You're not an asshole. That's rare."

I took the treat because it was weird not to. And he had a gun that he was clearly good with. And all I had was my loud mouth. While I chewed, an army of black SUVs swarmed the area. Any Vapors that were still alive scrambled to run.

I followed Felon out of the house and he secured the lock. One of the many SUVs swerved in front of us. Felon jumped into the back and I crawled into the passenger seat. We were on a roll out of the area in a hot minute. Felon was back to not talking. It wasn't lost on me that the scenario I had recommended was playing out for us now.

While we were carted back to the Feybi compound, I got the feeling that in this giant nightmare, I'd made the right decision. Like Dice had said before he was murdered, trying to be on the right side of wrong.

When I was dropped off at the warehouse, I expected some shit for disappearing with Felon. Volt and Skinny for sure would want to beat the life out of me. Instead, I was met with silence. And then some distance. I walked to my cot with squinted eyes. It didn't seem like this was the time for cooled jets. And I was the fresh meat, so...

"Good work out there, new kid." Skinny offered up his fist for tapping, face unreadable. I knew I was staring at his hand like I had no idea what to do with it. I'd abandoned the crew to go with Felon. The whole vibe of the van was not what I was getting now. I tapped his fist with my knuckles.

Volt offered, "Grab a quick nap, then the boss wants you on the garden shed watch." I studied him. He was saying one thing, but his anger was just under his skin. I watched as his hand closed, knuckles white. He was angry with me. And he was hiding it. Or so he thought. I didn't like it. I'd rather they punch me than plot against me.

Maybe Felon had more pull than these guys realized. All I knew was when I set my head down on my pillow, I wasn't entirely sure I would be alive to pick it up again.

When I woke up, Skinny told me it was time to do watch

duty. He wasn't trying to kill me. I was getting treated... well, I don't know how to explain it. Like I was a lit fuse or something.

I grabbed a sandwich and a bottle of water from the fridge, and then Skinny and I took the golf cart down to the shed to swap guard duty.

The guys on duty there had no part in this new, careful treating of me. So whatever was happening, it was localized. They started razzing me and complaining as soon as they saw I was the "new kid."

38

Animal

WE SECURED A PLACE in Valston. T and Nix were on Ember. Trying to find her. I was keeping the face of our particular business up and running. The people who needed to know who was in charge were taught. I kept up the money laundering and Internet gambling rings. We'd slowed down on our newest business venture—wind energy conversion—until we got this Ember situation sorted out. We didn't need to show weakness now. Ember's disappearance was essentially taking Nix out of the picture. He would be on the Ember hunt until she was found. T was doing her best to run two entire situations: staying on top of my needs and helping Nix. With his skeleton tats, sometimes he needed a person he could trust that could slip in and out of places easily in broad daylight.

The Feybis were making moves. That was for sure. After I spoke to Merck, he checked in with his old police station. I found out that entire gangs were being wiped out. The Cokes were mentioned. Ember disappearance wasn't. And it didn't take a genius to put Ember and one of her two boyfriends, the one from the Cokes, together in my head. T couldn't find Lock in his neighborhood. His mother and sister were still in residence at the address we had on him. Now wasn't the time to alert Merck about the Ember situation. He would come in barrels blazing if he knew. This needed a delicate touch.

I was hoping he'd gotten through to Ember and the two were holed up somewhere being young, dumb, and in love. But it was seeming less likely with every hour. I had meetings all day with the Kaleotos, the Feybi family's old enemy.

They pledged help and assistance if the Feybis were stepping out of bounds. I didn't want to toe that line yet. With the deaths of the Kaleotos lately, they were raring to go.

Nix had no new news. But I could bet he was getting all up in the Feybis' digital trails. As I sat at the desk, I blew out an exasperated breath. He'd been right. We should've never let Ember out of town.

39

Ember

THE LONELINESS CRASHED OVER me. My heart wanted the window to blow open. Wanted Nix, Animal, and T to come swooping in to save me. But there was only silence. Which meant I was still protecting them. The hammering of my pulse and the noise of the nervous gulps I was taking were all I could hear. I sat, ramrod straight, on the couch in the cottage. I regretted eating. I felt nauseous as it was.

There was a slight commotion at the front door, a changing of the guard, clearly. From the sound of it, there were two men in place of the one that had been there. I listened to a faint argument. I couldn't make out exact words, so I stood from the couch, trying my best not to mess with the makeup that Laura had put on me.

"You're too new. You fuck. Where the hell is Lucid?"

I heard a voice. And it made my heart start to pound. It sounded like...

"I don't know, dude. Seriously. I've only been here a few days. I go where I'm told."

Lock.

My Lock.

Here.

When the door swung open, I had to take a step back. I held my breath.

It was one thing to *try* to be strong. Remember the things I'd been telling myself over and over. To stand up straight. To be overly nice. To accept what was offered to me.

But to see his familiar face. Feel the butterflies in my stomach and the accompanying zing to my heart—and then remember to not react. Be confused and not react. We were both in a viper pit. Still, the floor seemed to be moving.

I felt his arms come around me. His scent and warmth were enough to break me. I was going to melt into a puddle. The strength to push him away surely came from my mom. That's the only way I could explain it. Because my spirit was falling right into him.

"You'll mess up my makeup."

He still had to steady me as I tried to stand.

"Ember?" His voice slammed into the part of me that I was desperate to get back to. I had to not fall apart. If I showed even a moment of weakness, the Feybis would hurt everyone I loved and I'd go to prison.

Lock's presence was disorientating.

"You know her?" The guy with Lock was suspicious.

He covered quickly. "Nah. She has an Instagram I follow. Haven't you seen it?" It was a quick lie. A decent one. I wouldn't make eye contact with him.

"Send me the link. I wanna see it." The guy moved next to Lock.

"I had to delete my Instagram. Now that I'm with Cosmo."

"See, Skinny. She had to delete it."

I could feel Lock staring at me. I'd tried to tip him off that things had changed drastically. Because he'd seemed as shocked to see me as I was him.

Skinny stepped to the side. "Well, either way, we better get you up there for your dinner."

The heels were tall and the trip out of my cage took us across the grounds and through a garden.

I grabbed Lock's arm. "Hey, I'm going to fall here. Can we walk slower?"

Skinny was too close for me to say anything to Lock; I squeezed his arm. We fell a few steps behind and Lock whispered, "What the hell?"

I shook my head. I had no idea if there were cameras on us. I looked up at him, despite my better judgment. He was baffled and extremely handsome. I had no idea why he was here.

He whispered again, "Cosmo?"

I shrugged and looked at my feet. I pictured the man dying in front of me again and again. And then Bowen. The last few days had been a tilt-a-whirl of nightmares. Still, I had to look at his face.

"Why are you here?" I mouthed to him.

"I work here." Lock glanced all around us. I wasn't even

paying attention to our surroundings. I toppled a little and he caught me full-out, swinging me to his chest. "Whoa. You okay?"

I was in his arms. Never before had I so fiercely wanted to tell someone something in my whole life. But it was a flash of Lock dead in my head that kept me from confessing.

I needed to know more. I had to center myself. Get information. Keep a clear head so my people would be safe from Olin.

All I could think to say was, "Stay alive."

I turned from his embrace and continued on my own. When we got to the long, stone steps, I reached for Skinny instead. I felt unnerved and grateful that Lock was behind me. We were coming up to a large outdoor entertaining space, complete with a pool and bar. There were guards stationed around the patio table with an umbrella, where Olin and Cosmo were already seated.

Cosmo was surly, and Olin had his giant, blindingly white teeth on display.

Skinny led me to the table. Olin Feybi stood and held out his hand. I took it and he made me spin. I struggled to keep myself upright on the heels.

"Magnificent. We're so lucky to have you here with us, Ember."

I nodded at him and smiled. Cosmo stood after his father slapped his palm on the glass top of the table.

"You look lovely," Cosmo offered in a half-hearted way.

I saw Lock tense, his fist curling out of my peripheral vision. Now that I'd gotten over the shock of his presence, my mind was swirling. *Was Lock really with the Feybis? Was he working for my brother? Why the hell was he here?* I took the seat that had been vacant and Cosmo and Olin sat as well.

Olin shooed the guards away. "We have family business to

discuss."

I watched Lock. His gaze was darting around, seemingly trying to make sense of this situation before we made eye contact. I tried to give him a smile so he knew I was okay.

He moved with the other guards, as naturally as if he truly belonged with them. They rimmed the edge of the pool patio.

I turned my attention back to Olin.

"There she is." He'd been waiting for me to meet his gaze. "Make sure you only have eyes for my son, yes?"

I swallowed hard. I knew a blush was creeping up on my face. Cosmo's hand was on the chair arm and I made a point of putting my hand over his.

"Nice. You are a quick learner, Ember." Olin flashed that smile again.

Cosmo didn't react to my hand on his. A waiter stepped up to the table, bearing drinks and plates of hors d'oeuvres. My stomach rumbled. Anxiety clearly made me hungry.

As I reached for a cracker, Olin slapped my hand. "No. We have to maintain that figure. Maybe start with a carrot."

"Fuck off, Dad." Cosmo took his hand from under mine and grabbed a cracker. He turned to me and offered it. "You want this? You can have it."

This was my first real inspection of his face up close. He had hazel eyes and classical good looks. He was trendy, though, making a few distinct decisions on clothing that made him stylish. The cut of his pants was skinny and tight, his shirt the same. The latest trend, on the nose.

I had to choose between the two directions. One from the father, one from the son. The tiny bit of empathy in Cosmo's face led me to him. I took the cracker and nibbled on it.

"All right. That's fine." Olin ruffled with his napkin, smoothing it and refolding it. "She's yours, so we'll let it slide this once."

"You've been bothering me for two years about getting a girl. If she's mine, she's mine. Period. Don't you touch her. No slapping her either." Cosmo grabbed a handful of food and doled it out. Crackers, cheeses, fruits, filling both of our plates.

Olin's smile could have been caked on by rage.

Cosmo fingered the gold chain around his neck while he gave the mansion's yard a glance, followed by pushing his lips to the side, his attitude revealing just how spoiled he was. "What about my party? The tents should be setting up by now."

"Soon. I wanted us to have this time to get to know Ember." Olin took some food as well.

I ate a piece of mozzarella. It felt like sand, my throat was so dry.

Lock was here.

It was like his presence was forcing my head to turn in his direction. But the old man had all his attention on me. As Cosmo listed things he wanted for his party, Olin watched me like a television set, so I kept my eyes where they were supposed to be.

Lock's appearance gave me a tender hope. Maybe the nightmare would be over soon. Before I had to do whatever it was I was supposed to do for Cosmo as his girl. I clued back into the conversation when my name was mentioned again. Cosmo was requesting something for me.

"So, I think we need to get her a tutor. Someone to help her stay up on her classes." Cosmo patted my shoulder. I flinched at the touch and then forced myself to stop reacting. I quickly checked Olin's face. Anger flashed over it before it was replaced by this mask he wore around his son.

"That's admirable, son. But, honestly, it's a waste. She's just a woman." Olin waved his hand airily, as if my education was something that could be released like a balloon.

"If you want this to work, she needs a tutor. Education stimulates me. I'll have my guy arrange it." Cosmo copied his father's hand gesture, emulating him, possibly on purpose.

Through my self-preservation I was starting to see these men's relationship for the toxic thing it was. Cosmo was manipulating his father, even as Olin controlled his life. Rich as hell, but still screwed up. Maybe all the murder in their lives tainted everything.

Cosmo stood quickly and I followed suit, my nervous system humming with fear.

"I've got to get the hell out of here. This party had better be *lit*, old man." Cosmo turned to me. "Good meeting you, Ellen."

I didn't bother to correct him. Cosmo was clearly a mixed bag of tricks. Very hard to read. Olin, on the other hand, was transparent, or at least his intentions were. He wanted things his way. When I moved to follow Cosmo, Olin caught my arm.

"Stay. Sit a spell, Ember. We have a few things to discuss." I looked at his hand and then felt Lock's eyes on me. I couldn't meet them. Instead, I turned my back so I'd have to ignore him.

After I sat back down, Olin took his seat and messed with his napkin again. I glanced at him. I knew better than to eat now that Cosmo was gone. I was full anyway, but still.

The waiter came over with a bottle of red wine. After Olin sipped a small taste, he submitted to having his glass filled, and then indicated that I'd be having one as well. I wasn't a wine drinking girl. Anything I had in the past was full of fruity concoctions that hid the liquor.

I lifted my glass to touch Olin's in the toast. After the first sip that I disliked, I took another. Olin watched me the whole time.

"You'll be perfect, after you're molded." He took a hissing sip of his drink.

His hands had age spots and prominent veins. His tan was

clearly applied by chemicals, despite his obvious access to a huge, gorgeous pool. This close, I was thinking the hair he had in the front might be plugs. This was a man who was clearly fighting his age.

"My son, his childhood wasn't the best. Honestly, and I think I do have to be honest with you, Ember." He reached his hand across the table and patted the top of mine. I made a mental note to stop making my hand so accessible.

Lock was here, still. At the perimeter. Part of my brain screamed to run to him. Tell him that I was kidnapped and this was all an act. And then I thought of Bowen again.

"You'll have access to my son. And despite the act he put on here, you're mine, not his. You work for me."

I felt my brow furrow and then quickly tried to smooth it.

"Yes. You work for me. Some payment isn't monetary, my dear. The lives of those you love are in your hands. You're a perfect fit for what I need. And my son? He's just a bonus. Do you doubt I can do what I say? That I can kill the people closest to you? I can prove it again to you, if I must. I'll prove it as many times as I have to." Olin's smile spread slowly like a cancer.

"I understand." I took another sip of the horrible wine, trying to not let my nerves show. Of course, the liquid in the glass was like a wave pool from my shaking.

"I'm glad. From this point forward, you're in love with my son. He should never doubt it. And neither should I." Olin crossed one leg over the other.

I nodded again. Across the sparkling pool, I could feel Lock's intent stare. I knew how to pretend to be in love, because I was pretty sure I was already there. With him.

"Very good. Tomorrow you'll be in a different outfit. The same girl will come, but also someone else to get those pesky colors out of your hair." He stood and I copied him. "You're going to thank me when all is said and done. I'll turn you into a wealthy, respectable woman. What more could you want?" Olin offered me his hand and walked me straight to where Lock stood with another guard. "You're the new one, correct?" Olin addressed him directly.

I was petrified I'd given away too much of Lock's and my connection with my stolen glances during the meeting.

"Yes, sir. Super new." Lock kept his hands tucked behind his back.

I darted my gaze all over to avoid looking at him.

"My brother really likes you. Thinks highly of you." Olin held my hand out to Lock. I felt the warmth of his hand as it enveloped mine. "See that she gets back to her cottage safely. Ravenous dogs these men are. And she's so very beautiful."

Lock pulled me closer to him. "She's gorgeous. Looks scared, though."

I silently prayed to all the gods ever worshipped that he would drop his threatening tone. He always seemed proud of his big mouth. I literally could still feel my heart beating from Olin's threats on my loved ones. I didn't want to see Lock die right here in front of me.

"She has a big day tomorrow. She's very happy. Right, Ember?" Olin was testing me.

"Yes. I can't wait to see Cosmo again." Even I could hear the tremor in my voice.

"I bet you can't. Look at those white knuckles! You're going to squeeze this guy's hand right off." Olin motioned toward my grip on Lock.

"My name's Sherlock, sir. And my hand can take it. No worries." Lock did a half-bow and led me off to the garden path.

I picked my way carefully, slowly. I didn't want to lose my

balance again. Lock's arms around me again would break me. And my farce would shatter on the ground like glass.

40

Lock

SHE WAS SHAKING. A shell of the girl I knew. Her confidence was dismantled. I raged, thinking about what could have taken it from her. Skinny stayed on me like glue, so all I could do was try to read her body language.

Volt was at the guest door, clearly doing my job of protecting the empty place, and he unlocked it as we approached. Ember went inside without turning around. Volt locked her back in. Skinny was assigned to be the second on the job.

A golf cart trundled down the garden path then. I looked up and locked eyes with the driver: Felon. He tapped on the steering wheel and then patted the passenger side. I expected a verbal jab from the guys for my special treatment. None came. I glanced at the windows of the cottage. Ember was sitting on her couch, not moving. I hated leaving her, but I had no choice. I climbed into the cart with Felon. He pulled us away from the scene.

I expected him to drive me to the warehouse, but instead, he veered right. After the crest of the next hill, a house came into view. It was clearly artsy. The roof mimicked an aircraft hangar. The windows seemed mismatched. There were trees stripped of bark that were performing support duty.

"This is awesome." The whole effect was incredible. It almost seemed like a prop from a fantasy movie.

There were carved details and at least three different doors visible from where we sat.

I peeked at Felon. He was grinning. It made him look so much younger.

"My pride and joy. I've been building this for at least two decades." Felon parked in front of it and pocketed his keys.

"You built this?" I stepped out of the golf cart and walked up to the closest wall. I ran my hands over it. Smooth wood of all different colors. There was clearly a lot of love in the place and I told him so. He let out a low chuckle.

"Can I see inside?" I had a ton of things on my mind, but seeing this art in the middle of nowhere seemed like the break I needed.

His eyes lit up. "Sure thing."

Instead of a key, there was a complicated wood puzzle to free the door, which rolled to the side. I marveled at the engineering. I knew jack shit about building, but anyone in his or her right mind would be able to tell this project was a labor of intense devotion.

The interior was amazing. It would take days to appreciate all the details in the nooks and crannies. But the overall impression was like a tree house; the walls were constructed of honey-golden logs, stripped of their bark and shined to perfection. There were plenty of places for the sunlight to stream in. Felon jerked on a rope and part of the ceiling shuttered out of the way. Railings made from the same logs as those lining the walls framed the stars. An ingenious way to make the night sky part of his décor.

"You're a genius." I wasn't trying to compliment him. It was an obvious fact. I watched him kick the floor with his foot. "You could make stuff like this. I bet people would pay serious change."

Felon walked over to another pulley. A wall slid to the side, revealing a hallway. "I have money. I just like to build. My hands need it."

Down the hall were four doors, all closed.

"I have these guest spaces. Never use them. You want to pick a room here instead of the warehouse?" He seemed almost shy in asking.

I put my tongue to one side of my mouth, considering. This place was far closer to Ember's cottage. "That'd be great. Thanks a lot."

I put out my hand for a shake, like my father had taught me. From one man to another, when there was an agreement, you shook hands. When there was a gift given, you shook hands.

Felon pumped my hand once and then smiled again. "Good to hear it. Each bedroom has a bathroom, so it's just a matter of choice. I'm going to bed. Good night, Lock."

"Thanks again, and night, Felon."

The older man worked his way up an elaborate spiral staircase. I had concerns; I'd be lying if I said I didn't. But there was something deep inside that drew me to Felon in this fucked-up situation. He could kill the hell out of me. After the Tootsie Roll show, I knew this was the truth.

But I had to play this right. Ember had done a complete 180-degree turn. Instead of being into me, she was tits high in a relationship with Cosmo? I didn't buy it for a second. She was here as unwillingly as I was, maybe more so. I thought about her security detail. As far as I knew, her brother was in charge of her situation. The Olin thing wasn't a match. I needed to get some online connection and do some research.

I toured each bedroom. They had different themes and colors. I picked the forest green one. From the window I could see Ember's cottage lights in the distance. She'd looked so lost. They'd taken her colors from her hair. Made a plastic doll version of the girl I'd fallen for. I could watch over her from here. And as little power as I had in this scenario, I would give it to her.

41

Ember

I THINK I SAT on the couch for an hour. Just sat. The dress and Spanx and everything I was wearing were so complicated that I just sat. Lock was here. I wasn't saved yet. Nix wasn't here. I had waves of panic attacks as I sat there. I lived and died a million different ways in my head without moving. I watched my loved ones die in my mind as well. Their safety hinged on me.

I felt resigned after hashing it all out. The best I could do was follow Olin's lead. I had no way to communicate with Nix. And I didn't even want to go down that path. I wasn't testing Olin. Not with Nix and Animal and T's lives. And Becca. And Lock. Not to mention the threat of jail time.

Lock. So handsome. I had no delusions that he was some kind of superhero who could swoop in and fix this whole situation, but having him here was good for my heart. For my hope. Knowing I wasn't alone mattered.

I finally stood and made my way into the bathroom. Laura had laid out a nighttime ritual for me to follow. It was far more elaborate than my usual toothbrush and face washing. By the time I got into bed, I didn't even care that I left my blinds open. I just collapsed.

———

It was weird waking up to a human that I didn't know really well, but Laura did her best to be gentle about it. She praised me on completing the new skin routine. I sat up and she handed me coffee. I felt bad telling her I didn't like it, so I took a few sips and set it aside.

Cosmo's party was that night and we devoted the entire day to getting me ready for it. She'd even called in one of the other girls to help with my hair, which was getting permanently dyed dark today.

I sat at the kitchen table as I was attended to. She thoughtfully put on a chick flick to give us safe things to talk about.

About an hour into the movie, the other girl, Colleen, arrived with the hair kit. She and Laura discussed my color stripes and how to bleach them and dye them to match the rest of my hair, as if all of our lives depended on it. And maybe they did. It got to the point that I felt guilty about even having them, and told the girls so. They fussed over me then, telling me to ignore the shoptalk.

My stomach started growling, and before I could comment, Laura was sending a text for some breakfast.

Lock walked in with a covered tray, followed by two other guys. My heart dropped out of my chest when he set the tray down with a smile. The dimples and everything.

"Hey," he offered.

I nodded and made a point to look at the food. He lifted the cloche. A healthy breakfast omelet was ready for me with fruit and cheese. There was only food for me. I knew the two other girls had to be hungry.

"There's not enough."

Lock and the other guys stopped in their tracks. "What?"

"The other girls are hungry, too. We need more."

Laura and Colleen started denying it, but it became a test. I wanted to see how much I could get from the main house.

"Skinny, can you call up and tell them?" Lock turned to one of the other guards, same one who'd walked with us the night before.

"I guess?" Skinny hesitantly stepped out the front door and started talking on his phone.

Lock tucked his hands behind his back and rocked forward on his toes.

Laura spoke up, "You're new."

"Yup. I'm staying up at Felon's house. You can see it right through that window." Lock pointed out at the artsy building in the distance.

He was telling me where he was. That he could see me.

"All the other guys stay at the warehouse. It's about a mile from here." Lock ran his hand through his hair and peeked at me.

Information. He was telling me all he could. I appreciated

it, but it scared me as well. Because I knew that the place was bugged. And Lock wasn't as slick as he thought he was.

"Can you wait outside? I like privacy while I get ready." I glanced out the window at Felon's house, but not before I saw the hurt pass over Lock's face.

The girls talked about how hot he was as soon as he was out the door. I had to feel my jealousy burn in my throat and act like it was fine.

We didn't have too much time to eat. Soon after Skinny came back with more food, we got word that Cosmo was stopping by.

The tension in the room and among the guys outside ratcheted up as Cosmo entered. Everyone stood taller and their jaws tensed. Cosmo was dressed in jeans and a T-shirt and he had a new guy with him. He was slightly shorter than Cosmo. He had a studious look about him that was exacerbated by the textbooks in his arms and the glasses on his face.

"This is your tutor, Felix," Cosmo said, gesturing to him. "We're going to have your first lesson today." He dragged up a chair; Felix sat across from me.

I gave the girls a quick side-eye. We were very, very involved in hair right now. I was sitting under the portable lamp while my hair color processed. Considering all the work Olin put into me before Cosmo was allowed to even lay eyes on me, I wondered how he would take this very pre-party version.

Lock was still outside. Guarding. Being involved. Being near. I caught his eye a few times through the window, even though I tried to remind myself to not look.

Felix had a copy of each of my textbooks from school. He explained that he was able to access my records and we could pick up where I left off.

I wanted to scream that I hadn't left off. I'd been kidnapped to be Cosmo's doll, but I swallowed the words and tried to concentrate on economics while the girls tugged on my hair. When we had to switch to makeup, Felix began reading to me.

Cosmo stayed the whole time, his attention rapt. It made me suspect this was his sneaky way of getting a college education. When it was time to rinse and style my hair, Felix set up the television to show me some graphs and charts.

I was doing my best to follow, but it was all staggering. Cosmo's presence was odd. Easy, almost. Everyone seemed to let their guard down a touch. When Felix was done for the day, he stood up and started gathering his books. "For a beautiful girl, I can't believe they're spending this much time on you." The compliment was awkward, but I shrugged and thanked him for his lesson. Cosmo offered to drive Felix back to his car and promised to see me in a few hours.

After he left, another batch of food came from the kitchen. A huge salad with enough sides for everyone. I asked Colleen to pass the leftovers outside with a few forks, because I hadn't seen any of the men take a dinner break. Lock winked at me through the window as he took his first bite.

And then I hated myself for the impulse to feed him. That wink could get him killed. Laura took me into the bedroom to the full-length mirror. This outfit required a lesson. It was a little black one with straps and a slit up the thigh. I had to learn how it was undone in case I needed the bathroom.

I asked Laura if she was going to the party and she shook her head no, the prospect seeming to scare her.

"I hear the party is for you and Cosmo to come out as a couple. Plus, it's his birthday." Laura tried to offer me a smile.

I looked at my reflection. The dark eye makeup and matte lips made me seem like a cover model. The darker hair was severe, but in a high glam way. These girls were amazing at their jobs. They made me look older and like I was cold as ice. I considered it armor. To keep the fear at bay. To keep my head cool. Make no mistakes.

Laura pointed to the earring in the shell of my ear. My mother's jewelry. My first gift from Nix.

"Olin sent diamonds. That doesn't really fit. Can we?" She held her hands up as if she would take it out for me. I covered the small gold stud.

"This stays." I stepped back from her, my heels clicking on the wood floor.

"Okay, no problem." Laura held up her hands as if I were holding a gun on her. "It's okay to have some personality."

The slight hesitancy in her reaction made me wonder if it really was okay. But that earring was a hard limit for me. I was a prisoner here, with a gun on everyone I loved. I needed this to keep me strong.

I straightened my shoulders and walked out to the living room. The guards were ready to take me back to the house. Laura had mentioned that I might need to stay away from the pool because if the dress got wet it would not react well. I joked a bit about jumping in, just to try to lighten the mood between us. She told me that the fabric was so delicate, that it might actually dissolve.

With that terrifying potential party trick, I got into the passenger seat, my heart hammering as Lock slid behind the wheel. Skinny and Volt were in the back seat, so I knew Lock wouldn't be able to talk to me. We shared a few poignant looks that explained nothing on the ride up.

When we arrived at the house, Skinny came around the SUV and held out an elbow to me. I used his help to get up to the patio. Over the past day, the pool area had been transformed. Already beautiful, it was decorated with white lights and strips of cloth that fluttered in the breeze.

The pool had a few submersible LED lights dropped into it

that gave it a gentle ombre blue. The music was classical and gently playing. There was a dance floor and a ton of tables with white tablecloths. Between the centerpieces and the flowers threaded in the trees the party could almost be a wedding. The huge banner stretched across the house proclaimed the event:

The fact that there were four bars set up displayed that alcohol was a huge part of this party. Everyone was in either black or white, and I was not overdressed at all. Laura had struck the perfect tone, actually. Skinny removed my hand and stepped away. I was being released into the crowd.

My heart started to pound. I had no idea who any of these people were. How many were dangerous. How many were actually employees of Olin's.

I didn't know which way to go, but Olin waltzed up to me and snagged the back of my neck. "Come, sweet girl. Stay with me until your Prince Charming arrives."

He pushed me as we threaded through tables and groups of people chatting. They leaned out of his way. "Have a seat, dear."

I did as I was told. The chair had a white cover and I

crossed my feet at the ankles. Olin stood behind me with his hands on my shoulders. I had to actively work at not recoiling.

Lock was standing guard along the perimeter. The mere sight of his face was comforting. The concern in his gaze was real. It was surreal, being at a cocktail party where I also was being kept as a prisoner.

The crowd started clapping. Olin grasped my hand and pulled me up. Cosmo had arrived. He was traveling with an entourage of his own. They were not nearly as dressed up as the rest of us were. Cosmo had a bottle in a brown bag that he took a glug from as he waved.

Olin's displeasure radiated from his body. I silently hoped that Cosmo would do whatever his father wanted. Olin took my hand and squeezed it, first gently and then more and more. He leaned and hissed into my ear, "You better get lover boy under control."

I snapped a confused gaze at the older man. What he expected me to say or do about his son was a conundrum. Cosmo laughed with his friends before setting down his bottle on a tablecloth. It tipped over and he didn't bother to try to right it.

Cosmo blurrily looked around the party until he spotted his father and then me. He made his way toward us, struggling to walk straight. He paused at the edge of the pool, as if just realizing it was there. He turned, wobbling off balance before giving his friends the middle finger.

Cosmo spread his arms and fell backwards into the pool. The surrounding crowd either gasped or laughed as the splash soaked more than a few. I was grateful that I was on the other side. Before Cosmo surfaced, I looked across the patio. There was a silhouette of a man confidently striding toward the party. He passed beneath the party lights, which illuminated his face. I inhaled sharply.

Nix.

Nix was coming to the party in an immaculate tux. There were gasps now as Cosmo pulled himself out of the pool. But they were for Nix. His face, etched in ink to create the façade of a skull, was shocking.

My hand that Olin still gripped was squeezed even tighter. I glanced down. Olin's fingers were digging into my skin. I tried to pull away, but he held fast.

A hand that was etched in bones soon grabbed Olin's arm.

"Let go of her hand, Olin."

Nix always had kindness in his eyes for me, even when he was frustrated. But as I looked at him, I found the part of my brother that I'd rarely seen. He radiated a current of anger. I felt it in my blood, and surely everyone else did, too. Olin released my hand. I rubbed at the bruises I knew had to be forming.

Nix turned his steely gaze at me. "You ready? Let's go."

Cosmo came to step near me. "There a problem?"

He draped his soaking wet arm around my shoulders. I winced, thinking about the dress that wasn't supposed to get wet under any circumstances. I curled my shoulders forward and crossed my arms over my chest.

Nix's eyes were a bit wild as he looked from Cosmo to my reaction and back again. He shrugged out of his suit jacket and spun it around so I could get in it quicker. I could feel the dress contracting, so I shimmied away from Cosmo and shoved my arms into the jacket. Nix put his arm where Cosmo's had been.

"She's leaving."

I wanted to go. So much. I wanted him to save me, but Olin Feybi had an expectant gaze. Everything he'd said echoed through my mind.

"If they take you? Everyone you love dies and you go to prison very quickly. Head spinningly quickly. Do you want me to prove it? I can."

Nix had come alone. I knew all of the guards here were armed, and those were just the ones I could see. I felt my eyes start to fill up with moisture.

"I'd like to stay. I'm serious about Cosmo," I said the words, staring at Olin's face. He barely lifted his eyebrow and his grim frown turned up a little bit. I'd made the correct guess. I had to lie to Nix like I'd never lied to anyone in my life. If I got it wrong, he wasn't living through the night, and I was getting arrested for murder.

42

Lock

MERCY HAD A REPUTATION. But in person he was like a dead James Bond in his damn suit. From my earpiece I heard everyone freaking out behind the scenes. No one knew how he'd gotten into the compound. He'd just appeared, as far as we could tell.

He was alone. The tux he had on was well-fitted, so no matter what he had on him, it was seriously low-profile. Mercy was focused on Ember and offered her his suit jacket—more proof that he was lightly armed, if at all.

I was rooting for Mercy to take his sister out of here. This was no place for her. And I sure as shit didn't want her anywhere near Cosmo. I was burning and secretly in awe that Ember was so close to Mercy.

Everyone was waiting for Olin to give a direction. Should they gun Mercy down? He was half-legend in all of our minds. I watched as Olin whispered to the guard closest to him. The chain of command started to trickle down. The play was to let Mercy talk to Ember. I was tasked with getting Felon from our house.

I hated leaving Ember here. There were obviously tense words being exchanged. I hot-stepped it to an ATV and revved it. The golf carts were too slow. I wanted to do my job and get the hell back here.

I solved the complicated wooden lock and found Felon inside, reading an old leather-bound book. He looked up pleasantly. I told him in a rush that Mercy had crashed the party and Olin wanted him at the pool.

Felon seemed to take forever to pack his bag. He also got a fistful of Tootsie Rolls. And that was my first indication that there could be a lot of death tonight. Felon asked a few basic questions about Mercy's setup and seemed mildly interested that he was by himself.

After nodding at the information, he requested that I abandon the ATV and drive the golf cart. I hated not taking the faster way, but Felon had the Tootsie Rolls so I knew what that meant. Death.

When we got back to the patio, Volt informed Felon that Mercy and Ember were in the sitting room off the patio with guards.

Felon tipped his chin at me, avoiding speech, as he liked to do. He wanted me to follow him in. Olin was watching the action happen from outside, but didn't protest as I followed Felon into the room. Ember and Mercy were sitting across from each other. She was sitting ramrod straight and he was leaning toward her, fingers tented under his chin. His ink was remarkable. There was so much artistry and attention to the details.

Ember was ice cold to him, shaking her head no. Cosmo was in the room as well, to the left of her chair. He was wobbling and soaking wet. Mercy only had eyes for his sister.

Once I'd taken up my spot on the perimeter of the room, I focused in on their conversation.

Mercy was calm as he told her his plan, "Say the word and I'll get you out right now. I'll kill every person here if I have to."

The guards bristled around me. From anyone else there probably would've been snickering. But the rep on Mercy was otherworldly. He was particularly hated in this circle of hell I was currently in.

Ember murmured something too quiet to make out, but the reaction from Mercy was to sit back as if she'd slapped him. I had to hand it to her. She had boss level balls to say anything that the man in front of her didn't like.

"Are you serious?" Mercy ran his hand through his hair.

Ember stood and turned to Cosmo. She planted a kiss on him that made my knees go weak. It was such a punch in my feelings and my balls at the same time. Cosmo immediately wrapped his arms around her, hauled her off her feet, bringing her closer to him.

There was obvious tongue.

I died. My soul fell out of my asshole and curled up into a ball. The girl I was crazy about was making out with a goddamn douchebag.

Volt reached over and closed my jaw for me. I bit the inside of my cheek. I wanted to kill Cosmo. I knew the veins in my neck were sticking out. My wild eyes landed on Mercy. He squinted at my obvious distress. I swept my gaze over to Felon, wondering what the hell was next. Was Ember's brother about to be killed in front of her? Shit. Even as mad as I was at this whole show, she didn't deserve to see her brother murdered.

I watched as Felon put his hand into his pocket and took out a Tootsie Roll. I stepped forward.

"Well, that's all she wrote. Let's move on out, Mercy. Ember's happy."

My words were clipped and rough. The force it took to say them was unnatural. I closed the space and put my hand on Mercy's upper arm, like I could lead him out. Ember was still kissing Cosmo; I was sure my head was going to pop off my neck like a firework.

Mercy leaned around me, shrugging off my hand. "Nice earring, Ember."

She stopped kissing Cosmo and her hand flew up to the small stud in the shell of her ear. "That's right. Thanks for reminding me. I don't need this anymore." She took out the earring and held it out to Mercy.

He reached past the earring and put his hand behind her neck, pulling her to him.

"What have they got on you?" His hiss was barely loud enough for me to hear.

"Nothing. I love him. Leave me alone." Ember pulled away from Mercy's grip, whipping him in the face with her hair.

The emotion was layered in her face. She was fighting something. I glanced at Cosmo's crotch. As far as I could tell, he wasn't turned on by Ember's kiss. But I was. And that was fucking confusing. I was angry and jealous and sad. And rock hard.

Felon was rolling a Tootsie Roll between his fingers. Things were about to go down. I knew from the time we were together that Ember loved her people. Seeing her brother gunned down in front of her was not going to sit well.

And I had serious concerns that Mercy was expecting this part. He wasn't scared or jumpy. Like he had a way out or a plan. Cosmo held out his hand and Ember took it, pulling herself against his elbow, rubbing her cheek on his shoulder.

I could hear Mercy's jaw snap shut. Cosmo turned and led Ember out of the room. She didn't look back. Mercy clenched both his fists. He was an angry fucking skeleton. I darted my gaze over to Felon who had unwrapped the candy.

"So, if we're all done, maybe we can move along?" I stepped toward Mercy with my hands in front of me.

I wanted him to take the out. Leave. Save himself. Mercy's stare was riveted on the door his sister had just walked through. Olin came in seconds later, taking Ember's place.

"She wants to be here. I'm sure that was clear." He waved his hand around like there was a fly he was trying to kill. "Young love...so difficult to predict."

Mercy lifted his chin. "If any harm comes to her, anything at all, I'll turn you inside out. And I'll make sure you're alive for the whole experience."

Olin feigned astonishment, like the conversation they were having was one he really expected to go cordially. "But of course, she'll be safe. I take care of my own."

"You didn't take care of your half-brother that I roasted like a goddamn marshmallow." Mercy folded his arms in front of his chest.

Olin took his flamboyancy down a few notches. "That was unnecessary. And as long as *you* don't kill her, Ember will be fine. You know, this could be a good thing, a very good thing for us both. I mean, think of the next generation. The children? This is the beginning of something lovely. My brilliance? Your... inherent deadliness. Of course, I hope they get my good looks."

Olin stepped to the side of the door on the opposite end of the room. "And as a show of good faith, I'm going to let you leave. You won't even have to sneak out. And let's meet up soon. Discuss our futures together. I'm excited." He pulled open the door.

I watched Felon rewrap the Tootsie Roll and put it back into his pocket. I heaved a mental sigh of relief. Mercy met my eyes before turning his back and leaving, the door hanging ajar behind him. Olin tipped it closed with his fingertips and whirled on his crew.

"I want to know how he got in and who I have to kill. That man should not have gotten past any of you." He pointed at each one of us around the room. I was too new to know how this all worked. Felon motioned for me to follow him again, so I did. We went outside and stood by the bushes along the patio.

"You love that girl."

My steps stuttered as panic shot through me. "What do you mean?"

"You wear your balls on your sleeve. You're crazy about her." Felon pointed at the golf cart. I guessed I was driving again when he got in the passenger side. I slid behind the wheel and didn't respond, but he shook his head. "That's some messy crap. She's on lockdown."

I shrugged before hitting the gas. I was here and she was here. There was only one thing to do: watch over her. Try to figure out what the fuck was going on. Feel the pain burn inside me. Okay, that was a whole lot more than one thing, but all of it was true.

43

Animal

MY MAN WAS DESPONDENT. I was expecting anger. Rage. But this total lack of emotion was troubling. He'd told me how it went down. That Ember had chosen Cosmo Feybi over him and the escape he was offering.

It had appeared that he was alone, but we'd all been on standby. T had been in the woods with a sniper rifle. We could've gotten them both out. But instead there was just Nix.

Becca, the love of his life, was busy rubbing his back. My man was dying a slow death in his head. He had rules he followed, and protecting his girls was the most important.

I wanted him to rant. Punch a wall or two.

"How could it happen so quickly? Like she's in love with this douchebag? What about the other guy? And why the hell is he there? Did we miss something? Is there a connection?" He stood, grabbed Becca's hand, and kissed the inside of her wrist.

T was on one computer and I was waiting on a few messages. The hotel penthouse we'd rented to run this operation from was racking up quite the tab. Nix had moved in a ton of surveillance equipment. We needed to find out how things with Ember had spiraled out of control so quickly. T was running more background on Sherlock Sonnet. It was too convenient that he was there, too. We had to figure out why. Was he really working for the Feybis, or was he a plant from another family?

T turned her monitor to face us. On it there was one pretty, older woman. "That's his mom. And it says she has two children. We've had his address since we worked up his background."

Nix took his phone out of his pocket. "Text it to me."

"What are you gonna do, Sweetness?" I was concerned about his stress level.

"Ember's my sister. And whether or not she's there of her own volition, I'm going to make sure this kid does everything to help her. His loved ones' lives depend on it." Nix went to the weapons closet and started picking his poison.

He usually left women and children out of things. But all bets were off as far as Ember was concerned.

44

Ember

I WAS ON THE patio, holding a drink as the party continued around me. When I realized the contents were splashing around too much, I set it on the table. I tried to see what was happening to Nix. I had to believe treating him the way I did was necessary. I reached up to touch my mother's earring and then remembered. Cosmo caught the movement. He was staying next to me, but he had dropped my hand when we got outside. As far as I could tell, Nix was leaving. I could see into the sitting room now that it was dark.

My brother was here. And as much as I'd pushed him away, it was hell watching him leave. Having him believe the lies I was telling. It occurred to me then that he may never know the truth. That I was trying to help him, not hurt him.

I'd been overwhelmed with indecision. But that room had been packed with men with guns and they made the decision for me, for Nix. I wasn't thinking about escape, just life.

I watched as Lock and another man got into a golf cart to leave. He didn't see me or was actively trying to not look my way. I touched the fabric of my brother's jacket. His pockets were empty. I'd checked discreetly.

"That was some kiss."

Cosmo, who was holding my glass and one of his own, snapped me out of my thoughts.

I took the glass, remembering Olin's words. We were in a circle of his friends who were loudly discussing pools.

I took a gulp of the wine instead of putting it down again.

"There you go. That's the answer. If you feel something, drink. That's what I do." He touched his glass to mine and we both drank together.

45

Lock

IT WAS TWO WEEKS ago today that Ember had arrived on the compound, and she was giving me nothing to go on. As far as I could tell, Cosmo was her new man. He was at her cottage any time she had her college tutor over. They spent time hunched over a book or an iPad.

I wasn't sure it was even a legal way to get a degree, but I was guessing that with the vast Feybi money, anything could happen. The more I saw, the deeper I believed the roots went.

Meanwhile, my friendship—if that's what you called it—with Felon was heading toward a doable routine. The guys didn't raz me the way the Cokes did. I expected to be called teacher's pet or whatever, but Felon had built a reputation of not hearing anyone. And not talking. So they treated him like deadwood. It was actually genius. Because he was privy to everyone's conversations. They forgot he was in the room.

Olin clearly trusted him. He was called into at least six meetings in the last two weeks, always with a handful of Tootsie Rolls. Sometimes he returned with the candy. Other times, the wrappers were empty.

The day after the Mercy scene, he'd offered to take me to the woods out back and show me some of his tricks. What the tricks were, I was pretty sure had everything to do with the duffle bag he meticulously packed with weapons before heading to meetings. I had to take him up on it one day. I didn't want to be rude, and I wasn't making any more friends here.

The duffle bag came with us, and my eyes couldn't help but follow it as we made our way through the trees. Just waiting to see what would come out like a deadly jack-in-the-box. Felon set it on a stump, unzipped it, and pulled out two hatchets.

"We start with the basics. People who pick up a gun first lose perspective. How to ground themselves. How to find the mark using your own power." He twirled the hatchet and faced the handle toward me. I took it and felt the weight in my palm. The forest was scarred with the rehearsal of death. Targets pinned up on various trees, some free-standing.

Felon started by showing me how to position my feet. We spent an inordinate amount of time on centering myself and feeling the direction of the target. It was a good hour before I heaved my first hatchet. It slapped against the red bull's-eye and tumbled to the forest floor.

Felon laughed. "You've got work to do. If you're not on detail, come out here. Do this until you can hit the mark with your eyes closed. Then we'll do more."

Felon embedded his hatchet into the stump after zipping the bag and tossing it over his shoulder.

Two weeks later, I was able to bring Felon back out. He was impressed with the new skill I'd learned. Maybe he attributed it to the motivation that could be seen from my bedroom window. He upgraded me to a pistol.

Now, he stayed with me, making minor adjustments to my stance, my shoulders, anything to get a more accurate shot. I released my fury here. Letting the anger I had at Dice's death. The frustration at my father's arrest. My sister and mother being alone. But mostly, it was about her.

Ember was acting like we meant nothing to each other. She was making every effort to ensure we were never alone for a second while she held Cosmo's hand.

There was something, though. Maybe it was my imagination—Ma always said I had a great one. But when she was looking at him, I couldn't shake the feeling that her soul was still facing me.

I was decent with the gun. Pretty goddamn good with the hatchet, after the endless days of practice. Then, four weeks after Ember's arrival, I got a text that Cosmo wanted to go out tonight with Ember. And I was on her detail.

I wanted to hit myself in the dick with the hatchet. But I would go. I'd watch. She'd be as safe as I could make her.

46

Ember

THE COLORS WERE GONE from my hair. It was insane to feel so alone in a place that had visitors in and out. Laura and her friends. The guards. Cosmo and the tutor. And, of course, Lock.

Lock was watchful, and in my head he was waiting for me. A knight outside my bedroom window in the distance. As the days piled on top of each other, I was waiting for the other shoe to drop. For Nix to burst in here and try to save me. I dreaded the moment he saw through the lies I told him. He needed to stay away. Stay safe. And despite everything, my brain insisted on trying to come up with plans for escape. And then I'd end up back to my original assessment. It was impossible to protect everyone the minute Olin wasn't getting what he wanted. And so the endless cycle continued, and I let myself plan escapes I would never act on.

Cosmo wanted to go out. Felix the tutor was coming and all of Cosmo's friends. Laura put me in the corresponding skintight dress and sky-high heels a nightclub required. Cosmo was late picking me up, but Lock was with him. I felt a whisper of relief. It looked like his job was to stay close to us.

Felix was right behind him. He was cordial to me. I thought it was weird that the tutor would come with us, but Cosmo was just that kind of person. He wanted to round up everyone, be the life of the party.

I had to take deep breaths as I walked out of the cottage. We were going into public. I knew the need to run would be strong. To collapse and give up the façade of going along with all of this nonsense. I could feel where Lock was, like my body had a radar just for his heat. Behind me. To the right a little. When we got to the set of stone stairs just beyond the pool patio that led to the driveway, I felt his hand touch my lower back. The heels were stupid. My ankles would be so sore in the morning.

As we descended the stairs to the driveway, the front door to the mansion opened. Olin stepped onto the porch. I nodded at him. The light from inside was a broken halo around him; his white hair almost looked like it was on fire. The devil himself, maybe.

I headed toward the waiting SUVs. All black with dark tint on the windows. Cosmo jumped in first, then Lock held the door open, offering a hand.

We hadn't touched. Not since...

I avoided his hand, instead climbing into the back in a fairly unladylike fashion. Touching Lock would break down my walls like a sledgehammer—at least, that's what I was afraid of.

He cleared his throat and closed the door once I was seated, avoiding my eyes. Cosmo opened the door closest to him and leaned out.

"Felix! Ride with us!" Cosmo left the door ajar. Soon enough, Felix was climbing past us and sat in between us.

It was cozier than it needed to be for an entire train of vehicles. Lock slipped into the front passenger seat. I was free to look at the back of his head all I wanted. And I did. Cosmo and Felix had a murmured conversation that didn't include me.

I pulled on my dress to try to keep my panties covered. Lock turned around in his seat to stare at me. We gazed into each other's eyes. My skin tingled. My lips parted as I inhaled. His pupils widened as he exhaled.

Cosmo broke the connection inadvertently by reaching across Felix and grabbing my hand. His fingers curled around mine. Lock dropped his gaze and turned back around.

The club was barely noticeable. It had a sign that wasn't illuminated, but there was a line out front. Cosmo and Felix got out of one side of the SUV, and I got out of the other. The driver tried to rush to my side, but I'd hopped out before he could help me.

Cosmo and Felix strode toward their friends, leaving me in the dust. I reached back into the Escalade and got my purse. I had some backup makeup in there that Laura insisted I take in case I needed some touch-ups. The door to the club opened and shut, each time allowing the music to pulse through the night. Cosmo started dancing every time he heard it.

As an afterthought, he trotted back to put his arm around

me. I was as important to him as my purse was to me. Felix and Cosmo cracked jokes around me. Lock trailed behind. Cosmo was insulated by the pretense of about fifteen Feybi men. They didn't have to stop to show their IDs or anything, just got waved through.

The interior of the club was wall-to-wall people. Cosmo pushed me in front and put his hands on my shoulders. After tiptoeing up the stairs, not letting my heels touch, we got to the VIP section. It was small, and only a few guys could fit with Felix, Cosmo's friends, and me. Lock was left below, on the dance floor.

Cosmo dragged out a chair and I sat. The table was soon covered with drinks. I had a glass of sweet wine that I drank heavily—the only way I could escape. The music was pounding. Cosmo, busy drinking and laughing at jokes I couldn't quite follow, seemed to be having a great time with his friends.

I could see through the glass divider. Lock was standing at the bottom of the stairs. Volt leaned over and spoke into his ear. Lock shrugged and started dancing. As I scanned the floor, I saw all of Olin's men trying to blend in. Some were dancing, some were chatting up girls, and others were holding drinks. Clearly, Lock had gotten the message.

My glass was getting refilled when it was halfway empty, so I stopped trying to count how many I'd had. I liked the way the alcohol slowed down the worry. It took away the terror at being a pawn in Olin's game. I drank more.

Cosmo touched my shoulder a few times, clinking his glass against mine. He was more interested in talking to Felix, though. I stood, because it was time to use the ladies' room. Check my makeup. Something. I walked to the railing on the balcony. I found Lock in the crowd; not one but two girls were grinding on him. Like he could feel my gaze, he looked up. I peered down my nose at him as my anger built.

How dare he?

Right here. While I was a prisoner, he was going to dance with two sluts? I finished my glass of wine and slapped it on the table. I wanted to storm downstairs, but these stupid heels were like shackles. I kicked them off. I walked much more assuredly over to the VIP stairs, and Cosmo didn't stop me. I wasn't his focus anyway. I made my way down the stairs, only stopping once to get my balance.

The guards nodded at me. They must be confident enough that they had the place secured to allow me to walk free. It was fine. I had one destination in mind. Well, one person in mind. I fought my way through the crowd of gyrating bodies. When I spied him again, he was watching me, unmoving while the girls around him danced.

I came up close to him and grabbed his hand. He allowed himself to be pulled. One of the girls clutched his suit jacket.

"Bitch."

She couldn't stop what was happening. Lock brushed her off. He squeezed my hand as I towed him through the crowd. I wasn't sure where the hell we were going, but my walls were crumbling. My determination was dissolving. I staggered. The wine was hitting me all at once. Lock switched hands so he could guide me with a hand on my back.

He hurried me up the stairs and pushed me toward the VIP bathroom. Since we'd clogged up the VIP section with dudes, the ladies' room was empty. He let go of me altogether to grab the door and hold it for me.

He tilted his chin, indicating for me to go through. He was waiting to see what I'd meant by bringing him with me. I turned around and backed through the door, grabbing his tie and pulling him with me. I was irrational now. This was far from the stiff upper lip I'd been presenting to the world for the past month.

Lock pulled the door closed behind him. I reached past him and locked it.

The bathroom was done up in a gaudy rose gold marble. The lights had a tint. I pushed Lock against the door. He was staring at me like I was a lit fuse. Distrustful. Scared.

In my head I had a million things to say to him. I bit my cheeks to keep the words inside. I could feel his heart pounding under my hands.

"Ember." The rumble of my name in his lungs.

"Don't..." I went to my tiptoes and put my hand behind his neck. Our lips were close as he dipped his head down, eyes growing heavy-lidded. "...dance with other girls."

I expected some fight. I was "with" another man. I'd ignored him as totally as I could since we discovered each other in this twisted Alice in Wonderland nightmare.

"Anything you ask, I'll do."

His breath on my face sent shivers over my shoulders and down my spine.

"Kiss me." The wine was talking. The lonely was talking. The scared was screaming.

He shifted and pulled me to his chest. I put my other hand in his hair. His eyes darkened like he might kill me, but instead, he kissed the living hell out of me. Twisting and pulling so I was straddling him and had my back against the door.

I melted into the comfort. The care. I felt the moisture in my eyes start. While we kissed, heart to heart, my tears went down my cheeks and traveled down my throat, creating a tiny river running between my breasts.

"Sweet Ember." He must've felt the tears and stopped kissing me. He set me on my feet and used his thumbs to wipe my tears away. "What's this? What is this?"

He reached down and grabbed my hands, kissing each of them. Oxygen burned in my chest. I wanted to fall into him.

Beg him to save me from it all. Call my brother, call Animal and T. Enough was enough. And then I dropped my hands. I pictured Bowen. I saw Files die in front of me all over again. I couldn't do it to him.

"I've made a mistake. Please leave." The words were a double-edged knife that sliced into both of us.

Lock's confusion clouded his face. He came toward me for another kiss. I put my hands up. His chest was under my palms. I unlocked the door and pushed it open behind me. He stepped out the door, then turned and said my name.

"Soften to me again just once—for a heartbeat and that's it. This place can blow up around us. You have this light inside you when you turn it toward me. I'm yours. That's all I am. Not a brother, not a son... None of that matters. I'm only yours. Be wary with that power, Ember. I'd end the world for you." He held his hands open like he was offering me something. And he was.

I let the door swing closed behind me.

47

Lock

I WAS PRETTY SURE I denounced everything I stood for because that gorgeous girl kissed me. She made me stupid, and I'd gladly take the dunce cap. Shit, I'd have to put it over my goddamn boner to get out of this ladies' room.

I was sure about something now, though. She was a prisoner. She wasn't here because she wanted to be. I'd bet my life on it. I *was* going to bet my life on it. As I snuck out of the bathroom, I had the start of a plan. It involved her brother and me taking a bunch of risks. And going down in flames. Hell, for her I'd swallow fire if I had to.

The rest of the night she stayed in the VIP room, and every time I looked she was facing a different way. But the memory of her lips on mine sealed my resolve.

The next day, I sent a letter to Ember's address at school when I went into town with Felon to buy more Tootsie Rolls. It was my hope that the mail would get forwarded to her brother somehow. I was holding my breath the whole time, but if Felon saw me he didn't mention it.

A week later, Volt and I escorted Ember to the pool again. It was evening and she was dressed in white. She wouldn't look at me, but my heart was aching for her to do just that. I was so focused on trying to make a connection that I missed the obvious. Her dress was very telling, almost bridal. Her makeup was light, reminding me with a pang of our date at her college. I realized it had been weeks since I'd heard her laugh.

That's what I was thinking when Cosmo went to one knee in front of her and the small crowd that had been invited to witness the proposal. I was thinking that I'd do anything to hear her laugh again. That her laugh was a soul cleanser. It reminded me of how happy my sister made me. How loved my mother made me feel. Ember's laugh was a part of my soul that clicked in such a way that I knew it was meant to be.

And that was the part, that part with her laugh in it shattered when she told Cosmo she would marry him. Each crack was a gunshot. I couldn't tell if it was my heart breaking or my soul dying. All I knew was my surprised, painful gasp made her look at me, concern written all over her face.

I put my hand to my chest and leaned forward. I felt Volt smacking me on the back, and went with it, acting like I was choking. Instead, I was drowning in pain. And then I felt her hand on my forehead and saw her beautiful eyes filled with worry and fire.

As soon as I stood, realizing that I was breaking our cover, risking Ember's life with my reaction, I straightened my shoulders and patted my throat like I had actually choked. I couldn't bring myself to say congratulations. I wasn't that good of an actor.

It turns out, you can still breathe after your heart breaks. You can still hear her pretend to be happy when your soul curls up and dies.

48

Animal

WE GOT WORD THAT Ember was now engaged to Cosmo Feybi. Nix was livid.

"How far is she going to take this? When will she throw in the towel?" Nix paced the basement.

"Well, according to Lock, he doesn't think she knows that she can." I shrugged my shoulders. Baby Girl had gotten herself into a big ol' situation. "Or she's in love with Feybi. And Lock has trouble dealing with moving on."

We'd gotten a letter from Lock, forwarded from Ember's school.

T spoke up, "Yeah, I think she'd ask for Lock's removal if she really was in love with Cosmo. She wouldn't have him hanging around. It puts him at risk. She's not a different person, despite her actions at the college."

My lady was right, though she usually was. Ember's turn-around was too much. Too convenient for the Feybis. Nix looked at his phone and slowly shook his head.

"What's going down, Sweetness?" I stood and walked closer.

"Olin Feybi is requesting a meeting in a neutral spot." Nix looked like he was going to throw the phone but thought better of it. "He left a message on the old server that Bat Feybi would use back in the day."

Nix could hack the living shit out of anything you could plug in. He used to do assassin jobs for whoever was paying top dollar. Oh, how things had changed.

"He'll get the meeting. I wonder if he'll leave dead or alive." Nix sounded genuinely interested and more than a little motivated.

49

Ember

THE ENGAGEMENT RING SPARKLED on my finger. It was a huge rock and the band was a little too big. It kept swinging around and dangling on the palm side of my hand.

I twisted the ring upright again; Laura complimented it as she put the finishing touches on my hair. We were going for beachy waves today because Cosmo had mentioned we might take our engagement photos. Down by the river, there were a beach area and a gazebo. Felix had texted that he wasn't feeling up to the tutoring session, so we had some extra time. I found myself staring out of my kitchen window at the sound of repetitive gunfire. It had made me nervous a few days ago, and I mentioned it to Cosmo and Felix. Cosmo had shared that his uncle, Felon, did target practice, but not to worry. He was an expert at it.

Lock was at Felon's house, so the gunfire could have been him working out his emotions. I heard his words all the time in my head, breaking my heart. And they'd broken my heart a little more when I said yes to Cosmo's proposal. We were in Olin's presence, so what the hell else was I supposed to say? Yes. I told Cosmo yes and plastered a fake smile on my face as Olin embraced me and whispered his foreboding congratulations into my ear.

Cosmo seemed almost as unimpressed with the engagement as I was. I saw Felix and Cosmo fighting, and later, it was Lock and Volt who saw me back to the cottage. It had possibly been the most somber engagement party in history.

The gunfire tapered off and I relaxed a little. It made me nervous. I watched through the window as a convoy of golf carts and ATVs arrived at the front of the cottage. Olin jumped out of one, grandiose and jovial. As far as he was concerned, everything was coming up aces. Skinny unlocked the front door and let him in. There was no knocking where Olin Feybi was concerned.

I walked from the window to stand near the kitchen table. Laura stopped putting away the makeup. Neither of us really knew what to do. The warden was in the building.

Olin's smile slid off his face like skin off a snake when he took in my appearance. "What's this?"

He gestured to Laura and then to my head. I put my hands on my hair. What could have made him so mad?

Laura started to apologize immediately. "Sir, I'm sorry. So sorry. I know you said straight hair on Ember, but Cosmo has been liking the curls on Instagram and the beach photos..."

Olin advanced on her and backhanded the rest of the words out of her mouth.

It had been brutal, watching Laura get beaten before I knew her. But now I considered her a friend. I'd had plans to stay quiet. Stay in the background. But I reacted before I could reconsider. As he pulled his hand back again, I rushed him and shoved him away.

I didn't want to hurt Olin, but I'd caught him off guard. He stumbled backwards. Skinny caught him before he could hit the floor.

Adrenaline coursed through my system, making me braver than common sense would dictate. "You'll have to go through me. Don't touch her again."

The silence in the cabin while Olin straightened his shirt felt like a death sentence. I felt Laura gently pull on the back of my dress. Maybe by way of thanks, because I might be about to die.

"You horrible little thing." His words dripped like venom into my veins. This man was so deadly. I put one hand behind my back and grabbed Laura's hand. It was my way of trying to tell her I'd tried my best.

Olin rolled his head on his neck before unfastening his belt buckle. I expected some violence. But fear rolled over me. There were levels of violence, and Olin was clearly ready to ratchet it up notches. He unthreaded his belt completely.

"You're going to be my daughter soon. So, I think you're not above a sound spanking." He folded the belt in half and snapped it. "Skinny. Hold that one." He pointed at Laura with his pinky. "Ember, darling. Go put your hands on the back of the couch."

I hated my shaking hands and the tears in my eyes. I had no idea how bad this would get. I did as he asked. Men with guns surrounded us. No Lock. He was off duty. No Cosmo, though I wasn't sure he'd step in. Olin flipped up my skirt. He ran his hand over my ass. The thong I was required to wear was as close to nothing as possible.

"Cross your ankles." Olin traced his fingers down my thighs. "And don't fall. Or cry out. Or I'll add ten more for each transgression."

My whole body was shaking. The anticipation was horrible. When he was done tracing patterns on my ass, I felt his hand on my lower back. The sound of the belt sliced through the air until it hit. The loud slap corresponded with my knees buckling. The pain made me see stars. The yelp echoed in my ears before I realized it was mine. I couldn't take one more, never mind ten more.

"Well, that was both falling and crying out. So that's twenty on top of the other twenty you were originally slated to get. You must like it, Ember." Olin adjusted his hand so he was supporting my stomach and hips on his forearm to prevent me from moving away. The belt sliced through the air, and the pain was twice as much, because I knew it was coming and it hit almost the same spot again. I cried out against my will. Olin's arm took my weight as I sagged. He leaned over me and whispered into my ear, "Oh, darling, that's another ten. My men and I may have to take turns so my arm doesn't get strained."

In the next moment I was tumbling to the floor. I rolled away. Cosmo was holding Olin by the throat.

"Dad. What the fuck? You're fucking spanking her? You perv." Cosmo let go of his father's neck and put his body between Olin and me.

Olin took a step back. "She hit me."

"So what? You can't take a hit from a girl?" Cosmo smelled like alcohol.

I could see Olin's feet. I heard the noise of the belt and flinched, but after peeking around Cosmo, I saw the old man was putting it back through his loopholes on his pants.

"She gets a new makeup girl. This one isn't cutting it." Olin pointed at Laura. The redness on her cheek was a dead give-away to the previous violence.

Cosmo shrugged. "Fine. But if anyone spanks my fiancée, it'll be me."

Olin seemed like he wanted to fight more, but he backed away from his son. Olin issued orders for Laura to be taken away.

"Wait!" I scrambled to my feet but stayed behind Cosmo. "Where are you taking her?"

Olin's smile went up on one side. "I'm going to kill her."

Laura went white and limp. Skinny caught her and dragged her toward the door.

"No! It's not her fault. It was my fault. I asked for the curls. My decision." I tried to step around Cosmo.

He turned and grabbed me around the waist. His hushed voice stopped me briefly. "No. Not now. We won this battle."

I struggled still and Cosmo wrapped me in a bear hug.

Skinny pulled Laura through the door; Olin followed and closed it behind them.

I watched through the front window, transfixed and horri-fied, as Olin motioned angrily until Volt placed a gun in his hand.

"No!" I yelled, but Cosmo adjusted his hold on me to put his hand over my mouth. The rest of my screams were muffled.

Olin cocked the gun. Laura turned her head away from her fate and locked eyes with me. She started to mouth something, but didn't get far. She was shot in the head. Skinny, who was standing off to the side, holding one of her arms, let go. She slipped below the windowpane. I screamed and sobbed.

Cosmo whirled me around and pulled me against his chest. "Shh. He has a gun. Let's just let it go. Let it go."

I sank to the floor and Cosmo went with me, comforting me. I don't know how long we sat there with him rubbing my back. Eventually, I started to feel the pain of my belt beating. Eventually, I started to feel my heart pumping. Hear my breathing. See my lungs bring my chest up and down. When I pushed away from Cosmo, I could read the real sadness on his face.

"It's like this with him. Now you know why I hate him."

I nodded. I hated his father, too. Cosmo saved me. But why couldn't he have saved Laura, too?

50

Lock

A T THE SOUND OF gunfire, Felon took off running. I jumped into his Jeep as well. Felon took the straightest path. I don't think I took a breath the entire time. The crowd of people around Ember's cottage was alarming. The fact that a woman-shaped person was being carried away put my heart in my throat. Felon grabbed my arm hard.

"It's not her. That's not Ember."

I had to look at his face to understand what he meant. He kept the grip on my arm until he saw me come to the realization that he was right. The girl's hair was different. She was taller. But she was definitely dead.

I didn't see Ember. Olin was getting into a golf cart. He didn't spare a glance in our direction. Business was completed here. I ran to the door of the cottage. Ember was on the floor in Cosmo's arms.

Relief surged through me. It actually outweighed the jealousy I was feeling. And that was saying something. Felon grabbed my shoulder and pulled. He wouldn't talk to me now. Not in front of anyone else.

I got what he was saying. I needed to keep quiet about my connection to Ember. Hell, I hadn't even said as much to Felon, but he was observant. He motioned for me to stay outside. I had to rock on my heels but managed it.

There was blood on the flagstone outside. A lot. It reminded me of Dice dying in front of me. The thought that it could have been Ember turned my stomach. The knowledge that it was someone else made me turn and puke into the bushes that rimmed the edge of the cottage. I stood back up as Volt brought a bucket, the smell of bleach wafting from it. The cleanup. That's the way it was in this new life. A beautiful girl was murdered and everyone seemed to know their chores.

I wasn't going to get used to this. I hoped I'd never march through a day where bleaching blood from stone was what I did before lunch.

Who was I kidding? I wasn't going to survive that long.

51

Animal

NIX WAITED UNDER THE bridge for news on Ember.
He was prepared to offer his services. He was
prepared to threaten Olin Feybi within an inch of
his life. But we weren't sure how it was going to go. When Olin
arrived wearing his suit jacket like a cape, I had a bad feeling.
He fed Nix the whole bullshit line that Ember was happy. That
she wanted to be with this sleaze bucket son.

We believed differently. Olin acted hurt when Nix ran through the options.

"Honestly, I'm here to send out the wedding invites. These two kids can't wait. They're having the ceremony in the backyard. So wonderful, the young love of it all."

"Ember wants me to come?" Nix cracked his knuckles, giving Olin an impassive glare.

"Of course. Well, she might not want you to come right this second, but we both know that down the line she'll want to have you in the picture. Let's do it for Ember's future."

"I killed your half-brother. Why is it okay now to invite me onto your property?" Nix rocked back on his heels. T piped in through my earpiece that more Feybi men were on their way. Almost like the conversation that we were having was a setup for something else.

A cold look came over Olin's face. "Quite a thing. The way Bat died. You infested our own family, gained his trust, and killed him. You'd think that someone might want revenge for something like that."

Nix tilted his head. Murder cloaked his eyes. He was perfectly willing to go down in flames right this second. I'd seen this look before. More often when we were younger, but still. It was a problem.

I stepped forward, hands out, ready to mend the situation if I had to. We needed Ember out of this deal. Olin saw me coming at him.

"I can't say it doesn't entice me to know what it is you offer. What your price is. But first, let's meld these families together so that your outcome and my outcome are the very same. Think about that for a while. Feybi and your organization together on equal footing. It was like when great houses and empires would combine their strength, combine their bloodlines. I love the whole idea of it."

Nix bit his bottom lip. Waiting.

Olin straightened his lapel. "Consider this a formal invitation. As soon as we decide on the date, we'll clue you in. Hopefully, you and Ember can make amends before the big day."

Olin gave a little wave.

While we watched him and his caravan of men leave, I stepped next to Nix. "Well, he's insane."

Nix nodded. "He's clever, too. Maybe too clever for his own good. I still think we run the numbers for an extraction."

I murmured out loud for T to follow the caravan back to Feybi property. She gave me her acknowledgement.

I was starting to agree. Get in, get our girl, and get the fuck out.

52

Ember

WE WERE STILL GOING to take the engagement pictures. And I was trying to get my feet to move. Ann, the madam from the brothel, was called in to fix my hair. Straighten it out. I wondered if I was going to have to tell her Laura, her employee, was killed. But as Cosmo left and Ann walked in, she made it clear with the judgment in her eyes that she already knew.

Cosmo was hoping to take the pictures at sunset. He

seemed pretty confident it was safe to leave me alone so he could go get dressed. Either he knew where his father was or he liked taking chances.

Ann looked me up and down. "So, you're the one that got Laura murdered."

I knew my eyebrows were damn near my hairline. "What?"

"Yes. Laura could've taken a beating, but you stepped in and got her killed. I can't get any work out of a dead person."

I held my stomach. This horrible woman was weighing her net losses. I wanted to kick her and cry. I did neither as she put her manicured hand on my shoulder and pushed me into a chair.

Flat ironing the curls that Laura had painstakingly put in felt sacrilegious. And Ann wasn't gentle. Clumps of my hair littered the floor, a harsh reminder of her rough handling. My bottom throbbed from the beating.

I felt my will to make it through this whole fiasco draining out like a bathtub. *Was my life even worth all of this?* Waves of despair washed over me as Ann repainted my eyes with liner and shadow.

Lock's face peered through the front window. He was worried about me. I could feel it coming from him even though he said nothing. I started doing some magical thinking. Imagining myself with Lock, out of this situation. Living a normal life together. Going to the movies. Being back at school, going for a slice of pizza.

"Don't you start crying again. You can cry in your bed. And that's it. And only if you're alone." Ann started cleaning up Laura's makeup and brushes.

Everyone was able to work Laura's death into the day. It was horrifying. After Ann had packed the last of the brushes, she went to the kitchen and got a glass of water and apple slices. I was surprised when she set them down in front of me.

"Eat. Can't have you passing out on the cliff over the water during your photo shoot. Though, honestly, it'd be a whole lot easier for me. None of the girls would come here to work on your face after Laura was killed."

I took a long swallow of the water.

I said nothing to this woman. She was part of the goddamn problem. She continued unprompted, "So now I have to take time out of running my business to be here every day. Starting tomorrow, I'll train you to do the basic stuff yourself. Together, we'll manage this less than optimal situation."

I forced myself to take a bite of an apple slice. Because she was right—about the need for food. I needed to stay strong for now. Move forward for now.

It wasn't until after the pictures were taken on the cliff that Cosmo told me that he was moving in. He told me it was for my own protection. That his father had a temper. In the next breath, he told me that Felix was also moving into the extra bedroom. He wanted to spend more time with me and really wanted me to work on my college degree. I listened and nodded. He would do as he wished. But the sex that I hadn't yet been forced to have with him would become expected.

Cosmo was handsome, but I didn't choose him. I wasn't interested in him. I wrapped my arms around myself on the way home. I wished I had my mother's earring to touch. To give me strength. Cosmo, Felix, and Felon took the security cameras out of the cottage. There would be no more interior surveillance. But I dreaded what the price of this small freedom would be.

53

Lock

I DIDN'T KNOW HOW the hell people slept when a girl was murdered less than a stone's throw from their bed. Gratefulness that it wasn't Ember was still with me. But man, that makeup girl had been here every day. Ember was a beautiful girl, but even I had to notice the artistry and talent that went into her makeup.

And like the snap of fingers, she was gone. Like Dice. Like I feared Ember and I would be someday soon. I hoped Nix had gotten my letter. I had a mini panic attack when I pictured Olin somehow intercepting it. I got out of bed in Felon's amazingly intricate house. The pacing started. I wanted to check on Ember. I wanted to check on my mother and Rhy.

I walked to the front door and unlocked the wood puzzle that barred the front door. I looked down at my sleeveless T-shirt and sweats. I wasn't dressed up. I put slides on and crossed the front lawn. In the darkness I could see her bedroom window better from the little knoll toward the front of the property.

I made out the silhouette of a woman moving around in the kitchen. Then she moved to the bedroom. Just staring out the window. I wasn't close enough to make out her face, but I could guess Ember was having trouble sleeping for the same reasons I was.

I peeked over my shoulder. Felon stood in the open door-way. "She's really special, huh?"

I bent down and pulled up a handful of grass. I started throwing the blades of grass like handfuls of pebbles.

"Yeah." I wanted to be honest with him, but he was blood with the Feybis so trust would be a tough ask.

"I saw how screwed up you were when you thought that girl was Ember." He stepped out farther onto the lawn.

"Aren't you supposed to be in bed?" I offered the obvious. He was usually headed in for the night by nine.

"Ah. Yeah. Usually. Hard to sleep on a night like this."

I took my eyes off the window that held the shape of Ember—the shape that I thought belonged to her—and gave him a disbelieving stare.

"She was an innocent. I mean, hell, she worked for Ann so I know she was no Girl Scout. But you never know why these girls get into the life. If it was even her choice..." Felon started stretching his arms.

"This was your family, though. Your brother lost his temper. How do you make peace with that?" I was toeing a line, though Felon and I *had* gotten to know each other quite a bit from the hours behind his house.

"I woulda stopped him if I'd been there." Felon looked off into the distance.

We both watched another figure approach the woman in the window. I stiffened until I watched her turn and hug him.

Cosmo. She was hugging Cosmo. It was really, really hard to see this.

"If you love her, hang in there. You never know." Felon turned and walked back into the house, leaving the door ajar for me.

I watched as Cosmo and Ember held each other. There was no kissing or anything, but I was jealous. And sad for the makeup girl.

54

Ember

THE FIRST NIGHT COSMO slept over he stayed on the couch. Felix was in the guest bedroom. By the second night, Cosmo had bought an air mattress and put it on the floor of my room. The only kiss we'd shared was the one I forced on him in front of Nix.

He didn't leer at my ass or linger on my boobs. I was grateful for that small kindness. By the third night, I figured out why. I was up to use the bathroom when I heard the moaning. And then it clicked. Felix and Cosmo were together.

My mind was blown. In this situation, I finally had an upper hand. I wasn't sure what the hell I was going to do with that information, but it gave me a shot of hope.

Cosmo was hiding his homosexuality from his dad. The ring on my finger was a cover. Felix, though a great guy and a good teacher, was here for Cosmo, not me.

Their relationship was incredibly obvious in the morning light. I was shocked it took moaning for me to figure it out. They shared secret looks and gentle smiles. Now that I was watching for it, I saw the little touches, moments when they brushed up against one another. It was almost cute. Except I was stuck here. And I didn't know the risks involved in any of this.

Ann came every day, earlier and earlier, to make me up for the day even though we didn't go anywhere. On Friday night, she had to return to enhance my makeup because Cosmo had a house party he wanted to go to.

She was less rough than she had been that first night, but there was no friendly banter like there had been with Laura. I missed her, plain and simple. And my heart hurt every time I thought of her.

After Ann had swept my hair up into a swirled bun, she shared that I needed to be seen on social media with Cosmo and my ring. Olin was getting ready to leave on business on the other side of the country and would be checking his son's Instagram for evidence that I was doing my part.

Lock, with a handful of guys, was escorting Cosmo and me to the party. And, of course, Felix was with us as well.

The house was huge and on the water. Cosmo explained that it belonged to his friend's uncle. I made sure that Cosmo took a few engagement pictures for Instagram, and then we split up. The crowd was young. The lights were low.

I got a glass of wine and put my back against a wall while Cosmo and Felix went upstairs. Across the crowded room, I spied Lock. He was all business in his suit with his earpiece in. I stared at him until he returned my gaze.

Instead of letting my stare scurry away, I held still.

The conversation we had didn't contain words. Just a tongue to the lips or a shake of the head.

He thought I looked nice. I thought he was crazy. A hint of who we used to be. I set my glass down on a nearby end table and left in search of a bathroom. I glanced over my shoulder and Lock followed.

The house was a maze of rooms and hallways. As I went deeper in, Lock got closer. After two left turns and two doors, I opened a door that led to a nondescript looking bedroom.

I waited inside with the door ajar, the lights off.

Lock slipped in and closed it behind me. "Are you okay?"

We were only illuminated by the slats of light that the blinds allowed in. His voice and the sweet tone got me. I walked right into his chest so he was forced to put his arms around me. I shook my head slowly. No, I wasn't all right. No, I wasn't okay. I was the reason a girl had died a few days ago. The man I was supposed to marry was leading a double life. I wasn't sure if this whole farce I was putting myself through was worth it. Was it even helping keep Nix and Animal and T alive? Or was I nothing more than a pawn in Olin's fucked-up game?

I didn't voice those concerns, but his kiss on my forehead was understanding enough. Lock still had feelings for me. Thank heavens. Because I needed the connection more than I could even admit to myself.

"It'll be okay, Ember." He rubbed my back.

"Not for Laura." I tilted my head up. Lock was so handsome in the moonlight that was making its way inside the room. "Are there cameras here? For Olin?"

It was always about him—that horrible murderer.

"No. Things aren't as tight in this house. I think that's why Cosmo picked it. We do have eyes on us, though." He tucked a bit of stray hair behind my ear.

"Okay. I get it. Just a quick visit." I touched his face. "I'm so sorry. For all of this. God, this can't get you in trouble. I can't deal with it if you're hurt."

I was saying too much. The last time I had wine I had taken risks. I couldn't do this to him. I needed to let him do his job.

"Does this mean we're friends? Because this feels like you softening to me." He was serious.

I shook my head. "Please don't put friendship on me. You've sacrificed so much, your sister, your family. I can't take that on right now. I need to just get through, day by day. And I think, if I have to do this to the very end, I would like hugs from you from time to time."

He had a sad smile for me. "That's okay. We can do that."

55

Lock

INHALED THE SCENT of her hair. Her arms were locked around my neck. I swayed a little, making her move with me. Almost a dance.

She didn't know how much had changed between the last time we were alone and now. Telling her wasn't an option, not in this moment anyway. Felon had been teaching me behind his house. How to aim. How to shoot. He had years and years of practice, but he was able to pare down a lot of his best tips into easily understood lessons. I was careful around him; I couldn't forget who he was. Who he was loyal to. But I was really starting to like him. And starting to trust him as well.

I was moving up in the Feybi organization at a breakneck speed. Another Felon perk. The guys didn't give me shit. And I was getting things that should take years to earn. Like the right to go to the store and grab food and stuff for Felon and me in my time off. During my second trip to the Shoppers Grocery Store, I'd learned I was being watched. Mercy, Ember's brother, had appeared at my side, a hood covering his elaborate tattoos.

A chill went through me. I knew he'd be able to kill me in no time flat. "Give T your list. She'll get the stuff you need. Come talk to me in the van."

Was anyone brave enough to stand up to this guy without an army? I hadn't met them yet. And I certainly was smart enough to do whatever he said.

In the white "free candy" van in the parking lot, Animal was sitting in the driver's seat. He nodded at me when our gaze connected in the rearview mirror. I returned it.

Nix opened up a laptop. I saw the screen and my blood went as cold as a slushy.

My sister and mother were in a picture, smiling. "I know who these people are to you. I've been to see them."

And then I flipped. This man, Ember's brother or not, was an assassin. His visit could only mean one thing—he'd threatened them or killed them to get my compliance. I started swinging.

Nix moved fast, ducking out of the way of my first two punches. He wrapped my wrists up and used my own weight against me. Before I knew it, he was sitting on my back, hissing into my ear, "They're alive. Calm the fuck down." Nix waited until I stopped struggling, then let me up slowly. I was still fuming and close to primitive in my need to protect my girls.

In the driver's seat, Animal had a gun pointed at me. He shrugged as if to say he was reluctant to do it, but my obvious violent impulses required it.

"Your mom was running out of money despite what you've sent her. Your sister's doing great in the new school, but there are a lot of extra expenses." Nix reached past me and flipped through some more pictures. Obviously candid, security camera style.

My sister and mother were being tailed by Nix and company. I was raging. Fury washed over me, despite the firearm pointed at my head.

"Settle down, Lock. Your sister's tuition is now paid in full through to her senior year in high school. Including programs and extra stuff for your mom and sister to do together."

I felt my eyes narrow. There had to be a catch.

"I now own the building they live in. They're living rent free. T put money into a trust for your sister, so she has what she needs for the foreseeable future." Nix folded his arms in front of him.

He scrolled through the paperwork that had been completed. My signature was forged all over it. For as much as Ma would ever know, I had provided for her and Rhy.

I copied his movement. "Thanks? I think? I'd rather they weren't being tailed by a bunch of murderers. What do you want?"

Nix tipped his chin up. "My sister. I want you to watch her. Take care of her until I can get her the hell out of there."

I nodded. "I was already doing that."

"Yeah. But I wanted you to know that your responsibilities are covered. As far as your family. So..."

"So, if I get killed, I can die in peace." I tilted my head to the side.

He bobbed his chin in agreement. "I hope it doesn't come

to that. I need a bit of time to get her out. And to make sure that she *wants* to get out."

"I sent you a letter saying as much. Did you get it?" At the rear of the van, the tailgate doors opened. T climbed inside with the bags and Felon's credit card.

Her appearance clearly signaled that I had to get moving back to the compound. I couldn't be gone longer than a reasonable amount of time.

"I got it." He waited while I gathered up my stuff. "You're telling me Ember needs to be removed from the Feybis?"

I had to be clear. "Hell yes. But it's tricky. Olin's got her scared. Real scared."

"Whenever you come out to the store, one of us will be here. Give me updates on Ember. Let me know what's going on. You'll be our guy on the inside. Don't tell Ember, though. She has to keep doing what she's doing. I don't want Olin to be able to torture her for information." Nix half stood.

"And in exchange? My sister and mother are taken care of. But if I don't do as you ask?"

I needed to know how deep in the shit I was.

Animal spoke up, "Nix doesn't kill women and children. They'll be taken care of as long as one of us is alive, no matter what you choose to do."

T nodded and Nix gave me his steely stare. I knew then they were on the right side of wrong—the kind of guys Dice and I always wanted to be. They were the good bad guys, if there was such a thing.

I left the van and got into the SUV I'd driven there. I knew that I was going to watch Ember either way, but I felt a whole lot better knowing my sister and mother would be taken care of. Nix and his crew could've threatened them to control me. Instead, they'd earned my eternal loyalty. They were taking care of Rhy. Somehow, by existing and doing this thing, I was providing for them both.

Back in the present, the peacefulness of my moment with Ember washed over me. She didn't know that we were moving to end this for her. And as I held her in the bedroom, I vowed to get her out alive. Get her back to Nix. Even if I didn't make it.

I was doing the best I could to get her what she needed. And right now, she needed a little hugging. I was down for that. I'd report this whole thing to Nix next time I went to the store.

She seemed more trapped than ever. Before she slipped away, I put her face in my hands. I kissed her forehead, the top of her nose, and then her lips.

Ember seemed ready to crumble at my feet. She clearly thought she was fighting this battle alone. I needed the element of surprise.

56

Ember

WALKING AWAY FROM A cuddly, understanding Lock sucked. But I didn't want to get caught in a bedroom alone with him, no matter how much my soul wanted to stay there.

I was fortunate I'd kissed him back quickly and left the room, because Felix and Cosmo didn't want to party anymore. They both wanted to go home, not even an hour after arriving.

I wasn't sure what they had done while we were separated,

but when we returned, they quickly made it back to their bedroom. Lock saluted me and swapped spots with Volt before trudging away to Felon's house.

I went to my room and touched my brother's jacket, the one he'd wrapped around my shoulder's at Cosmo's birthday party. Sometimes, when I reached down to the bottom of the closet, I would sniff it. It still held a hint of his cologne. And it made me feel homesick and happy at the same time. I had to make it sneaky though, because even though I knew the cameras were off, I was wary of dropping this cover I had that I was angry at Nix.

After a quick shower, I toweled off my hair, as the familiar moans began emanating from the guest room. Then the front door unlocked. I opened the bathroom door a crack and saw that Feybi's men were entering the cottage.

I was stunned silent with panic. The bedroom doors didn't lock, a feature I discovered soon after coming to this place. I assumed it was so I couldn't deny Cosmo any conjugal visits, but as the guest bedroom door was flung open, I wished there had been a lock. Just anything to give Cosmo and Felix a few minutes to cover up. Olin Feybi's rage and disbelief manifested in a noise that was a combination of a scream and a sob. I ran into the room; Cosmo and Felix were in a lovers' embrace. Naked.

I covered my mouth with my hand as I watched Olin scream yet again like he was falling from a building. The side of his face that I could see was almost purple with fierce emotion. It clicked for me then. If Cosmo was killed, I would be, too. Or possibly used as bait against my brother. There'd be no reason to keep me alive.

The men with Feybi looked truly bewildered. I saw one toss his hands up. A solution, and possibly my only choice appeared in my mind's eye. A solution. Or a death sentence.

I stripped down and stepped into the guest bedroom. A heartbeat before Olin started slapping his son, I stepped between Cosmo and Felix. The air hit my skin, as did the gaze of every man in the room. I touched Cosmo's dick and Felix's face at the same time.

"Let's not get too carried away, Mr. Feybi. A girl's got needs. And my fiancé was kind enough to indulge me."

Cosmo and I looked at each other. He bent his head to give me a kiss. Felix reached around me to cup my breasts. I never felt so exposed, but I knew I had to do this. This was the only way to keep Cosmo alive. I'd seen Olin murder before, and I had no doubt he'd shoot his son if he knew the truth. Cosmo stepped into my kiss and slipped his hand between my legs.

They were covering me as best they could and making it seem like they were into the scene.

Olin teetered backwards. "Cosmo?"

I turned my face from Cosmo. "Have an open mind. People our age are all about pleasure."

Lock came running up behind Olin, and horizontal wrinkles appeared on his forehead. I saw the betrayal in his face.

I could feel my throat closing up. This had been a huge risk. And I had to watch as the love of my life stumbled away from the scene in front of him. Cosmo twirled me so I was chest to chest with Felix and stormed toward the door.

He shouted at Olin, pushing him and his men out of the cottage and slamming the cottage door behind them. Felix was clutching me to his chest when Cosmo turned back to us.

We all took halting breaths, waiting to see what was next. Through the window, we could see Olin striding away from the cottage. Cosmo let out a sharp bark of laughter. He walked naked to the bar in the cottage and poured himself, Felix, and me tall glasses of bourbon.

Felix reached behind us and grabbed me a blanket from the

back of the couch. He swung it around my shoulders. I walked over to the bar and grabbed a glass. The guys did the same. We all locked eyes. Something was changing right here, right now. I'd protected them both with my actions.

Cosmo held up his glass. "To Ember thinking on her feet."

Felix tapped my glass and Cosmo's before draining his. I managed a few gulps before coughing on the amber liquid. Looking up, I caught Felix and Cosmo trading a look of pure love.

I set my glass down and walked to the kitchen window. In the distance there was repetitive gunfire. Practice. Someone was practicing to kill. And I was positive about who it was. My Lock. I drained the glass. This place, where I was, it was hopeless. Depression crashed around me. I might never get out.

57

Lock

I RAGED THROUGH THE night. There was no sleep, but there was exhaustion. The next morning, I got a text that Cosmo and Felix had to go investigate a boat, but Ember had asked that I not accompany them. The boat was supposed to be Ember's wedding gift, maybe from them both. I was simmering. A slow burn. I knew what I'd seen last night. My girl was in a dick sandwich. I wanted to throw my shit everywhere. As the sun set, I'd emptied tons of clips behind Felon's house.

Turned out, that rage and jealousy made me a much better shot. Felon kicked the empty shells at my feet.

"You got some anger, kid."

I made sure the gun I just emptied was, in fact, empty before slamming the safety back.

I shrugged. "Don't we all."

"Heard from the guys what happened." Felon reached into his pocket and held out a Tootsie Roll. "I'll give you a freebie. If you want, I'll handle the girl. No guilt for you."

I turned my head so fast I damn near pulled a muscle. "No. Shit. Never."

Felon gave me a flat smile. "You have your answer then." He pocketed the candy.

"An answer for what?" I was still dealing with my shock at the "gift" Felon had offered me.

"There was a girl for me. Years ago. I'd do anything for her. Did everything for her." He heaved a heavy sigh. "And when I caught her with my brother, I still took her back."

I whistled a low tone. "Olin?"

He gave me a slow nod. "I'd do anything for her. She knew it. Turned up pregnant after a while."

We were going deep, standing in spent bullets. I gave him the space to tell his tale.

"Olin was sure it was his. Told me that I was a sucker for her. Let me really have it, you know?" He bent and picked up a handful of brass. "But that baby? He was mine. I knew it. Didn't have the evil in him like my brother did."

"Cosmo?" This was some straight crazy shit.

"Yeah. But she went to Olin. I offered her what I had. This house. My heart. My protection." He let the shells flow from one hand to the other. "I stay here for her now. Watch over him. He grew up to be a little jackass. Entitled shithead."

I stared out at the cottage in the distance. Ember was moving from window to window. Restless.

"She killed herself. Ten years ago yesterday. Left me a note taped to this door. Blamed me for not saving her. Angry that I would watch him with her all these years." He poured the metal into the bucket we had for that purpose.

"So, what's the lesson?" I bent, grabbing up handfuls as well.

"I don't have one. I did what I had to do. I was here if she had the courage to be with me. I was here if she didn't. My son is better off inheriting the family business. I stay here for him now." Felon and I finished cleaning up. I had a few minutes before I started my guard duty.

"Do you regret it?" It was a peek into his soul.

"Hell yeah. I shoulda taken her from here. I made every wrong choice. Now I kill people to keep Cosmo's inheritance viable. What a waste." Felon hit me with his regretful stare. "Feels like I'm watching history repeat itself here."

I clapped him on the shoulder, giving him the thanks I had for sharing. Maybe I had to grab her up and run. Forget the dudes she was screwing. She was mine. And she made me happy. Or miserable. Or both. Either way, I had to go stand guard.

The walk to the cottage was shorter tonight, maybe because I was half-dreading what I would find. I swapped out with Volt. He didn't say much to me. If I was trying to get in with the other guys, my friendship with Felon was preventing me. I was fine with that.

I rounded the side of the cottage, checking the perimeters. When I checked the window to make sure it was closed, I was met with a surprise.

Ember was leaning out of it, a glass balanced on the sill beside her. Her long, dark hair was cascading over one shoulder. Although the cottage was one story, the foundation gave her a good three feet above the ground. The lack of surprise on her face said she'd been expecting me.

She pinned me with all of her emotion.

Trapped. Scared. Fierce.

I thought of seeing her window at her dorm. And here we were. She folded her arms on the sill.

"I had to. What you saw. I had to do it."

"Really? You *had* to get sandwiched between two dudes?" I wanted to run, but she was here so my feet refused to move.

She grabbed a glass that had been near her arm. She drained half of it like it was nothing. It was then I noticed how out of focus her eyes were. She'd been drinking a lot lately.

"I think I'm going to die here." She dropped the glass outside and it rolled out from under the bush there.

"Nah. You don't have to do that." I stepped closer to the window, kicking the glass back under the shrub,

After regarding me for a beat, she started to move. She was wearing a T-shirt and not much else. She pushed herself up onto the sill and swung her legs around to the front.

She was swaying a bit. "If this was higher, I could just...slip off. Right?"

Her fingers danced over her knees. She pushed off the window and I stepped up through the foliage to catch her.

I wrapped one arm around her hips. I let her slide down me. Her shirt rode up.

This woman. She was pretty at a distance. But when close enough to kiss, Ember would melt any man's brain. She touched my face. I turned toward her palm.

She whispered to me, "They're gay. Felix and Cosmo. And his father was going to kill him. So I had to."

I felt my eyebrows knit together. "What the fuck?"

She stepped backwards, out of my arms. I kept a hand on her hip so she wouldn't fall into the bush. "I shouldn't have said anything."

"Cosmo's gay?" I wasn't letting her get away that quickly. She looked over my shoulder and past me.

"Yeah. It seems obvious now." She tipped her head up and closed her eyes. I felt her body relaxing into mine. Like being in my arms took tension away from her.

"What's going on here, baby?" I was sorely tempted to toss her over my shoulder and heft her out of the entire compound. It was stupid. I knew the cottage's cameras had been taken away, but there were guys on the perimeter with guns. They wouldn't think twice about putting a bullet in me.

"I can't. This weight is too much. Tell me to be braver." Ember put her hands in her hair, messing it up.

"I dream of you every night. I think about you every day." I wasn't going to tell her what she wanted to hear. But I could tell her what I needed to say.

Her glassy eyes were unfocused. "That's the opposite of what I need." She turned and pointed to the window. "Get me back in there. Please."

We were messy intruders. I gave her a boost, patting her ass. She reached down and yanked on my forearm. I pulled up on the sill and slid inside. This was her room.

No Cosmo. No Felix. Just us. The door was already closed.

Ember walked over to her bed and flopped backwards on it. She started laughing, and that's when I knew she was at the edge of sanity.

Because this wasn't funny. She was trapped in this house, with a fiancé she didn't love. There were bridal magazines on the floor, still wrapped in the plastic packaging they were mailed in. I walked to her mirror and touched the Polaroids I'd sent her in our other life. The time before all the death. My heart swelled. She'd brought them here. Had them here. I moved close and sat next to her. The mattress dipped in the center.

"What did they tell you to keep you here?" I asked.

Her weight was shifted to me. I put my arm around her shoulders. Small. She was small against me.

She didn't answer, but she ran her fingers along my face. "I've wanted you since we met."

I felt the lust rise in me. With her it was always right there, but now it was an active fight I was losing. Maybe I would never forget this moment. Somehow, we weren't kids anymore. There was a haunting in her face that etched the hole in my soul. We matched for how broken we'd become.

And I should've stopped myself, but I didn't. I dipped my head lower to her lips. We were just a wish away from a kiss. Her diamond ring from another man danced in the moonlight, cutting a white sliver across her bedspread.

"Lock. Let's take tonight. Maybe. Let's just take it." And then she moved her hips and pushed toward me. She closed the gap, and I could taste the explosion of her. Her lips. And then the tinge of the alcohol she'd swallowed.

This was more than lust. It was a rebirth of a girl who'd passed away weeks ago. I knew that her hair was brown now, but I could feel the colors emerging from her. Red, blue, and purple. She straddled my lap, and I had everything that I could hope for. She was so beautiful, writhing on me. And it was wrong. This moment was awful; the street-smart part of me trying to send alarms to my brain, but it was gone. I was all heart. All love. All sex. For her.

She went to her knees and kissed my mouth like it had done her wrong and she would punish it with kisses. And tongue. I ran my hands up the back of her thighs, running my fingers beneath her thong.

The noise she made was a sound I could die to. I guided her onto her back. There was too much here. I tried to memorize this version of her. Her messy brown hair, the white T-shirt pulled above her toned stomach. I pulled it up even higher. I ran my hands over her like I was using the moonlight to sculpt her from my dreams.

Ember reached for my hands, pulling them to her lips. She kissed my palms. "Make me forget that I'm here."

I leaned over her and kissed her throat, letting my hand slip under her neck. She arched her back just enough for me to hold her. I brought my mouth from her neck back to her lips while pushing the fabric of her shirt up farther.

She was braless, and her breasts were spectacular, but that wasn't surprising. She was made of diamonds and fire. For me.

I took a nipple into my mouth, thumbing the other one.

"Yes. Please." And she ran her hands under my shirt, up my back, my spine under her fingertips. My skin ignited with every inch.

I let her go so I could pull my shirt above my head, taking my gun out of the back of my pants and setting it on the nightstand.

I didn't want it far away. If anyone tried to stop what was about to happen, I'd kill them.

After pulling her panties down her legs and casting them aside, I watched as she spread her legs for me. Ember pulled her shirt off and then lay back, waiting.

In her eyes there was a promise. And a threat even. I slid her by her hips lower on the bed. I kneeled in front of her, letting her be the offering on the altar that her bed had turned into.

She tipped her chin toward the ceiling, nipples taut. Exceptional. And we hadn't even started. Kissing the inside of her thighs should've taken forever, but I needed to make sure she forgot where she was. I put my mouth on her.

With my lips, tongue, and fingers, I let her know how often I thought of doing this very thing to her. My dick ached for her. I'd be willing to screw it off and leave it here for her, because it would want to be here forever anyway.

She alternated between tossing her head around and digging her fingers into my hair and scalp. I felt her first orgasm clench around my fingers and I uttered a litany of horrible curses as I watched her lose control.

And like the first tip of the heroin needle, I was addicted, hooked on her. The scent of her. The feel of her against my fingers. The way her smoothness touched my forehead.

I had to have her. I needed to have her. There was a part of me that begged my mind to go slowly. To know that I can only have this first once.

But I was losing any battle I ever had about self-control. I pulled away from her and slid my pants and briefs over my hips. When she put her gaze on my dick, I felt my ears flare red with the intimacy of it.

Somehow, right now, this second was more revealing than anything in my life had ever been. When she was able to focus, a slow smile appeared on her face, and then she crooked her finger and pointed to her mouth. I'd have run through a lava wall to get there.

Her beautiful lips weren't just made for blowjobs, I know that. But my dick had other plans. He was all about fucking the hell out of her mouth. The silk of her hair tipped between my legs and she adjusted her angle. She lay on her side, opening her throat to take as much of me as she could.

At my disposal was her beautiful, naked body. I had serious concerns that she would rush me into an embarrassingly quick orgasm, where I might scream just like a monkey beating up another monkey.

But my dick didn't care; it didn't care about anything but the beautiful pleasures of her mouth. Her tongue was warm and so, so busy. Her tongue was so busy it probably had its own Google calendar. Maybe a briefcase.

Oh shit. I had gone full mental. I was giving her mouth its own career. I clenched hard on my release, knowing my eyes were probably pointing in different directions.

A quiet voice deep in my head started screaming to mount her, to stop looking like a disaster and try to be sexy if I could.

I pushed on her hips and stared at her gorgeous face. I positioned myself over her and stopped. "You are..." and I stopped. Her beauty had gotten her kidnapped. She touched my cheeks and then slid her hands behind my neck.

She bit her bottom lip and looked from my eyes, to my lips, to between her legs. It was the single hottest thing I'd ever experienced. And I slid inside her. If I thought her mouth was heaven, then her vagina was heaven on fire. I grabbed her leg and pushed it up. And then I let go of any restraint I had been pretending to have.

58

Ember

I'D BEEN LOOKING AT the door, half-concerned that it
was unlocked until he was on me. And then there was
only him.

Lock. His hands on my hips. He was strong and he was
home somehow. This wasn't sex. It was salvation. A tiny bit.
Since I'd been here I'd been on the edge, waiting for my
demise.

But this took everything away. There was only his beautiful

face and muscles working for my pleasure. When he was inside me, the tension that I'd been feeling ripped through me. He hushed me as I moaned out loud.

If there was something the opposite of a punch, Lock had found it and used it between my legs. I was getting slammed with adoration.

The second orgasm was all clenching until it was spellbinding. I became softness. And he followed soon after. I reached up for him and encouraged him to land on top of me. The weight of him pressing me into the mattress grounded me. Made me feel real. Reminded me who I'd been before this whole nightmare.

Our night became a test of our endurance and pent-up feelings.

Even when morning came, and Lock had left, I could still feel his hands all over me. I tried to catch them, which was pointless. He'd added color back into my life, even if only for a night. I was missing him and our old lives. We'd just been starting out. Discovering each other.

But he'd given me hope. It was time to try to get out. Olin Feybi was dangerous. Cosmo and Felix were very, very grateful that I'd stepped between them when they were caught. But this morning over coffee, they both looked worried. I was in with them both now. I had not touched my mug. Cosmo leaned toward Felix. Felix glanced at Cosmo's hand over and over like he wanted to hold it.

"How long do we have before your father comes back?" I hated to bring it up, but we were all living in suspended reality.

Cosmo took out his phone. "Not anytime soon. Dad left on the plane this morning. So the guys say."

Felix stood and got my textbooks from the ottoman in the living room. "Maybe we learn while we wait?"

Cosmo tapped his fingers on the table. "Who was it last night?"

I felt my face grow pale. I was positive we'd been quiet enough. I didn't answer.

Cosmo cleared his throat as Felix put the books down on the table. "Because, we could maybe go on a little trip? And I'd want you to bring whoever that was."

I snapped my gaze at him, my eyes narrowing. Naming Lock seemed like a horrible idea for keeping him safe.

"What do you mean?" I needed more information.

"Well, I wanted to go skiing. And if we went together, you could bring someone as protection—your choice. Like whoever was here last night, as a guard. And we'd keep your education going as well. With Felix. We have a cabin..." Cosmo rubbed his thumbs on his fingertips.

Cosmo was living in a dream world. I was no expert on the Feybi family, but I knew the mask of rage on Olin's face would come to some sort of reckoning. But then there was last night.

In Lock's arms. Feeling almost safe. Feeling almost home. It could get him killed. I was already on track for either death or prison. A shiver ran up my spine and over my shoulders.

"Let's say we saw it was Lock? Would you be amenable to having him come along?" Felix flipped open my math textbook. He posed the question like it was part of a pop quiz.

The selfish part of me nodded once. Affirmative. I wanted Lock to come with me. I wasn't sure if I'd just signed his death warrant with my neediness.

But I was in love with him. And my heart wanted him. If this was the only power I got to have, I just prayed it wasn't going to hurt him.

———

It turned out that the Feybis had more than one plane. I was dressed in jeans and a T-shirt. So incredibly understated for what was usually asked of me. Ann was staying here. We brought Felon, Lock, Volt, and Skinny. Felix and Cosmo stayed on opposite sides of the plane, letting me know that not all the men here were to be trusted. Lock acted like I hadn't had my legs wrapped around his neck last night, though I felt like the information was broadcast on my forehead.

How was he even hotter now?

He'd packed a light bag. I watched him as he checked the contents in his chair. I was more than a little curious about the hatchet he shined up briefly before tucking it back inside the bag. He caught my eye as I watched. His tongue peeked out, then a slow smile pulled up his lips on one side. When I bit my lips together, it evolved into a full grin. And then he dropped his attention back to his bag.

Cosmo leaned over to me and whispered, "Breathe, rainbow girl."

I gave him a quick look. "How'd you know about that?"

"I Googled you. I preferred the colors. I like rainbows." He gave me a wink, and I shook my head, chuckling.

"Thank you again," he whispered into my ear as the plane began its takeoff. "I damn near shit myself when you stepped between us."

I knew what he meant. It had been an impulse. I was still waiting to see if it made sense. I felt like every breath I took was through Olin's stranglehold on my neck.

59

Animal

THEY HAD LEFT ON a plane. That was the last intel I had. We were working hard on taking down not only Olin Feybi but also his entire empire. I was pulling in the big guns. When we got Ember out, no one would be left alive to mess with us. Or her.

Merck pulled his old man car next to my SUV. This man was my secret weapon. He may have been a retired cop, but he loved his own. It was time to clue him in to the danger Ember was facing.

I held the envelope that proved that Ember was his daughter. I'd broken into his house myself to get the sample from his brush. Ember's hair was all over her room. After getting it tested, it was beyond a reasonable doubt that he was Ember's father.

Ember and Nix's mother had tried to leave Nix's dad years and years ago. Ember was the only evidence that she had loved Merck. He didn't need this proof to help me. He'd help because I'd asked. Just because Ember's mom, Elise, had asked.

Patrick Merck was a true man. A good man. He was devoted to his horrible wife. He was almost my adoptive father. Circumstances had changed the paperwork but not the reality that he was devoted to me. And I was to him.

I got out of the driver's side and embraced the man. He seemed a bit faded now. His hair grayer, his midsection a little soft. But he whacked my back with the same vigor.

"Hey! How's it going? You got me any grandchildren yet?" He kept a hand on my shoulder and squeezed.

He insisted on treating me like a son and I never missed it. We shared a mutual respect that ran deep.

"Nah. Not yet, big man. T's holding off on that for a bit." I smiled wide and it was echoed on his face. We didn't mention that T was a talented assassin and that play dates at the local park weren't in her future anytime soon.

"Listen, I hate to cut to the chase, but we have a situation that requires all hands on deck. Even yours." I handed him the envelope that would confirm what he'd known unofficially for the entirely of Ember's life.

He took it and held it. Whatever I was asking, he knew I was desperate, because I'd never tapped into his contacts on the right side of the law before.

Merck let go of my shoulder to hold the envelope with both hands. The smile fell from his face. I'd gotten serious fast on him. I needed to remedy that with a visit if we all lived through what I was proposing.

Merck tore into the envelope like it was a bill to be paid. It was so much more. I watched his eyes as they raked over the page. I knew he was seeing that he had for sure fathered a child with the woman he loved. Nineteen years earlier. I saw the goose bumps raise on his forearms. He swayed a bit and I put out an arm to steady him.

"She's mine." He looked from the page to the sky.

"I knew you said that you didn't need to know. But..." I watched as his knees almost collapsed. I stepped up to him and held his shoulders.

"She's so beautiful. Just like Elise. So much fire in her." Emotion hit him. His eyes filled up. It brought a lump to my throat.

"She's amazing. And I'm not surprised that you're her dad." I made sure he was solidly on his feet before stepping back.

"Why are you telling me this?" He patted the paper with one hand.

I sighed deeply. This was the part I needed to have him trust me with. "She's being held."

And like that, his professional demeanor snapped over him like war paint. He wanted details, time, places. And I'd give him all the things he was asking for. "But first, I need you to understand what's at stake. And how illegal this is all going to be."

"I'll save her if it's the last thing I do." I'd heard that said in the past, but I'd never seen a gun cocked in someone's eyes before. He meant it.

60

Lock

S HE WAS NESTLED NEXT to Cosmo and they were
trading confidences. Well, that's how I thought of it.
And I didn't want to think about it.

When Felon told me I was going on the plane with Ember
and her boys, I thought it was a shit idea. Taking off to a
different part of the country seemed like a needless risk. But
then I realized that we'd be off the compound, which would

increase the possibility of getting away without getting about 400 million bullets lodged in our backs.

Felon was sitting in the back. I was so used to him being quiet in front of others that I didn't even try to ask him questions anymore. I'd shined my hatchet. I pictured chopping off Olin's head. I put it back and then she smiled at me. Over her shoulder, full-on smiling at me. Then she seemed to remember herself. She turned to talk to Cosmo again.

Her naked body slammed into my imagination again. Between them both. And then on her bed for me. So different. When she was for me, spread for me. Coming for me.

I had to adjust myself. Thinking of her like that was complicated surrounded by dudes. I couldn't stop the boner, so I moved my hands to cover it as casually as I possibly could. I needed to stay on point. Ready to move. She was clouding my head. Well, she always did, but now I had actual images of her nude body in my head.

I didn't have time to tell Nix, Animal, and T about the impromptu visit to the mountains to ski. I hoped they knew. I tried to imagine where we were going, but no one was even telling me if we were going across country or north a few states. I glanced back at Felon. He was sensing my restlessness because he raised his hand and lowered it, as if to request that I turn down my anxiousness a notch. I listened and took my seat.

We'd been on the plane at least three hours, so I was figuring we were up by Canada, maybe. When we landed, it seemed like a private airport, judging from the staircase they rolled over to us to disembark. After Cosmo helped Ember down the stairs, we all carried the bags behind them to the waiting cars.

I didn't like it. Too many ways for Olin to track us. But then

I realized Cosmo didn't mind if his father knew where we were. He wanted the whole "your future wife is a giant bed swapping maniac" thing to blow over.

I flashed to her, her face etched with pleasure. It had been so special, I felt rage that she had to use her body to save Cosmo. Though doing it had saved her as well, I think she'd put that together when she saw them naked. The minute that Olin realized they were a gay couple Ember was doomed. She was a clever girl. Quick on her feet. Thank God.

Cosmo, Felix, and Ember led the way. Rumors had gotten around, so I saw Volt and Skinny hitting each other and wiggling their eyebrows. They didn't know about me. Felon and I went in our own car. He still said nothing, but offered me a piece of gum. Happy it wasn't a Tootsie Roll, I took it.

We sat in silence for the hour ride. Judging from the signs we were in upstate New York. We'd passed the sign for Poughkeepsie a while back.

Pulling up to the cabin, I realized it was more like a resort. Or a wooden mansion. The layout was perfect if you wanted to sequester yourself and your gay lover far away from prying eyes.

There was a bottom floor for security and the upper three floors were for Cosmo, Felix, and Ember. Felon was picky about rooms. He chose a weirdly laid out one for me, which required me to go through his room to even enter. There were no windows either. It was almost as if a walk-in closet was renovated to be a bedroom. There was a bathroom between Felon's room and mine.

After we'd unpacked our weapons and checked that they were properly working, Felon closed his door to the hallway. He opened a closet in my bedroom and pointed up to the air vent.

I went to my tiptoes and pushed on the vent. It lifted to reveal the inner working of the old cabin. Felon pointed to it.

"If your girl gets this bedroom on the third floor, that goes up a floor and you can climb up in there." I nodded and pulled the door closed behind me. "I've made mistakes. But I think you deserve a bit of happiness, even if you only get it here." Felon unpacked his stuff. The giant, bulk store-sized bag of Tootsie Rolls had a drawer of its own.

Later that evening, I passed a note to Ember letting her know that I'd be climbing up the air vent to see her. Felon had assured me there were no cameras in her room. I said I would knock.

I wasn't sure what happened upstairs for dinner after the pizza man left the food with us. Felon volunteered to start guard duty and told me that I could swap off with him at six a.m.

I showered and waited, wearing sweatpants and an old T-shirt. I thought of Mom and Rhy. This might be a place I could pinch off a note to them. I pictured the snowfall on the sloping hill behind the "cabin" until the dark fell as well.

When it was solidly evening, I walked over to the closet and pulled open the door. The climb through the air vent was easy. I used the pipes to help me pull myself up. Clearly, I wasn't the only one who'd done this climb. There were worn spots that had shoe treads on them. Then I wondered how Felon had known about it. Maybe he took the same trek to see Cosmo's mom.

There was a good amount of light shining above me, which was puzzling until I arrived at the top of the vent. Her closet was wide open and my girl was sitting there cross-legged, waiting for me.

She yanked on my shoulders and then my pants as she lay

back and drew me on top of her. I kissed her gratefully for a few minutes. Eventually, I had to pull her forward underneath me until I could kick the closet door closed with my foot.

We made out like it was stolen time, because it was.

61

Ember

I RIPPED HIS SHIRT off his body. I should get details. How were we going to manage this? Should we set an alarm? It didn't matter because his lips tasted like a promise of pleasure. And I was a junkie for that feeling. I wanted him before I was trapped, but now that I'd had him, he was the answer to the hole in my heart. The emptiness I'd had since I pushed my brother and Animal and T away. He knew I was a prisoner. And he made everything melt away. I kissed his shoulder and then flipped him on his back. He held my thighs as I straddled him. I had lace panties under my T-shirt. He skimmed the hem of them with his fingers. I leaned forward and kissed his chest, licking and nipping from one nipple to the other. I pushed up to capture his earlobe between my teeth.

He slid my panties to the side and found my clit. I swiveled my hips to encourage him. With his other hand he cupped my breast, rubbing my nipple though my T-shirt.

I tilted my head back, sitting harder on his hand. He had a wicked smile as he let go of my breast and used both hands to bring me closer to the edge. Between the rubbing and having his fingers inside of me I knew I'd be done soon. His chest was lean, but the muscles moved as he watched me with lust in his expression. I pulled off my shirt, because he deserved the tits.

His pupils widened. And then it was as if the sight of me in my panties sitting on him was too much. He growled a little and then lifted me off his hips.

I waited to see what he planned for me. He picked me up and carried me to the bed, stopping to put his mouth all over my breasts. I arched my back in his arms.

Like this for him, with him I wasn't afraid of anything. The desire for him tripped a safety switch for me. There was only a carnal need to get his dick inside me. He tossed me onto the bed and slid my panties off.

He looked between my legs and sighed. "That's the prettiest pussy in the world."

I laughed as he treated me like I was art hanging in a museum. He pushed his sweatpants down and stood naked for me.

I went to my knees and met him halfway in the middle of the bed. Like this, on our knees, we kissed. And then it switched. It went from playful to serious. He kissed me deeper.

His hands skimmed my back and grabbed my ass, pulling me against his chest.

"Ember," he breathed my name before kissing the crown of my head, then my nose, then my lips gently.

"Lock," I said his name and kissed his chin.

"If I'm the lock, you're the key." He arranged my legs so I was straddling him again and then used the motion of falling on the bed to enter me. I threw my head back. He was perfection.

62

Lock

L YING ON HER BED with her on my chest, I thought
my heart would explode. I wanted this with her. I was
shit for planning for my future since my dad had gone
to prison. She made me a superhero. Her eyes on me made me
stronger. Smarter. Stupider, too.

I had it for her so bad. Felon's story hit me in the balls,
because I was starting to wonder if I was doomed to repeat it.
My brain fought me.

I ran my fingers through her hair. "I miss the colors."

"You're my colors." She grabbed my hand and put it on her breast. I slid it over to feel her heartbeat. "Do you trust Felon?"

She was thinking, too. Hoping, too, maybe.

"I trust him with your life. And that means more to me than mine." I kissed her forehead and she rolled her hips.

"God, just being near you turns me on."

And then I handled her all over again. There'd never be enough. Making love to her was like dipping my dick into heroin. I wanted it all the time. I was pretty sure I would die to get a taste.

The clock on the wall told me our evening was nearing an end. We had to talk about more stuff. Prepare us for the eventuality that all of this was going to shit. Cosmo was a gay man in love with Felix, or so it seemed.

His father was going to react. Shit. Olin had kidnapped Ember, knowing she was Mercy's sister. He had a big, giant pair of balls. It was either because he was good at what he was doing or crazy. Maybe both, which made me more afraid than anything else.

63

Ember

I HELD THE BEDSPREAD around my naked body as Lock
disappeared into the closet. It was not lost on me that my
fiancé was hiding in the closet and my lover was coming
out of one.

I closed the door and sat back down on the floor. I needed
to come up with a plan. A plan that was so good that it could
save him. Save my brother and Animal and T. I felt despondent.
I was only a nineteen-year-old chick. What the hell was I going

to do? When the solution hit me, I bit my bottom lip. There was something that I could do that none of these guys could. Maybe I was onto something. It'd require me to do something I never thought I could. It made me braver, though. His love and my plan were doing good things to my head. I had to do what my mother hadn't.

Exhausted from our night of making love, I tossed on a nightgown and crawled into bed. When I got up to check the heat, because it was sweltering in my part of the house, I ran into Cosmo.

He handed me one of the cold bottles of beer he was carrying. They already had the tops popped off. "Here, take this. I'll grab Felix another."

I took the bottle and tipped it back for a swallow. The thermostat was set at eighty degrees. I tapped the beer against the display. "We cooking meat here?"

Cosmo raised his eyebrow. "We certainly have some hot sausage upstairs." I couldn't help but laugh. His grin in return was beyond carefree.

"It can't last forever, though, right? I wish it could." I pushed the button down until the numbers read seventy.

"It maybe can? Like after you and I get married? We can sort of do what we're doing now? And well, after a few years, I'm sure the watch will lighten up. We do a few outings like this, show that we come back and can be trusted?"

I heard the word "years" and I felt it in my soul at the same time. Being with Lock was so much better than it was before he was coming to my room. But it was far from the life I wished I could have with him.

"That's a lot of time and what-ifs."

The door opened above and Felix stepped out onto the landing, smiling and without his glasses. He looked much younger that way.

"We can talk about it when we go back home. I think we can make it work. Stick with me, Ember." And with that, Cosmo trotted back up the stairs. Felix took Cosmo's beer from him, but snatched his hand and pulled him back into the room before Cosmo could go back downstairs to get another.

Maybe there was a crazy way to make it all work. Not ideal. And pretty dangerous...but maybe.

———

The week in the cabin was heaven compared to what I'd been through. Felix and Cosmo had the topmost floor to themselves. For the most part, they stayed up there. Felon had arranged for Lock to have the "flu."

His "flu" was being upstairs and living with me for the week.

We had sex, made love, and fucked. All different flavors of making the most of our time and our bodies. It was the worst idea, because with every hour we spent together, we realized how much we were missing when we were apart.

He was hilarious. His stories about being a young kid in his neighborhood were amazing and heartbreaking. He loved his sister so much. His mom was a spitfire. His father was a good man who did a hard job, and it was devastating that he was in prison for murders he didn't commit.

And then there was Lock. His big mouth got him into a lot of trouble. He let me draw him. We binged on some of the movies that were stocked in the TV. He showered up here, with me. There were a few games of strip poker. So much cuddling. We held hands all the time. We danced. It was like we were trying to fit an entire lifetime into a week.

"You're the inhale; I'm the exhale. One is useless without the other," he murmured with his head on my naked chest.

I learned what he looked like growing his five o'clock shadow. We both sucked at cooking. The pantry at the cabin was stocked. We kept the blinds tightly closed, despite the breathtaking view. Though it was supposed to be a skiing trip, none of us hit the slopes.

The morning everything changed, we were starting the routine. I was in the small kitchen attached to my room, wearing nothing but Lock's T-shirt. He was wearing his sweats and sitting shirtless at the table. Toast and eggs was the attempt today. A loud thwack made us both turn our heads. I turned off the stove. Lock was up in a second, headed toward where he thought he heard the noise when it sounded again.

It was coming from my closet. Felon shouted up, "Get down here, kid. Olin's in the driveway."

I didn't even know Felon could talk, but Lock didn't seem alarmed. He kissed me quickly. "Get dressed. Hide anything that gives us away."

He kissed me deeply and then dropped into the vent. I slid the cover over the top. I rushed around, doing what he said, making it look like I was here by myself. Then I realized that Felix and Cosmo didn't know.

Shit, shit, shit.

I ran out onto the landing and looked down the stairs. The door was opening. Olin pegged me with his creepy stare. His fur jacket was dusted with snow. I sprinted up the stairs. As I banged on the door with a flat hand, Olin was starting up the stairs. What the hell I thought was going to go on, I wasn't sure.

When Felix answered the door in a towel, I felt my stomach drop. Then Olin arrived behind me, pushing me roughly through the door. Cosmo was sitting, dressed in the kitchen. He stood when he saw his father.

"Dad. What are you doing here?"

"You're gay. You good-for-nothing, slippery little asshole." His father advanced on Cosmo.

He'd changed. Olin. He wasn't treating Cosmo with reverent kid gloves anymore. This was not the relationship between a spoiled boy and his adoring father.

The murder was back in his eyes. He slapped Cosmo across the face. Cosmo shook his head. "No. Dad. It's not like that. We really enjoy his company. Ember and I. We really like it."

It sounded hollow in my ears, and I knew it felt hollow in Olin's evil soul.

Lock was outside the door with Felon and Volt. Skinny was nowhere to be found. I had put on soft sleep shorts in my haste. Cosmo's two bodyguards stood behind him. I turned toward Lock. Felon had his hand on his arm.

I shook my head. *No, don't come in. I've got it,* I told him with my eyes. With my begging gaze. My heart was pounding in my throat.

If Cosmo died, I died. That's what I knew for sure. Olin raised his hand to hit Cosmo again. Felix caught the old man's wrist. There was fight in Felix's eyes.

"Don't hit him."

Olin ripped away from Felix's grasp and grabbed his bodyguard's gun. I saw the mask of rage. The one I'd been dreading.

Olin put the gun to Felix's head and pulled the trigger. I screamed because I couldn't not. I would see the snap back of his head over and over and over when I closed my eyes. Laura. Now Felix.

Lock was behind me, picking me up off the floor. I didn't realize that I had fallen to my knees. I felt like I was scrambling, trying to run, but my feet wouldn't take me.

Cosmo's face lost all emotion, as if watching Felix crumble to the floor was attached to his human feelings. And then he started to scream. Low and deep.

"No. No!"

I stepped back as if the horror was something I could get away from. Felix's head was a mess. It was very clear he'd stopped breathing. Stopped living. Stopped loving.

"You useless old fucking shit!" Cosmo stepped toward his father, rage unbridled. One of the bodyguards stepped up to him. No one was touching Olin.

Olin had lost his mind. "Felon. Kill her as well. We'll start from scratch."

He pointed at me, and I felt Lock's grip tighten on my arms. I shook my head no. It was an idea. A horrible one. But an idea.

"I'm pregnant with Cosmo's baby," I uttered the words and then started to pray. Pray that no one else knew about Lock. Prayed that Cosmo wasn't going to rat me out in his grief.

"That's right. Fuck you, Dad. She's got the next heir on board. How about fucking that?" Cosmo lurched forward and grabbed me. Lock was reluctant to let me go.

I felt like I was going to pass out. I wasn't breathing. We weren't breathing. Olin's eyes had prominent red veins. The air was thick with emotion and decision. And Felix's murdered body.

I felt a rush of nausea and I covered my mouth. I made it to the trash can where I hurled. I felt someone rubbing my back. I peeked over my shoulder to see Cosmo.

When I turned, Olin was straightening his jacket. He painted a garishly inappropriate smile on his face. I grabbed the hand towel off of the oven and wiped my lips.

"This is great news. Great news. Glad you were able to knock her up. That's marvelous. So let's assume the wedding will go on as planned."

Olin strode forward and took my hand. "This is good. We'll get you the best care possible. You'll come with me now. Of course."

He tugged me behind him. Felon stepped in front of Lock. I couldn't see what was going on between them, but as I was pulled down the stairs and pushed into the limo that had quietly brought death to our door, I realized I was being kidnapped from my kidnappers. And I wasn't safe anymore.

64

Ember

ON OLIN'S PLANE I was in the seat in the back. Olin was ignoring me. His two huge bodyguards kept watch over me. I felt chilly and tried to warm myself up. The larger of the two bodyguards on the plane stood and got me a thin airplane blanket. I nodded when I took it, my mind replaying the horror of the last few hours. I'd just reacted to the situation. I knew if Cosmo died, I was next. And there had to be a way to keep Lock and me alive. Claiming to be pregnant worked. But I doubted it would buy me much more time before the wedding.

I'd saved my life and hopefully Lock's, but just for a little while, only as much time as it took to get a pregnancy test. Once Olin realized I was lying, it was over. And Cosmo had tried to help, but he was an emotional basket case. The thought of watching Lock die was terrifying. I felt sick again. I tried to bat it down but took off running for the bathroom. After I dry-heaved, one of the bodyguards offered me a water.

I sat back down in my seat, my mind swimming in irrational thoughts. Maybe I could jump out of the airplane. Maybe I could attack them all right now.

Without Lock I was losing it. His presence had been my only balm. A way to calm myself. The plane started on its descent. It was time to pay the piper. As we disembarked the plane, I was starting to feel faint.

"We're going to take a quick pregnancy test to make sure you weren't lying to save your hide." Olin patted my back and I pulled away.

I expected a test from the drugstore, but instead, we were at an Urgent Care. A blood test. I was doomed. This was it. This was the way it ended for me. I searched for a pen to maybe write a quick note to Lock, to Nix. Tell them I loved them both. In the waiting room my gaze was drawn to a sick kid blowing his nose. Such a normal sight on an unreal day.

Olin stayed with me. I'd had a wild thought. Maybe I could attack the nurse. Run. But when the woman walked in, she looked like everybody's grandma. She was sweet with me, though clearly confused by Olin's presence. She handed me a cup for a urine sample and explained that she would also be taking a blood test.

I hopped off the table and took the cup. I glanced at the exit door on my way to the bathroom, but the exam room door was still open. I could feel Olin's stare on me.

Inside the bathroom, I did what was necessary. As I opened the little metal door to place my sample inside, I saw a piece of paper.

"If you need help and don't feel safe, please tell one of our staff that we are out of paper towels."

The bathroom had a hand blower. It was clever. There was no need for towels, but it wasn't something that would stir an alarm.

My mind began racing, trying to figure out what the best decision would be. I didn't want the kindly nurse killed. And I had no doubt that Olin would order his men to do just that. I thought of the kid in the waiting room with the stuffy nose. I didn't want to put him in danger either.

But I knew I wasn't pregnant. Or if I was, it would be too soon for a test to give a positive result. When I came back into the exam room, I felt like I uttered the sign's words while someone had my throat in a chokehold. But I got them out.

The nurse didn't react. Maybe she didn't know about the code phrase?

"Are you two related?" She checked her chart.

Olin responded, "Yes, I'm her father."

There was a way about her, so in charge of her space and environment, that when she handled Olin, he listened.

"Sir, you can't stay in here. She and I will have to discuss her menstruation at length."

I tried not to let my excitement show.

She ushered him out the door and then closed it. She pulled her phone out and set it to a loud white noise app. Then she came close to me.

"What's going on?"

Her gentle brown eyes went steely. From caretaker to

superhero. I had chills. I couldn't ask to be saved. That wasn't going to work. But maybe, just maybe, she could help me.

"That man I'm with? It's okay. He's okay. But I need him to think I'm pregnant. It's the only way." I touched her forearm. She had to trust me. And not overreact. I was taking a huge risk. Maybe too huge.

"I can help you get away. I have ways. We can admit you. I can get the cops here."

She spoke in between her sentences, regular questions about my period. She was good at this. Really good.

"If you want to save me, please tell him I'm pregnant. It's everything I need right now. If I'm not, I'm in danger. And it's not just me. It's other people, including you and everyone in the waiting room. There's a little boy out there. Please. Just tell him that I am, and I promise you I will be okay." I held my hope in my chest with my breath.

She assessed me once and then twice. Then she cued up the needle. She tapped the vein she needed and extracted the blood. I had flashbacks to Felix. Flashbacks to Laura. The nurse left, saying she'd have the results soon. Olin walked in behind her.

I felt faint again. Olin snorted and then stepped closer. "Feeling unsure? Honestly, I picked you for this very reason. To create an heir. Cosmo has been a disappointment. I kept hoping he would be more."

I gave Olin a tired stare. "You're the very worst. I hate you so much. Fuck you."

Olin's eyes rolled into his head. If the nurse didn't do as I asked...who knows what would happen next.

In less than ten minutes, the nurse came back into the room. She looked hesitant, but said what I needed her to.

"I have good news. You're pregnant. Congratulations."

I snapped into the role. I covered my stomach with my hands.

Olin started to clap like this was great news. Like he'd waited all his life to hear it. "Oh, you'll marry Cosmo. And soon. This'll be fascinating. Look at you! Managed to get a baby in you, after all."

Olin put his hand on my back and helped me down from the table. I was an asset now. I squeezed the nurse's hand as I went by. She'd just saved a lot of lives, at least for a little while. I didn't even catch her name.

65

Lock

COSMO FEYBI WOULDN'T LET go of Felix's body. Felon was tracking Olin, or so he said. I was trying to run and stay at the same time. It was like I was going to tear myself in half.

I could run away. That was a choice now. But then I wouldn't have access to Felon anymore. Or maybe I would. Felon showed me his text from Olin. He was taking Ember to the doctor. A blood test. I sent a message to the emergency cell service that Animal had made me memorize. I gave them all the information I could.

I got a quick response:

> Stay with Cosmo

And that was all I had to go by. Cosmo's deep, repetitive sobs were horrible to listen to. His pain was so acute. You could almost see his heart trying to beat around the blade of the knife.

Our plane was getting readied. Skinny and Volt were visibly uncomfortable. Felon was the one to pick Cosmo up and somehow calm him enough to transport him. I followed behind. Skinny and Volt would stay here to handle the dead body. Felon and I were in charge of the guy who wished he were dead.

It was almost a white noise of panic in my head. All this time I'd been in the Feybis I was able to pin my gaze on Ember when I was worried about her. And now...after this past week...she was more mine than ever.

Was she really pregnant? Did girls just know shit like that? I didn't think so. I thought of Ma and Rhy. Maybe they would love a little baby. How dare I think like that? Ember was now with Olin who'd just shot the love of his son's life to prove a point.

She was anything but safe right now. Felon offered Cosmo a stiff drink on the plane. He downed it. Felon and I sat in the back of the plane.

He glanced at a text message and whispered to me, "She's okay. Pregnancy is confirmed. We have to keep Cosmo alive because he wants them married."

Relief and fear collided in my mind. Ember would be kept alive—that was good. But I was going to be a dad? I thought about Felon's scenario. Staying within a stone's throw of his own child all this time. If I lived long enough. Ember was in Feybi's care. And now she was actually pregnant. It was a mind scrambler.

The next time Felon went up to refill Cosmo's drink, I texted the information to Animal's emergency number.

Seconds later, I had another message:

> Destroy the phone

I got up and went to the bathroom. I tore the phone apart. I stomped on the sim card and flushed the pieces. When I came out, Felon was waiting for me with a drink of my own. He had the same. Cosmo was lying on the leather couch, quietly dying inside. For now, keeping him alive was my way back to Ember.

Was she pregnant? Seemed so if the blood test said yes. I trusted her. I loved her. But I never asked what had happened to her before I was able to be with her. Could it be someone else's baby? Not that it mattered. She had to stay alive.

I sat next to Felon and we finished our drinks.

66

Animal

WE'D HAD TROUBLE LOCATING them at first. But then there was a ping on the tracker and we knew they were in New York. They stayed there for a week. And then the shit hit the fan. Both T and I were working furiously while Nix lost his cool. When we heard from Lock that Ember was with Olin, he went straight to the weapons room and loaded himself up for a battle. I heard him mumble,

"Pregnant?" Then as he stood behind me, getting real-time reports, he took a knee. Like a knight waiting to serve a queen.

But this queen was his sister. I didn't want to imagine what it was like for him. Was he reliving his mother's turbulent pregnancy with Ember?

When T yelled that she had contact with Lock, Nix was on both his knees. A suffering skeleton.

"He says she's getting a blood test."

Nix snapped to and made his way to his computer, using two at once. "It's best she is? Right?"

T and I made the decision. Olin seemed obsessed with an heir. We'd done our research. He was investing in LLCs and making trusts.

"I can't find them. We'll watch to see if any of Ember's files are pulled for medical information, but we can go to the airport and research from there." Nix stood from his computer and unplugged his laptop from the power source. "Now. We go now. Whatever we have to do. I'm not playing games anymore. I'm going to get my sister."

And I knew our time was limited. I wanted to get Ember and Lock out. Maybe I was the worst of all because I was thinking about losing her, and the ramifications that would have on Nix and our company. He didn't know about Merck...yet.

T packed a bag. They would go. I would stay. Ember was to be saved, or we would all go down in flames with her.

67

Ember

OLIN WAS AN ABSOLUTE psycho. Not even dealing with the news that his son was gay. He glossed over the whole thing in his head. Like killing Felix would make the fairy tale in his head true.

I looked at my stomach. I wasn't pregnant, despite all the throwing up I'd been doing. Maybe I couldn't make murder work in my head. And I was okay with that. My psyche was reacting to the violence. Olin had taken me to a house on the ocean, the off-season lending itself to privacy. That, coupled with the hugeness of the estates surrounding us, made me lose hope of alerting a neighbor. To what, I wasn't sure.

I wanted to get to Lock. And as far as I knew, our week in heaven was secret from everyone except Felon. And he didn't talk, though that didn't mean he couldn't tell people things.

It's crazy that your body can only stay at a heightened state of panic for blocks of time. And then you think.

And then you plan.

And then you get angry.

I was in a pretty room with a view of the ocean. The white curtains were billowing. I stood between them. In my head I compared myself to whom I thought my mother was. In my memory. I knew she was beaten. I knew she was killed. The few pictures I had of her were not clear enough. Since knowing Nix, he'd shown me more about her.

But there was the knowledge that Merck could be my father. The man with the kind eyes that I'd met with Animal. A baby would be his grandchild, if he was truly my father.

Olin knocked on the open door. "Pardon me?"

I could see his reflection in the window next to me. His shock of white hair. I turned around because I didn't want to have my back to him, not because I wanted to see him.

I lifted an eyebrow. He was asking like I was a guest he didn't want to trouble.

"I wanted to make sure that you had everything you need." He almost bowed.

"I'm captive. So everything sucks." My mouth got away from me. Maybe it was the exhaustion talking. The lack of Lock talking.

"Of course, of course. I understand. I just wanted to know for your health. Do you need food?" He stepped into my space, all humble. The last two days he had left me be. His minions delivered food.

It didn't make sense. He didn't make sense. I tested him. "I know that fruits and vegetables would be good. And a nice water cooler. I'm thirsty all the time."

He deferred to me, promising to see to my needs. Instead of thanking him, I nodded. I recognized this version of Olin. It was the way he'd treated Cosmo before he killed Felix. I wasn't a psychologist, and I'm sure someone somewhere could write one hell of a paper on him, but maybe, if he didn't snap, I might be able to play this game with him. Treat him like a spoiled child would.

He shuffled out of the room, very unlike the booming, insane person that I was used to. I narrowed my eyes.

"Close the door," I demanded.

His old, orange-tan hand grasped the doorknob. "Of course, my dear. Of course."

It popped back open and his creepy face hovered there. "You can't ignore the wedding plans. I want to make sure it's the event of your dreams. White dress, handsome groom. All the trappings of a wedding."

I crossed my arms and turned my back on him. The door clicked shut, but I could hear Olin chuckling like a madman. I let Lock's smile fill my mind and bring me courage.

68

Lock

WHEN WE TOUCHED DOWN in Denver, we had to pass the famous horse with the glowing eyes. It felt ominous. Felon updated me that we were going to a safe house with Cosmo. Soon, Ember and Olin would arrive for an impromptu wedding. It was surreal. I'd destroyed the phone I had, so I was looking for opportunities to contact Nix and Animal.

Cosmo was lying on the beat-up couch in the house Olin

apparently rented or owned. I felt a little bad for him, but more so for me. The week we'd spent together was stupid. Because I'd tasted what forever could be like with Ember. And it was amazing.

We were too young. We were too far in for each other. And we were both captives. Felon was whittling. I wasn't sure what he was making; he always seemed to be moving his hands. In the quiet, Cosmo fell asleep and started snoring.

Felon set down his work and motioned for me to sit down at the kitchen table with him.

The seats creaked and groaned as we pulled them under us.

"How are you?" Felon folded his hands and waited.

"Not sure. Nothing feels real. Thank you. For giving me that time with Ember." I had to thank him, even though we were all in this purgatory.

"He's gay." Felon indicated with a tilt of his head to Cosmo.

"Seems like." I wasn't sure where he stood on the subject. He was from a different generation.

"Olin won't go for that. He's pretending now. He can wish away things he doesn't want to face." Felon's eyes clouded with sadness.

"Do you think Ember's okay with him?" I tapped my fingers on the table, making sure to keep my voice hushed.

"Yeah. She's part of the dream. As long as she's got a baby, she's in the clear." Felon sat back and looked over at the sleeping Cosmo.

I felt helpless and useless sitting here while she was trapped somewhere without me. It was all a mirage anyway. Me believing I could keep her safe while I worked for Feybi.

"We'll get back to her. Don't worry," Felon offered

It would be another two days before I saw her.

69

Animal

PART OF BEING IN charge was turning off your heart and tuning into your head. I was doing that. Letting the Ember situation just run in the background of my thoughts.

I moved forward with some property purchases. I met with our guys and gave them orders they already knew about Midville. Stay ready. Stay observant. Really I just wanted to maintain the control in my city.

I was straightening my tie when Nix called. He rarely called. He was more of a texter, so immediately, I was concerned.

"Brother. I had some facial recognition software scanning security cameras, and I found that Ember was at an Urgent Care in Chicago just a few days ago. She left with Olin."

There was hope then. At least she had been alive enough to need any medical care at all.

"T and I are pulling up now. I'll keep you on speaker, but mute your side." I did as he asked.

Now I was privy to whatever he and T found out. T posed as a patient and requested someone named Wanda. Within ten minutes, I was listening while Nix spoke to what sounded like an elderly women. At first, she was not willing to discuss it and claimed HIPPA rules were a problem. Then Nix let his heart bleed out in front of her. That his sister had been kidnapped and he would do anything to find her. That the people she was with were dangerous.

Wanda's voice was lowered in a whisper while she told Nix that she was concerned. A girl and an older man had been in and the girl begged her to reveal fake results to the man.

Bingo. Wanda even had a son who worked at the local airport, so Nix thanked her and promised to find his sister. When they were back in their rented vehicle, I took off the mute button.

"So Baby Girl caught a break. Thank fuck."

Nix responded, "She's keeping herself alive however she can. Next stop is the airport to meet Wanda's son. As soon as we have a location..."

I finished his thought, "I'll be on the next flight. We'll get our girl back."

I just hoped we were in time. And that Ember could keep up with her lies.

70

Ember

I WAS IN A wedding dress. I was about to marry a gay man who had a broken heart. Olin rubbed his hands together.

"You do paint a beautiful picture of a bride. I wanted a big party back at the compound, but considering it's only been three days since I learned I'm going to be a grandpa, this is the best we can do. We'll just get it done quickly. Then, after the baby, we can have a big party. When you're back to your fighting weight." He was wearing a white tuxedo. Battling me for the spotlight I didn't want. Nor would it have an audience.

Ann was here in this old church in Denver with a view of the mountains, having hustled in before I was even in my gown this morning. A priest had been in and out with one of Olin's guards. He looked terrified, so I was assuming he was under duress.

Ann's hand shook a little when she applied my makeup. She had always seemed unflappable, and now she was flapped. If that was even a thing.

I ran my hands down my body. A simple, strapless gown. Olin proudly brought it to me before we boarded the plane to get here before dawn.

He went with simple, but it had a train and a veil. Ann fastened it in my hair.

I was hoping like hell that Lock was with Cosmo. Olin didn't mention it. It seemed that he'd transitioned his treatment of Cosmo to me, or at least my supposed baby. But I was toeing a line. Just like Cosmo had saved me from the spanking, but hadn't been able to save Laura's life, I could only ask for so much. At least this was the conclusion I'd drawn during the few days he kept me prisoner in his house by the ocean.

Ann emerged from the bathroom where her bags were and produced a pregnancy test. "How about we double-check for Olin? Make sure everything is moving along?"

I swallowed hard. I'd gotten my period forty-five minutes ago. Luckily, the ladies' room in this church had tampons. But it didn't bode well that I was wearing white. My nerves were rattled. I locked the bathroom door after taking the test from her hand. I studied the box. Two pink lines, I was expecting. One, I wasn't. And then the jig was up. I dug around in Ann's bag and found a thin pink lip liner. I sat down on the toilet and did what I had to. After waiting the required two minutes, with

Ann knocking on the door, I added the second line with the lip liner. When I tossed the liner back into the bag, I saw a knife. Madams were ready for everything, clearly.

When I handed my test to Ann, she accepted it with a smile, though thankfully didn't study it too hard. "Very good. Nice work."

As Ann fussed with how the veil hung in the back, we overheard Olin on the phone in the hallway.

"Yes. That's fine. Just bring Cosmo and those two. I have a few tuxes here for him. You know what? We'll use one of the guards as his best man. Well, I'm walking my new daughter-in-law down the aisle. Yes. Okay. In an hour." He slid his phone into his pocket.

Ann had toned down her madam flourish a ton. Olin walked back in and tutted over my appearance. "I chose well. So convenient, really, for our families." He started walking in a slow circle around me. "And your brother will be indebted to me because we'll be family. Surely, you recognize the genius in this?"

I shrugged. "If you say so."

I felt Ann bristle behind me. Of course, my new attitude was a bit shocking to her. I was taking chances that were paying off, slightly anyway. I was still here in this dress, so the man got what he wanted, eventually.

The loud sigh of disappointment filled the room, and then I realized it was coming from me.

Olin tilted his head. "Why so sad, princess?"

His use of "princess" reminded me of Animal. Reminded me of Lock.

Olin's phone sounded a tone, and he dug it out of his pocket, putting on his jovial attitude.

Ann started packing up her makeup. "You've made yourself a place here, I see."

She was reaching out to talk, when it wasn't something she did normally. I didn't trust her, so I stilled my lips.

"What happened with Cosmo?" She was fishing.

I turned my mouth down in the corners. "Nothing. The wedding was moved up since I'm pregnant. That's it." After sliding my high heels on, I waited to see what else she would say. She offered nothing, but went to the corner and swapped out her less formal attire for a black gown. I averted my eyes when she was in her underthings. She snickered when she noticed.

"Sweetheart, enough people have seen this old vessel. I'm not shy."

I still gave her my version of privacy, though Olin could clearly see her from where he was huddled on the phone in the hallway.

"I would've married him a million years ago if he'd asked." Ann fixed her hair in the mirror. I must've made a face because she laughed. "We weren't old our whole lives."

The whole conversation was confusing. "He's a murderer."

I mean, that had to be common knowledge. Ann licked her lips like I'd shown her something distasteful. In a wave, I realized that she was probably as deranged as he was if I had to remind her about the murders. About Laura. I still saw her death when I closed my eyes.

I stood in a wedding dress, not in school, having witnessed multiple murders. Scared, trying to control the uncontrollable. I felt the change within me. I'd gotten harder. Meaner. Maybe I was more like my brother than I thought.

I had a fleeting thought about my possible father, Merck. His kind eyes. In that moment, I wanted the life I knew I should be in. These people were using my fear against me. The people I was protecting weren't innocent lambs. They could take care of themselves. I felt the courage start to fill my lungs with hope and plans and the air I was breathing. I could do something. Right now. Lock wouldn't see it coming. No one would.

When I opened my eyes, I saw Lock in the hallway wearing a tuxedo. I smiled at him. Cosmo lumbered into his shoulder. He was either drunk or dying of a broken heart. Probably a bit of both. But I kept my eyes on Lock. So thankful he was here.

Ann put her hand on my waist. "It's showtime."

71

Lock

THE LIGHT FROM THE window behind her made the edge of her dress and veil look like it was glowing. I was stunned. Breathless. She opened her eyes and pierced right into my soul.

If there was a more beautiful sight than Ember in her wedding dress, I didn't want to see it, because I felt like my heart was going to explode already. And then she smiled. Cosmo bumped into my shoulder. I snapped back into reality.

She was about to marry the guy next to me. Not me. I'd stay in their employ as long as I could. After sliding an arm around Cosmo and propping him up, Ember was still smiling.

She said, "I love you," out loud. To me. Well, she was looking right at me. And Cosmo was staring at the floor.

I pointed to my chest, confused.

"So much. Thank you. You did more than you know." A woman stepped next to her. Ann from the guesthouse was dressed up like a bridesmaid.

This farce. This absolute farce made me rage. Like play actors. None of it mattered. Marriage was an ancient ritual ol' Olin thought made him win.

Ember curtsied to me. Then she kissed the tips of her fingers and blew the imaginary kiss my way.

Olin Feybi came sashaying into the hallway. "Oh. No! Is the door open? He's not supposed to see the bride. It's bad luck."

He came forward and pushed Cosmo and me toward the church doors. I risked a final glance over my shoulder. Ember looked radiant, even peaceful. It was off. The terror she normally kept right under the surface of her skin was gone. It was like seeing the old Ember, the girl I first fell for, on the floor of that pizza parlor a lifetime ago.

I took my place at the end of the aisle. Cosmo was softly weeping. I swallowed hard and felt like the whole church could hear me. The edges of the pews had at least ten armed guards. I knew there would be more outside. The priest stood next to Cosmo.

Ember was smiling at me when the music was piped in. The stained glass created a pattern on her dress as she moved forward. One whole side of her became a kaleidoscope of religion. She held onto Olin's arm. She came to a stop halfway down the aisle, though the music continued to play.

Ember handed Olin her bouquet. He was the picture of a

loving grandfather figure. He took the handful of white roses with a puzzled face. She bent at the waist and pulled up her long gown. The glint of silver sticking out of her traditional blue garter was instantly confusing.

She unsheathed the blade and stood. In one swift motion she buried the knife into Olin's throat. His eyes rolled into his head and his tongue stuck out.

Blood spurted down the front of Ember's dress. She turned to me, one last glance before spreading her arms wide. I was running toward her when the first shot hit. And then the second. The gunmen on the side of the church were doing what they were paid to do. I slid toward her on my knees as she fell. I covered her with my body as best I could, cradling her.

Olin was dying a slow, gasping death, insultingly close to Ember and me. Gunfire exploded above me. I stayed low.

"Why did you do that? Ember, why did you do it?" I ran my hand down her body. Her dress was more red than white. I pulled my jacket off and tried to figure out where the fuck the bullet wounds were. The color was draining from her face and lips. I kissed her gently.

"Say it back." Ember tried to lift her hand, but it flopped next to her. I picked it up. Above my head there was an all out gunfight. Screams and grunts from fallen men.

I realized what she'd done. She'd said goodbye to me before she even started to walk down the aisle. She'd told me she loved me.

Her eyes closed. She took a deep breath and then didn't exhale.

You're the inhale; I'm the exhale.

The terror filled me. Losing her. Losing her now. We were just getting started. I screamed at the top of my lungs. I let her lie at my feet as I stood, black suit covered in her blood. Olin finally sputtering to a stop.

Not without her. I couldn't do it. I waited for a bullet to hit me.

She had taken her last inhale, and I committed to my matching exhale.

Romeo and Juliet. How we started was how we would end.

Breathe in.

Breathe out.

Please breathe...

72

Animal

BY THE TIME I got to the church, police surrounded it. Ambulances and hearses were loud and silent, in that order.

I was glad I'd brought Merck. He was able to speak to the cop in charge. He got a list of patients from him and the hospitals they were taken to. And then he dropped the bomb.

"They have one female inside. DOA. The rest are male."

Nix almost went to his knees and I caught up to him. He

and T had arrived just moments before. We'd had a wild goose chase. Following Olin's plane to the beach house, though it was empty by the time we arrived, took a lot of effort to track. After using some satellite footage, we made it to church. Finally reuniting, but on the scene of our worst fears.

Merck was all business. He was using his police voice and demeanor.

T came out of the church before I realized she'd slipped away. Always under the radar one way or another.

"That's an older female. Not Ember." She patted Nix's shoulder. In her other hand she showed me a handful of Tootsie Roll wrappers.

The adrenaline was a rush; it wasn't Ember. And then a push because we needed to get to her. Nix beat himself up the whole time, saying he should have believed his gut when she said she was happy with Cosmo—that she wasn't.

Merck found out where the other female was taken. The cop fluctuated between talking about her in the past tense and present. I saw Merck lean over and ask him softly if she was alive. The cop grimaced, then amended himself, "They haven't called it yet...so..."

Nix headed to one of the SUVs we had rented, ready to leave. T, Merck, and I rushed over to him. He was driving and we were letting him. Merck fed him the directions from his phone.

When we got to the hospital, Nix ditched the SUV in a set of bushes. No time to park. We hoofed it after him, and I caught up and pulled his hood over his face.

He was clearly beyond reasonable thought when he forgot he was a skeleton to the outside world. I looked at T. One of her hands was balled in a fist.

We all hurried into the elevator together. Merck took the time between the floors to update us. He'd gotten a text from someone in the local police department. "They've got one male patient. Young guy. Sounds like your friend Lock. Should we check there first?"

Nix grunted one word, "Ember."

Merck nodded. After we got off the elevator, Merck went with his police badge to the nurses' station. He found out Ember had been taken into surgery. She didn't have updates, but she'd go herself to get one.

The police were posted outside one room, and if I had to guess, I would say that Lock was in there. Merck obviously worked this out as well and asked the cop to let him inside. We followed behind him because we—honestly, as a group—were going crazy. And Nix was almost beyond speech. I was stunned that he wasn't trying to tear down the walls to get to her.

Lock was sitting up and uttered the same word when he saw Nix's face and then mine, "Ember?"

Merck took hold of the narrative. "She's in surgery. We'll get an update soon. Matter of fact, I'm going to stay in the hallway to make sure the nurse sees where I am."

I slapped Merck on the back. Having him here was priceless. We would've been met with more resistance otherwise. We would've found out all this shit anyway, but it would've taken time. Better to just point Nix in the right direction.

Lock put his head in his hands before mumbling, "She's still with us, though. I mean, they're still working on her."

Nix walked close to Lock and snaked his skeleton inked hand through his wrists to grab his throat. "You had a job."

Lock didn't even flinch at the attempt to hurt him. "She took it upon herself. She snapped. Whatever it was, she just lost it. She was walking down the aisle with Olin, and then she pulled out a knife and stabbed him in the throat. And then I caught her so her head wouldn't hit the ground. Her wedding dress was bright red. It went from white to red."

Tears were tracking down his face. He was in the room with us, but clearly his eyes saw the scene all over again.

"It didn't make sense. She's pregnant. I never expected..." He stopped talking as Nix's hand started to close.

I pulled Nix away, having to really force his hand that was an open claw. "Hey, Sweetness. Fenix. She loved him. She was crazy about him."

I made sure to stay between them, but he stopped fighting to choke Lock to death.

"She was breathing, and then she wasn't. She told me she loved me. I should've known she was saying goodbye. All her fear was gone. She was just Ember again." Lock sat back in the bed.

T cleared her throat. "What happened exactly?"

Lock gestured past her, and T had to ask the question again.

Finally, he set the scene for us. "It was just Cosmo, Olin, Ann, and me. The rest were guards... I just don't know where she got the knife... Anyway, so when they saw Ember stab Olin, they opened fire. After I caught her, I stood up. I wanted to die, too. Her lips were so blue. Her breath had stopped. There was so much blood." Lock looked at his hands. I could see dark red caked under his nails. He seemed to get distracted by it as well.

"I didn't get to tell her how crazy I was about her. I'm so crazy about her." Lock tilted his head up to study the ceiling drop tiles.

Nix was curling into a ball, sitting down in the room's one chair as he did so. There was a ghostly whispering coming from inside his hood. I met T's eyes across the room.

I mouthed, "Becca," to her. Nix would need his woman to remember himself. To grieve.

Hell, I'd need mine.

Lock continued, "So I stood up and I wanted to get tagged by the bullets. And Felon, he shot me in the leg. Took me out."

After T was done texting, she went to Lock and moved his blanket over. She peeled back the bandage to see what his wound looked like. "Felon like you?"

T could've punched Lock in the face over and over. I doubt he would feel anything.

Lock shook his head. "I mean, I guess he does. He shot me, though."

T replaced the bandage. "It was like a surgeon put that bullet in your leg. Best place to get shot. Either you're real lucky or he could sign his name on somebody's torso with bullets from 400 paces."

Lock gazed at his leg despondently. "He's a genius with a gun."

T shrugged. "Then he wasn't trying to kill you."

Lock looked at her feet. A few Tootsie Roll wrappers had fallen from her hoodie pocket. "Where'd you get those?"

"The church." T stooped to pick them up.

"That was Felon. He eats one when he kills people." Lock sighed deeply.

"Damn, son," was all I had to offer. Because that was pretty fucking specific.

Merck's voice in the hallway was a distraction. I stepped to the door. The nurse he spoke to before was there with a clipboard. "She's still in surgery. There's extensive damage."

"She's pregnant," Lock offered.

T stepped near to Lock. "She wasn't. We spoke with the nurse at the clinic. Ember was *not* pregnant. Just said she was to stay alive."

Lock was crushed.

The nurse absorbed the information and continued, "She was defibrillated twice in the ambulance. She was gone a few times on the table, too. It's been a lot of blood loss. Just prepare yourselves. We're doing everything that can be done, though." The nurse touched Merck's forearm; he looked like he might pass out.

I stepped next to him and wrapped my arm around him. "She's a fighter. Understand that."

Merck leaned inward. I moved past the nurse after Merck rubbed his shoulder against the doorframe. I walked to the waiting room close by and grabbed two chairs, carrying them back to Lock's room. One for Merck and one for T. We'd be here a while. I'd need another couple chairs. The policemen stationed at the door nodded as I moved past them.

We were going to sit together as the people who loved Ember. And maybe we were going to do some praying.

73

Lock

HER BLOOD WAS ON my fingers. Her love was under my skin. There were times in my life I thought I knew pain. The beating into the Cokes comes to mind. Nothing came close to holding her and feeling her soul leave her body.

In front of me was her family. Her brother. Animal. T. There were a lot of mistakes in this room. But I blamed myself the most. Waiting for the perfect moment. Believing she was doing anything but loving everyone here.

I wanted to say we should have moved sooner. Should have coordinated better. But words were just frames around the failures. She was still with us. Still fighting. That's what the nurse said.

Time never stretched on so long. We saw a rush in the hallway, two nurses running. That had to mean something bad. I wasn't sure if it was about Ember, but it felt that way.

They said I had blood loss. A nurse came in to take my vitals. I was doing just fine.

But her blood was under my nails.

And her love was under my skin.

74

Lock

THIRTEEN HOURS LATER AND she was out of surgery. Ember was still alive. Well, her body was still alive. They had me on pain pills I was against taking. But T had given me a look that made me take them. So I was floating a little bit.

No one was sleeping, but there was pacing, grumbling, and hugging. The fact they stayed with me made me think that they wanted to support me. The other possibility was that her crew was waiting to kill me. They'd be the second to try it in twenty-four hours. Me being the first.

There was a time and place to deal with the fact that I stood up in the middle of a gunfight to try to join Ember. And that Felon shot me to force me back to the ground.

He was gone by the time the ambulances and cops got there. Nix and I quietly worked out that Felon had taken the guys on. That the firefight was likely Felon's response to the guards taking out Ember.

The surgeon knocked on my doorframe. Everyone in the room stood at attention except me.

She nodded as she walked in. "We've got her still. She's in the recovery room. Her vitals are good."

The details of the surgery and the cautions issued washed over me. This was stage two, the struggle. She lost enough blood and her heart had stopped long enough that they were monitoring everything. Nix went in to see her first, with a lady named Becca who arrived just behind the surgeon.

Animal stood at the window of my hospital room as morning rose around him. T rubbed his lower back. Merck sat back down in one of the chairs and held his head.

They took turns, Becca swapping out with a new person. And finally, after Merck had been to see her, they offered to move me to a wheelchair to visit her.

They said that she looked as comfortable as possible, but to prepare myself. The nurse helped transfer me out of bed and into my transportation.

Animal handed me the blanket off my bed to cover my legs. A few hallways over and up an elevator, I was wheeled into the room. Nix was holding Ember's hand, resting his forehead on her knuckles.

She was delicate and healing. The nurse put me on her

other side and I touched her arm. The monitors set the tone for the room.

Nix peered over her hand to me. If looks could kill, I would've been dead. Clearly, I was to blame for where his sister was. And if he wanted to kill me, I'd be easy pickings.

"She talked about you the last time she and I were together." My voice was scratchy.

His gaze didn't soften.

"She said she missed you. And that she was upset that you'd put her kidnapping on yourself." I cleared my throat to try to get a more manly sound to come out. "She loves you."

Nix narrowed his eyes, tilted his head forward, and then gazed back at Ember. We were silent for the rest of my visit. I kissed her forearm just before the nurse took me back. I wanted to tell Ember more. That she was amazing, that she was beautiful, that she was brave for trying to protect her family and to take out Olin. But all that would have to wait. Nix wasn't going anywhere anytime soon.

75

Ember

THE DREAM WAS THE realest thing in the world. I was in my bed at Aunt Dor's house. I looked at my hands. They were smaller than I remembered. I glanced around; the room was different, or rather, looked the way it did before I restyled it in middle school. I sat up and the reflection in the mirror that hung on my closet door was like a video come to life. Fifth grade me.

I lifted my hand and waved, and then mussed up my hair. Yup. It was definitely my reflection. I couldn't remember what I'd done yesterday. Or what day it was. My pink comforter was soft. And the scent in the air washed over me—my childhood in a wave. Muffins baking somewhere. Nail polish remover was a note in there as well. Aunt Dor was doing her own manicure and making snacks for her book club buddies.

I looked back to the mirror, and the older version of myself was there instead. Standing, walking to the mirror. I was transfixed. Still in my bed. Still young. The closer the older me got, the more I realized it wasn't me; it was a person who looked just like me.

Mom.

It was my mother. She stepped through the mirror and into my bedroom. My heart swelled with love and welcome.

"Ember. My sweet girl."

She sat on my bed in a graceful movement and laid her hand on my forehead. I lay back as she tucked the blanket around me.

"Mom?"

She stopped fussing and smiled. "I always wondered what it'd be like to hear you say that. The most beautiful sound."

I sat back up and wrapped my arms around her. She hugged me back hard and started rocking as well. An instinctual thing that I'd seen other moms do with their kids.

"I'm so proud of you. You're strong. And you fight to be happy. I love watching every moment. And I can't wait to see the rest of it. But you have to take all that fire in you and fight. Right now. Get back to Nix. Get back to Lock."

I didn't want to let her go. I didn't know there was a cure for my yearning for a mother. But in that moment, her arms healed me. Centered me. I inhaled. She smelled like cookies and something else...a familiar scent that I couldn't place.

"You can do it. I love you so much. My beautiful warrior. Fight for it. The happiness. Love Fenix and Lock. And him, too."

I was so tired. I had an entire lifetime of questions on the tip of my tongue, but they faded as my mom helped me lie back down, tucking the blankets once again. She kissed the top of my head, and then I slipped into deep blackness again.

———

I wished someone would turn off the beeping alarm, because my head was pounding. My mouth was super dry. And I was pretty sure that my eyeballs had withered under my lids.

The scent of the room was something very specific that I couldn't place for a while.

Dentist?

Maybe. I tried to remember what the hell had happened. Because clearly I wasn't home.

That beeping. Goddamn it. I needed to sit up. It was for sure time to get up to...do something?

I spent another few minutes trying to peel open my eyes. My right one was more successful than my left one. Focusing took another few beats. I looked to my left and to my right. White room. Hospital? That's the scent. It smelled like a hospital. My right hand was imprisoned. I brought it into focus and saw it was covered in bones.

Nix.

My brother.

I needed to warn him about something.

Someone.

I pulled on my hand and his head popped up from where he'd been resting it on the mattress.

Relief and then worry crowded over his decorated face. "You're awake?"

I tried to swallow, but my mouth was super dry. I took my left hand and pointed to my mouth.

"Sure? You're thirsty." He let go of my hand to press the call button on my bedrail that was collapsed under the mattress.

He hopped out and grabbed a plastic cup, filling it from the tap.

By the time he came back, I had tried to sit up. Something horrible had happened to my torso. It felt like I had giant slices taken out of my body.

"Don't move. The nurse is coming. Here, take this." He passed the cup to me. I tipped the water into my mouth and it spilled from the glass onto my chest. I stopped pouring and licked my lips. They were so dry and cracked.

"Lock?" As soon as I swallowed, I got that question out. It was like my brain needed just a spot of water to expand with worry.

Like an explosion, the memory of what brought me here blasted through my mind. Olin, Cosmo, Felix, Animal, T, Nix. *Lock.*

"You have to be careful. Olin..."

I couldn't figure out how in the world that he was in danger, but he was. The nurse trotted through the door and started talking to me sweetly while taking my vitals. Nix patted my hand. "It's okay. Everyone is okay."

"Everyone?" I needed to know about Lock.

"Yeah. Everybody. Lock, too. Felon and Cosmo are unaccounted for." He kept looking at my face and taking deep breaths.

I felt faint, but I was lying down. "Not too much at once, okay, Ember?" The nurse adjusted my pillow, which made the dull pain in my torso a bit better. "You've got to heal quite a bit."

The gunshots. Lock. Nix. He nodded without me having to say a word. I needed to see Lock.

76

Lock

SEEING NIX IN MY room was startling because he'd
spent all his time in Ember's. At first, I feared the worst.
Today was my last day in the hospital. I was actually
dressed in sweats and a T-shirt. I could walk, but I had a cane.
Physical therapy had been brutal, but I was grateful when I
was able to stand with my concern.

"She's asking for you." Nix stepped to the side and gestured
to the doorway.

I pointed at my chest. "Me? Ember's awake?"

Nix seemed like he might shoot me again if I didn't move as quickly as possible. It was unnecessary because I moved the quickest I had yet. My therapist would've been thrilled.

By the time we got to Ember's door, I'd gleaned that she was talking and seemed to remember what had happened. The relief was immense. But to see her.

When I made it to the door, her eyes were waiting for mine. "Thank God."

Ember teared up when she saw me. I didn't realize I was crying until I got to her and bent to lay my head near her shoulder. She patted the side of my face with her hand.

She was just out of it. She seemed numb, but she knew who I was. And that meant she remembered things. Comprehended things. I felt a chair get slipped behind my knees and collapsed in it. We held hands after I wiped my eyes.

"It's going to be okay." She was comforting me. Me.

"It will be. All your people are safe. You're safe." I tried my hand at comforting her in return.

To see her eyes moving, see her lips moving, I'd never been so touched. I moved forward so I could push up enough to kiss her forehead.

She nodded and held tight to my hand. "Don't go anywhere. I'm so sleepy."

The nurse nodded. It'd be okay to let her sleep, even though she'd just woken up. I stayed through the doctor's exam and then the surgeon's. Ember was going to make a comeback.

Nix collapsed in the other chair in her room. "You can sleep if you want. I'm not going anywhere."

He crossed his arms in front of his chest. He slipped into a nap like a cat. I knew he'd been awake for days. I made myself comfortable. I was checking out of the hospital to check right back in. Ember and I would walk out together. No matter how long it took.

77

Ember

THE THERAPIST SAID THAT I'd had a momentary lapse of sanity. That being under stress and duress can do that to a person. And it did that to me. The thing is, I'm not that kind of person. I can't just take a life, see lives taken in front of me, and brush it off. I shouldn't be jealous of that skill that T had, that my brother evidently had. Maybe Animal had, too.

But I didn't have that capacity. I was torn from my sleep by the nightmare of watching my hand stab Olin in the neck. Lock was an immovable force next to me. They let him stay in the chair or a cot, depending who was on duty. He would talk me through the confusion as I walked my pulse back down from a ten to a two.

And we'd talk. And he'd make me laugh. Tease me with dark humor, like telling me if I wanted a red wedding dress, there were easier ways of getting it dyed.

And then he'd climb into bed carefully next to me and let me put my head on his shoulder. And then I could fall asleep again.

Healing and Lock went hand in hand. He was as dedicated to me as I was to getting out of this bed. He was in sweats and a T-shirt and I was in the matching outfit. My hair was in a giant messy bun. And we were holding hands. Lock seemed relaxed and devoted. His concern about my welfare was the sexiest thing in the world. I couldn't do anything about it, but he preened and flexed when I told him, so I did that more than a few times.

Today he was filling up my water bottle when Nix tapped on the doorframe with his knuckles. I nodded to him, admitting him without words. He put his hands in his hoodie pockets and angled toward the bathroom. Lock startled when he saw my brother mid cap twist. The water splashed on his T-shirt and he yelped.

I burst out laughing and Nix sheepishly joined in. Lock rolled his eyes and then went back to refill it, topping off the liquid he'd lost. He handed me my bottle as I tried to swallow my smile. Laughing hurt, so I tried to stop. My mind kept picturing the splash and I'd chuckle all over again.

"I'm going to grab a new shirt from the car. You need anything from the store?"

I shook my head. Animal and T had already brought over armfuls of supplies. I was all set. Lock left for the first time since I woke.

It was time to apologize to my brother. To make him understand. He didn't want to press me, but I felt strong enough to relive at least a little bit for him.

He grabbed a stool and straddled it near my bed. "How you feeling?"

"Better. Every day is better. I think that physical therapist is trying to kill me. But after she leaves, I can always do more stuff than before she came." I stretched my arms above my head like she insisted I do in between sessions.

"Yeah. After I was injured at the Feybis, I had one therapist who I wanted to punch in the face. Worked miracles, though."

Maybe it was because I was trapped for so long, but the kindness in Nix's eyes slayed me. I glanced down when I felt the tears stir up. I never wanted to be a pawn again.

Nix reached out to hold my hand after I dropped my arms. "What's up?"

I wiped at my cheeks and swallowed. "I'm sorry. I'm so sorry for not trusting you. If I had gone with you that first time you came, or even at the dorm... I was so scared that he'd hurt you and Animal and T. He'd killed Bowen. He killed another man in front of me. He said he'd frame me for it if I didn't comply. I'm so sorry."

I watched as his face went from confused to sympathetic to what I would only call vengeful. "No apology necessary." His voice was rough and scratchy. "I'm sorry I didn't see through what he was doing to you. I'll never forgive myself for not just taking you." He gripped my hand. "It's my one job."

"No. I forgive you. And I forgive me. We're alive. We did it. We're here, together. Mom, I think she would have been so happy." I covered his hand with mine. "Do you still have it? I mean, I know I gave it back..."

"Mom's earring?" He let go of my hand to stand and dig out a small paper wrapped package from his pocket. He handed it to me.

I unwrapped it and stuck it in my ear. The nurse had said no jewelry, but I was never taking this out again.

"She would've been so proud of you," he lowered his voice, "that you had the courage to kill him. I wish she'd been able to do that to my father."

I was fortunate that Ann had let me test myself before the wedding and that I'd gotten my period. If I'd really been pregnant, I wouldn't have tried to kill Olin. I told Nix as much. That if I was going to have a baby, I would've never even tried. That Mom was probably putting our lives in front of hers way back when she was killed. Nix sighed. A lifetime's worth of what-ifs expressed with a simple noise.

After a silence, he broached a new topic. "Animal did a thing with your DNA. He got hair from one of your brushes while you were gone."

"Okay?" It was an unusual statement.

"And with Merck's." He bit his bottom lip.

"Oh." And then the meaning slammed into me. He'd tested to see if Merck was my biological father. Without my permission. I was annoyed, but at the same time I felt ready to know the truth. I met Nix's gaze. "And?"

"You're his kid, Merck and Mom's." Nix held my hand again. "You tell me if you want to do something or nothing at all. Whatever you want."

I wasn't even sure what I did want. Almost dying had changed some of my perspective. Lock had told me about Felon and his secret love affair with Cosmo's mom. So many secrets. And all at once I didn't want to have any more. Maybe I aged since I was technically dead. Since I was pretty sure I saw my mother in the afterlife. Or what I thought was my mom. Maybe it was just my dearest wish. But what she said made sense now.

"Love Fenix and Lock. And him, too."

She'd meant Merck. "Okay. Tell him I want to see him."

I heard Lock in the hallway, and then a deep, grumbly voice. I narrowed my eyes with suspicion. "He's in the hallway?"

Nix shrugged. "I really thought you would agree."

Lock walked to the doorway and waved to Merck to come in. Then he seemed to look harder at Merck.

Nix countered the confusion with a quick offer of, "Tell Merck it's okay. She wants to see him."

Lock didn't have to say anything, because Merck was in the door with a bouquet of daisies. "Uh. Hi." He gave me an awkward wave.

I waved back and then gestured to the chair that normally had Lock in it. Merck sat and shifted a few times.

"So, you're my biological father?"

He leaned over and gave me the flowers and then held his hands, palms up, as if he was unsure if flowers were appropriate.

"Animal ran a DNA test," he offered.

I looked for myself in his face.

"You're so much like her. I know people tell you that." He was adorably awkward.

"Tell me something about her. From an adult point of view."

He ran his hand over his tie. "Oh. Um. Wow. Let me think." He shifted in his chair again. "She was crazy about Nix. So proud of him. Would talk about whatever he was doing in school. Showed me pictures he'd drawn. Little things like that. She liked to hold hands. She'd listen to my heartbeat and say that she heard it say her name." He stopped and blushed. He stammered a little.

I tried to comfort him. "It's okay. I know just what Nix can remember. I really like hearing the sweet stuff."

I smiled at him, hopefully in an encouraging way.

"She wanted to leave. I often think he had something on her to get her to come back after she lived with your Aunt Dorothy. I wished she'd told me. I would've done anything. I would've done everything to help her." He tapped his fingers on his knee.

There was a silence. I decided then to tell them both. "When I wasn't breathing on the way to the hospital, I felt myself sort of slipping. And then I felt like I was caught. By Mom. It felt like a visit in my old bedroom."

They both snapped their heads up.

"She was really pretty and smelled lovely. She had a birthmark just at the base of her neck." I pointed to the place just under my hair. "It looked like..."

Nix and Merck filled it in for me, "...a heart."

They were both astonished. Clearly, this was not something I would've known from the few blurry pictures I had of her.

"She hugged me and told me she loved me. And she said to tell you two that she loved you." I left out the part where she tucked me in and then I woke up in the most pain of my life.

Nix held his head and Merck seemed stunned.

"I mean, maybe it was the lack of blood to my brain, but it felt real." I messed with my daisies in the silence.

Nix smiled. "I think that was real. I mean, the birthmark is something you'd never know."

Merck nodded as well. "I bet she saved you. Loved you back into your body. She would've done anything for you kids."

I reached out and grabbed Nix's hand and then grabbed Merck's with my other. I didn't say anything because I didn't need to.

78

Lock

WE'D SAY IT SOMETIMES. That she was the inhale and I was the exhale. It meant more now that I watched her stop breathing. I also reminded her that I was the lock and she was the key. She liked that, would wrinkle her nose every time I said it.

I mean, we were boyfriend and girlfriend. At least that was what the hospital staff called us. Clearly, whatever Ember wanted to call me, I was down for. We had such a similar trauma that having each other was essential.

She was funny, my girl. She liked to give me a hard time, still, and I was lapping it up. When the nurse kicked me out at night, I'd run a few errands. Get Ember some of the girl things she wanted. Animal had seen to it that I had a credit card that worked. He also saw to it that we had a few bodyguards and I had a decent knife.

The bodyguards were required to stay in the waiting room by the elevator, though they'd take turns watching the hallway with the stairs as well.

I had a burner phone with a connection. I'd called my mom a few times. Rhy and I played on the phone as well. She was doing well and my mother was, too. Nix had taken care of them just like he'd promised.

A few weeks into Ember's recovery, I was on a trip to the pharmacy for her favorite hand lotion. After I put down the bottle to pay, a bag of Tootsie Rolls was slapped down next to it.

I didn't have to turn to know who it was. Felon's hand pushed me out of the way and he paid for the lotion and the candy. I followed him out to the parking lot. He had a rental car that he tossed the candy into but then motioned for me to take him to my vehicle.

Animal had left a Charger for me to borrow while Ember was at the facility. When we were in the car and the doors were shut, Felon cleared his throat.

"You okay?" His focus was straight out of the car's front windshield.

"I'm good. Ember's alive. That's what matters." He turned his head to make eye contact.

"Sorry about shooting you. But I needed you to get down." Felon looked at my leg.

"They say it's like a surgeon shot me. I was walking in about two days." I touched the wound on my leg through my jeans.

A smile tipped on one side of his lips. "How's Ember doing? She recovering?" Felon was bouncing his leg.

"She's healing. Has a long way to go. But we'll make it." I put my hands on the steering wheel just to give them something to do.

"I should've seen it happening. It was out of nowhere. Out of character for Ember." Felon sucked on his teeth.

"She said she snapped. Walking to another man when I was right there."

"Sure enough." Felon shook his head as if he was witnessing it again.

"How's Cosmo?" I didn't really care, but I knew Ember would want to know.

"He's a mess. Not recovering mentally yet. Really loved that Felix guy." Felon stopped making his leg jump. "I'm here just to say hey. But also, the family, it's looking to me to take over."

"Shit? Yeah?" I winced. "That seems...risky."

Felon nodded. "Also, few people even know I talk. I let them know I'd think about it, but I wouldn't run it like Olin. Or Bat. I want to try to make it go legit. Reinvest money in the right places. Clean it up. I mean, I know it can't get all the way out, but I want to give Cosmo something that won't get him killed when he inherits it."

"That's commendable." I had some serious doubts. But a lot of the men very loyal to Olin had died in the church that night.

"I was wondering if you'd set up a meeting with Mercy and Havoc for me."

Now I tilted my head. "For?"

I didn't have a bad feeling in my gut yet, but I couldn't see how the family that kidnapped Ember could ever get into their good graces. As far as I knew, they were dismantling the whole organization from the ground up.

"I want to live in my house. I want to meet Cosmo's next boyfriend. Maybe they'll have kids. I just want to be around. I have to protect Cosmo. He's my kid. But I want to make things easier for him. And you." Felon tipped his head toward me. "They good to you?"

"Oh yeah. Taking care of my people and everything." He'd defended Ember and me in that church, by himself. "Thank you. By the way. For taking out everyone. They told me about the wrappers at the church and I knew it was you."

Felon swallowed hard. "No problem. Just sorry they got to Ember. She moved so fast. They just got her twice?"

I nodded. I trusted Felon with information about Ember. Which meant I trusted the hell out of him.

"Yeah. That's hell to recoup from. I wish her quick healing." Felon opened the passenger door. He tossed a burner phone near me. "I have my number programmed in there. Call me if Mercy and Havoc want to talk."

79

Ember

W HEN I WAS MOVED to the physical therapy
facility, Lock could no longer stay with me. I had a
roommate. As soon as he was allowed to visit, he
was there and stayed until the night nurse kicked him out.

He was gorgeous. Not just his face. His attentiveness to me.
The way he joked with all the personnel at the facility, and
beyond. How he took even quiet moments seriously. His focus

and ability to help me were humbling. Hugging me through my guilt over Bowen and Laura's death.

We had this weird thing in common, the Feybis and being taken against our will. He told me one night all about how he wound up as a guard on their property. We interwove our fingers and he told me about Dice being killed. About Olin showing up. About the crooked frames. That he had to leave his mother and Rhy and expected to die every moment he was at Feybi's. Until he met Felon. The non-talker that had a soft spot for Lock's big mouth. He told me that the Tootsie Rolls were found at the scene of the church, that Felon had taken out the guards and he'd shot Lock so he would get down.

When I asked him why he'd stood up during the gunfight, he just shook his head and smiled. "Let's not think about that part. We're here now."

Lock and I played Uno and checkers. He read out loud to me from some of my favorite books. We watched movies on my phone. Nix, Animal, and T all came to visit, though they seemed very busy and happy that I was in one place and that I was staying there. Lock suspected that the fallout from the church massacre was going to be driving their free time for a long time.

My job was to heal. Lock's wound was just shaping up to be a sexy scar. Mine were still bandaged and the locations of my incisions were in rough spots. One close to my shoulder and one near my hip. Moving was trouble. But I had Lock's strong arms a lot of the time. And I had to do it by myself as well. Building up my stamina was required. My PT sessions were grueling.

But I would fight for this part of my life that felt like I wasn't meant to have.

80

Animal

EMBER STAYED IN THE hospital for two weeks. Then she was moved to the physical therapy facility. Lock stayed with her, as did Nix. I went back to Midville with T. We had to play catch-up. Our soldiers had held it down, but some things were still brewing. The Feybi family was recoiling from the death of yet another family leader. The Internet chatter was vague. The only people who knew what really went down were Ember, Lock, Felon, Olin, and Cosmo.

Kaleotos and I met, and I told them now was not the time to overtake the Feybi family. They were at a flash point. And Olin had built up quite an empire. We had to restore business as usual and that's what we did. Nix had moved Lock's sister and mother to a local house in Midville, and T had set up a new service for Rhy. Midville had the headquarters for the school that Rhy had loved in Valston.

I knew that Lock had Facetimed his mother and sister a number of times, even introduced Ember to them digitally.

But today was a big day. After months, Ember was coming home. Nix had changed his shirt three times. We'd all made sure her new room was ready.

The family was getting back together. Lock was due to move in with her. It was the safest way to be. When Lock pulled up carefully in the Charger, Nix opened the front door and we all barreled through it.

Baby Girl was home. She'd thought she was saving all of our lives while staying with Olin Feybi. And maybe she had. And she'd been "framed" for the killing of a man named Files. T handled the evidence one evening. There wasn't much, a gun with bloody prints, some bloody clothes. My poor, sweet Ember.

But now, this was the happiest I'd ever seen Nix. He was like a mama hen with all her eggs set down under her getting warm. I told him as much, only to get a skeleton middle finger in my direction.

After we walked into the house, I came in for a gentle hug and Ember got me back with surprising force. She was strong. PT was doing great stuff for her. Her hair was streaked with fresh rainbow colors. It was really nice to see them. It suited her. T walked next to her and took her purse off her shoulder. Ember navigated the steps easily, but we would have broken all the bones in our bodies before she fell.

We took her to the elevator Nix had installed, which whisked us all to her wing downstairs. He'd stocked the place with presents, food, and balloons. Ember was delighted. She was doing great until she staggered a little, and Lock and Nix insisted she sit down on the couch. Once there, she regained her color.

It was going to be a long road for our girl, but we were happy she was here. Proud, too.

Just the day before, Mercy and I had a meeting with Felon Feybi and Lock. It'd taken quite a bit of restraint not to kill the remaining Feybi for his half-brother's sins.

Lock insisted Felon was good. And he'd helped save Ember and himself that evil day in the church.

It was worth hearing what he had to say. He came to our location without any entourage. He submitted to my pat-down willingly. And then he apologized. He said that he should've taken Olin out himself years ago. He was willing to turn over any and all territory to us in reparations. Felon wasn't interested in the business. He'd lost the woman he loved and just wanted to make things right for his son, Cosmo.

He put a lot of trust right on the table. He was telling us stuff Cosmo didn't even know. We told him we'd think about it and sent him on his way.

I could see a truce down the line. Maybe. But right now, it was magic looking at Nix with a full house. A guy who thought he was alone was anything but.

81

Ember

THE ELEVATOR WAS EXTRA. I could do stairs. But I loved Nix for the thoughtfulness. It was a given that Lock would stay with me. We were inseparable. After we were all moved in, Rhy and his mother were coming over for dinner.

We'd met on Facetime, and I was looking forward to meeting them both in person. I made Lock stop on our way to

Nix's so I could get a toy for Rhy. She was a fan of the smooshie cupcake toys that smelled like vanilla and reduced stress, so we grabbed three.

I held Lock's hand. I thought about Merck saying that my mom liked holding hands. I could get where that came from. Merck was coming over tonight, too, for a homecoming dinner. Becca and Animal were making a feast. It was like a mini Thanksgiving. I put my head on Lock's shoulder.

"We just need to get your dad out of prison," I offered.

He snorted. "You reading minds now, pretty lady?"

"Yeah. I don't know. Dying made me really think hard about living. I want us all to be next to each other. If I could have my mom here, I would. If Nix thinks he knows a good lawyer and Merck has some pull, maybe we can get him an appeal?" I put my other hand on the center of his chest.

"That would be great. For Rhy in particular. She misses Dad harder than any of us. She loves straight on, you know?" He kissed my forehead.

We were quiet for a while before making out. We hadn't been physical since I came back to life. I was far too injured, but we could still touch one another. Revel in the fact that we made it out alive.

He pulled out a box from his pocket. A jewelry box. It was about the size for a necklace, so I wasn't getting marriage thoughts.

He opened it for me. It was a silver lock on a chain. I laughed.

"This is perfect."

He helped me put it on.

Then he revealed a key on a ball chain and slipped it over his neck. "It fits in your lock."

"That's pretty sexual," I offered.

"I hope so." He whispered into my ear, "So, does this mean we're going out now? Like you're my girlfriend?"

I nodded. "Yes."

I tucked myself under his arm carefully. Safe.

EPILOGUE

ONE YEAR LATER . . .

LOCK ZIPPED UP MY pale yellow dress and kissed my shoulder when he was done. I leaned toward him and was rewarded with a head kiss, too.

I looked at him in the mirror. He was amazing in a tuxedo. I touched my lock necklace and he responded by touching his own key one.

"It was nice of Becca to have the wedding here at the house." I turned and put my hands on his shoulders. The fabric on his jacket was stiff. I straightened his bowtie.

"I don't think anyone here will have a wedding in a church after what you went through." He trailed his index finger on the sweetheart neckline of my dress.

"*We* went through. You got shot, too." I lifted his finger to my lips and licked it gently.

"Pretty. You can't start that now. We have to be upstairs in one minute."

Lock looked like he could be easily convinced to do something else. I took his hand and led him behind me. I slid my feet into my flats. I was healing. I was doing great, but pushing my hips forward into a pair of heels for a whole evening would be too much.

After pretending to put his elbow on the top of my head, he laughed when I faked a punch to his middle.

We took the stairs up to the main floor, avoiding the elevator and enjoying my strength. Once up top, Lock shook hands with Nix and Animal, who both had tuxedos on as well. Nix was smiling widely.

Both greeted him with his hated street name.

"Thanks, Asshole."

"Hey, Asshole, put 'er here."

Lock rolled his eyes, but laughed it off.

Nix was marrying his Becca today. He already had the wedding band tatted on the correct finger. Becca had done the honors a few days ago. She had added a slim band to her "engagement ring," which had been a skull tat on her ring finger.

I kissed my brother's cheek and then smacked Animal on the ass as I walked by.

Lock gave a very loud, "Hey!" but I kept going right up the

stairs to find Becca and T.

I liked to make Lock jealous with my adoration of Animal. There were usually sexual "claiming" benefits to be had later from him. When I got to the master bedroom, Becca was fussing with her custom veil.

T looked relieved to see me. "Can you try this? I can't make it stay securely."

I grabbed a brush and worked the combs into the right place. T and I were wearing similar gowns. She was the matron of honor and I was doing double duty as the flower girl and bridesmaid.

Becca's makeup looked lovely. She had such an artist's eye and human skin was her regular canvas. Half of her face was etched with a hint of a skull tat, matching Nix's. Her dress continued the theme, with half of it featuring a full skeleton, outlined in silver. Her shoes were mismatched as well, with one showing the bones in her foot.

After I had the veil all set, she stood and shook out her hands. "I guess I'm ready?"

"You nervous?" She and my brother were so perfect for each other; I couldn't imagine her having anything but joy.

"Well." She walked past me and opened the closet.

Hanging there was a very sexy black teddy. It had a full skeleton embroidered on it. Upon closer inspection, I saw there was a tiny baby skeleton on the tummy.

"What?" I whirled on Becca. T covered her mouth.

"Just found out. Nix doesn't know yet. At least I don't think so. He's pretty in tune with my body and..." Becca put her hand on her belly.

The three of us did a group hug. "He's going to lose his mind."

Becca was glowing with her excitement.

"We're aunts!" I put my arm around T. She let out a very un-T-like squeal.

The wedding was everything. I managed to keep my mouth shut about the baby, despite the fact that I almost messed up twice. I danced with Nix and Animal and Merck, who I called Dad for the first time.

My friends from high school stopped by. Lock acted suspicious of my guy friends and I ate it up.

Lock's mother and Rhy were a hit. The legal prognosis for Lock's father's appeal was looking great. He was being protected in prison as well—Nix and Animal had connections there.

Lock and I worked our way through the party and danced as much as possible. After the last song was played, the lights were dimmed and our guests cleared out, we returned to our wing of the place with a nice chunk of wedding cake. My middle was a little achy. When I had a huge day, it would sometimes act up.

Lock followed me down the stairs and into our apartment. After our door was shut, I climbed up onto the kitchen counter and Lock placed himself between my legs. We fed each other bits of cake while we talked about weddings. After we were full, I set the plate into the sink. Lock licked my fingers clean.

"You look happy, Miss Ember." He kissed my wrist and then my palm.

"I'm alive, Mr. Sherlock Sonnet. And you're here. How could I not be happy?" I sat back, propping myself up on my arms.

Lock pushed away and started frontin'. I knew what he was doing. I told him it was hot when he was being a badass so he would do it for me.

"So, you like slapping some ass that's not mine?" He was

using the big gestures. Someone else might think he was threatening me.

I crossed my legs and bounced my foot. "Sometimes. What are you gonna do about it, tough guy?"

He wiped his lips with his thumb and dropped his shoulder. "Imma go upstairs and teach that man a lesson."

I lifted my eyebrow. "Really. The giant muscle-bound murderer?"

"Yes." He fake boxed in my direction.

I leaned forward. "And what are you going to do to *me*? Isn't that kinda sexist? I mean, I'm the one who harassed him."

Lock narrowed his eyes, then started walking toward me, dragging one leg like we were about to get in a bar brawl.

"Still. His ass touched your hand." He bobbed and weaved until he was pressed against the counter between my legs.

"And, actually, out of the two of us..." I dipped my finger into the sink and got some white icing on the tip. I touched it to his nose and then to his lip. "I'm the only murderer in this room."

Dark humor. Here, in this little cave, I would joke. He knew how much I was tortured by nightmares where I saw Olin's face. We used laughter as medicine.

I watched as the façade slid from his eyes, the playacting over. "I wish I could have done it for you."

"It's okay. We don't have to be serious." I licked the icing off his nose. "Let's love on each other. That's what tonight is for."

We heard a shout from above. Lock smoothly removed himself from my arms and found his hatchets.

"Stay in the closet." He pointed in the direction of the closet in our bedroom. It was a fully functioning panic room.

I shook my head. "No. It's good news."

Lock relaxed his stance just in time.

Our door flew open and Nix ran in like a madman. "A baby! I'm going to be a dad!"

He had on just his tux pants and no shoes. I hopped down from the counter and ran over, giving him a huge hug. He spun me around before putting me down quickly. "Are you okay? I'm sorry. I was so excited."

I watched as the excitement dulled a bit. Like the thought of hurting me set his mind on a roller coaster of emotions that led back to his murdering dad.

I put my hand on his face. "No. Don't go there. We're made of pure love when it comes to our people."

Nix nodded against my hand.

"You get to be excited and feel all the things." I hugged him again.

Lock stuck out his hand and gave Nix a congratulatory slap on the back.

"Thanks so much, Asshole. I appreciate it." Nix beamed again. "Well, you can be Uncle Asshole."

After the excitement was over and Nix vaulted back up the stairs to Becca, I led Lock back into our bedroom.

"Time to let me deal with all this sexy in a tux." I lifted my hair so he could unzip me.

I let the dress fall to the floor. Lock grabbed up my hair in a fist and used it to make me tilt my head. He gave me whisper kisses praising my beauty. His other hand covered the scars on my stomach. He said he loved those as well, and I believed him.

He turned me after he dropped my hair. His eyes were fire. After leaning down, he kissed me as if we'd just come back to life, again.

"You're the inhale, Ember." He cradled my face in his hands.

"You're the exhale, Asshole," I offered.

I watched as his dimples were brought out by his smile.

"Oh, you'll pay for that." He went to his knees and removed my panties. After tossing my leg over his shoulder, I paid over and over and over.

Animal

I clicked the door to our bedroom closed. T was on her side, eyes closed. White panties and a white tank top should be illegal in every state—the way she wore them anyway. She knew I was there. I'd not been able to sneak up on her yet. Though I never really wanted to try.

I trailed my hand from her ankle to her thigh before she cracked a smile. The goose bumps followed the path my fingers had taken. I smiled in return. She opened her eyes and looked at me with all the love and forgiveness that only any angel could.

"He okay?" T asked.

I rest my palm against her chilled torso.

"You knew?" Of course, she knew. When she'd heard the screaming from below, she didn't react.

"Becca told us before the wedding. Said she wasn't sure it'd be a surprise. Because Nix is..."

I knew the answer to this one. "Nix."

She twisted in the bed so she was lying on her back. "Another person for him to follow."

"He's going to be a nightmare. But who are we kidding? We'll all follow that kid around making sure they're okay." I sat on the edge of the bed, in the me-sized space T had cleared.

T covered my hand. "How about you? With the kids? Is that something you see in your future?"

I knew what she was getting at. How it would end. T was worried that the disease that kept her from spending time with her mother would be passed on to any biological children we had.

"The only future I see belongs to the both of us. As long I have you, I'll have what I need." I kissed her gently on the lips. She puckered and then smiled, her mouth letting me know she was pleased with my answer.

I sat back up. "Someone's got to take care of all our new people, too."

"Rhy looked so happy today."

We were both fools for Lock's little sister. She was the purest sunshine in the world.

T pulled herself to sitting. "You know, after everyone's settled, I was looking online and..."

I put my hands on either side of her thighs, letting my thumbs rub her skin. Touching, always touching. She was my miracle. I didn't rush her. My girl would get to what she wanted to say. I let her have the silence of my focus.

"A lot of adoptable kids have special needs like Rhy. Some with even more needs, and I feel like we have this big house..."

"You want to adopt?" I felt a spark in my chest.

"Stupid idea, I know. I mean, how are we going to pass any inspections?" She put her hands on her bare lap.

"T, Merck loves us both. Can you think of a better recommendation?" I took her hands into mine, stilling them from their worry.

This time T looked at me like I was the miracle. "I'd really love to do that. Be parents to a kid who needs help."

I started laughing, picturing our very own child. "Not to be too full of ourselves, but I think we'd be amazing at it."

She put her hands on my chest. "Maybe we can spend more time with Rhy? Let her teach us what it might be like?"

I pulled her to my chest and kissed the top of her head. "I can't wait."

————————

Need more Lock and Ember? I've got you covered!
Read about their New Year's Eve Surprise
Go here: https://dl.bookfunnel.com/1yk4gf8oxb
Or scan the code below:

ABOUT THE AUTHOR

Debra creates pretend people in her head and paints them on the giant, beautiful canvas of your imagination. She has a Bachelor of Science degree in political science and writes new adult angst and romantic comedies. She lives in Maryland with her husband and two amazing children. She doesn't trust mannequins, but does trust bears. Also, her chunky tuxedo cat talks with communication buttons. So that's fun. DebraAnastasia.com for more information.

Pretty please review this book if you enjoyed it. It is one of the very best ways to support indy authors. Thank you!

Scan the code below to stay connected to Debra:

tiktok.com/@debraanastasia
facebook.com/debra.anastasia
instagram.com/debra_anastasia

ALSO BY DEBRA ANASTASIA

Angst with Feels:

CRUEL PINK

DROWNING IN STARS

STEALING THE STARS

Mafia Romance:

MERCY

HAVOC

LOCK

Silly Humor:

FIRE DOWN BELOW

FIRE IN THE HOLE

Funny Humor:

FLICKER

BEAST

BOOTY CAMP

FELONY EVER AFTER

BEFORE YOU GHOST (with Helena Hunting)

Paranormal:

THE REVENGER

FOR ALL THE EVERS

CRUSHED SERAPHIM (BOOK 1)

BITTERSWEET SERAPHIM (BOOK 2)

Ingram Content Group UK Ltd.
Milton Keynes UK
UKHW040718070623
423012UK00004B/20/J